IN THE WET

Nevil Shute Norway was born on 17 January 1899 in Ealing, London. After attending the Dragon School and Shrewsbury School, he studied Engineering Science at Balliol College, Oxford. He worked as an aeronautical engineer and published his first novel, *Marazan*, in 1926. In 1931 he married Frances Mary Heaton and they went on to have two daughters. During the Second World War he joined the Royal Navy Volunteer Reserve where he worked on developing secret weapons. After the war he continued to write and settled in Australia where he lived until his death on 12 January 1960. His most celebrated novels include *Pied Piper* (1942), *No Highway* (1948), *A Town Like Alice* (1950) and *On the Beach* (1957).

OTHER WORKS BY NEVIL SHUTE

Novels

Marazan

So Disdained

Lonely Road

Ruined City

What Happened to the Corbetts

An Old Captivity

Landfall

Pied Piper

Pastoral

Most Secret

The Chequer Board

No Highway

A Town Like Alice

Round the Bend

The Far Country

Requiem for a Wren

Beyond the Black Stump

On the Beach

The Rainbow and the Rose

Trustee from the Toolroom

Stephen Morris and *Pilotage*

Autobiography

Slide Rule

EX LIBRIS

VINTAGE CLASSICS

NEVIL SHUTE

In the Wet

VINTAGE BOOKS
London

Published by Vintage 2009

Copyright © The Trustees of the Estate of Nevil Shute Norway

Nevil Shute has asserted his right under the Copyright, Designs
and Patents Act 1988 to be identified as the author of this work

First published by William Heinemann in 1953

Vintage
Random House, 20 Vauxhall Bridge Road,
London SW1V 2SA

www.vintage-classics.info

Addresses for companies within The Random House Group Limited
can be found at: www.randomhouse.co.uk/offices.htm

The Random House Group Limited Reg. No. 954009

A CIP catalogue record for this book
is available from the British Library

ISBN 9780099530046

10

The Random House Group Limited supports The Forest Stewardship
Council® (FSC®), the leading international forest-certification organisation.
Our books carrying the FSC label are printed on FSC®-certified paper.
FSC is the only forest-certification scheme supported by the leading
environmental organisations, including Greenpeace. Our
paper procurement policy can be found at
www.randomhouse.co.uk/environment

Printed and bound in Great Britain by Clays Ltd, St Ives plc

Lord God of Hosts, through whom alone
    A Prince can rule his nation,
Who settest Kings upon their throne
    And orderest each man's station;
Now, and through ages following,
    This grace to us be given:
To serve and love an earthly King
    Who serves our King in Heaven.

C. A. ALINGTON
(from a hymn sung at
Shrewsbury School)

One

I HAVE never before sat down to write anything so long as this may be, though I have written plenty of sermons and articles for parish magazines. I don't really know how to set about it, or how much I shall have to write, but as nobody is very likely to read it but myself perhaps that is of no great consequence. The fact is, however, that I have been so troubled in my mind since I came back from Blazing Downs that I have not been able to sleep very well or to work whole-heartedly upon my parish business, and my services in the church have been mechanical and absent minded. I think it will help me if I try to write down what it is that has been bothering me, and then I think that I may send it to the Bishop for him to look over. Perhaps the trouble is that I am getting a little old for duty in this somewhat unusual parish, and if that should prove to be the case I must accept whatever he decides.

Writing materials are not very easy to come by here, because Landsborough is only a small town. I went down to Art Duncan's store just now to buy some paper, but all he had was pads of thin airmail paper and these exercise books that Miss Foster uses for the older children in the school when they have got past using slates. I got six of these books and I expect I shall want more before I have written all that I have to say, but that only leaves nine books in the store and I would not like to think that I was running the school short. I have asked Art to get in some more, and he will send an order out to Townsville by next week's aeroplane.

In fairness to anybody who should read what I am writing I think I should begin by putting down something about myself, so that he can form his own judgment on the credibility of my account. My name is Roger Hargreaves and I have been ordained as a priest in the Church of England for forty-one years; I was sixty-three years old last month. I was born in the year 1890 at Portsmouth in the south of England and I was educated at Portsmouth Grammar School. I was ordained in 1912 and became curate of St. Mark's, at Guildford. In 1914 when the war broke out I went into the army as a chaplain, and I saw service in Gallipoli and in France. I was very fortunate in the war, because although I was blown up by a shell at Delville Wood during the Somme battle I was only in hospital for a few weeks, and I was able to return to the front line in less than four months.

After the war I was rather unsettled, and disinclined to return to parochial work in an English town. I was twenty-eight years old, unmarried, and with nothing very much to keep me in England. It seemed to me that while I was still young and vigorous I should give a few years of my life to service in more difficult places, and after talking it over with the Bishop I left for Australia to join the Bush Brotherhood in Queensland.

I served in the Bush Brotherhood for fourteen years, travelling very widely from Cloncurry to Toowoomba, from Birdsville to Burdekin. During that fourteen years I had no settled home, and I did not very often sleep more than two nights in one place. I drew fifty pounds a year from the Brotherhood, which was quite sufficient for my clothes and personal expenses, and I had a small expense account for travelling though I seldom had to draw upon it. The people of the outback were most generous in helping me to travel from station to station for my christenings and weddings and funerals and services. They would always take me on to the next place in a truck or a utility, and in the wet when the roads are impassable to motors because of the mud I have been given the loan of a horse for as long as three months, so that I have been able to continue with my duties all through the rainy season.

In 1934 I got appendicitis at a place called Goodwood near Boulia, three hundred miles west of Longreach, where there was a hospital. There was no Flying Doctor in those days, of course, and I had to travel for two days in a truck in very hot weather over rough country roads to get to the hospital. I had peritonitis by the time I got there and I very nearly died, and might have done if Billy Shaw of Goodwood station hadn't driven me all through the night. I was poorly after the operation and I didn't pick up very well, so very reluctantly I had to resign from the Brotherhood, and I went back to England. The Bishop was most kind and gave me a very good living, St. Peter's at Godalming, and there I settled down and met my dear wife, Ethel. Our few years of married life together were so happy I can hardly bear to write about them, so I shall not try to do so.

Ethel died in 1943, and we had no children. In wartime England there was much work for a vicar, and I did not feel the call to greater service till the war was over. But then it seemed to me that Godalming required a married priest more than a widower, and that there were still parts of Queensland where a man of my experience could be of use, even though he were fifty-six years old. I gave up my parish and went back to Australia as the clergyman of an emigrant ship, and to my great delight I found that the Brotherhood were willing to take me back into their service again in spite of my age.

I soon found that work in the outback was much easier than it had been ten years before. The war had brought improvements to the roads, for one thing, and small wireless receivers and transmitters were in general use on the more isolated stations, so that all communications were vastly easier. Most important of all was the greater use of aeroplanes; there seemed to be airfields all over the place, and even regular passenger services from them. All these developments made it possible for a priest to do a great deal more for the people than had been the case before, and I found that over much of my district it was possible to visit a given town or station as frequently as once in six months instead of once in two years as was the case when I first came to the country.

In 1950 an acute shortage of clergy developed in New Guinea; at one time owing to leave and sickness there was only one priest of the Church of England there to serve an area of a hundred and eighty-one thousand square miles in Papua and the Mandated Territory. It seemed to me that their needs were even greater than those of the Queenslanders, and with the consent of the Brotherhood I volunteered to go there for a few months to help them out of their difficulty. I was fifty-nine when I flew up to Port Moresby, much too old for such a job, I suppose, but there was nobody else to go. I travelled widely in the country for a year, from the Fly River to Rabaul and from the goldfields at Wau to the plantations of Samarai. I am afraid that I was careless in taking my Paludrine because in September 1951 I went down with a severe attack of malaria at Salamaua, and I was in hospital at Port Moresby for some weeks. That was the end of my service in New Guinea.

I mention that attack of malaria because I still get

4

recurrences of it from time to time, though in a milder form. It has a place in the events that I am trying to write down. I am told that these malarial fevers are likely to go on for some years after the first attack before they gradually die away, and the recurrences that I get now are already much less severe than the first bout I had at Salamaua. I find now that I can go on with my work quite well when the fever is on me, certainly as regards travelling, although occasionally I still have to postpone a service for a day while I go to bed and sweat it out. However, that first bout was a severe one and left me rather weak, so that I was glad to give up New Guinea and to go and stay with friends up on the Atherton Tableland behind Cairns in North Queensland while I recovered and regained my health.

The Bishop was travelling in the district at that time, and he wrote to me proposing that he should come to see me, and saying things that I did not deserve. I travelled down to meet him at Innisfail because I was quite well enough to go to him, and we had a very friendly talk in which he spoke about my age and the desirability that I should take on less exacting work. He told me then that he was anxious to re-open the parish church at Landsborough and to provide a resident priest for the parish. He spoke about my experience of the country, and asked me if I would like to go there for a few years to start up the church again in that district. He said that he would not expect me to travel very widely in the parish, which is about twenty-eight thousand square miles in area though sparsely populated, because he hoped to be able to provide me with a young man as a curate within a year. Money is always a difficulty in the Church, of course, but he said that he would send me a truck in a few months time, although it might have to be rather an old one. It hasn't come yet, but I really get on very well without it.

Landsborough is a town at the head of the Gulf of Carpentaria in what is known as the Gulf Country. The town was much larger fifty years ago than it is now; at the time of the gold-mining boom it had about twenty-five hotels—probably mere drinking shops, most of them—but now it has only two. There are about eighty permanent white residents there, counting men, women, and children, and a floating population of two or three hundred blacks who live in deplorable conditions in iron shanties outside the town. The place is about two hundred miles from Cloncurry and five hundred by air from Cairns and Townsville on the coast. It has a hospital staffed by a couple of nursing sisters, and it has a house for a doctor though no doctor has ever been induced to practise there. In an emergency they speak upon the radio to Cloncurry and the Flying Doctor comes in the air ambulance; there is a very good aerodrome built during the war, and an aeroplane calls with mail and supplies once a week.

My church at Landsborough is a very simple weatherboard building that was rebuilt about thirty years ago after a bush fire. I am afraid it is rather sparsely furnished, and it could do with a coat of paint both inside and out as soon as we can get the money for it. It has chairs instead of pews, and this is a great convenience because once every two or three months we get a travelling cinema in Landsborough and then we can take the chairs out of the church and put them in the Shire Hall, or in Art Duncan's yard in the hot weather. It is a convenience to me personally, too, because my vicarage is rather short of furniture, so that if I have notice of anybody coming to see me I can go and borrow a chair from the church and take it back before the next service.

Both church and vicarage have been rather neglected, because the last incumbent died of snake bite in 1935 and since then there had been no resident priest at Landsborough till I arrived in the autumn of 1952. Of course, the church had been used from time to time for services by visiting priests, and I used it myself on several occasions when I was in the district, so that I knew all about Landsborough. I was very glad to go there, because although by English standards it's not much of a parish, perhaps by English standards I'm not much of a clergyman, and for me it was a place where I could carry on the work that I was used to from a base where I could gather a few books around me and live in comparative rest and comfort. In spite of what I told the Bishop, I must privately admit that I'm not the man I was before the malaria. It's probably only a passing weakness, and as the thing wears off I shall get back my strength again. I hope so, because there's so much to be done, and so few years now left to do it in.

The Bishop, when I met him at Innisfail, forbade me to take up my living at Landsborough until April, when the rains would be over in the Gulf Country, and although I was a little annoyed about that at the time I think perhaps that he was acting wisely in view of my infirmity and the state of the vicarage. In the seventeen years that had elapsed since the death of the last incumbent there had been little money available for the maintenance of either church or vicarage, and what money there was had been spent on the church to keep the roof in order and to repair the ravages of the white ants. Not very much had been done to the vicarage in those years; most of the corrugated iron roof was rusted through, and there was little glass left in the windows. However, I bought some corrugated iron in Atherton and took it with me in the mail truck when I went to Landsborough in April. It was so expensive that I thought it best to leave the windows for the time being; one doesn't really need glass in the windows in the tropics.

It took five days for the mail truck to get from Cairns to Landsborough because we stopped at a great many places. Moreover, it was early in the season and the roads are never very good in April; we got bogged three times in one day near the Gilbert River. It seemed a long time to me, because of course I was impatient to get to my living and commence my ministry. When finally we drove into Landsborough and unloaded my corrugated iron and my swag in front of the church, I found that the vicarage was not in quite such good condition as I had thought. It has two rooms with a verandah in front, but the white ants had got into the floor of the verandah and one room. However, the other room was quite safe and that is all I need, and I soon had the new corrugated iron nailed down on the roof beams with the help of Jim Phillips the constable and one of his black trackers, called Sammy Three, to distinguish him from all the other Sammies. They were most kind, and found me some packing cases and beer crates, because the vicarage had little furniture. Within a few hours I was very comfortably installed, with my camp bed set up and my swag unrolled upon it under my mosquito net, and a chair out of the church, and a packing case for a table with my hurricane lamp on it, and a little book case made out of a beer crate for the half-dozen books I had brought with me, and my tin trunk with my clothes in it.

My parish is a large one. It extends about a hundred and sixty miles to the south, to the border of the Northern Territory a hundred and twenty miles to the west, and about fifty miles to the east in the direction of Normanton. It has two other churches in it, St. Mary's at Leichardt Crossing and St. Jude's at Godstow. St. Mary's is in good repair though very small, seating no more than fifteen people; it stands on Horizon station and Mr. Kimbell the manager has seen that it was kept in order. St. Jude's, I am afraid, is little more than a ruin, but I make a point of holding a Celebration there twice a year, and I am hoping that we may be able to get some iron for the roof in a few months.

In the dry months of the year, from April to the end of November, I can get about in this large parish fairly easily. The roads are not metalled, of course, and in England they would be described as cart tracks, but in a truck you can depend on averaging fifteen miles an hour, so that most of my parish lies within a couple of days' journey of the vicarage. In the wet season, however, travelling is very difficult. About fifty or sixty inches of rain falls in three months; the rivers, which are dry for the rest of the year, turn into swollen torrents, and much of the country is submerged in floods. In the wet no motor vehicle can move a hundred yards outside the town without getting bogged, so that there is little movement in the countryside; station managers get in the stores that they require for four months in November and seldom appear again in Landsborough before the beginning of April. A horse is the best way to get about the country then if one must travel, but the crocodiles are rather a nuisance in the floods and the incessant rain makes camping very unpleasant.

Like every other parish in the world, the parish of St. Peter's, Landsborough, has its own special problems. There are only nineteen white families in Landsborough itself, seven of whom are Roman Catholic, so that much of the local parish work revolves around the school and the hospital and the office of the Protector of Aboriginals. The town, however, is the social centre for a number of cattle stations in the country round about, the smallest of which is eight hundred square miles and the largest over three thousand. The managers and stockmen from these stations total nearly a hundred Europeans and perhaps twice that

9

number of half-castes and aboriginals, who usually make very good stockmen. The white stockmen come into town frequently on business and to spend the evening in the hotel, and everyone from the whole countryside comes in to town for the race meetings, which are held twice a year in the dry. Each meeting lasts for four days and the town is then very full with men sleeping everywhere, in bedrooms, on the verandahs, in their utilities or on the bare earth of the paddocks rolled up in their swags, drunk or sober, but more frequently the former.

A parson who arrives to live in such a town, the first parson for seventeen years, must act with some discretion. The problem of drink in outback towns like Landsborough is not an easy one; right is not wholly right nor wrong completely wrong in such communities. Landsborough lies at sea level only seventeen degrees from the Equator; it can be very hot indeed at certain times of the year. In such places the body requires not less than a gallon of liquid each day to replace the losses due to evaporation, and there are few liquids more palatable and more refreshing in hot climates than the cold, light Australian beer. The two bars in the town are the natural meeting place for men in from the stations; indeed they are about the only places in Landsborough where men can meet and talk their business. If a stockman from a station far out in the bush comes into town to meet his friends and to hear new voices stating new ideas, he must stand in the bar all day, for there is nowhere else for him to go. If then with his starved mind refreshed with news and human company he lies in drunken slumber in the back of his truck, should the parson rail against him from the pulpit? I do not know if he should or not; I only know that I have never done so.

I started modestly and rather cautiously in Landsborough. I visited each of my white parishioners in the first week and got a Sunday School going for the children. That went all right, and presently I got some of the women to come to matins; I found, as I had found in other places, that the half-caste women and quadroons were more devout than the pure whites. Presently I started a short children's service each morning five minutes before school, consisting of one hymn and a short Bible reading, and a lot of the children used to come to that because my church is on their way to school. I visited the hospital each morning and the iron shanties of the blacks each afternoon, and I engaged in a good deal of correspondence to try to get hold of an old cinema projector for the town to make a diversion from the bars.

All this was well enough, but it did little to touch the major social problems of the district, which concerned the men. I had hardly been six weeks in Landsborough when the first race meeting brought all the stockmen into the town in one body. At that time I was taking all my meals at the Post Office Hotel, the larger of the two, run by Bill Roberts and his wife. Cooking a meal is hardly practicable in my vicarage; I have a Primus stove on which I can boil a kettle for a cup of tea for my breakfast, but dinner and tea I usually take at the hotels, changing from one to the other every week to avoid offence.

For the next four days the hotel was a bedlam. Normally only one or two of the ten bedrooms would be occupied, but for the race week Bill Roberts set up seventeen extra beds in the verandahs, and the other place had as many. A travelling roundabout for the children turned up from Cloncurry and was erected in the main street; it had a great loudspeaker that blared canned dance tunes every night till one in the morning, and could be heard ten miles out in the bush. Two pedlars arrived in trucks that opened up as shops, and to crown everything the cinema truck arrived on one of its infrequent visits, displaying films that I had seen ten years before in distant Godalming on the far side of the world. Miss Foster closed her school, and all the town went to the races.

A race meeting at Landsborough has one or two features that distinguish it from Ascot. All the horses must be bred in the district and they come straight off the cattle stations, ungroomed of course, and sometimes covered in mud where they have been rolling. The jockeys are the stockmen from the stations decked out in brilliant racing colours, each riding a horse that he has picked out from the mob of two or three hundred in the horse paddock of his own station, and that he confidently believes will one day win the Melbourne Cup. The racecourse itself is in a natural clearing in the bush, the posts and rails are rough, untrimmed saplings cut a hundred yards away. The centre of the racecourse is the aerodrome and the ambulance aeroplane was there in case of accidents, and for a more mundane reason, because its crew were busily running a gambling wheel to pay for the aeroplane. There is no grand stand, but over the horse lines and the bar rough roofs of gum tree boughs with the leaves on them have been erected to provide a little shade. There is a stockyard for the Rodeo which comes on the last day of the meeting. There is a great deal of unrelieved sunshine, a great deal of beer, and a great deal of dust.

I drove out to the races with Mrs. Roberts and her coloured maid, a girl of about seventeen called Coty. We were a little late in starting because they had served over sixty hot dinners cooked on an old fashioned kitchen range with the shade temperature in the yard outside at a hundred and five. It seemed only fair to stay and help them with the washing up, so it was after three o'clock when we got out to the racecourse. I knew a number of the managers and stockmen by that time, of course, and I spent the afternoon with them pleasantly enough, drinking one beer to every three of theirs and putting my two shillings on the tote each race on their advice.

Towards the last race, I met Stevie for the first time in my life. I was standing with a little group that included Jim Maclaren, manager of Beverley station, when I saw a very tattered old man zig-zagging towards me. He wore a dirty blue shirt without a collar, open to show his skinny chest, and dirty drill trousers held up by a ringer's belt with a leather slot for the knife and a leather pocket for the tin box of matches. He had no hat; he was very tanned, with lean, not unpleasant features; he had worn out elastic sided riding boots upon his feet. He was unshaven and rather drunk; indeed, he looked as if he had been rather drunk for some considerable time.

He came up to us and stood swaying a little, and said, "You're the new parson."

"That's right," I said, and held out my hand to him. "My name's Roger Hargreaves."

He took my hand and shook it, and went on shaking it; he wouldn't let it go. "Roger Hargreaves," he said seriously. There was a pause while he considered that information. "That's your name."

"That's right," I said. "That's my name." I knew that everyone beside me was smiling a little, watching to see how the new parson reacted to this drunk old man.

"Good on you," he said at last, after another pause. "The Reverend Roger Hargreaves. That's what they call you."

"That's right," I assured him. "That's my name."

He stood motionless, still holding my hand, while his mind changed gear. "I heard about you," he said. "You're a Pommie. A bloody Pommie."

"Aw, cut it out," Jim Maclaren beside me said. "Mr. Hargreaves, he's been in Queensland twenty years. Buzz off and buy yourself a beer, Stevie. I'll shout you one."

"Mr. Hargreaves!" said the old man scornfully. He still had me by the hand. "If he's right, why don't you call him by his name? His name's Roger."

"He's right," said Jim. "I called him Mr. Hargreaves because he's the vicar. Buzz off and get yourself a beer. Tell Albert that I'm shouting for you—I'll be along in a minute."

"He's all right," I said to Jim. I turned to the old man. "What's *your* name?"

"Stevie," he said.

"Stevie what?"

"Stevie," he repeated. "I'm Stevie and you're Roger. Put it there, chum." He shook my hand vigorously. He peered up into my face and breathed stale beer at me. "Cobbers, ain't we?"

"That's right," I said. "You're Stevie, and we're cobbers."

He released my hand at last, and stood swaying before us. "He's right," he informed Jim, "even if he is a bloody Pommie." He turned to me, full of goodwill. "Who're you betting on?"

I smiled. "I'm the vicar," I said. "Two bob on the tote is my limit. I was thinking of going on Frenzy."

"Don't do it," he said earnestly. "Don't do it, Roger. Black Joke. You go on Black Joke and you'll be right."

"Aw, you're nuts, Stevie," said Fred Hanson. "Come on over 'n I'll shout you one." He took the old man by the arm and drew him away towards the bar.

I glanced at Jim Maclaren, and we were both smiling. "Who's he?" I asked.

"Stevie? Oh, he's always about. Lives with a Chinaman about ten miles out. He don't do nothing now—he's too old. Used to be a good man once, they tell me. I did hear he was manager of Wonamboola, years ago." He hesitated, and glanced at me. "Bit of a nuisance, now and then."

I turned and looked at the tote board behind us; up till then only one punter had fancied Black Joke. "What about Black Joke?" I asked.

"He's a joke all right," said Jim. "You stay on Frenzy, Mr. Hargreaves."

I wandered away just before the race and had a look at the horses as they cantered down to the start. Frenzy was the only one with any breeding; Black Joke was a thin, starved looking animal with a big head and a small rump. I strolled towards the tote and there was still only one backer for Stevie's fancy, against over forty on Frenzy. The dividend, if certain, would be very small. I thought of old Stevie, whom I was sure to meet again, and who was sure to ask me what I had backed, and I put my two bob on Black Joke.

I sometimes think that Ascot misses something that places like Landsborough have got. Tommy Ford was riding Frenzy, and Tommy was resolved to win that race; he came surging forward at each start and spoiled six starts in quick succession. By that time every horse was dancing on its toes and practically out of control, and the starter had a rock in his hand. On the seventh start he flung this stone at Tommy's head and checked his rush as the two-pound rock whizzed by within an inch of his ear. One of the other horses spoiled that start. On the eighth start Tommy came surging forward again and the starter flung another rock which ricocheted off Frenzy's head between the ears and hit Tommy fair and square in the chest. Frenzy, startled by the blow upon his head and the yank on his mouth, went bush; the start was a good one but fifty yards down the course Frenzy crossed the field, barging against Daisy Bell, who fell, and Coral Sea, who sat down on his haunches for a rest, while Frenzy jumped the low rail and made off into the gum trees with Tommy standing in the stirrups sawing at his mouth and cursing. Black Joke was left to race against a poor little mare called Cleopatra, and won by a length. I collected two pounds seventeen and sixpence from the tote.

I looked around for Stevie, but he was nowhere to be seen. I was rather glad of that, because if I had seen him then I could hardly have avoided standing him a beer, and he had had quite enough. Jim told me later that he had gone to sleep in one of the horse stalls, on the ground, where there was a patch of shade. Most of the horses stayed out at the racecourse for the night with a few of the black stockmen to look after them. When Stevie woke up it was dark and starry, one of the magnificent Queensland winter nights, cool and balmy, when the stars burn right down to the horizon and it is a pleasure to sleep out on the bare earth. The black boys had built a fire to boil up and they were sitting around and yarning. They gave Stevie a mug of tea out of their billy and a tin plate of meat, and presently he left them and started on the mile and a half walk into town, to the bar.

I did not see Stevie again that night. I had my tea at the hotel and helped them with the washing up. Then I made off towards my vicarage, but Jim Maclaren saw me as I passed by the bar out in the street and I had to go in and have a drink with them, and shout one in return out of my winnings. I found that my bet was the main topic of the evening; not only was the whole of the last race an interest and an amusement to the men who thronged the bar, including Tommy Ford, but they all showed genuine and unaffected pleasure in the fact that the parson had won two pounds seventeen and sixpence on a long shot. North Queensland is a rewarding place to work in.

I tried to find out a little more about Stevie in the half

hour that I was in the bar before I could withdraw without offence, but I did not get very far. He was much older than most of the men present, and he had been in the Gulf Country for as long as they could remember. There was a tradition, backed by the pilot of the air ambulance, that Stevie had served in the Royal Flying Corps in the 1914–1918 war, and that he had been a pilot. He was known to have been manager of Wonamboola station some time in the Twenties, probably soon after that war, but nobody was old enough to remember that time personally. Since then he had gone steadily downhill. He had worked as a saddler and as a cook on various stations at various times; nobody in the bar that night knew his surname and nobody knew of any relatives that he might have. He was now unemployable, but he had a pension of some kind that he drew from the post office. He lived with an old Chinaman called Liang Shih who ran a market garden ten or twelve miles out of town, and he helped in the garden in return for his keep. These two men lived alone. Stevie never had any money in his pocket because his habit was to go straight from the post office to the hotel and drink his pension before going home, but when his clothes became indecent Sergeant Donovan of the mounted police would wait for him outside the post office and take him to the store and make him buy a new pair of pants before releasing him to the bar.

I knew a little bit about Liang Shih, because he was the only source of fresh vegetables in Landsborough. At that time I had not seen his house, though I saw plenty of it later on. He had his garden between two long waterholes on rather a remote part of Dorset Downs station, about fifteen miles from the homestead. The waterholes were really part of a river that ran only in the wet season and joined the Dorset River lower down; in the dry the land between these waterholes was very fertile and adjacent to permanent

17

water for irrigation. Here Liang Shih cultivated two or
three acres of land and on it he grew every kind of vegetable
in great profusion; he had an old iron windmill to pump
water, and he worked from dawn till dark. He had a house
built on a little rising knoll of ground near by, above the
level of the floods. Twice a week, on Mondays and Thurs-
days, he would drive into town in a two wheeled cart drawn
by an old horse to sell his vegetables, and then he would go
straight back home. He did not drink at all.

I met Stevie next morning in the street as I was on my way
to the hospital. The bar did not open until ten o'clock, and
he was looking pretty bad; his hair was matted, his eyes
bloodshot, and his hand shaking. Clearly he had slept out
somewhere, because his shirt and trousers were dirty with
earth, and there was a little hen manure on his left shoulder.

I stopped by him, and said, "I got on Black Joke, like you
told me to."

He mouthed his dry lips, and said, "Good on you. They
told me last night in the hotel. You're Roger, aren't
you?"

"That's right," I assured him. "I'm Roger, and you're
Stevie."

"Got a drink in your place, cobber?"

"I'm afraid I haven't," I said. "I don't keep it in the
vicarage." I paused, and then I said, because his distress
was evident, "The bar opens at ten."

"Too long," he muttered. "The last one, he was better
than this bloody chap. He'd give you a drink any time. This
mugger, he's scared of the bloody policeman."

"I tell you what," I said. "Go up to my place, the first
house this side of the church, and have a shower and wash
your shirt and pants. They'll be dry before ten, and it'll pass
the time. I've got to go up to the hospital, but I'll be back
by then, and I'll shout you a drink for Black Joke."

"It might pass the time, at that," he said. "Up by the church?"

"That's right," I said. "You'll find soap and everything up there. A razor, if you want to use it. I'll be back before ten, and then we'll come back here and have a beer."

I went up to the hospital—I forget what for, or who the patients were. I didn't stay long in the wards; I call them wards for courtesy, though they were no more than three bedrooms with two beds in each. When I was ready to go Sister Finlay asked me to stay for a cup of tea; they usually gave me morning tea when I went to the hospital.

I went into the sitting room, where Nurse Templeton was pouring out. There were only the two of them to staff the little place. "I mustn't stay long," I said. "I've got Stevie up in my house waiting for me."

"For Heaven's sake!" said Sister Finlay. "What's he doing there?"

"Having a bath," I replied.

Nurse Templeton looked up, giggling. "He usually has that here."

"Do you see a lot of him?" I asked.

"Do we not!" said Sister Finlay, sighing a little. "He's a horrible old man. He gets drunk or gets in a fight, or just falls down and hurts himself, and then he comes to us and we have to patch him up. Last time he went to sleep in Jeff Cumming's yard behind the house, and Jeff's dog came and bit him in the arm."

"Sister would have bitten him herself, only he smelt too bad," said Templeton. "Here's your tea, Mr. Hargreaves."

"I made him go and have a bath before I dressed his arm," the sister said. "Templeton washed his clothes and turned him out spruce as a soldier. But he didn't stay that way."

"He's a bit of a nuisance, is he?"

19

She nodded. He'd be all right if it wasn't for the drink. It's not as if he was a vicious man. But the drink's got him now, and he's got to have it. That, or something else."

"Something else?"

She said, "He lives out in the bush, with that Chinaman who brings in vegetables. Out on Dorset Downs."

"I know. I ought to go out there some time and visit them."

She glanced at me, and hesitated. "I don't know that they're very Christian, Mr. Hargreaves," she said at last. "I think you ought to know that, if you're thinking of going there. I don't know about Stevie, but Liang Shih's a Hindoo or a Buddhist or something, and there's an idol stuck up in a sort of niche in the wall." She hesitated again. "It's none of my business, but I wouldn't like you to get a surprise."

I smiled. "Thanks for the tip. Is Stevie a Buddhist, too?"

She laughed. "Oh—him! I shouldn't think he's anything, except a Beerist." She paused, and then she said, "Sergeant Donovan took me out there with a party one day when they were shooting duck on the waterholes, and we looked in and called on them. Stevie was sober, and he looked ever so much better—quite respectable. The Sergeant says it's only when he gets some money and comes into town he gets like this. He's all right living with Liang Shih out in the bush."

I left the hospital soon after that and went back to the vicarage. Stevie had washed himself and he had made an attempt to shave, but he had cut himself and given it up; he was now sitting on the rotten verandah steps with my towel around his waist while his shirt and trousers, newly washed, hung in the sun over the rail. Clothes dry in ten minutes in North Queensland, in the dry.

"I had a shower," he said. "My word, I'm crook today."
He licked his dry lips. "You got a whiskey, cobber?"

"I'm afraid I haven't," I replied. "I don't keep anything
up here. The hotel will be open in ten minutes." I paused.
"Going out to the track today?"

"Suppose so," he said listlessly. "I done my money, so I
won't be betting." He reached for his shirt and trousers
and began to clothe his skinny, scarred body.

"That was a good tip you gave me yesterday," I remarked.
"What made you think that Black Joke was in the running
against Frenzy?"

"Aw, something was bound to happen in the last race,"
he said. "Nothing hadn't happened up till then, but something was bound to happen. I knew that three nights ago,
out in the bush. I know when something's going to happen
—I do, cobber." He rambled on as he pulled his dirty boots
on his bare feet. "Pisspot Stevie," he said resentfully.
"That's what they call me. But I know more'n any of them.
I'll show them all one day. I know more than any of them.
Mark my words."

"Of course you do," I said. "Come on down to the hotel
and I'll shout a beer, if it'll clear your head."

He came forward with alacrity, buttoning his trousers as
he came. "I done my money," he explained ingenuously.
"I got to wait now till some other bastard shouts."

"They tell me you were in the Flying Corps in the first
war," I remarked. "Is that right?"

"Ninth Batt. and R.F.C.," he told me. "That's what I
was. Sergeant Pilot, maternity jacket 'n all, 'n wings on it,
flying R.E.8s artillery spotting. Armentears, St. Omer,
Bethune—I know all them places, 'n what they look like
from on top. I know more than any of them, cobber.
Pisspot Stevie!"

He walked down to the hotel. "I'll stand you one beer

21

and then I'll have to go," I told him. "If you'll take my advice, you'll go, too." He did not answer that, and when I left the bar he was deeply involved in rounds of drinks, and looking a lot better, I must say.

I did not see him that day at the races. He was in the bar at tea time, rather drunk, but I avoided getting drawn into the bar that night. I went to the dance later on to put in an appearance for half an hour. The Ladies' Committee had done their best to decorate our rather sombre Shire Hall, and they managed to produce an orchestra composed of Mrs. Fraser at the piano, the half caste Miss O'Brian with her violin, and Peter Collins with his cornet. Everybody seemed to be having a good time and I stayed there till about eleven o'clock, when the fight took place.

It happened on the verandah outside the bar of the Post Office Hotel. When I heard about it and got out into the street to try and stop it, it was all over. The police were marching Ted Lawson off to spend the night in the cooler, one on each side of him dragging him along and standing no nonsense; the crowd were putting Stevie, streaming blood, into a utility to take him to the hospital. It seemed that Ted had been very rude to Stevie, calling him Pisspot, and Stevie, very drunk, had hit out at Ted and by a most incredible fluke had knocked him down. Ted was a man of about twenty-five, a ringer on Helena Waters station, too young by far to hit such an old man. However, they fought on the verandah, and with the first blow Ted knocked Stevie out; as he fell he caught his left ear on the edge of the verandah or against a post and tore it half off, which made another job for Sister Finlay. There was nothing much that the parson could do about it till the morning, so I went back to the vicarage and said a prayer before I went to bed for wandering, foolish men.

When I got to the hospital next morning Stevie was just

leaving for the hotel. Sister Finlay had put a couple of stitches in his ear and dressed it, and he now wore a large white bandage all around his head. He had little to say to me, and we watched him as he shambled down the hot, dusty road to the town a quarter of a mile away. "I'd like to see him put into a truck and taken out to Dorset Downs, where he belongs," the sister said. "He's all right when he's out there."

"I could try that," I said. "One of the men would run him out, if I asked them."

"He's got to have the stitches taken out on Sunday," she replied. "This meeting will be over by then, and he'll go on his own."

The police let Ted out of their little gaol about the middle of the morning after giving him a good dressing down for hitting an old man, and Ted came back into circulation rather ashamed of himself. To make amends, for Ted was quite a decent lad, he went straight to find Stevie and to stand him a drink, so that bygones should be bygones. Bygones were still being bygones that afternoon out at the rodeo; Stevie and Ted were firm friends and half drunk, and the name Pisspot was being bandied about in the most amicable way without any offence at all.

That was the last day of the races, and there was a fancy dress dance that night in the Shire Hall at which I had to help in judging the costumes and giving away the prizes. Few of the men had managed to do anything about a fancy dress, but all the girls had attempted it and it had given them a great deal of pleasure; there were two Carmens and four Pierrettes. The prizegiving was not till about half past eleven, and when it was over I was shepherded into the hotel by Jim Maclaren for some refreshment as a reward for my labours.

Ted and Stevie were there, still drinking, still the firmest of friends, and Stevie was singing 'My Little Grey Home in the West' for the entertainment of the company, singing in a cracked voice as many of the words as he could remember, and beating time with one hand. I stood at the other end of the bar drinking the one beer with which I hoped to escape, and chatting to the men. Presently Stevie saw me and made towards me unsteadily, clutching the bar as he came to steady his course.

He came to a standstill before me. "You're Roger," he said.

"That's right," I replied. "And you're Stevie."

He held out his hand. "Put it there, cobber."

I shook hands with him, and again he held my hand. "He's the parson," he told the men. "His name's Roger."

I disengaged my hand. "That's right, Stevie," said Jim a little wearily. "He's the parson, and his name is Roger. Now you beat it."

The old man stood holding on to the bar, swaying a little, his head grotesque in the white bandage. It suddenly occurred to me that he was half asleep. "He's a good cobber, even if he is the parson," he said at last. "He's a good cobber."

"That's right," said Jim patiently. "He's a good cobber, and he's the parson. Now you buzz off and leave him be. We've got business to talk here."

"He's in the wrong job," said Stevie. There was a long pause, and then he said, "He's a good cobber, but he's in the wrong job."

"Aw, cut it out, Stevie."

"He believes people go to Heaven when they die," said Stevie. "Harps and angels' wings." He turned to me. "That's right, cobber?"

"Pretty well," I said. And beside me Jack Picton said, "You're not going to Heaven when *you* die, Stevie, and if

24

you don't stop annoying Mr. Hargreaves I'll dot you one and bust the other ear."

I put a hand upon Jack's arm. "He's right—he's doing no one any harm." To Stevie I said, "I don't know if you'll go to Heaven, but I do know that it's time you went to bed, with that ear. Where are you sleeping, Stevie?"

There was no answer. One of the men said, "He hasn't got a bed, Mr. Hargreaves. He just sleeps around, any place he fancies."

I turned to Mr. Roberts behind the bar. "Got a spare bed, Bill? He should sleep somewhere on a bed tonight, with that bandage."

"That's right," said the innkeeper. "There's a spare bed on the back verandah. He can sleep on that."

I turned to the men. "Let's take him up there."

Jim and Jack Picton grasped Stevie by each arm and marched him out into the back yard; I followed them. They stopped there in the still moonlight for a certain purpose, and then they took him up the outside stairs to the back verandah and deposited him upon the vacant bed. "Now see here, Stevie," said Jim Maclaren. "The parson's got you this bed, and you've got to stay up here and sleep on it. If I see you downstairs again tonight I'll break your bloody neck."

"Let's take his boots off," I said.

We took his boots off and dropped them down beside the bed, and pushed him down on it. Jim said, "Want a blanket, Stevie? You'd better have a blanket. Here, take this." He threw one over the old man. "Now just you stay there. Nobody's shouting you another drink tonight, and if you come downstairs again I'll break your neck. That's straight. I will."

"Harps and angels' wings," the old man muttered. "That's no way to talk."

25

Jim laughed shortly. "Come on down, Mr. Hargreaves. He's right now."

"I could tell you things," Stevie said from the semi-darkness of the bed. "I could tell you better 'n that, but you wouldn't believe me." There was a pause, and then he muttered, "Pisspot Stevie. Nobody believes what Pisspot Stevie says."

I said in a low tone to Jim Maclaren, "I'll stay up here till he goes off to sleep. He won't be long. I'll see you downstairs later." It was a subterfuge, of course. I wanted to avoid going back with Jim to the bar.

"All right, Mr. Hargreaves." He went clattering down the stairs with the other men, laughing and talking, and their voices died away into the bar. It was very still on the verandah after they had gone. Half of the verandah was in brilliant, silvery moonlight, half in deep black shadow, hiding the beds. Under the deep blue sky a flying fox or two wheeled silently round the hotel in the light of the moon.

"I could tell you things," the old man muttered from the darkness. "You think I told you something when I said Black Joke, but that ain't nothing. I could tell you things."

"What could you tell me?" I asked quietly.

"Being born again," he muttered sleepily. "All you think about is harps and angels' wings, but Liang's a Buddhist, 'n he knows. Old Liang, he knows, all right. He tol' me all about it. He knows."

It was somewhat dangerous, but the night was quiet, and I wanted to explore the depths of this old man. "What does Liang know?" I asked.

"About another chance," he muttered. "About being born again, 'n always another chance of doing better next time. I know. I got the most beautiful dreams, 'n more and

26

more the older that I get. Soon I'll be living next time more'n this time. That's a mystery, that is." There was a long, long pause; I thought that he had gone to sleep, but then he said again, "A mystery. Liang says it's right, 'n no one ever dies. Just slide off into the next time, into the dream."

It wasn't very comprehensible, but one would hardly have expected it to be because Stevie was very drunk. I asked for curiosity, "What do you dream about?"

"You want a pipe for it," he said drowsily. "Lie down with a pipe, 'n the dreams come. All about Queens and Princes and that, and flying, and being in love. All across the world, backwards and forwards, backwards and forwards, all across the world, and carrying the Queen."

I stood by the verandah rail in silence, wondering at the jumble of words generated by the muddled, alcohol-poisoned brain. Flying, because this man long ago had been a pilot, though that seemed incredible now. Being in love—well, that lasts till the grave in some men. The Queens and Princes—figures on a pack of cards, perhaps. The pipe, and lying down—did that mean opium? It was at least a possibility for one who shared a home with an old China-man. A phrase of Sister Finlay's came into my mind; had she been hinting at that?

I stood there silent under the bright moon thinking about all these things till the steady rhythm of breathing from the darkness told me that Stevie was asleep. Then I went quietly down the wooden stairway to the yard and slipped away from the hotel, and went back to my vicarage to go to bed.

I did not see much more of Stevie after that. The race meeting was over, and most of the people left town early next morning to go back to their stations. Stevie hung around for a couple of days, moody and bad-tempered

27   B

because he was out of money and there was nobody left in town to stand him a drink except a couple of engineers belonging to the Post Office and Reg McAuliffe selling life insurance to the residents. Finally Sister Finlay took the stitches out of Stevie's ear, started him off with a clean bandage, and dismissed him. Somebody going out to Dorset Downs gave him a lift in a truck, and that was the end of him. Everybody in the town was glad to see him go.

I started then to get acquainted with my parish. Miss Foster very kindly undertook to carry on the little daily hymn service for the school children, and I set out one day to go to Godstow to see what was to be done about St. Jude's. I travelled on the mail truck and we stopped at every house and station on the way, of course—perhaps once every twenty miles or so. It was very hot and dusty and I wore a khaki shirt and shorts, but I had my case with me, of course, containing my cassock and surplice and the sacramental vessels, and I baptised three children on the first day, and held two Celebrations. The driver of the mail truck was most kind and waited for me while I held these services, although it meant that he would have to drive far on into the night to keep his schedule.

Sergeant Donovan was riding in the truck with us, because he had police business out in the same direction. We stayed at Beverley that first night with Mr. and Mrs. Maclaren. One or two matters that concerned Stevie were still running through my mind, and rather foolishly I raised the question of opium at the tea table.

I said, "Old Stevie said one thing that night in the hotel, Jim, after you went down. He said he got beautiful dreams."

"I bet he does."

"I know. But he said he gets them when he's lying down

28

with a pipe. Would you say he smokes opium? He lives with that Chinese."

Sergeant Donovan said a little tersely, "No reason to think that. He could smoke tobacco, couldn't he?"

"I suppose so." Something in his tone pulled me up, and made me feel that there was more in this than I quite understood. I said no more, but later in the evening Jim Maclaren had a word with me privately. "About Stevie and that Chinaman, Liang Shih," he said. "I wouldn't talk about opium to Donovan unless you've got some reason."

"You think they smoke it?"

"Of course they do. Liang Shih smokes opium—what Chink doesn't? It doesn't do them any harm, no more than smoking tobacco. Liang grows the poppies in his garden out on Dorset Downs, along with all the other stuff. Donovan knows all about it."

I said, "But that's illegal. If Donovan knows all about it, why does he let it go on?"

He grinned. "Arthur likes fresh vegetables."

I was silent for a moment. "You mean, if Liang Shih was prosecuted he might go away?"

"Of course he would. He'd pack up and go and grow his lettuces and poppies somewhere else, and then there'd be nothing but tinned peas in Landsborough. Arthur reckons that it's more important that the town should get fresh vegetables than that he should go out of his way to persecute one old Chinaman for doing what he's done all his life and that doesn't hurt him anyway." He paused. "Only, if people get to talking about it too much, he'll have to do something or else lose his job."

Right is not wholly right nor wrong completely wrong in the Gulf Country. I said no more about the opium.

With that, I put Stevie out of my mind. I had more important things to think about, because the dry season was

29

already well advanced and I had determined that before the rains came in December and stopped travelling I would visit every family in my rather extensive parish, and hold a service upon every cattle station. That may not seem a very ambitious programme for five months because there are only a hundred and ten families all told, but it meant a great deal of travelling. I did not care to leave Landsborough for longer than a week; I was trying to get the people of the town into the habit of going to their parish church again, and I felt it to be very important that I should be there on Sundays if it were humanly possible. I had no transport of my own, so I had to depend on the mail truck or on lifts in casual vehicles travelling about the area, and these seldom fitted in with my desire to be back in Landsborough every Sunday.

I worked hard all through the dry that year, and I succeeded in getting to know most of my parishioners. I think they appreciated it, because as time went on I began to get messages more and more frequently asking that I should go back to some family to comfort some dying old woman, or to conduct a funeral service over a new, hastily dug grave, or to baptise a baby. These calls set back my schedule, of course, but I was able to attend to all of them and get to the place where I was needed within two or three days.

There was another race meeting at Landsborough in September, but I did not go to it. A clergyman can do little in a town that is enjoying a race meeting; his opportunity for service comes at quieter times. It seemed to me that I was better occupied in visiting in the more distant parts of the parish, and I did not bother to return to Landsborough until that Saturday. By then the meeting was over and most of the people had gone back to their stations, but half a dozen station owners and managers had stayed in the town with their wives to come to church on Sunday, and that was a great encouragement to me.

I asked Sister Finlay if she had had Stevie up at the hospital. "No, not this time," she said. "He was in town for the races, but Liang Shih came in with the vegetables on Friday, and I think he went back with him." She paused. "He wasn't looking at all well."

I smiled. "I'm not surprised at that."

"No . . ." She thought for a minute. "I believe he's got something the matter with him," she said. "I was saying so to Templeton only the other night. He's got that sort of grey look about him." She paused. "Dr. Curtis was here with the flying ambulance and I asked him to have a look at Stevie if he got a chance, but they got a call to go to Forest Range on the second day to take an Abo stockman to the hospital at the Curry with broken ribs. I don't think he ever saw Stevie."

"Is there another doctor coming here, at any time?"

"There's nothing fixed," she said. "I've got it in mind. But it's a bit difficult, with him living out there in the bush. I don't suppose he'd come in to see a doctor, and anyway the doctor would be gone before we could get a message to him, probably. It's only a fancy that I got when I saw him this time. It may have been just that he had a hangover that day."

I kept it in my mind that I should go out to the market garden upon Dorset Downs before the wet, to visit Liang Shih and Stevie in their home. But a visit such as that came low down on my list of priorities; I could not hope to do much for them spiritually, and their house was off the beaten track and difficult for me to get to without a truck of my own. I always meant to go to them before the wet, and I never went.

Those last few weeks were very exhausting. November is always a hot month in North Queensland, and that year it

31

was particularly trying. I was hurrying against time, moreover, to finish getting around my parish while travelling was still easy, and I took a good deal out of myself. I knew that when the rains set in about Christmas time I should have plenty of time for rest in my vicarage, since it would be impossible to move very far from Landsborough till March or April. I drove myself hard in those last few weeks; I'm not a young man any longer, and I must confess that I got very tired indeed.

We got a few short rainstorms early in December and as usual these made conditions worse than ever, for they did little to relieve the heat and brought the humidity up very high. Every movement now made one sweat profusely, and once wet one's clothes stayed wet for a long time. I got prickly heat, which is a thing I seldom suffer from, and the continuous itching made it very difficult to sleep. Everyone began to suffer from nervous irritability and bad temper, and everyone looked anxiously each day for the rains that would bring this difficult season to an end.

The rains came at last, a few days before Christmas. For three days it rained practically without ceasing, heavily and continuously. The dusty roads gradually turned into mud wallows, and motor traffic ceased for the time being. Landsborough retired into winter quarters, so to speak. I lay on my bed for most of those three days revelling in the moderation of the heat and in the absence of sunshine, and reading the fourth volume of Winston Churchill's war memoirs which an old friend had sent me from Godalming.

The wet brought its own problems, of course. I had to go down to the hotel twice a day for my meals and it was still so hot that a raincoat was almost unbearable; if one walked down in a coat one got as wet from sweat as if one went without one. If the rain was light I went without a coat, because wet clothes are no great hardship in the tropics. The difficulty, of course, lay in getting any dry clothes to put on; my vicarage has no fireplace and there was now no sunshine to dry anything. Mrs. Roberts was very kind and let me dry some of my washing by her kitchen fire, but the difficulty was a real one, and I often had to wear wet clothes all day and sleep in a wet bed.

Christmas came and went. We had a carol service in the church with *Good King Wenceslas* and *See amid the Winter Snow*, and Miss Foster had to spend some time and energy in explaining to the children what snow was, a task made more difficult by the fact that she had never seen it herself. We had a children's party in the Shire Hall with a Christmas tree with imitation snow on it, and I dressed up as Santa Claus and gave the presents away. The aeroplane from Cloncurry brought us the cinema operator with his projector, three dramas, and *Snow White*, which none of the children had ever seen, so altogether we had quite a merry time.

After these excitements things went rather flat in Landsborough, and the rain fell steadily. In these conditions and although I had been taking my pills, I fell ill with an attack of malaria. It was nothing like so bad as the first bout that I had had in Salamaua, and I knew what to do about it now. I lay in bed sweating and a little delirious for a day, dosing myself; Mrs. Roberts was very kind and brought some things up to my vicarage and either she or Coty looked in every two hours to make me a cup of tea. On the second day Sister Finlay heard that I was ill and came to see what was the matter, and gave me a good dressing down, and wrapped me up in blankets and took me to the hospital in Art Duncan's utility, which got bogged a hundred yards from the hospital, so that I had to get out and walk the rest of the way. Finlay and Templeton put me to bed in more comfortable surroundings than I had been in for some time, and I stayed in hospital for the next week.

The fever spent its force after the first few days, as I had known it would, and they let me get up for dinner and sit in a dressing gown to write my parish magazine, going to bed again before tea. My temperature was generally normal at that time though it rose a point or so each evening, but that was nothing to worry about. I was sitting writing in their sitting room on the afternoon of January the 8th; I remember the date particularly because it was two days after Epiphany. I had not been able to preach in church the previous day, the first Sunday after Epiphany, and so I was writing what I wanted to tell my parishioners in the magazine. January the 8th it was, and I was sitting writing in the middle of the afternoon when I heard the sound of a horse and wheels. I got up and went to the verandah, and I saw Liang Shih draw up before the hospital in the vegetable cart.

I was surprised to see him, because we had had no fresh vegetables since Christmas and we all thought that we should see no more until the rains were over and the roads improved. Sister Finlay and Templeton were lying down; I went and called them, and then went back to the verandah. It was raining a little; Liang was getting down from his two wheeled vehicle and tying the reins to the fence. He had an old Army waterproof sheet tied with a bit of string around his shoulders to serve as a cape; under that he was in his working shirt and dirty, soaked trousers; he wore a battered old felt hat upon his head to shed the rain.

I said, "Come in out of the wet, Liang. Nice to see you."

He came on to the verandah. "Sister, she here?" he asked.

"She's just coming," I replied. "We didn't expect to see you for a bit. What have you got for us?"

"I no got vegetables," he said. "Garden all under the water. I come see Sister. Stevie, he got sick in stomach."

"Sick in the stomach, is he?" I asked. "What sort of sickness, Liang?"

He put his hand upon his lower abdomen. "He got pain here, big pain. He been sick three days."

"Is he very bad, Liang?"

He nodded. "Very bad now. I want Sister come see him, or perhaps he die."

Two

SISTER FINLAY came out on to the verandah behind me. I turned, and told her that Stevie was sick. She nodded briefly, and I knew that she had been expecting this. "Where is he sick, Liang?" she asked. "Show me just where the place is."

He put his hand upon his abdomen and rubbed it over a fairly wide area. "He sick here."

"Does that mean anything to you?" I asked her.

She shook her head. "It might be almost anything." She turned to Liang. "Has he been taking anything for it?"

Perhaps there was a tiny hesitation. "Hot cloths," he said. "I put hot cloths on belly. Very hot water, Sister."

"And that didn't do any good?"

"No, Sister."

"Why didn't you bring him in here with you?"

Liang said, "He no understand me—him mind away. I no can lift him, put in jinker. I no know what to do, and then I think better come for help."

She stood biting her lip for a minute. "We'll have to get him in here, Liang," she said. "He can't be nursed out there."

"He very sick," he said. "We take stretcher and put stretcher on the cart, maybe."

"What's the road like?" I asked. "Did you have much difficulty getting in here, Liang?"

"Or-right," he said. "Water near house, one mile, two mile." He put his hand down to within nine or ten inches of the floor. "Deep like that. Then road or-right."

A mile or more of shallow water wasn't quite so good, but the old horse could pull the light two wheeled cart where no motor vehicle could go.

"All right, Liang," said Sister Finlay. "I'll come back with you. If we go at once, can we get to your place before dark?"

He nodded. "We start quick, Sister."

I turned to him. "How long did it take you to get in here, Liang?"

"I no got watch," he said. "I think two hours, maybe."

It was nearly three in the afternoon, and in that overcast weather it would be dark before six. I had never been to Liang's house but I had been told that it was ten miles out; clearly in the conditions the old horse would not go very fast. I turned to Sister Finlay. "We'd better get away as soon as we can. I'll come with you, Sister."

She hesitated for a moment. "You'd better stay here," she said. "I'll get Sergeant Donovan to come out with us. I don't want you getting a relapse."

"I ought to go," I said. "If the man's likely to die, I should be with him."

"He won't die before we get him back here to the hospital," she said. "I'll take some dopes with me. All I want is somebody to help me get him on the cart and bring him in. No, you stay here. I'll pick up Donovan on the way out."

It was sensible, of course; I had only been out of bed a day or two. "I tell you what I'll do," I said. "While you're getting ready, I'll go on down and warn Donovan, so that he'll be ready to start when you come past with Liang." There are no telephones in Landsborough.

37

"That 'ld be a help," she said. "I'll be about a quarter of an hour."

I went and slipped on a pair of trousers and a raincoat and shoes, and set off down the road to the police sergeant's house. Mrs. Donovan came out to meet me on the verandah. "Afternoon, Mrs. Donovan," I said. "Is Arthur in?"

"Why, Mr. Hargreaves!" she said. "I heard you'd been sick—I do hope you're recovered. Art's gone to Millangarra—he rode out this morning."

"When's he coming back?"

"He'll have stayed for dinner," she said. "He said he'd be back before dark. Is it anything important?"

I told her briefly what had happened. "Jim Phillips is still on leave?"

"I'm afraid he is, Mr. Hargreaves. I don't know what to suggest, unless she took one of the black boys. Dicky might go."

I shook my head. "I'll go with her myself. When Arthur comes in, tell him where we've gone, will you? If we're not back by ten o'clock tomorrow morning, ask him to ride out that way and have a look. I'm just a bit afraid that with all this rain the water may be rising."

"I think it will," she said. "Liang Shih got through all right, did he?"

"Didn't have any difficulty," I told her. "If you'd just tell Art when he comes in."

I met Liang and Sister coming towards me in the cart as I walked back towards the hospital. "Donovan's away," I said. "He's gone to Millangarra—I left a message." I swung myself up into the cart. "I'll come with you, sister."

"I don't like it, Mr. Hargreaves. There must be *someone* who could come."

"I'll be all right," I said. "If we waste time looking for somebody you won't get there in daylight."

38

She said no more, because it would be most dangerous to go wandering about in darkness in the flooded Queensland bush; it was imperative that the journey should be finished in daylight. We stopped for a minute or two at the vicarage while I went in and picked up my little case of sacramental vessels and a small electric torch, and then we started out upon the road to Dorset Downs. It was raining steadily.

One of the characteristics of that part of North Queensland is that it is entirely featureless; it is a flat country with no hills or mountain ranges, covered in sparse forest and intersected with river beds. The view is exactly the same whichever way you look, and the sun gives little guidance in the middle of the day at that time of the year, for it is directly overhead. It is a very easy country to get bushed in; the sense of direction can be easily lost, and when that happens the only safe course is to camp till the evening when the setting sun will show the direction of the west.

That afternoon there was no sun in any case; we plodded on through the rain, the old horse sometimes trotting on hard patches but more often walking and labouring in the shafts to pull the jinker over the soft ground. In half an hour I had lost all sense of direction; we might have been going north or south, or east or west for all I knew. Liang, however, knew the way; from time to time he showed us broken trees or a side track branching off into the bush that were familiar signposts to him on the road he knew so well.

We were all of us wet through in a very short time, of course, but with the temperature still in the eighties that was no great matter; there was little risk of a chill, because there was no wind at all. We sat there in a row on the bench seat of the jinker, motionless but for the movement of our bodies as the wheels bumped and swayed over the uneven ground, not talking, depressed. The grey, monotonous scene and the hot, steaming rain, and perhaps a sense of the futility of our mission to relieve this drink sodden old man, all these conspired to rob us of all wish to talk. For my part, although it was my duty to go to offer spiritual consolation to any man near to his death, I went with the knowledge that my offer to Stevie would almost certainly be spurned, and I could not help thinking of the cheerful, green painted hospital rooms that I had left to come upon this somewhat worthless errand.

Presently we came to pools and standing water on the road, and soon the pools were continuous and we were driving through water several inches deep, the old horse making a great splashing as he plodded on. I roused myself, and said to Liang, "Has the water risen much since you came out this morning?"

He said, "No water here this morning. Water deeper now."

"What do you think about it? Will we be able to get to your house?"

"Or-right," he said. "We get to house or-right."

He kept on steadily, and though now we could seldom see the track it was clear that he never left it, for the wheels rolled beneath the water on fairly hard ground. With the approach of evening the light began to fail, or possibly it was that the clouds were getting thicker. I asked Liang, "How much further have we got to go? How long before we get there?"

He shrugged his shoulders. "Two-three mile, maybe."

"Think we'll get there before dark?"

"Or-right," he said. "We get there before dark."

Presently we came to land that undulated slightly, so that islands of dry land appeared among the floods, and here we had to go more cautiously, for we were getting to a region that was cut up by tributaries of the Dorset River. We crossed one or two small creeks, places that Liang identified carefully and where the depth of water reached almost to the wheel hubs. Presently, as we drove cautiously through one of these rising creeks, we saw a very unpleasant sight.

There were three or four Hereford cows standing on a dry piece of land quite near to us, part of the Dorset Downs station. One of these cows standing near the water's edge had a small calf running with her, only two or three days old. The cow raised her head to look at us as we splashed past, and moved in curiosity a little nearer to us, and to the water's edge. The calf moved nearer to the water, too.

I happened to be looking at them, and I saw the whole thing happen. The long nose of a crocodile thrust quietly up out of the water and the jaws closed upon the near foreleg of the calf; there was a great thrashing in the water and a struggling as the brute dragged the calf under. The thrashing and the struggling went on under the water for a time, and then everything was still. The cow did nothing about it, but stood looking puzzled.

Sister Finlay said, "We should have brought a rifle."

"I never thought of it," I said. "I should have borrowed one from Mrs. Donovan."

We went on in silence after that, busy with our own thoughts, and now the water was over a foot deep, and the light was definitely going. Presently Liang pointed with his whip to a ridge of dry land ahead of us, perhaps a mile away across the surface of the water. "House," he said. "House on land."

"That's your house is it?" I asked him. "Where we're going to?"

He nodded, and at that moment we went down into the hole. It was impossible, of course, to see the track ahead of us, and perhaps I had distracted Liang's attention from the course. Whatever was the reason, one moment we were on firm ground and the next moment the old horse was swimming, and the jinker was rolling down an underwater bank pushing the horse further out.

Liang dropped the reins and stood up, and plunged over the side to go to the horse's head; he must have known the ground, for he was wading hardly more than waist deep. I hesitated for a moment, and then, shamed by the old Chinaman, I plunged in from my side to go to the horse on the near side and to lighten the jinker. The water was out of my depth, and I swam to the horse's head with the thought of a crocodile searing on my mind, terrified. My feet touched ground at the same moment as the horse's feet, and then Liang and I were on each side of his head as he fought and strained to climb the steep underwater bank and pull the sinking jinker up it. Sister Finlay was standing up, uncertain whether to get out and swim. I shouted to her to stay where she was.

With a series of strains and heaves the horse pulled the jinker up the bank and stood in a foot of water, quivering with fright. I was quivering no less, and even Liang was disturbed, I think, because we all got back into the jinker in remarkably short time, out of the way of the crocodiles.

"Well, that's all right," I said rather stupidly, because one has to say something when one is frightened. "There must have been a hole there." And then I looked around, "Everything all right?"

And then I saw that everything was far from right. The tailboard of the jinker had fallen down, and Sister Finlay's case, and my case of sacramental vessels, were no longer in the cart with us. They must have slid out as the jinker was pulled up the bank, and they were nowhere to be seen.

"Hold on a minute," I said to Liang. "We've lost the cases." I looked under the seat, but they were not there. Darkness was falling quickly, and the water behind us looked grey and menacing, and deep enough, I knew, to hold a crocodile. My own case could lie there till the dry weather, perhaps, for in emergency I could give the Sacrament in a teacup and had often done so, but the sister's case was essential. Without her drugs and medicines she could do little to relieve her patient.

"Wait a minute while I find them," I said, and slipped down into the water again, absolutely terrified. Sister Finlay said, "Come back, Mr. Hargreaves!" but I did up the tailboard of the jinker and started to walk slowly back, feeling under water with my feet to find the cases, miserable with fear. When I was about waist deep down the sub-merged bank my foot touched one of them and I stooped down in the water and picked it out; as luck would have it, it was my own case of sacramental vessels.

"Here's one of them," I said. "The other one won't be far off," and I waded back and put it in the jinker. Liang and Sister Finlay were expostulating with me, but I was too shaken with my terror to answer them, and I started back into the pool to look for the other case. I could not touch it with my feet, and when the water was up to my shoulders I dived down, and searched for it under water with my hands among the mud and grass. When I came to the surface Liang and Sister Finlay were splashing through the water to me; they seized me one on each side and began to propel me back to the jinker.

"I'll find it in a minute," I said. "Let me have one more try." And Sister Finlay said, "You're absolutely crazy. This place is full of crocodiles. I can manage without it tonight."

"But it's got all your medicines in it," I said.

She was quite angry. "Get back into that cart at once," she said. "I don't know how you could be such a fool." We were all very frightened secretly, of course, or she wouldn't have spoken to me in that way.

We all got back into the jinker in silence, and Liang touched the old horse with the whip; he strained and we moved forward. It was really getting quite dark now; we could still see the loom of the dry land ahead of us, but I could see no sign of the house. I found out soon that the land on which the house stood was a ridge a mile or so in length between two creeks, which was so high that it was never flooded; the house was at one end of this dry ridge and we were approaching it from the other.

We plodded on through the water in the dusk; the water grew shallower and the old horse went faster, and presently in the dim light the track appeared before us winding through the gum trees, and we were on dry land. And then we saw a most extraordinary sight. The ground under the trees was covered as usual with a light growth of stunted scrub and grass and bracken fern, and in this undergrowth were animals, hundreds and hundreds of them. I saw Hereford cows and bulls, and Brahmah bulls, and scores of wallabies, and several enormous black wild pigs with long faces and savage tusks. There were dogs there, too— dingoes, perhaps, or cattle dogs gone wild and breeding in the bush. There were plains turkeys there stalking about like little emus, and there were goannas and lizards and snakes upon the track ahead of us, gliding off out of our way. All these animals had swum and walked and crawled and hopped and crept to this sanctuary of dry land among the floods, and now they stood looking at us as we passed in the half light.

I said to Liang, "Do you get all these animals here every year, in the wet?"

He nodded. "Every year." He turned and grinned at me. "I Buddhist. Animals, they know. I no eat 'um."

We plodded on through the trees, and now I was impatient to arrive. We had sat upon the hard seat of the jinker for about three hours, and I was beginning to feel quite unwell. As I have said, my temperature had been rising every evening just a point or so, but now I was feeling hot and I was having difficulty in focusing my eyes and thinking clearly. I was very much annoyed at the thought that my fever might be coming back again; at all costs I must suppress it till I got back to Landsborough next day. I felt that if I could get down out of the jinker and have a long drink of cold water and sit quietly in a comfortable chair for a little I should be all right, and able to carry on with what I had to do that night without letting Sister Finlay see that I was not very well.

I was thankful when at last we saw the house in the last of the light. It was a poor little place of two rooms built of weatherboard with an iron roof; whatever paint there might once have been on it was now bleached and blown away, and it had weathered to the normal grey colour of ancient wood. It was built on posts as usual in that country, and a short flight of steps led up to a rickety verandah. A tumble-down fence surrounded it and stretched away into the darkness.

There was no light in the house.

Liang got down from the jinker and tied the reins to the fence and went up the steps; we followed him. It was quite dark under the roof and we heard him striking a match; a sputter of flame followed, and Liang made some kind of exclamation. Then he lit a candle that was standing in a saucer on a table; as the light slowly grew we could take in the scene.

There was a bed in the room with a mosquito net, but this net was thrown back disclosing the soiled, rumped sheet and pillow. Stevie was lying on this bed clothed in shirt and trousers, with bare feet; only the top button of the trousers was done up. On a chair beside the bed was a small spirit lamp, and a slender metal pipe with a tiny bowl, and a saucer with some brown stuff in it; there was a heavy, acrid smell about the room. On the floor beside the bed a cheap paraffin lamp, the sort that hangs upon a wall, lay over-turned; the oil had flowed out of this and made a pool upon the wooden floor. Stevie did not appear to be conscious.

Liang went forward and picked up the lamp and swept away the pipe and spirit lamp and saucer, but not before we had seen them. Sister Finlay went forward to the bed. "Evening, Stevie," she said. "I'm Sister Finlay from the hospital. What's the matter with you?"

There was no answer; the old man was clean out, but whether from the opium or from the march of his disease I could not say. Finlay threw off her raincoat and took Stevie's wrist to feel his pulse, peering at her wrist watch. "Would you see if you can get that lamp lit, Mr. Hargreaves?" she asked. "We'll have to have more light than this."

I picked up the lamp from the floor and examined it; the glass was unbroken. I asked Liang, "Where's your drum of kerosene?" He did not answer me, but began to hunt about the cluttered room for something, and finally produced about an inch of candle end. I said, "I've got a torch here," and opened my soaked case; the torch was lying in a puddle of water with my cassock, but it lit all right. Liang grinned, and led the way down from the verandah underneath the house, which stood on posts as many of these houses do.

The drum of kerosene was there, and that's about all there was—just the drum. Somebody—it could only have been Stevie—had left the tap running, and there was paraffin all over the earth floor, soaking in and running away with the water. We shall never know exactly how he did it, but I think he must have gone down to refill the lamp, and probably a spasm of his abdominal pain took him while

46

he was down there, so that it was all that he could do to get back to his bed. Anyway, the barrel was just about empty.

Liang picked up a can and made me hold it while he tilted the drum forward, but only about a teacupful ran out into the can because the drum had already been tilted down a little as it lay. "Is that all you've got, Liang?" I asked. "Have you got another drum?"

He shook his head. "No more drum."

"No more kerosene than this?"

"No more."

It was bad, but there was nothing to be done about it. He produced a funnel and we emptied the can carefully into the lamp, filling it about a quarter full. We went back up into the house, and I explained the position to Sister Finlay. "I'm sorry, Sister," I said, "but this is all the kerosene there is. I shouldn't think it would last through the night, but it may. We'd better turn the wick down when you've finished —make it last as long as possible."

I helped her to get Stevie's trousers off so that she could examine him. We laid him on his back, and he did not wake, and then I held the lamp while she examined the man's abdomen. There was a swelling which was evidently tender, because when she pressed it gently he stirred and complained even in his deep, drugged sleep. Presently she pulled the sheet over him to the waist, and stood there looking down at him in silence. "Peritonitis, I should think," she said at last. "He's so heavily doped there's not much we can do."

She turned to Liang. "Show me the things that were on this chair, Liang," she said, and there was no acrimony in her tone. "The pipe, and the opium."

He brought them out and showed them to her in silence.

"Does he smoke much of this?" she asked.

"Three," he said. "Three, when it is dark, to sleep. Not good smoke more."

47

"You smoke it yourself, I suppose?" I asked.

He nodded.

Sister Finlay asked him, "Do three pipes send a man to sleep like that?"

He shook his head. "He smoke more yesterday, today. Good for pain."

"How many pipes do you think he's had today?"

He picked up the saucer and looked at the remnant of brown, treacle paste smeared on the bottom. "Ten— eleven," he said. "I not know. I think when he wake up he smoke one, two pipes, good for pain, and then he sleeps again, one, two hours."

She leaned over the patient and raised one eyelid carefully; I held the lamp for her while she looked at the eye. Then she stood back again from the bed. "It's not a bad thing, in a way," she said at last. "We'll have to get him to the aerodrome tomorrow somehow, and get the ambulance to fly him to the Curry. There'll have to be an operation. If I'd had my case with me I'd probably have had to give him a dope, and now he's doped himself. In a way, and in the circumstances, it may be rather a good thing."

I nodded. "What *is* opium?" I asked.

"It's morphine," she said. "I don't know what else it is, but that's the element that works in it. It's what I should have given him in any case, so far as the narcotic goes."

There was nothing to be done, and I sat down wearily on a packing case beside a table that was littered with the remains of a meal; my head was swimming and I was very hot. From a great distance I heard Finlay say, "We'll just have to watch him tonight, and hope we can get him out of this tomorrow, somehow."

I forced attention to what she was saying. "The water will be higher, with all this rain," I said.

48

"I know. That's what I've been thinking about." There was a pause, and then she said, "Are you feeling all right, Mr. Hargreaves?"

"I'm all right," I said. The next thing that I knew was that her hand was on my wrist taking my pulse. "You're not all right at all," she said. "You've got a temperature."

"Not bad," I said. "I'd like a drink of water, though."

She spoke to Liang, and in a dream I heard her arguing about something with him, but I could not comprehend what it was all about. Then she was giving me a glass of water, thick in colour and tasting of the floods, but it refreshed me, and I felt more myself.

Presently Liang appeared from the other room, where there was a wood fuel cooking stove, and began to lay the table for a meal. He produced three large wooden bowls, three cheap spoons, and bread that was mis-shapen and home made as a sort of a flat bun. Lastly he brought in from the other room a copper saucepan full of hot, steaming soup, thickened with many vegetables. This was our supper, and very good it was; I had two bowls of the soup and felt a great deal better. At the end of the meal there was a cup of black tea, without sugar.

It was while we were drinking our tea, sitting at the table in silence, that the rain stopped. The drumming on the iron roof had made a background noise that we had been unconscious of, but now it reduced, and finally stopped altogether. I raised my head and looked at Sister Finlay, and she looked at me.

"That's better," I said. "I was beginning to get a little bit worried about getting him away tomorrow."

"I was thinking of that, too," she said. "If it gets any deeper we shall have to have a boat."

"They've got a boat at Dorset Downs," I said. "Donovan

knows we're here, and he'll organise something for us in the morning." I turned to the Chinaman. "How far are you from Dorset Downs homestead, Liang?" I asked.

"Ten—fifteen miles, maybe," he said. "Not far."

There was nothing much for either Sister Finlay or myself to do; Stevie lay in a coma, though he stirred once or twice. I got up presently and went out on to the verandah; it was cooler there, with a faint whisper of a breeze that cooled my fever. The clouds were breaking up and a full moon was showing now and then, illuminating the natural clearing in which the house stood and the gum tree forest beyond.

I stood there letting the light breeze play through my clothes, while my eyes gradually adjusted to night vision. And then I saw a most extraordinary sight.

The animals were there, standing or sitting at the far edge of the clearing, grouped in a rough semi-circle round the house, their heads all turned in our direction, watching. The cattle were there, and the wild dogs, and the dingoes, and the wild pigs, and the wallabies, all at a distance of about a hundred yards from the verandah. They did not seem to be grazing or moving about much, although they were not motionless; one or two of the dogs were scratching and the cattle were changing their position a little. They were just standing or sitting there in a semi-circle round the house, watching us.

I turned and went back into the room, and said to Sister Finlay, "Come and look at this." She came out on the verandah, and when her eyes became accustomed to the moonlight she saw them too. "It's the lamp," I said. "I suppose they've been attracted by the light."

Behind us, Liang grunted; he had come out quietly, and I had not realised that he was there. The sister turned to him. "Do you often get them like this?"

He said something that neither of us could quite understand, and then he turned and went back into the house. We stayed on the verandah watching the animals for a time, and because Liang was not with us I could speak more freely to the sister. "What's the position with Stevie?" I asked her. "Do you think he'll get through?"

She said, "I doubt it. I don't know what's wrong with him. I think it's peritonitis by now; if it is, I doubt if he'll get as far as Cloncurry. It's quite possible that he might die tonight."

I nodded; I had been thinking the same thing. "I'm very sorry about your medicine case, Sister. I ought to have looked after the things better."

"It doesn't matter," she said. "It doesn't look as if I'll have much use for what was in it."

We stayed out on the verandah for a time. I was still hct and it was cool there and refreshing, but presently I got a cold spell and began to shiver a little, and I made some excuse and we went back into the room. Liang was not there, and now there was a faint odour of fragrance in the room that I had not noticed before. I went and looked into the other room, to see what was there.

It was lit by the candle, now burnt down quite low. There was a small, tawdry little shrine set up in one corner of the room, with dirty Chinese hangings; in it was a battered Chinese Buddha mostly painted red and very dirty. There was a stick of incense burning in front of this, a joss stick, I suppose, and Liang was kneeling in front of it in silent prayer. I withdrew quietly.

"He's in there, praying," I whispered to the sister. "In front of an idol."

She raised her eyebrows, but there was nothing we could do about it, and it was none of our business. We turned the lamp low to conserve the kerosene, and settled down to wait

51

for something to happen. I sat dozing on a chair, hot and feverish; my clothes were dry by that time, but I was very uncomfortable. From time to time I got up and drank a glass of the muddy water, and sat down again.

I don't know what time it was when Stevie came to; perhaps about eleven o'clock, or midnight. We had been there for several hours. I was dozing in my chair, and woke to see Sister Finlay get up and go to the bedside. I got up also, and went over to the bed. She was feeling the pulse, and Stevie was now restless. Once or twice the eyes opened and shut. He had drawn his knees up tight against his stomach, evidently in pain.

"He's coming round," she said quietly. "This is where our job begins, Mr. Hargreaves. We could have done with that case, after all."

I crossed to the table and turned up the lamp, and then went back to the bed. Liang came out of the next room, roused, perhaps, by our movements; he stood with us in silence for a time watching the gradual return to consciousness and pain. Then he went softly to the verandah and stood looking out.

There was nothing I could do, and so I went out with him, and stood there while my eyes became accustomed. It was intermittent moonlight and darkness as the thick clouds parted and drifted across the moon, and in the passing, silvery light I saw that the animals were still there watching us, much as I had seen them before. I said to Liang again, "Do the animals usually come around like this, in the wet?"

He said, "Stevie die tonight."

"I hope not," I replied. "We'll get him to the hospital tomorrow."

He shook his head. "Animals, they come. I think he die."

I stared at him. "You think the animals know?"

He nodded. "Animals, they know."

I didn't see why the death of one drunken, dissolute old man should excite the animal kingdom very much, but there was no good arguing it with Liang, if indeed the language difficulties had permitted argument. I stayed with him in silence for a minute or two, and then went back into the room, to Sister Finlay and her patient.

Stevie was fully conscious now, and evidently in considerable pain. He was moaning a little; from time to time his face became distorted as the spasm racked him, and this was more eloquent to me than the noise that he was making.

When he saw me he said to Sister Finlay, "What's that Pommie parson doing here?" I think it was parson that he said, but Sister Finlay is sure that it was bastard, and says that she didn't know which way to look when he called the vicar a Pommie bastard. Whichever way it was, it doesn't matter. I went over to the bed and said, "I came out with Sister Finlay when we heard you were sick. Sergeant Donovan would have brought her out here, but he was away at Millangarra, so I came instead. How are you feeling, cobber?"

"I'm bad," he muttered. "I been bad three days. Got a bottle of whiskey, Roger?"

"I haven't," I said. "I didn't bring any, and anyway it wouldn't be good for you."

He stared at me for a minute. "Your name's Roger?"

"That's right," I said. "I'm Roger and you're Stevie."

"I know," he said. "Harps and angels' wings. Pack of bloody lies, that's what I think."

I felt Sister Finlay beside me quiver with indignation, and I must say it didn't look as though Stevie was likely to accept the sort of spiritual consolation that I could offer him.

"That's all right," I said. "We'll argue that one out when you're well. We'll get you into Landsborough tomorrow, and then the ambulance will come and fly you to Cloncurry."

"I flown further than that," he muttered. "Up 'n down, up 'n down, all across the world, carrying the Queen. Ottawa, Keeling Cocos, Nanyuki, Ratmalana—I know all them places. I got the Seventh Vote—did you know that, cobber? Did you know I got the Seventh Vote?"

I glanced at the sister, and she raised her eyebrows. He was wandering in his mind, of course, but anything that would take his thoughts off his pain was probably useful, since we had no morphia to ease it. "I never heard that," I replied. "How did you come to get the Seventh Vote?"

The pain hit him again, and his face contorted with the spasm. The current of his thought was broken, because presently he said, "I been sick in the belly three days. Got any whiskey, cobber?"

"I'm sorry," I said patiently. "I didn't bring any with me."

Sister Finlay said, "Lie down, and try and get some sleep, Stevie. It won't be long till morning, now, and then we'll get you to the hospital."

I withdrew a little from the bed, partly because I could not help her in her treatment of the disease, and partly because I was hot and sweating again, and my head was swimming, and I did not want her to see my condition. The old man's hallucinations went round and round in my tired brain, the Seventh Vote, Ottawa, Keeling Cocos, carrying the Queen. I seemed to remember that he had talked to me like that before. Where did it all come from, what vagrant memories had come together to be expressed in those words? Old copies of some travel magazine for Ottawa and Keeling Cocos? Some article in the *Australian Women's Weekly* about the Queen? And then the flying motif once again. But that was easier, because I knew that once a man has piloted an aeroplane the memory lies deep within his brain, and he can never forget it.

I sat there in a hot discomfort while the crisis rose upon the bed. From a great distance I watched the spasms, and watched Sister Finlay doing her best to help her patient; it was little enough that she could do. Liang was bringing hot, steaming cloths now from the other room, and they were laying them upon the skinny, rigid abdomen. And presently, as the hot fit passed and I grew temporarily more comfortable, I heard the old man say,

"Is Liang there?"

"He's just in the next room," said Sister Finlay. "Do you want to speak to him?"

Stevie nodded, and the sister called Liang, who came to the bedside. He said, "You want something, Stevie?"

"Too right, I want something," the old man said. "Give us a pipe, mate."

The Chinaman glanced at the sister, who shook her head, and Liang withdrew softly to the other room, leaving her to fight her patient. "Not now, Stevie," she said. "You've had enough of that for today—it would be dangerous to take any more. Come on—I'll give you another of these cloths."

There was a long, long pause. At last I heard him say in a weak voice, "Give us a whiskey, Sister. I'm bloody crook."

She said a little desperately, "I haven't got a whiskey, Stevie, and it wouldn't be good for you. Lie still, and try and get some rest."

The spasm came to him again, and I saw her holding him down upon the bed with both hands on his shoulders. Liang must have been somewhere in the background watching, because he came forward softly and helped her, and together they fought with Stevie till the spasm passed. I felt ashamed that I was not helping her myself, and that I had given in to my weakness, and I got to my feet, holding on to the table.

"Can I do anything?" I asked stupidly.

The patient was quiet again now, for the moment and until the next spasm. She turned to me, and she was sweating with her exertions, and a wisp of her damp hair had fallen down over her eyes. "How are you feeling, Mr. Hargreaves?" she asked.

"I'm all right," I said. "I felt a bit queer just then, but I'm all right now."

She brushed the hair back from her eyes. "Come out on the verandah."

We went out of the room, and the moon was still fitfully lighting up the clearing and the forest, and the animals were still there watching us. She turned to me, and said in a low tone, "I know you're feverish. Can you understand what I'm saying, Mr. Hargreaves?"

"Of course," I said. "I understand you perfectly."

She nodded. "I don't think he's got a chance," she said quietly. She glanced at her wrist watch. "It's an hour and ten minutes since he came to, and he's much weaker now than he was then. I think he'll die before morning, Mr. Hargreaves."

I nodded. "I should think so. There's nothing we can do?"

"Nothing," she said. "The only possible thing would be an operation now, at once, and I can't do that. Even if I had my medicine case I couldn't do anything for him, except give him a dope to ease the pain. He's having a great deal of pain."

"I know," I said. "I can see that."

"I think our job now is to make things easy for him," she said quietly. "I don't think it would hurt him to have a few pipes of that opium stuff. I don't think it will make any difference, now." She looked up at me. "Would you think that very terrible?"

I shook my head. "No. I should think it was the kindest thing that you could do."

"It's very unprofessional," she muttered. "I don't know . . . If he were quieter, it might conserve his strength . . ."

I said, "I should let him have it."

She nodded gravely. "I think one ought to." She hesitated, and then turned to me. "I don't think it will kill him," she said quietly, "but if he takes enough to put him under, I think he may die before he comes to. I want you to understand exactly the position, Mr. Hargreaves."

"Nevertheless," I said, "I think you ought to let him have it." I hesitated, and then I said, "If I may, I should like to sit and talk to him a little, while he's going off."

Behind us, the darkness was closing down. "Of course," she said. "I've never seen this stuff work, and I don't know how long it will take. If it's like any of the others, there'll be a drowsy period when the pain is almost gone, before he goes to sleep. He may be able to talk sensibly for a few minutes then."

The shadows crept out of the room behind and enveloped us; on the far side of the clearing we could see the beasts of the field, waiting. She shivered a little. "Those animals . . ." she said. She turned back to her patient, and then said, "For goodness sake!"

"What is it, Sister?" And then I saw what it was. The room behind us was indeed nearly in darkness, because the kerosene in the lamp had come to an end, and there was now only a small flickering blue flame above the wick. "Never mind," I said. "There's a candle somewhere."

I went into the room, and called, "Liang!" He came at once from the other room, and a ray of candlelight shone from the door. He looked at the lamp with concern and went straight to it and shook it, but it was bone dry. I went to my case and opened it, and took out my torch. "I've got this," I said, and it shone a pool of yellow light upon the floor. "Have you got any more candles, Liang?"

"Little candle," he said ruefully. "Very small." He went back into the other room, and returned with about an inch of candle burning in a saucer.

"Is that all there is?" I asked.

He nodded.

"No more candles?"

He shook his head.

"No kerosene? Nothing more to burn for a light?"

He shook his head again.

I turned to the sister. "We'll be in darkness before morning, I'm afraid. The candle won't last long, and this torch is very dim."

She laughed shortly. "It's just one thing after another tonight, Mr. Hargreaves. It doesn't matter much, after he's gone to sleep. We'll have to keep watch over him, but when he's dropped off we'd better put the lights out, so as to have them if we need them later on. He may come to again."

"I should think that's the best thing to do," I said.

She turned to Liang. "Give him a pipe now, if he wants it."

"One pipe?" he asked.

"Give him as many as he wants, to kill the pain and send him to sleep," she said.

He took the torch from me, and padded off into the next room. He came back presently with the long metal pipe and the spirit lamp and the brown stuff in the saucer that we had seen upon the chair beside the bed as we came in. He put them down upon the chair again, and drew the chair up to the bed.

Sister Finlay said, "Liang's got a pipe for you, if you want it, Stevie. You can have one now."

He did not speak, but lying on his back he made an effort

to roll over on to his right side, towards the room. He seemed to be incapable of moving the lower part of his body; Liang moved forward and with Sister Finlay helping him arranged the old man's limbs in a comfortable and reclining position on his side. Then Liang lit the spirit stove upon the chair, and took a sort of skewer and dipped it in the brown substance, and picked up a morsel about the size of a pea, and began to toast it in the blue flame while it burned and sizzled. Then he transferred it carefully to the tiny bowl of the metal pipe, put the bowl to the flame, and drew in slowly to get the morsel glowing; he exhaled at once. Then he gave the pipe to Stevie.

The old man took it, and put it to his mouth; he inhaled deeply, held it for a few moments, and exhaled it from his nose; the smoke was acrid and unpleasant. He did this four or five times, and it appeared to give him almost instantaneous relief, because within a minute or two he was lying more relaxed, and the strained lines of pain were smoothing on his face. The pipe was apparently finished with those few inhalations, because he handed it back to Liang.

"Another?" asked the Chinaman.

The old man nodded, and Liang set about preparing another pipe. I moved forward and sat down on the edge of the bed.

"Stevie," I said. "I'm Roger Hargreaves. You know me; I'm the parson from Landsborough. Remember?"

"Too right," he said weakly. "You got on Black Joke."

"That's right," I said. "You and I are cobbers. You're a sick man now, Stevie. You'll go off to sleep after you've had these pipes, and while you're asleep we're going to take you into hospital for an operation. I think it's going to be successful, and you'll be strong and well again, but there's a risk in every operation. I've got to die some time, and so has Liang here, and Sister Finlay; we've all got to face it when the time comes. You've got to face it too, Stevie. You may die tonight. Would you like me to say a prayer or two before you go to sleep?"

"Harps and angels' wings," he muttered. "I don't hold with that."

"I know you don't," I said. "What creed were you baptised in to, Stevie? What church did you go to when you were a boy?"

"I never went to no church," he said. "I was raised out on the station."

"When you were in the army, what did you have on your identity disc?" I asked him. "C. of E., or R.C., or what?"

"Church of England," he said sleepily. "That's what they said I was."

"Then you're one of my parishioners," I said. "Look, Stevie, I'm going to say two little prayers, and then I want you to answer one or two questions. They're very simple. Now listen carefully."

So I did what I had to do, and he was quite good about it, and I gave him the Absolution. Then Liang was ready with the second pipe, and he took that and smoked it, and now he was much easier, and apparently in little pain.

He handed the pipe back to Liang.

"Another?" asked the Chinaman, and Stevie nodded. I glanced at Sister Finlay; she shrugged her shoulders slightly, and then nodded.

Stevie said, "I'm dying, aren't I?"

"I hope not," I replied. "If you are, there's nothing to be afraid of."

"I'm crook all right," he muttered. "She wouldn't let me have three pipes, 'less I was bloody crook. I ain't afraid of dying. I'll go carrying the Queen."

The hallucinations were returning; no doubt that was

the opium. Perhaps the fading mind was poisoned through and through with that outlandish drug. "You'll be all right," I said quietly. "God is very merciful, and he won't judge you too hard."

"You don't know nothing," the old man muttered weakly. "I could tell you things. Old Liang here, he's got the rights of it. I ain't done so good. I know it. I'll start lower down next time. But I'll be right. Everyone gets another shot, however low you go, and I'll be right."

He seemed to be convinced about reincarnation in some form, and he was too weak for me to argue with him. I was weak myself; the hot fit had come on me again, and I was restless and sweating.

"You'll be right," I said. "God will look after you."

There was a long, long pause while Liang fiddled about preparing the next pipe. "I ain't afraid of dying," Stevie muttered at last. "That's nothing. Old Liang here, he knows a thing or two. It's just going off to sleep and sliding off into the next time, into the dream. I reckon that I'd rather be there than here."

I was too hot and fuddled with my fever to say anything to that. Liang lit the pellet in the bowl of the third pipe and gave it to Stevie; the old man inhaled deeply four or five times, and gave it back to Liang.

"Another?"

Stevie gave an almost imperceptible shake of the head, and relaxed on to the pillow. Liang gathered up the spirit lamp and the pipe and the saucer of opium, and padded off with them to the next room. I moved and sat down on the chair beside the bed. Sister Finlay bent over and held the old man's pulse for a minute, and then stood up again.

"Going off now," she said in a whisper.

I nodded. "I'll sit with him for a bit." I glanced at the

candle; it was burning very low. "You can put that candle out and save it, sister, if you like. We may need it later on. I've got the torch here."

She moved to the table and blew out the candle; I switched the torch on for a moment. Stevie's hand was lying on the sheet. I took it and held it in my own; it was rather cold. I was concerned at that, and then I thought that part of the effect, at least, lay in my own high temperature. I switched the torch off, and sat holding him by the hand. A little light filtered into the room from outside in the glade, but it was waning, and as I sat there a few raindrops fell on the iron roof again, and steadied to an even drumming.

I knew that there was something that I had intended to ask Stevie, and that I had forgotten. I sat there in the darkness holding his cold hand, fuddled and incompetent in my fever, trying to remember what it was that I had forgotten to do. The drumming of the rain upon the roof perplexed me, making it difficult to think clearly; I felt myself falling into a coma, and I had to jerk myself awake. What was it that I had to ask?

And then it came to me—it was about relatives. I had forgotten to ask if there was a wife anywhere, or any children—any relatives who should be told if the old man should die. It was quite doubtful if anyone in Landsborough knew much about him, because they were all so very much younger. Even Liang probably knew little about his relations. As for myself, I did not even know his name.

I pressed his cold hand, doubtful if I had not left it too late. "Stevie," I said. "Stevie, can you understand me? This is Roger here—the parson. Tell me, before you go to sleep—what's your other name, your surname? What's your full name?"

I felt the hand that I was holding stir a little in my own,

and I forced my fuddled mind to concentrate upon what he was saying. .

"Anderson," he muttered, "David Anderson. Me cobbers call me Nigger."

Three

IT was no novelty to me to come upon a man known by two names, and I can remember a feeling of relief that he was still able to talk, because it was important to find out about any dependants. The country districts of Queensland are full of men like Stevie; I know several sailors who have jumped their ships and have worked for years upon the cattle stations under false names, and one or two husbands who have escaped from intolerable marriages in some city. The police know all about these men in most cases and turn a blind eye, because white labour on the cattle stations is getting scarcer every year. Like Liang with his lettuces and poppies, they see no point in persecuting a man doing a good job unless there is some compelling reason forcing them to do so.

"David Anderson," I said hazily. "Are you married, David?"

"Too right," he muttered.

"Any children?"

"Two."

In my heat and my fatigue I was immensely relieved that I had time to get this matter straightened out. "I'll write a letter to your wife when you're in hospital, and tell her how you're going on," I said. "Where does she live?"

"Letchworth," he muttered.

"Where's that?"

"Outside Canberra."

"What's the name of the house, or the road?"

"Three Ways, in the Yarrow Road."

I was so ill and feverish that there seemed to be nothing incongruous in that to me. "I'll write to her as soon as we get you into hospital."

"Pommie bastard," he mumbled, or it might have been parson. And then he said, "She come from England, too."

"She's English, is she? What part of England does she come from?"

"Oxford," he told me. "Her Dad and Mum, they live at Oxford, at a place called Boars Hill. But we met at Buck House."

Even in my fatigue, I knew that this was nonsense. There was nothing serious in this that the old man was telling me; he was not married, least of all to an English wife from Oxford, and he had no home in Canberra. These were hallucinations, fantasies from the dream world that he slid into when opium or drink had gripped him. In the disappointment of this discovery I had to force myself to concentrate again upon the problem I was trying to solve. "Try and tell me what's real," I said wearily.

He did not answer that, but his hand stirred in mine, and he said, "Where am I, cobber?"

"You're in Liang Shih's house on Dorset Downs," I told him. "We've got to keep you here tonight, but we'll get you into hospital tomorrow. There's too much water on the track to move you tonight."

"The Butterfly Spirit," he muttered inconsequently, "what goes out of you, flipping about all sorts of places while you sleep. Liang tol' me. This ain't real."

It was no good; he was too far gone in drugs and in disease. One cannot argue with hallucinations, or make sense of them. I said, "Don't worry about it now."

There was a silence. I glanced around me as I sat by the bed. My eyes had become accustomed to the faint light now, and I looked to see what Sister Finlay was doing. She was sitting by the table, one arm resting on it; her head had fallen forward on this arm, and she seemed to be asleep. I was glad of that, because she had had a very tiring day, and there was no sense in both of us staying awake at the same time. Better to let her rest, and save her energies till they were needed.

Liang was nowhere to be seen; probably he was in the next room. A faint odour of burning incense drifted round me as I sat there in the darkness, and I thought that he had probably lit another of his joss sticks before the Buddha. The rain still drummed upon the roof, but the clouds cannot have been very thick because to my night-accustomed eyes it was light enough to see a little way across the open clearing, looking through the open door from where I sat. The animals were still there; they had come closer, and I could see them sitting or standing on the edge of visibility. Perhaps they had come closer in the darkness so that they could still watch the house, though now the lights had been extinguished.

From the bed Stevie spoke suddenly. He said, "This place on Dorset Downs?"

"That's right," I told him. "We're near the Dorset River, about fifteen miles from the homestead. Where you live with Liang Shih."

He muttered inconsequently, "I was born near here. My Dad was a drover."

It was queer how fact and hallucination were mixed up in his mind. It was entirely credible that his father had been a stockman or a drover, as it was incredible that he had married a girl from Oxford. I would remember the address

66

that he had given me at Canberra, but it was most unlikely that he had a wife and family living there. And then I thought, it really didn't matter. I could find out about him from the Post Office, because he drew a pension once a month. Some Government office would have most of the particulars of his life; indeed, Sergeant Donovan probably knew a good deal about him. I should only have to ask the sergeant.

"I'm sick, aren't I?" he asked. "On Dorset Downs, up in the Gulf Country?"

"That's right," I repeated. "We'll get you into hospital tomorrow."

"There's one thing you can do, cobber," he muttered. I bent to catch his words. He said, "Send a telegram to Rosemary at Letchworth. Air Vice-Marshall Watkins. Got that, cobber? Air Vice-Marshal Watkins. Say to see Air Vice-Marshal Watkins, 'n the R.A.A.F. 'll fly her up to Group at Invergarry, 'n she can come on in one of them helicopters."

It was all delusions, of course, a hotchpotch of war memories. Invergarry was real enough. It was a bomber station in the second war, from which the Liberators had flown against the Japanese in Timor and New Guinea. I knew it as two vast bitumen runways in the bush, that would endure for ever. No aeroplane had landed there since 1946, except perhaps the ambulance to take away some injured stockman. There were no buildings there, no installations, and no people; nothing but wild pigs and wallabies.

"I'll see to that in the morning," I said quietly. "Now try and get some sleep."

It seemed to me that he stirred restlessly in the darkness. "I got to get in touch with Rosemary," he muttered, and it seemed to me that he was sobbing. "I got to get to her. This ain't real. She'll get me out o' this. . . ."

There was nothing I could do for him. I sat holding his hand, and listening to him sobbing in the darkness. Death sometimes comes in very distressing forms. After a time I asked him, "If you can't sleep, shall I ask Liang Shih to make you another pipe?" I knew that Sister Finlay would allow it, if it would give him rest.

"I don't smoke a pipe," he muttered. "Never did. I *got* to get to Rosemary."

He lay twisting and turning on the bed in his delirium, so far as the paralysis would allow. I had a raging thirst; half in a dream I got up and went to the table—I think—and took a long drink of the muddy water. As I moved across the room I seemed to be gliding in mid air; I could not feel my feet upon the ground or hear my movements, and when I picked up the glass I could not feel it in my hands. I was intolerably hot and my body was streaming sweat; my clothes were drenched, and sticking to me with each movement, and I could not think very clearly. After I had had the drink I went fumbling around to try and find my torch, because I wanted to switch it on, to look at Stevie lying on the bed. In my feverish state I had a strange thought that it wasn't Stevie who was talking, and though with my intellect I knew this to be nonsense I wanted to switch on the torch and look at the old man. But I couldn't find the torch, and then it didn't seem to be important any longer, and I went back to the chair and sat down again, holding his limp hand.

He was still restless, muttering something incoherent. I bent to hear what he was saying but I could make no sense of it, though I heard the name Rosemary again. I straightened up wearily and sat there in a daze. His insistence on the name worried me. It was just possible that some part of all this rigmarole was true, and that he really

68

had a wife called Rosemary who had been born in England. My lips were thick and dry again in spite of the drink that I had taken, too parched to speak, but I managed to ask him somehow, "How did you come to meet Rosemary?"

The drumming of the rain upon the tin roof was insistent, too loud for me to hear his weak voice, but he answered, "I got sent to Boscombe Down after the war. And then I got sent to White Waltham. I met her at the Palace."

In my fever I asked him, "What Palace?"

"Buckingham Palace," he said. "Where the Queen lives, cobber."

I knew with my intellect, of course, that this was nonsense. He was delirious, and I was not much better. I knew it was all rubbish, but I was too dazed and fuddled to be able to think clearly why it should be so. I sat there holding his hand, thinking that presently Sister Finlay would wake up and hear what I could not, that he was talking, and she would do something to relieve me. In the meantime, I could sink into the daze, and we could go on talking without speaking; it was easier that way.

"Where's Boscombe Down?" I asked.

"In England," he said. "West o' London." He said that it was where new aeroplanes for the R.A.F. were tested in flight. In a dazed stupor I remembered that this man had been a pilot in France in the first war, so it was possible that he had been to such a place. He said it was a very big place on an aerodrome, staffed by many engineers and scientists, all testing these aeroplanes. The pilots were a mixture of every nationality in the British Commonwealth because each country used to send its best pilots to Boscombe Down, so that there were British and Canadian and Australian and Rhodesian and Indian pilots, and many others, all working together test flying these aeroplanes and living in the same mess.

I sat there, feverish and confused, listening to his fantasy while the rain drummed down upon the roof, drowning all sound. He said that he had been there for about six weeks, flying on some experimental test flight every day, when he first met Group Captain Cox. He had done a job early in the morning which had involved a climb to eighty thousand feet in an experimental fighter followed by a long dive down to a lower altitude, but the refrigeration had been unsatisfactory and he had had to pull out and reduce speed at forty thousand feet as the temperature in the cockpit became unbearable. He went up and tried it again, and managed to hold the dive down to thirty-two thousand feet; he landed after an hour and ten minutes in the air, very exhausted. He wrote some notes for his report while the details were still fresh in his mind, and went back to his quarters for a shower and a change. Then he went over to the mess for lunch.

There were three Australian pilots on the course at that time, one from the Navy and one other with himself from the Air Force. In the ante-room he saw the other two standing with the C.O. and this strange Group Captain. The C.O. called him over, and introduced him to Cox. "This is Squadron Leader Anderson."

The Group Captain was evidently English, and an officer of the old type, lean and soldierly and handsome, with perfect manners. "Morning," he said. "I'm in the book. What are you drinking?"

He said, "Tomato juice, sir."

"Flying this afternoon?"

He shook his head. "I grounded my thing for a refrigeration check. It's got to go into the hot hangar; it won't be ready till tomorrow."

"Have a sherry, then."

"No, thanks. I never do."

70

He found that the Group Captain was interested in the work that he had been doing on the fighter, and wanted to know a good deal about it. Quite early in the conversation David Anderson became mindful of security and parried one particularly direct question skilfully by turning it into a joke, which made the C.O. and the Group Captain laugh, not altogether at the joke. "It's all right, Anderson," the C.O. said. "You can talk to him."

"Everything?"

"Oh yes, everything. We're not afraid of him."

They lunched together, and in conversation it became evident to David that the Group Captain's main interest lay in the flight trials of the new de Havilland 316, later to be known as the de Havilland *Ceres*. This was of interest to the Australian, too. Before he had left Laverton to come to England for this course, David had had an interview at Canberra with the Australian Minister for Air. The Minister had told him about this new mail carrier which was then beginning its flight trials in England, and he had told him that the Australian air line, Qantas, had placed an initial order for six of the new machines to expedite the air mail service from England. Because of this order, and because the aircraft might be interesting to the Royal Australian Air Force for other purposes, the Minister had written to the Air Ministry in London to request that Squadron Leader Anderson should participate so far as possible in the flight trials of the aircraft while it was at Boscombe Down. So far, David had had nothing to do with it.

He spent that afternoon, however, with Group Captain Cox and with the firm's test pilot examining the new machine in the hangar. The mail carrier was designed to fly from England to Australia with one stop at Colombo, which is almost exactly halfway between London and Canberra. The cruising speed of the machine was about five hundred knots at fifty thousand feet, so that the journey from England to Australia would be completed in about twenty hours, carrying three tons of mail. The manufacturers, with an eye to other markets for this fast, long range aeroplane, had designed the fuselage to be sufficiently large to carry twenty passengers in lieu of freight, so that the 316 was quite an interesting aircraft capable of a variety of uses.

It was not until the evening that David Anderson discovered the identity of the officer with whom he had spent the afternoon. At dinner in the mess he asked the C.O. what appointment this Group Captain held; he was still slightly troubled about security, because he had been talking to him very freely.

The C.O. said, "He's the Captain of the Queen's Flight. Didn't you know?"

David shook his head. He knew vaguely that the post existed and that it had to do with the air travel of the Royal Family, but he knew little of the organisation. "What is that, sir?" he asked. "Do they have their own aeroplanes?"

The C.O. shook his head. "Not now," he said. "They used to in the very early days, but now they charter machines for their journeys from one of the Corporations, or borrow them from the Royal Air Force. It's nominally an independent organisation paid for out of the Privy Purse, but nowadays there's not much more than a typist charged up to the Royal Family. Cox is an R.A.F. officer, of course." He paused. "They've got a hangar at White Waltham aerodrome still, and a little ground equipment. The Prince of Wales had an Auster there at one time, but I think he's sold it now."

David had not been in England long enough to know all the aerodromes, and he had never been to White Waltham. "That's a civil aerodrome, isn't it?" he asked.

The other nodded. "Near Maidenhead. It's quiet for them there, and close to Windsor."

In the fortnight that followed, David saw a good deal of Group Captain Cox. He found himself allocated to the flight trials of the mail carrier next day, and Cox was evidently deeply interested in the machine. When David began to fly in it on trials as second pilot he found that Cox was frequently a passenger in the bare fuselage behind him with the scientific test observers and their gear. Several times when the test work was over and before landing, at the instigation of the Chief Pilot, David slid out of his seat and the Group Captain took his place to fly the 316 for a time. He was a very good pilot still, though he had grey hair and he was well over fifty years of age.

When this had been going on for about a month, David was mildly surprised to receive an invitation from the Group Captain to dine with him at his home. He lived in a small Georgian house in Windsor, standing in about an acre of ground that adjoined Windsor Great Park, so that the house looked out over a wide expanse of park land, and a herd of deer grazed up to the garden fence. It was a very stately little house, beautifully kept and very well furnished; it was a Grace and Favour house. Here Frank Cox lived with his wife and family of three young children, in a dignified and gracious way of life that David had never seen before.

It was a somewhat formal dinner party, conducted with such ease that it did not seem formal to the Australian. The other guests were a Major and Mrs. Macmahon, and a sister of Mrs. Cox. Macmahon was a man of forty-five or fifty, cast in the same mould as the Group Captain, a pleasant man with easy manners but with quite a keen business sense, and widely travelled. He had evidently spent some time in Australia and could talk about it with some inner knowledge; David did not learn who he was or what he did, and wondered about it a little.

Like many test pilots, David was a keen sailing man. Since he was likely to remain in England for a year, he was planning to buy a small five ton yacht and to keep her in the Hamble River, and he was about to clinch this deal. He found that both Macmahon and Cox were yachtsmen, and this made a bond and enabled him to keep his end up in the conversation on that topic. They talked a good deal about flying, too, and about the recent war when he had been an acting Wing Commander in charge of an Australian bomber squadron operating from Luzon. Altogether, the evening passed very pleasantly and quickly for David Anderson; it was a surprise to him to find at the end of his cigar that it was eleven o'clock, and time for him to take his leave and drive back to Boscombe Down in his small sports car.

A week or ten days later he got a letter from the High Commissioner for Australia instructing him to call on the Commissioner at Australia House, and giving him an appointment in the afternoon. Somewhat surprised, and wondering what this was all about, he took the day off and went up to London, and was shown into the office of the High Commissioner, a Mr. Harry Ferguson. He had met Mr. Ferguson for a few minutes formally when he had arrived in England, but he had not seen him since.

Mr. Ferguson got up from his desk to greet him. Like all Australians, he believed in using Christian names. "Come on in, David," he said. "I've been wanting to see you." He made him sit down in a comfortable chair by the desk, and sat down again himself, a heavy, genial man in a grey business suit.

He gave David a cigarette. "Well," he said, "how are you liking your job down at Boscombe Down?"

The pilot said, "I couldn't like it better. I've been flying the 316 a good deal recently." It was in his mind that Ferguson wanted to know about the Qantas order.

"I know. It's a good machine, isn't it?"

"It's a bonza job," David said. "They've got a few bugs to get out of it, but nothing serious."

"I know. You're quite happy in your work there?"

"Absolutely," David said in wonder.

"Would you consider a change?"

"I don't suppose I'd like it," said the pilot. "It couldn't be a better job than I've got now." He paused. "What sort of change?"

"You've been seeing a good deal of Frank Cox recently, haven't you?"

"Group Captain Cox? He's been down there a good deal, flying the 316. I had dinner at his house one night."

"I know," said Ferguson. He sat in thought for a moment, and then said, "How would you like to join the Queen's Flight?"

David stared at him amazed. "Me? The Queen's Flight?"

Ferguson said, "That's the proposal, David. They didn't want to raise the matter with you before consulting me, in case the Federal Government and the R.A.A.F. should object. I've been in touch with Canberra about it, and there would be no objection from our side. But it's entirely up to you. It means a break in your service career, of course, but you wouldn't be required to leave the Air Force. It means immediate promotion to the rank of Wing Commander with pay and allowances for that rank in Australian currency, as usual. But you would be detached for special duties with the Queen's Flight."

David sat in silence for a minute, thinking over this extraordinary proposal. It was undoubtedly an honour and

75

a compliment to his ability, but it was unwelcome. Like all Australians, he venerated Royalty, but to spend his career in Court circles was another matter.

"What made them pick on me?" he asked. "They've got plenty of good pilots in England. And anyway, they haven't any aeroplanes."

"That's true enough . . ." The Commissioner hesitated. "I don't know how much you know of what's been going on," he said at last. "Did you know that the House of Representatives have voted the funds to present a de Havilland 316 to the Queen's Flight?"

A vague memory of a small paragraph in *The Aeroplane* stirred in the pilot's mind. "I think I did read something about it."

Ferguson nodded. "The Canadians are doing the same thing."

"Are they?" the pilot said in wonder. "The Queen's Flight is going to have two 316s?"

"That is so . . ." Ferguson hesitated. "If you should take this job, David, the first thing you'll have to learn is to keep out of politics. There are some things you'll have to know, of course, but your business is to think as little as you can about them, and just stick to your flying."

The pilot nodded. "I never bother about politics," he said.

"That's fine." The High Commissioner paused, and sat in thought for a moment or two. "In the beginning, when the King's Flight was first founded in the Thirties, aeroplanes were small and cheap, and the Civil List was larger in terms of real money than it is now. The aeroplanes were then the property of the Monarch, and naturally they were at his sole disposal; he could go anywhere he wanted to, at any time, without consulting anyone." He paused again. "Since then aircraft have grown vastly more expensive to buy and to maintain, and the Privy Purse has been drastically reduced in purchasing power. For many years the aeroplanes for the journeys of the Royal Family have been paid for by the State." He glanced at David. "You understand that this is all completely confidential, Squadron Leader?"

"Of course, sir."

"Yes. Well . . . It has now been proposed that the Queen's Flight should be abolished on the grounds of economy, and that the Royal Family should make arrangements with Transport Command of the R.A.F. whenever they wish to make a journey by air. And this proposal has come forward when the 316 will make it possible for Royalty to get from Windsor to the Royal Residence at Canberra in twenty hours, and to their residence at Ottawa in less than six hours."

He paused. "The Federal Government," he said quietly, "and the Canadian Government also—we think it very wrong that the freedom of movement of the Monarch in the Commonwealth should be in any way controlled by the British Government through the Royal Air Force, however generously that control may be exercised. To prevent that situation from arising our Government, and that of Canada, have each offered to present a 316 to the Queen's Flight, and to pay all running and maintenance costs of the machines. Her Majesty has accepted this offer, and she has asked that the crews for these machines shall be composed entirely of Canadian and Australian personnel. That's how this job comes to be offered to you, David. You're the officer they've picked to be captain of this aircraft, representing Australia."

David sat in thought, in gloomy silence for a minute or two. The whole thing was unwelcome to him. It meant leaving the test work that interested him and that he was

77

good at, to enter on an unknown regime of Court life. It meant interrupting his career in the R.A.A.F. It meant many other changes in his life, most of which, he felt, would not be for the better.

"Whose idea was this?" he said at last.

"Frank Cox suggested your name first," the High Commissioner replied. "When it was agreed in principle that the crew of this machine should be Australians. Cox put your name forward as a suitable officer for the captain."

"He doesn't know anything about me," David said. "I don't think I should be suitable at all."

Ferguson smiled. "They've taken a good deal of trouble to investigate you, of course. They asked for details of your Service record, which we gave them. You've met the Assistant Private Secretary, haven't you?"

"What Secretary?"

"The Assistant Private Secretary to the Queen—Major Macmahon. You had dinner with him, didn't you?"

"There was a chap called Macmahon there when I went to dinner with Frank Cox," the pilot said. "Is that who he was?"

"That's right. You made a good impression."

"Didn't eat my tucker with my fingers?"

The High Commissioner laughed. "That's right."

David sat in silence. At last he said, "Can I have a day or two to think it over?"

"Of course. It might be a good thing if you had a talk with Frank Cox."

"I think it would be," the pilot said. "There are a lot of things he ought to know before I take a job like this."

Ferguson eyed him for a minute. "I see that you don't care about it much," he said presently. "What's the trouble?"

The pilot shrugged his shoulders. "I don't care all that

about this country," he said. "All these empty houses and shops get me down. They're still the best engineers in the world, and they build the best aeroplanes. But anyone can have the rest of it, so far as I'm concerned."

"How long have you been over here?" the High Commissioner asked. "Two months?"

"Nearly three," the pilot said. "I've only got another nine months to do here before I get back to Australia."

"Never been in England before?"

David shook his head.

"You want to look beyond the low standard of living," the High Commissioner said. "They're a great people still, and they can still teach us a thing or two. But anyway, you think it over, and have a talk with Frank Cox. Give me a ring on Monday or Tuesday of next week and let me know what you've decided."

David Anderson went away and lunched at the Royal Automobile Club in Pall Mall; like many officers in the Australian services he had found a welcome and hospitality in that club. In the lounge he met an Australian naval officer, a Queenslander like himself, that he knew fairly well. Lieutenant-Commander Fawcett said, "Hullo, Nigger. Come and have a drink."

"Have a tomato juice," said David. They went into the bar.

"What are you doing in Town?"

"Mooching around and seeing the sights," said David.

"Have a pink gin."

"No, thanks. I never do."

He lunched with his friend, who was serving a tour of duty at the Admiralty, but he did not tell him anything about the Queen's Flight. Commander Fawcett had just come back from a holiday in which he had motored to Scotland up one side of England and down the

79

other. "Didn't spend a single night in a hotel," he said.

"Camping?"

"Empty houses," the Commander said. "They're the shot in this country. We had our swags, of course, and camp beds. It's far better than messing about with a tent. The only thing is, in Scotland they take the roofs off."

"I heard about that," said David. "That's to keep up the value of the others, isn't it?"

"That's right. I don't know that it really does it, though. You can get a new house up there for the price of the roof, plus five quid for the rest of it. That's the exempted houses —not owned by the Government."

"Down here it only costs the fiver."

"That's right."

"You didn't have any difficulty in finding a house when you wanted it?"

"Not really. They lock the doors, of course, but you can usually find one that's been broken into before. There are masses of them in the north. In the suburbs, mostly, fairly far out from the centre of the towns—that's where you find them. People move in towards the centre as the houses become empty, because the bus fares are less. Places like Nottingham and Darlington, every other house is empty in the outer suburbs. There's no difficulty at all in finding one to sleep in."

"Pity they can't shift 'em all out to Australia," said David. "We could do with them."

"Too right we could. They should have built them portable, when they were building all these houses in the Fifties."

"It's the hell of a waste."

"You can't take twelve or thirteen million people out of England without waste," said Fawcett. "This place had a population of fifty millions when these houses were built.

They're thick enough on the ground now. My word, they must have been rubbing shoulders then."

Over the coffee David asked, "How are you liking it here?"

"I like it all right," said Fawcett. "There's something about it that we haven't got at home."

"What?"

The naval officer laughed. "I don't know. Something."

"We'll have more people in ten years."

"Maybe. You don't like it much?"

"Australia's good enough for me," said David. "It's interesting over here, and I'm glad I've been, but I don't care how soon I get back."

He rang up Group Captain Cox after lunch, and found he was in town and not far off, at the office of the Queen's Flight in St. James's Palace. David went round to see him. He found the Queen's Flight in those rambling buildings with some difficulty; it occupied a three room flat on the first floor overlooking Engine Court, a flat consisting of office and sitting room and a bedroom used by Frank Cox when he stayed in Town. A girl typing in the office by the telephone welcomed him, and showed him into the sitting room.

The Group Captain got up to meet him. "Afternoon, David," he said genially. He held out his cigarette case. "Seen the High Commissioner?"

"My cobbers call me Nigger," the Australian said directly.

Cox glanced at him. "Oh? Why do they call you that?"

"Because I am one. I'm a quadroon."

The Captain of the Queen's Flight smiled. "Do you know—I *did* wonder about that. Which side was the colour on?"

"My mother's," said David. "I'm a dinkum Aussie—

81

more than most. My grandmother was a full blood Aboriginal from somewhere up in the Cape York Peninsula. I don't know who my grandfather was, but he was white. My mother was an illegitimate half-caste. I've got a lot of coffee coloured uncles and aunts scattered round the Gulf Country. My aunt Phoebe had fourteen children; she works as a servant in the hotel at Chillagoe."

"I see. Were your father and mother married?"

The pilot nodded. "I've got a birth certificate. He died last year, my father—he ran the store in a little town called Forsayth. My mother died about five years ago."

The Group Captain said, "Well, what's all this got to do with me, David? Have a cigarette."

Anderson took one and lit it. "Nigger's the name."

"All right—Nigger, if you like it." He held a match for the younger man's cigarette. "You'd rather be called that?"

The pilot blew a long cloud of smoke. "I've always been called that—ever since I joined the R.A.A.F. as a boy. I've always been called Nigger Anderson. I'd just as soon that people called me that in England. Then we'll all know where we are."

Frank Cox nodded. "As you like. Did the High Commissioner tell you what we want you to do?"

"He told me."

"And what did you think about it? Sit down." He dropped down into a Chippendale armchair himself.

The pilot sat down by the table and rested his arms upon it, facing the Group Captain. "It's a very great compliment," he said slowly. "The only thing is, I'm not the right man for the job."

"Why not?"

"Colour, for one thing," said the pilot bluntly. "I'm not white. That might make a lot of trouble some time or another, and you don't want that."

"Do you find that really happens?" the Group Captain asked with interest. "Do you get waiters being rude in restaurants, people refusing to sit at table—anything of that sort?"

David hesitated. "Not recently," he said. "It happened once in Sydney."

"How long ago?"

"It was a good long time ago—I was about eighteen. But it could happen any time."

"I rather doubt that," said Frank Cox. "You don't look coloured. You look a bit tanned, that's all. You never had any trouble in the R.A.A.F., did you?"

The pilot shook his head. "I've always been called Nigger," he said. "I think that helps, if you don't try going under false pretences."

They sat in silence for a minute. "I don't think that's any real obstacle to you taking this job," Cox said at last. "As a matter of fact, the point came up a few days ago—after you dined with us. Macmahon said you were coloured, and I said that I didn't think you were. We talked it over on the assumption that he was correct, and we decided that it really didn't matter—bearing in mind your other qualifications."

"I'm not the man in other ways," David said. "I've not got the right background. I'm not like you, or Mr. Macmahon. I couldn't get alongside the sort of people that you deal with here, in this place." He glanced around him at the panelled walls, at the leaded casement window. "I started as a grocer's boy in Townsville." He struggled to express himself. "I mean, this is a social job, where you've got to know what to say to a Duchess, or perhaps even the Queen herself. You want somebody who knows the ropes, and not say the wrong thing and make everybody look stupid."

"We know what we want," said Cox. "Leave that to us. The chief thing that we want is an Australian who is very

thorough and reliable, and who can take a 316 safely to
Australia or any other part of the world practically in his
sleep. We've been into this with a great deal of care, and
our first choice was you."

"I could find you others who were just as good, born
white."

"We aren't asking you to find us others," said Frank Cox.
"We're asking you to take charge of a 316 and train the
crew and fly it as required. As for the colour, you can put
that out of your mind. We aren't asking you to marry into
the Royal Family."

David sat in silence. At last he said, "How long would
the job be for?"

"Indefinite," said Cox. "If you take it on, I think you
should stay for at least three years. We must have con-
tinuity, so that everybody works together as a team."

"And the main base is here, in England, of course?"

"That's right," the Group Captain said. "At White
Waltham. We've got a hangar at Canberra, at Fairbairn
airport, as you probably know. The present plan is that the
Monarch intends to spend two months of each year in
Australia, and two months in Canada. But the main base is
at White Waltham. If you want to set up a home, it would
probably have to be in England, near White Waltham. Are
you intending to get married in the near future?"

The pilot shook his head. "No. The colour makes that a
bit difficult."

"I see. Well, anyway, the main base is here."

David sat in silence. He could think of no good reason
for refusing this job, nothing more that he could say to
excuse himself. He knew that the vast majority of officers
serving in the R.A.A.F. would have jumped at the opportunity and he knew that it was a tremendous compliment
that the job had been offered to him first, a greater com-

pliment than any of his decorations. He knew also that it was practically impossible to refuse it, and the thought depressed him, so that he hesitated, and said nothing.

"What's the trouble?" the Group Captain asked at last.

The pilot raised his head. "I'm an Australian," he said, "and not out of the top drawer at that. I'm all right in my own country. They understand about people like me there —specially up in Queensland, my own state. I'm glad to have had the chance of this trip home, but I wouldn't want to spend my life here. It's just a trip to me, this is. I don't want to stay and spend my life in England."

Cox said, "You don't care about this country?"

"Not much," the pilot said. "I like a place where everybody's got the chance to make a fortune and spend it, like people do at home. I like a steak with two fried eggs on it."

"You don't like our Socialism?"

"I don't know much about it," David said. "That's one thing that *does* fit me for this job. Harry Ferguson said, if I took this thing I wasn't to take any part in politics—well, I never think about them much. The only thing I know is that we've had mostly Liberal Governments at Canberra for the last thirty years, and you've mostly had Labour. And your Conservatives, so far as I can see, are redder than our Labour." He paused. "I know a Labour Government suits England best," he said. "Too many people in the country, and so everyone hard up, everything in short supply, and so everybody's got to pull together. I know that's where the Socialism comes from. Everyone knows that. But I don't have to like it."

"There's another thing," said the Group Captain. "You've got a lot of our Conservatives in your country, as emigrants. It's where they like to go. On balance, you've moved further to the Right and we've moved further to the Left."

"I know," the pilot said. He smiled. "I still don't have to like it."

"Do you like the Commonwealth at all?" asked the Group Captain. "Do you want Australia to be independent, or to join up with the States?"

David was shocked. Although he took little interest in politics, he had heard of this heresy, and he disliked it very much. "Of course I don't," he said. "We're part of the old country. I only meant that, personally, I'd rather live in Queensland than in England."

"You feel that England still does something for Australia?"

"Of course," said the pilot. "You've only got to look at the 316, or at Rolls-Royce. We couldn't get along without England."

The Group Captain nodded. "I shall be sorry if you don't join our show," he said. "Perhaps England can't get along so easily without you."

"Without me?" said David.

"You and people like you," said Cox. He paused. "You think we want somebody in the Queen's Flight who knows how to talk to a Duchess. One of the Berkeley Boys, but Australian born. Well, that's not what we want at all. Australia is giving this machine to the Queen's Flight, and Her Majesty has asked that the crew shall be Australians. She's no fool . . . Nigger. When she says she wants Australians, she means real Australians—not ones that have been brought up in Mayfair. She's Queen of Australia as well as Queen of England. When she says she wants Australians and Canadians in the Queen's Flight as well as English, she's got some very good reason. I don't know what that reason is. I don't have to know. I only have to do what she wants, to the best of my ability. If you turn down this job, I shall look for another chap like you whose spiritual home is in Wagga-Wagga or Kalgoorlie. But I very much hope that you won't turn it down, because I think that you're the sort of man she has in mind in saying that she wants Australians."

The pilot grinned. "I've got a birth certificate, anyway," he said. "That's something. . . . Can I take an hour or so to think it over?"

"Of course."

David glanced at his wrist watch. "I'll give you a ring about five o'clock."

He left the Palace, and walked along Pall Mall in deep thought. He was vaguely on his way to the club, but when he got near to the R.A.C. and saw the streams of people going in and out, he gave up the idea, and walked on slowly down the street. It was quieter in the street, in that he could think without the chance of some acquaintance bothering him to come and have a drink. He walked on, wondering what Cox had meant by saying that England could not get along without people like himself, what the Queen had meant—if she had meant anything at all. England had plenty of first class pilots in the R.A.F.

It was May, and a warm evening. He came to the National Gallery on the north side of Trafalgar Square and crossed the road, and stood for a time looking out over the square at the corner by Canada House. There was a bus stop near him, and a long queue of white faced, patient Londoners waiting to go home. He thought of the vigour and beauty of the people in similar bus queues in Brisbane and in Adelaide, comparing the tanned skins with the sallow, the upright carriage with the tired slouch. It wasn't the fault of these people that they looked white and tired; hardships had made them so, and overwork, and the errors of dietary scientists who planned the rationing back in the Forties and the Fifties, when most of them were children. Badly treated people, out of luck, yet with a quality of greatness in them still, in spite of everything. No reason in all that why he should want to live with them, however.

He turned from them, and looked out over the Square, at the sheer beauty of the new buildings on the other side. The new Home Office between the Strand and Northumberland Avenue, the pillared white grace of the Ministry of Pensions at the head of Whitehall and Northumberland Avenue, the straight classic lines of the new Ministry of Fuel and Power at the end of Cockspur Street, still building but already visible through the steel scaffolding. These people were the greatest engineers, the greatest architects in the whole world, he felt, and now that housebuilding was at a standstill all the energy and talent of their building industry was concentrated on these marvellous public buildings, going up all over England. The new London, with its narrow streets and towering white palaces to house the civil servants, was fast becoming the most lovely city in the world, with Liverpool and Manchester not far behind. Sydney and Melbourne were shabby and old fashioned in comparison, and Brisbane puerile, where housebuilding lagged far behind the immigrants.

He turned, and looked at the bus queue once again. It said in the papers that things in England were on the upgrade after many years now that the population had reduced by twenty-five per cent; there was a suggestion that next year a private citizen would be allowed to buy a motor car and petrol for his own use. It might be so, but looking at the bus queue David felt it inconceivable that these tired people would regain the careless rapture of Australians within his own lifetime. And yet from their poverty and hardships they produced these marvellous things, these shining palaces in London, these superb aeroplanes and aero engines. Their radio and television programmes were the admiration of the world. Australia had now nearly as many people and Australia was a happy and a prosperous country, yet Australia did not produce one tenth the marvels that came out of England. Perhaps prosperity itself became a hindrance to great creative genius; raised on the stock route David knew that if a cow became too fat it was difficult for her to get in calf.

He could not make up his mind. He hated these people for their lack of spirit, for their subservience to civil servants, for their outmoded political system of one man one vote that kept them in the chains of demagogues. He venerated them for their technical achievements. To spend three years or more in England would be like living in a home for incurables, but not to do so would be to miss an opportunity he might regret his whole life through. Difficult.

He thrust his hand down into his pocket, grinning a little with his brown face. There were three coins there, two pennies and a shilling. He pulled them out impulsively and slammed them down upon the granite parapet beside him, and withdrew his hand.

The Queen's head gleamed up at him from all three. The shilling was an old one dated 1963 which showed the head of a young woman; the pennies, one of 1976 and one quite new of 1982, showed her middle aged and mature. He stared down at them, smiling quietly; the omens were definite. He was glad it had turned out that way. He would not enjoy three years or more away from his own country, but it was impossible to put aside this job.

He swept the coins up into his pocket with a lean brown hand, and turned, and walked back to the R.A.C. He stood in the telephone booth at the turn of the stairs and rang up the Group Captain in St. James's Palace. "This is Nigger

Anderson," he said. "I've thought this over, and I'll take the job if you still want me."

For the next few months Anderson did very little flying. Deliveries of the 316 could not begin until the prototype was through its trials, and actually it was four months after his appointment to the Queen's Flight that David took delivery of the Australian machine. In the meantime, however, he found he had a good deal of work upon the ground to do. He consulted with Cox and with his opposite number from Canada, a Wing Commander Dewar, and they set up Canadian and Australian offices in the annexe to the hangar housing the Queen's Flight upon White Waltham aerodrome. David moved from Boscombe Down to a small flat over a shop in Maidenhead; it was one advantage of life in England that there was never any difficulty now in getting a house or a flat on easy tenancy and at a very low rent from the National Housing Bureau. He began a series of meetings with the Air Attaché in Australia House to get together an aircrew. Then, with Cox and Dewar, he faced up to the problems of accountancy.

Here he found that they were breaking quite new ground. Hitherto all the expenses of the Queen's Flight had been passed by Cox straight to the Assistant Private Secretary, Major Dennis Macmahon, who had scrutinised them, queried anything that might seem relevant to him, and passed them for payment. Now a new system had to be thrashed out separating the costs of the Canadian and the Australian machines from the basic organisational costs, and passing those to the High Commissioners for settlement; it was complicated by the fact that spares and fuel and oil were held in common for the Australian and the Canadian machines, necessitating a complete revision of the rather simple system of accounting that had existed in the Queen's Flight up to date. These matters, with a number of others, were thrashed out at a full dress meeting held in a conference room in St. James's Palace. It was decided that in principle accounts for each machine should still pass through the Secretaries' Office in Buckingham Palace for check against the Royal use of the machines, before the separate accounts were sent for payment to the High Commissioners. Within those terms of reference the officers concerned were left to settle the new system in its details.

"Gee," said Wing Commander Dewar. "This thing 'll drive me nuts."

"Too right," said Wing Commander Anderson.

They had a meeting with Group Captain Cox in Major Macmahon's office in Buckingham Palace. It was the first time that either Anderson or Dewar had been inside the Palace and they were properly impressed, with a tendency to walk softly and to talk in a low tone of voice. The Assistant Private Secretary had a large, white painted office looking out upon the Park on the north front; he greeted them cheerfully and they settled down to business. He pressed a button on his desk, a buzzer sounded in the next room, and a girl came in, notebook and pencil in hand. "This is Miss Long," he said. The men got up and bowed. "She'll be handling the routine work of this thing when we've got a system going."

For an hour and a half they laboured to design a system to deal with matters of accountancy that were simple to the Assistant Private Secretary and Miss Long, but seemed difficult and complicated to the officers. Finally they got it straightened out, and Macmahon told the girl to type a memorandum of the decisions and to circulate it; later he told her privately to make it very simple and to put it in a form that they could refer back to if they had forgotten what to do. The business finished, the three officers got up to go.

Macmahon held them in conversation for a few minutes, asking the Canadian and the Australian about their living accommodation; Dewar was married, and had taken a small house in Maidenhead. Anderson told the Secretary about his flat; then for a time they talked in general about the aircrews and their accommodation. Finally Macmahon said to David, "Got your boat yet?"

The pilot smiled. "I've had her about six weeks. I bought her a few days after we had dinner with Frank. I spend every week end on her."

"Where do you keep her?"

"In the Hamble River—off Luke's yard."

Miss Long asked, "What sort of boat is she, Commander Anderson?" Macmahon said, "Rosemary's a great sailor."

The Australian turned to the girl with a new interest. "She's a Bermudian cutter, five and a half ton. She's pretty old; she was built in fifty three. But she's quite sound still. A chap called Laurent Giles designed her."

The girl nodded. "He was a very good designer in his day." She paused in thought.

"You sail yourself?" he asked.

"Dinghies," she said. "International fourteen footers. I've got a boat at Itchenor."

"Where's that?" he asked.

"Itchenor? It's in Chichester Harbour. I've done a bit of cruising with my uncle in a fifteen tonner—I was out with him last week end." She paused. "Your Laurent Giles five tonner isn't painted blue, is she? Blue with tanned sails?"

"Why—yes," the Australian said. "She's called *Nicolette*. Do you know her?"

The girl smiled. "It wasn't you by any chance aground at the entrance to the Beaulieu River last Sunday?"

The Australian coloured beneath his dark skin, and laughed self consciously. "The leading marks are wrong," he said. "Did you see us?"

"We passed you, going out," she said. "Lots of people go on to that bank. You took the outer boom for the leading mark probably."

"I wasn't bothering," the pilot said. "Maybe that's what I did. I thought it was all deep water."

She smiled. "I hope you don't do that when you're flying."

"I haven't yet," said David drily. "You only do that once."

For the next few weeks the pilots moved between their base at White Waltham, the test establishment at Boscombe Down, and the works of the manufacturers at Hatfield. Two of the 316 aircraft, now known as the *Ceres*, had been set aside for the Queen's Flight, and these were to be furnished specially, of course. The quarters for the crew remained as standard; the passenger accommodation was remodelled to provide three small single cabins each with a seat facing to the rear that turned into a full length bed at night, a dining room to seat six, and twelve reclining chairs of airline type for members of the Royal household travelling with the Queen. Accommodation was provided for a steward and a stewardess. The crew was to consist of the Captain of the Queen's Flight, the captain of the aircraft, a second pilot, two engineers, and two radio and radar officers.

All this gave the Canadian and Australian captains plenty to do without being overworked; David found that he could get away for most week ends on Friday afternoon to drive down to his little yacht moored in the Hamble River. He generally went alone for these week ends upon the Solent; he knew few people in England, and he did not cultivate the opportunities for social life that did occur. He was always quite happy in his boat alone and he preferred it so; from his boyhood he had been accustomed to the sea and boats and his five tonner was no problem for him; he could manage her single handed and the solitude gave him a sense of freedom. In England the sense of people pressing on him from every side worried the Queenslander; alone in his small yacht at sea the pressure was relieved and he felt something of the spaciousness of his own country. His quarter Aboriginal descent may have had something to do with this preference; whatever the cause was, David Anderson preferred to sail alone.

One Saturday morning in July he got up early at his moorings in the Hamble River and cooked his breakfast before seven o'clock. Like many Australian officers serving in England he found it difficult to adjust his habits of eating to the English rationing, and he went to some considerable pains to secure food from home. That week a bomber on a training flight from Brisbane had brought him two hams, a hundred eggs packed in sawdust in a carton, and six pineapples; he had cooked one of the hams in his flat and so he breakfasted that day on ham and eggs. He got under way at about eight o'clock and sailed down Southampton Water past Calshot in a moderate southwesterly breeze, and turned westwards down the Solent with the tide. All morning he beat to the west in tacks; as the sun came up the breeze dropped light, but the tide ran stronger. By lunchtime he was past Hurst Castle heading out to sea. He hove to off the Needles and had a lunch of ham sandwiches and fruit; then for a couple of hours he cruised up and down the steep cliffs to the southwards of the Needles fishing for mackerel. He caught three and gave up, having no use for more, and turned into the Solent again on the flowing tide and made for the small town of Yarmouth for the night.

In that fine summer weather Yarmouth was full of yachts

moored bow and stern two and three deep to the many piles within the harbour. The harbourmaster in a dinghy showed David a berth and took his warp to help him to make fast; in a quarter of an hour everything was snug. He launched his dinghy from the cabin top and put her astern, and then sat in the cockpit for a time, resting and watching the pageant of the vessels as he smoked. England, he reflected, still led the Commonwealth in the design of little yachts, as in most other techniques.

A girl in a thin shirt and abbreviated shorts rowed down the line of vessels in a dinghy, and rested on her oars opposite *Nicolette*. "Hullo, Commander Anderson," she said quietly.

He stared at her in surprise, and realised that it was Miss Long, in different attire from that which she wore in the Palace. He got to his feet. "Hullo, Miss Long," he exclaimed. "I didn't recognise you."

"I saw you come in," she said. "I'm with my uncle in the outer tier—the black yawl over there. The one with the R.N.S.A. burgee."

"Have you been here long?"

"We got in about half an hour before you did. We've just been messing about in the Solent. My uncle's got a mooring in the Beaulieu River—he lives at Bucklers Hard."

"I came down from the Hamble this morning," David said. "I took the tide down to the Needles and caught a few mackerel and came back here. Would you like to come aboard?"

She smiled. "I'd love to see your boat." She gave a couple of strokes, shipped her oars, and laid the dinghy gently alongside; taking the painter she stepped on to the counter and made her boat fast. Then she came down into the cockpit and peered down into the saloon. "She's very neat," she said. She glanced around the deck. "I like your winches." She fingered the rope knotting on the tiller head. "Did you do this Turk's head thing yourself?"

He grinned. "I got a book on it. I did that last week end. The first one that I did came off."

"I couldn't do a thing like that," she said. "I can do ordinary splicing, but not the ornamental stuff."

He reached into the saloon and produced a packet of cigarettes and gave her one. Together they sat smoking in the cockpit, watching the pageant of the yachts and the bustle of the little harbour. "It's a pretty place this," he said. "As pretty a little harbour as I've seen."

"I love it," she said. "We often come here. Do you have this sort of harbour for yachts in Australia?"

"Not quite the same," he said. "You do in Tasmania. But the coast of Australia hasn't got the same number of inlets—you've got to go further between harbours. It's not quite the same as it is here—you don't get so much small yacht cruising there, Miss Long."

"Where did you learn your sailing, then, Commander?"

He smiled. "I was in a place called Townsville when I was a boy," he said. "That's on the coast of Queensland. I went there when I was twelve years old to work in a shop, delivering the groceries. I used to go sailing a lot at Townsville, out to Magnetic Island and the Barrier Reef, in all sorts of old wrecks. That was before I went into the R.A.A.F." He paused. "I've had several boats at one time or another. I had an old Dragon before coming to England, when I was at Laverton."

"Have you ever done any ocean racing?" she asked.

"I sailed in the Hobart Race two years, in a boat called *Stormy Petrel*," he said. "We didn't do any good, but it was fun. It takes about six days usually—Sydney to Hobart."

She smiled. "Hard work?"

"Too right," he said. "You get a lot of gales down there, without much warning." He paused. "Will you have a cup of tea, Miss Long—or a glass of sherry?"

"Sherry's easier," she said. "I'd love a glass of sherry." She hesitated, and then said, "The name's Rosemary."

"I'll remember."

"Yours is David, isn't it?"

He went down into the saloon and found the bottle and the glasses, and passed them up to her with an open tin of tomato juice. "I've got a cake, or I've got a pineapple," he said. "Which would you rather have?"

"A pineapple!" she exclaimed. "Wherever did you get that from?"

"Brisbane," he said. He grinned up at her from the saloon. "The R.A.A.F. do what they can for officers who have to come to England. I've got a ham here, too."

"Not a whole ham?"

"I'm afraid so. I keep it tucked away in greaseproof paper in case I get murdered for it."

"I haven't seen a pineapple for years," she said. "I'd like a bit of pineapple with my sherry if you can spare it, David."

He cut a round off the pineapple on the cabin table. "David's the name," he said. "But most people call me Nigger. Nigger Anderson." He passed the pineapple up to her in the cockpit on a plate, with a bowl of sugar and a knife and fork.

"Why do they call you that?" she asked.

"Because my mother was a half caste," he replied. "I'm a quadroon." He climbed out into the cockpit and filled her glass with the sherry and his own with the tomato juice. He raised his to her. "Here's to the black and white."

97

"It's pretty mean to call you that," she said. "Not many people do that, do they?"

"Everybody," he said cheerfully. "Everybody calls me Nigger Anderson. I rather like it."

"I can see that you put up with it," she said quietly. "I can't believe you like it."

"Well, I do," he said. "I don't know much about the white side of my family, but on the black side I'm an older Australian than any of them. My grandmother's tribe were the Kanyu, and they ruled the Cape York Peninsula before Captain Cook was born or thought of."

She smiled. "And Wing Commander Anderson doesn't give a damn who knows about it."

"That's right," he said. "I don't. I'd rather people called me Nigger Anderson than that they went creeping round the subject trying to avoid it."

"I see you're big enough to carry it now without it hurting," she said. "It must have hurt a bit when you were younger. Or didn't they do it then?"

"I used to fight them if they said it to hurt," he replied. "I suppose I was rather a tough little boy. I was brought up on the station, because my Dad was a stockman. I could rope a steer from horseback when I was ten, and I won a prize at the Croydon rodeo when I was twelve for staying on a bullock. I don't remember fighting very much, but when I did I think I generally won."

She said, "What does it mean, to rope a steer? It sounds like something on the movies."

"It's when you're mustering," he said. "To brand the calves, and mark them. You drive a mob of three or four hundred into a stockyard built at the station or out in the bush if it's a big place that has several; then a couple of you go in amongst them on horseback and chuck a rope lasso over the head of the one you want. The

98

other end of the rope is made fast to a horn on the saddle, and you fight him with the horse and tow him out of the mob to the branding posts, and there the stockmen grab him and throw him to be branded. It's easy enough when you know the knack of it, but you want a good, steady horse."

She stared at him. "Do you mean to say that you were doing that when you were ten?"

"That's right," he said. "With little steers—not full grown beasts. My Dad was head stockman on Tavistock Forest, and he taught me."

"But however old were you when you learnt to ride a horse?"

"Three or four, I suppose," he said. "Dad told me once that he thought a boy shouldn't ride alone before he's five because if he fell it might put him off it, but I was riding much sooner than that. I don't think I could mount a horse alone before I was about seven, though, because of reaching the stirrup."

She said curiously, "Did you go to school at all?"

"Not what you'd call school," he replied. "Mrs. Beeman used to teach us—she was the manager's wife, and she'd been a teacher before she married. She had a class for all the kids upon the station. I was up to average when I went to Townsville, I think. They had evening classes there—I went to those."

She sat in silence for a minute, looking at the familiar harbour scene, the crowded yachts. What he had told her all seemed very strange and foreign. "How are you liking England?" she said at last. "It must be very different to Australia."

"It's different," he said. "But Australia isn't all cattle stations and horses, you know. I left the Gulf Country when I was twelve and I've not been back since, except

99

for six months in the R.A.A.F. at Invergarry. It's over ten years since I was astride a horse."

"Are you liking it over here?" she asked again.

He smiled. "Not very much. The job's a bonza one—I wouldn't give that up. But one day I'll be glad to get back home."

"How long have you been here?"

"Five months."

"Do you know many people in England?"

"Not many," said the pilot. "But that doesn't worry me. I don't know many people in Australia."

"Are you alone on board now?"

"That's right," he said. "She's all right for two, but you're on top of each other all the time. I generally cruise alone."

"Would you like to come and have supper with us, in *Evadne*?" she asked. "There's only my uncle and me—he's a retired captain, R.N."

He hesitated. "It's very kind of you to ask me," he said. "What about the food, though?"

"That's all right," she said. "We've got a lot of tins."

"Shall I bring my ham?" he suggested.

"We couldn't eat your ham," she said. "We'll be all right. There's heaps to eat on board."

"I'd better bring the ham," he said. "It'll go bad if it's not eaten. The last one did."

She was startled, and a little shocked. "Went bad?"

"I couldn't get through it," he explained. "I had to throw half of it away."

What was normal to him seemed an inconceivable blunder to her. "If that's what's going to happen we'd better help you eat it," she said firmly. "Let's have a look at it."

Down in the saloon they held a small conference over the ham, an enormous mass of meat to her. "How big is it— Nigger?" she asked.

100

He smiled. "Eighteen pounds—Rosemary."

"Whatever are you going to do with it? It'll take you months to get through that alone."

He looked puzzled. "I don't think so. One eats a pound or so a day. The other only went bad because I was away."

"You couldn't possibly eat that!"

"Why—I should think so. Look, that bit that's cut—that was supper last night and breakfast this morning."

"Just you alone?" He nodded, and she stared at the gap: what he said was probably true. "I suppose we don't eat so much meat in England," she said.

"Too right," he remarked drily. "I've noticed that already."

They wrapped the ham up and took it up into the cockpit. "How long have you been working at the Palace?" he asked.

"Three years," she said.

"Like it?"

She nodded. "One feels so much in the centre of things. It would be awfully flat working anywhere else, after being there."

He said curiously, "Do you see much of the Queen?"

She laughed. "Not me. Miss Porson takes her letters if she ever wants to write one herself, to be typed. Mostly she writes in her own hand, or else one of the Secretaries writes for her." She paused. "I've seen her often enough, of course—taking things to Major Macmahon when he's in with her, or passing in the corridor. I don't think she knows my name."

"What's she like?" he asked. "I've only seen her on the pictures."

"You'll be meeting her before long, of course," she said. "She's much smaller than you'd think from photographs." She stared out across the harbour. "She's a very wonderful person," she said quietly. "She's got such courage . . ."

"Courage?"

"That's what I said." She turned to him, smiling a little. "We're gossiping too much," she said. "That's one of the things we have to learn in our job—not to gossip about our betters. And when I say betters, I mean betters."

She turned to her boat. "Come over about six o'clock," she said. "Uncle Ted wants to go on shore first, but we'll be back by then. I think I'll make some ham toasts of this ham. I won't take too much."

She rowed off in her dinghy, and David watched her thread her way between the yachts and climb up on to the deck of the yawl.

He rowed across later in the evening, and was met by the uncle, a man of about seventy still lean and athletic, called Captain Osborne. He greeted the Australian warmly, and offered him a drink, but the pilot refused. "I don't at all," he said. "I never have. But please don't let me stop you."

From the saloon Rosemary said, "I've got some tomato juice. I could make you a tomato juice cocktail."

"I'd like that." So they sat in the cockpit while the girl cooked dinner, appearing now and then for a glass of sherry with the men and going down again, while the captain drank pink gins and David drank tomato juice.

For half an hour they chatted. Then his host said, "There's one thing about Australia I wish you'd tell me. How does your multiple vote work? It's quite an issue here in England, as perhaps you know."

The pilot raised his eyebrows. "I didn't know that. You don't have it, do you?"

"No. How does it work out in practice?"

"I don't really know," said David. "I've never thought about it much."

Captain Osborne asked, "Have you got more than one vote, yourself?"

The pilot nodded. "I'm a three vote man."

"I hope you don't mind me asking these questions," the captain said. "It really is getting rather important now in England."

"I don't mind," David said. "The only thing is, I'm afraid I don't know much about it. I've never bothered."

"What do you get your three votes for?" the captain asked.

"Basic, education, and foreign travel."

"The basic vote—that's what everybody gets, is it?"

"That's right," the pilot said. "Everybody gets that at the age of twenty one."

"And education?"

"That's for higher education," David said. "You get it if you take a university degree. There's a whole list of other things you get it for, like being a solicitor or a doctor. Officers get it when they're commissioned. That's how I got mine."

"And foreign travel?"

"That's for earning your living outside Australia for two years. It's a bit of a racket, that one, because in the war a lot of people got it for their war service. I got mine that way. I didn't know anything about the Philippines, really, when I came away, although I'd been there for three years, off and on."

"You had a wider outlook than if you'd stayed at home," the captain said. "I suppose that's worth something."

"I suppose it is."

"So you've got three votes. How does that work out in practice, at an election?"

"You get three voting papers given to you, and fill in all three, and put them in the box," the pilot said.

"You're on the register as having three votes?"

"That's right. You have to register again when you get an extra vote—produce some sort of a certificate."

They sat in silence for a time, looking out over the crowded harbour in the sunset light. Rosemary came to the saloon ladder and spoke up to them. "You can get more votes than three, can't you?" she said. "Is it seven?"

David glanced down at her. "The seventh is hardly ever given," he said. "Only the Queen can give that."

She nodded. "I know. We get them coming through the office. I should think there must be about ten a year."

"The others are straightforward," David said. "You get a vote if you raise two children to the age of fourteen without getting a divorce. That's the family vote."

"You can't get it if you're divorced?" asked Rosemary smiling.

"No. That puts you out."

"Do you both get it?"

"Husband and wife both get it," David said.

"What's the fifth one?" asked the captain.

"The achievement vote," said David. "You get an extra vote if your personal exertion income—what you call earned income here—if that was over something or other in the year before the election—five thousand a year, I think. I don't aspire to that one. It's supposed to cater for the man who's got no education and has never been out of Australia and quarrelled with his wife, but built up a big business. They reckon that he ought to have more say in the affairs of the country than his junior typist."

"Maybe. And the sixth?"

"That's if you're an official of a church. Any recognised Christian church—they've got a list of them. You don't have to be a minister. I think churchwardens get it as well as vicars, but I'm really not quite sure. What it boils down to is that you get an extra vote if you're doing a real job for a church."

"That's an interesting one."

"It's never interested *me* much," said the pilot. "I suppose I'm not ambitious. But I think it's quite a good idea, all the same."

"So that's six votes," Captain Osborne said. "The basic vote, and education, and foreign travel, and the family vote, and the achievement vote, and the church vote. What's the seventh?"

"That's given at the Queen's pleasure," said David. "It's more like a decoration. You get it if you're such a hell of a chap that the Queen thinks you ought to have another vote."

"Aren't there any rules about getting it?"

"I don't think so," said the pilot. "I think you just get it for being a good boy."

From the cabin hatch Rosemary said, "That's right, Uncle Ted. It's given by a Royal Charter in each case." She added, "I'm just dishing up."

They went down into the cabin of the yawl and sat down to the ham toasts. For a time they talked about yachts and the Solent, and of Rosemary's cooking, and of English food, but Captain Osborne was absent minded. Presently he brought the conversation back to the Australian system of voting. "About this multiple voting," he said. "They do it in New Zealand too, don't they?"

"I think they do," said David. "Yes, I'm pretty sure they do."

"They do it in Canada," said Rosemary. "Most of the Commonwealth countries have the multiple vote in one form or another, except England."

David smiled. "You're pretty conservative here."

The naval officer nodded slowly. "Yes," he said. "We

don't take up new things like that till they're well proved."
He paused, and then he said. "Of course, you've got your
States. You can try a thing like that out in your State
elections, and see how it goes."

"That's how women got the vote in the Commonwealth,"
Rosemary said. "New Zealand started it, in 1893, and
then South Australia gave women the vote in 1894. When
the Australian Federal constitution was drafted in 1902 they
gave women the vote. They didn't get it in England till
1918."

David stared at her. "Is that right? Where did you get
that from?"

"It's right enough," the girl said coolly. "I did History
at Oxford, and women take an interest in the women's vote.
But it was the same with the secret ballot in elections.
South Australia started that in 1856, but English voters
didn't get a secret ballot till 1872."

"Some time like that," the pilot said. "A bit before my
time, and I never did much history. I remember when
the multiple vote started, though. It was when I was in
Townsville, in 1963. They brought it in for West Australia."

"Why did West Australia start it?" asked Rosemary.
"Why not New South Wales, or Queensland?"

"I don't know," said David. "Labour was very much
against it."

"They're against it here," said Captain Osborne drily.

"West Australia was always pretty Liberal," the pilot said.
"People had been talking about multiple voting for a long
time before that. I reckon it was easier to get it through in
West Australia."

"How did it come to be taken up by the other States, if
Labour was so much against it?" asked Rosemary.

"Aw, look," said David. "West Australia was walking
away with everything. We got a totally different sort of

politician when we got the multiple vote. Before that, when it was one man one vote, the politicians were all tub-thumping nonentities and union bosses. Sensible people didn't stand for Parliament, and if they stood they didn't get in. When we got multiple voting we got a better class of politician altogether, people who got elected by sensible voters." He paused. "Before that, when a man got elected to the Legislative Assembly, he was an engine driver or a dock labourer, maybe. He got made a minister and top man of a government department. Well, he couldn't do a thing. The public servants had him all wrapped up, because he didn't know anything."

"And after the multiple voting came in, was it different?"

"My word," said the Australian. "We got some real men in charge. Did the Public Service catch a cold! Half of them were out on their ear within a year, and then West Australia started getting all the coal and all the industry away from New South Wales and Victoria. And then these chaps who had been running West Australia started to get into Canberra. In 1973, when the multiple vote came in for the whole country, sixty per cent of the Federal Cabinet were West Australians. It got so they were running every bloody thing."

"Because they were better people?" asked the captain.

"That's right." The pilot paused. "It was that multiple voting made a nation of Australia, I think," he said. "Before then we weren't much, no more than England."

Miss Long laughed. "Thanks."

He was confused. "I'm sorry—I didn't mean it that way."

"It's all right," she said. "I've never yet met anybody who could defend our way of doing things."

She switched the conversation, and began to talk about boats; no more was said of politics. Later in the evening, when he said good night to go back to his own vessel, the captain stayed below and Rosemary went up on deck to see the pilot into his dinghy. The moon was rising over the little town, the harbour bathed in silvery light reflected from the water. The pilot stood on deck, looking around him at the many yachts, the harbour, and the down. "My word," he said quietly. "It's a beautiful place, this."

Beside him the girl said, "You don't like England much, do you?"

"I don't know," he said quietly. "I love the scenery, like this. I'd always want to come back here again to see what's new in aviation, or in engineering, or techniques." He hesitated. "I don't like what I've seen of the way you govern yourselves. I think a lot of that is obsolete and stupid."

"Maybe some of us think that ourselves," she said.

He glanced at her, slim and straight beside him in the moonlight, holding the ham wrapped up in greaseproof paper. He took the ham from her. "Your uncle seemed very interested in our way of voting."

"Yes," she said. "It's coming to be quite an issue here, like the women's vote was back at the beginning of the century. I suppose history's going to repeat itself—it usually does. We'll end by copying Australia." She turned to him. "Be careful how you go, Nigger," she said. "Some of the politicians don't much care for the Dominions getting into the Queen's Flight. Be careful not to get mixed up in anything."

He smiled. "I'm here to fly the aeroplane," he said. "I don't intend to get mixed up in British politics."

He stooped and untied the painter of the dinghy. "Thanks for everything, Rosemary," he said. "See you some time at Buck House."

She smiled at him. "Don't go bumping on a rock, or on

the Beaulieu spit," she said. "And don't let anybody get you into anything."

"I won't," he said. "Good night, Rosemary."

She said, "Good night, Nigger."

Four

DAVID took delivery of the Australian Ceres for the Queen's Flight in September, a fortnight after Dewar had taken over the Canadian one. Before delivery both crews had put in a month of intensive work upon the crew trainer, a full-scale representation of the flight deck of a Ceres set up by the manufacturers in a vacant hangar; when the time came to take over the aircraft and to fly it away from Hatfield the crew knew their job.

Besides familiarisation training with the aircraft, the crew had to be trained to work as a team in radar controlled landings carried out in fog or bad weather. They were all experienced individually; indeed their experience of bad weather flying had been one of the chief factors in their selection for the Queen's Flight, but now they had to be exercised together on the Ceres till they could put it down upon the runway accurately and safely in the thickest fog, at night. They did this at the B.O.A.C. training aerodrome at Hurn, in Hampshire; twice a week they would fly down there to practise their blind landings all night long. Being members of the Royal Australian Air Force no civil certificates were issued to them, but Group Captain Cox kept them at it till he was assured that they were equal to the best B.O.A.C. pilots in this technique. Throughout their time in the Queen's Flight they went to Hurn for a refresher course once a month, whenever they were in England.

It was the Queen's wish that year to spend the late fall in Canada, and it was proposed that she should leave England in the Canadian Ceres on the evening of the twelfth of November and fly direct to Edmonton to open the Clearwater hydro-electric scheme, a flight of about eight hours, go on to Vancouver for a few days' holiday and then back to Ottawa. It seemed desirable to make a trial flight over this route before starting with the Queen, and the Canadian machine was quietly prepared to make this flight, carrying the Australian crew as passengers for general experience.

Before this trial flight took place, the crews of the Queen's Flight were plagued with visitors, exalted personages who took the afternoon off from their offices to motor down to White Waltham in the fine autumn weather to see the new machines. The High Commissioners were fair enough, because they after all had paid for the aeroplanes as representatives of their countries. Air Chief Marshal Sir William Bradbury came frankly for the drive in the country, and said so. So did eight civil servants from various ministries on eight separate visits, but they did not say so. All these people had to be entertained. Finally Frank Cox received a telephone call from the Secretary of State for Air, Lord Coles of Northfield, to say that he was coming down that afternoon.

He broke the news to the Canadian and Australian captains. "Lord Coles is coming down this afternoon."

"For the love of Pete," said Wing Commander Dewar, "what's it got to do with him? We aren't in his parish."

"I am," said Cox. "So is the aerodrome."

"Well, hell," said the Canadian. "Let him inspect you

and the aerodrome and leave us be. I've got the radar schedule three to do this afternoon. I can't have people in and out of the machine."

"He'll have to look at Nigger's aircraft," said Cox. "I'll tell him yours is just the same."

"Who is Lord Coles?" asked David. "Apart from being Secretary of State for Air?"

"Shop steward at an iron foundry," said Dewar. "He's been a good union man, and got to be head of the Royal Air Force."

David's lips tightened, but Frank Cox was there, and the Australians and Canadians were careful not to say what they might think about the British system of government. He turned to the Group Captain. "I can show them Tare," he said. "The upholsterers are in the port cabin, and they're checking the flap indicators, but that doesn't matter." They spoke of the Canadian and Australian machines as Sugar and Tare respectively, from the last letters of the registration call signs.

The Group Captain nodded. "I'll keep him in my office for a few minutes when he arrives, and send a message over —you'll be on the aircraft? Come over to the office, and we'll show him the machine together. Better warn Ryder." Flight Lieutenant Ryder was the Australian second pilot of Tare.

David was working with his crew on the machine when he saw the telephone girl crossing the floor of the hangar to him, in the middle of the afternoon. He went to meet her. "Want me?"

She said, "The Group Captain said I was to tell you that the Prime Minister is in his office, with Lord Coles."

David started. "Iorwerth Jones?"

"Yes, sir. The Prime Minister."

"Tell him I'll be there in just a minute. I'd better wash

my hands." As he did so, he speculated glumly on the afternoon before him. The Prime Minister of England had never been out of England but for one short holiday at Dinard, and he thought little of the Commonwealth; in return the Commonwealth thought little of him. Born in a Welsh mining valley, he had worked as a miner for some years and as a youth had been a member of the Party; Communism was no longer politically expedient in England since the Russian war and he had long abandoned it, but the class hatred of his youth still hung around him and influenced all that he did. In energy and in intellectual capacity he was a giant, a head and shoulders above the remainder of his Cabinet. He had sat in Parliament representing South Cardiff for twenty years, and he would sit there till he died.

David went into the Group Captain's office and was introduced. He had not met either of the two visitors before, though he had seen pictures and movies of the Prime Minister many times and was familiar with the broad, white face, the iron grey shock of hair, and the glowering eyes. He did not know Lord Coles at all, and found him to be a tubby, rubicund little man who liked his beer and carpet slippers, and who knew absolutely nothing about aircraft or the Royal Air Force.

After the introductions, David said, "Tare is all ready, sir. There are men working in her; shall I get them out of the machine?"

Lord Coles said quickly, "Working bonus or piece work?"

David glanced at him uncertainly. Frank Cox said, "No, sir—they work time rate on the maintenance."

The Secretary of State for Air was pleased. "Eh, then, give them a stand easy," he said. They went out into the hangar.

113

The hangar doors were open, and Tare stood just inside, a great smooth gleaming mass of bright duralumin, white painted on the upper surfaces. Outside on a concrete circle off the runway Sugar stood lined up upon the radar target on a mast a mile away upon the far side of the field. It was easier to see the shape and lines of the machine upon the distant aircraft, the delta wing, the long protruding nose, the buried engines indicated by the air inlets. The two officers stood for five minutes describing the form of the machines and their general characteristics to their guests, as they had so often had to describe them before, and as they talked they knew that what they said meant very little to these politicians. Once, when they said that the range of the machine was about eight thousand nautical miles, the Secretary of State for Air asked if that was far enough to take the machine to Aden without landing. They told him that it could safely fly as far as Colombo without landing and still have a forty per cent reserve of fuel, and he asked if Colombo was further than Aden.

This was all normal to the officers, and they turned to the aircraft in the hangar. Before going up the gangway into it, the two politicians withdrew a little from the officers and stood looking at it together, talking in low tones. Then Mr. Jones summoned the Group Captain, and said, "What did this bloody nonsense cost?"

The Group Captain said, "The aircraft, sir? I'm afraid I couldn't tell you that exactly. The High Commissioners handle the accounts. I think the machines cost about four hundred thousand pounds each, but I'm afraid that's only rumour."

The Prime Minister turned quickly to David. "Do you know what this cost?"

"No, sir," said the Australian. "I don't know anything about that side of it. It's not my business."

Mr. Iorwerth Jones stared at David. "What's your position in this thing? Who pays you?"

"I'm an officer of the Royal Australian Air Force, sir," the pilot said equably. "I'm paid by the Federal Government."

"How many of you are there here, paid by Australia?"

"Eight, sir—counting myself. That's the aircrew."

"How many people are there here paid by the British Government?"

Group Captain Cox said, "Myself and the telephone girl, sir. The High Commissioners for Canada and for Australia are meeting the whole of the expenses of the Flight, except those which pertain expressly to the Royal Household."

"It seems to me a bloody waste of money," said the Prime Minister. "If the Queen wants to go to Australia she can book a seat on the air line like everybody else, or go by sea."

There was an awkward silence. Lord Coles broke it by saying, "Well, let's 'ave a look at it, now we're here. It won't take long."

"The gangway is just here, sir," said David, frigidly polite. Inwardly he was furious, but he did not quite know why. He had the good sense not to show his anger, but commenced upon his description of the aircraft, now so often repeated to officials that it had degenerated into a sort of patter. He showed them everything inside the fuselage from the luggage compartment in the tail to the radar compartment in the nose. The Prime Minister found nothing to his taste.

"Waste of the working man's money," he said once.

He paused once at the entrance to the Royal cabin, quietly furnished in dove grey fabrics and silky oak veneers. "I know who put them up to this," he said. "That bloody old fool Bob Menzies. He's the nigger in the wood pile.

He'll have to learn to keep his nose out of what doesn't concern him."

David said quietly, "I don't know anything about it, but I'm sure you're wrong. Sir Robert Menzies retired from politics when I was a boy. He's a very old man, about eighty five. He couldn't have had anything to do with the decision to provide this aircraft."

"Don't you give me that," said the Prime Minister. "I know his stink."

The wonders of design meant nothing to these men. In the pilot's cockpit the Secretary of State for Air said, "Where d'you keep the Very pistol?"

Vague memories of the equipment of early Army Co-operation aircraft came to the pilot's mind. "Very pistol? We don't carry one of those."

"How do you signal to the folks on the ground, if you want to come down, like?"

"I don't think you'd do that, sir. We've got plenty of radio." It was difficult to commence from the beginning, to explain that travelling at fifty thousand feet no pyrotechnic would be seen, that an aircraft of that nature could not land in any field.

"You should 'ave a Very pistol," said the Secretary of State. "See he gets a Very pistol, Cox."

"Very good, sir."

Lord Coles turned to Mr. Jones. "You got to look after things yourself," he said. "If I'd not come this afternoon they might 'ave gone without a Very pistol."

At last the visitors departed to drive back to London in their official car, and David was left in the office with his Group Captain. For a minute each found it difficult to make the first remark. At last Frank Cox said dully, "I'll see if I can get a Very pistol for you, Nigger. They might have one in the Army."

David smiled. "Cheer up," he said. "We've people like that in Australia."

"Maybe," said the Group Captain. "But not as Secretary of State for Air."

There did not seem to be anything useful to be said between the Australian and the Englishman, and David found it equally difficult to discuss the events of the afternoon with Dewar when he came in from the radar check on Sugar. He went back to his office and sat in troubled thought for half an hour. Then he lifted the telephone and asked the girl to get Miss Long in the Assistant Secretary's office at the Palace.

She came on the line presently. "Miss Long," he said. "This is Nigger Anderson."

"Hullo, Nigger," she said. "Where are you speaking from?"

"White Waltham," he said. "We've just had Lord Coles down with the Prime Minister to have a look at the machines."

"Oh . . ." she said. "I don't think Major Macmahon knew that."

He said, "Will you have dinner with me, Rosemary? I want to talk to you."

"About your little friends, Nigger?"

"Yes."

"I don't know that you'd better."

"I don't want to talk very much. Just one or two questions that I think I ought to know the answers to. We might have dinner at the R.A.C. and go out to a picture afterwards."

She said, "I'd love to do that, but I don't know that I'm going to answer any questions. We don't gossip in this servants' hall, you know. When do you want to meet me?"

"Tomorrow night?"

"I'm free tomorrow night." They fixed the time, and rang off.

They met next night in the ladies' annexe of the club. He went forward to meet her. "It was good of you to come," he said. "I don't know that I've really got much to worry you about." He helped her out of her coat, and ordered a dry sherry and a tomato juice cocktail. "I've been looking at the movies," he said. "Have you seen *Red Coral*—Judy March?"

She shook her head. "They say it's awfully good."

He went to organise the seats, and when he came back to her they talked of unimportant things till it was time for them to go to dinner. The dining room was fairly full, the tables close together; the girl glanced round her thoughtfully as she sat down. Over the oysters she said, "What's the first question, Commander?"

He smiled. "Can I start off by telling you what happened?"

"If you like," she said. "I probably know most of it. Frank Cox was talking to Major Macmahon this morning, and after that there were some memorandums. Anyway, go ahead and tell me."

He gave her a short account of the events of the afternoon, making his story as dispassionate as he was able. As he talked the girl glanced round the room once or twice. In the end he said, "Well, that's what happened. I didn't like it much."

"No," she replied. "I don't suppose you did."

David sat in thought for a minute. "I can see that there might be difficulties when Canada and Australia come forward to do things for the Crown which England can't afford to do, or doesn't want to do," he said at last. "Small difficulties. But he seemed so vindictive . . ." He glanced

118

at her. "I know I'm only here to fly the aeroplane. But if this sort of thing is going to happen, I'll have to know the general situation some time or other. I'd rather that you told me." He met her eyes. "Are things getting bad between the Government and the Crown?"

She glanced around the crowded room again. "I can't possibly discuss that, Nigger," she said. "At any rate, not here."

"I don't want to press you to answer that," he said. "But I can tell you this, I'm going to find out how matters stand." He paused. "She's my Queen as well as yours," he said. "She's Queen of Australia as well as Queen of England. My Government have sent me here to work for her, to work for our Queen. I'll have to know a little bit about her difficulties."

She said, "Did anybody brief you when you took this job?"

He shook his head.

She said, "They should have told you. Something of this sort was bound to happen sooner or later."

"I can find out," he said. "I can go nosing round and listening to tittle-tattle, and putting two and two together. I'll get to know what's going on in no time. But I'd rather that you told me candidly, because you know."

"I'm not going to talk about it any more," she said. "There's John Llewellyn Davies sitting at the next table but one, and Henry Forbes over there. Let's talk about something different."

The names meant nothing to him, but he smiled, and said, "All right."

Over the coffee in the lounge she said, "Are you very keen to see this movie?"

"Not particularly," he replied. "Do you want to do something else?"

119

"I've got a flat up on the top floor of a house in Dover Street," she said. "We could talk up there."

They left the club and walked along Pall Mall and up St. James's Street. As they went, she asked, "Did you ever read much history?"

He shook his head. "No. All my schooling was done with a view to getting into the Air Force. It didn't leave much time for history."

She walked on in silence for a few minutes. Then she said, "It's a pity that something always has to be left out."

"Too right," he replied. "It's always that one that turns out to be important in the end."

They came to Dover Street, and she let herself into a doorway with a key, between a hairdresser's shop and a chemist. The entrance was well carpeted and decorated because it led to the studio of a photographer on the first and second floor; above that the decoration deteriorated. On the top floor she opened another door and they entered her sitting room; another door led out of that to bedroom, kitchenette, and bathroom.

She crossed to the fireplace and lit two reading lamps beside the two chintz covered armchairs. "Sit down and make yourself at home," she said. "I won't be a minute." She went into the bedroom and reappeared without her coat. "Would you like a cup of coffee?"

"Not if it's got to be made," he said.

She smiled. "I've got a lot of my breakfast coffee in the percolator. It'll heat up all right."

He went through to the kitchenette with her, and watched her as she made her small preparations. "You've got a nice little place here," he said.

"It's not bad," she agreed. "It's very central, and it's handy for the Palace. I just walk across the Park. I've been here for three years."

He stood watching her slim grace as she made coffee for him, wondering how old she was. Twenty six, or twenty seven probably, he thought; she wore no rings. She looked up presently, and handed him a steaming cup, and took her own, and went with him into the sitting room. She turned on one element of an electric stove, and they sat down in the armchairs.

Presently she said, "You'll have to understand the general situation, David. If you understand that thoroughly, I don't think there'll be any need for us to talk about the details, because you'll understand those too—as much as you'll need to. What's the population of Australia?"

"About twenty seven million, I think," he replied. "It goes up every year."

She nodded. "I think that's about right. Canada has about thirty two million people, and she's still increasing fast. Britain has thirty eight million people, and she's still going down, decreasing at the rate of nearly a million a year."

"That's right," he said. "As I understand it, about three hundred thousand immigrants a year come from England to Australia and New Zealand, about four hundred thousand go to Canada, and the rest go to Africa and the colonies."

"That's right," she said. She paused. "I think the first thing is the sort of people that these immigrants are. A very large proportion of them are politically Right Wing in their views. A man who leaves his country to go to Australia is a man who's taking a gamble on his own ability. He gives up everything he knows, gives up what security he's got at home in England, and he goes to Canada or to Australia to start again. He knows there's nothing like so much welfare in your countries. He knows that if he fails in life he may be much worse off in Canada or in Australia than he would be if he stayed here at home. He goes because he likes that sort of country, where he's got a chance to make a fortune for himself."

"I think that's right," said David. "There aren't a great many enthusiastic Socialists among the immigrants from England."

She nodded. "That's why you've had such a run of Liberal governments in Australia. Let's see—you had a Labour Government from 1970 to 1973, and before that there was the Calwell Government, and the Evatt one. I don't believe you've had more than ten years of Labour governments in the last thirty."

"I suppose that's true," said David thoughtfully. The curl behind her ear was fascinating. "You think that's because the immigrants are Liberal?"

"I'm sure of it," she said. "That, and the fact that your country has remained so prosperous. That's partly due to your expanding economy. But here in England the effect has been the opposite. We've only had about ten years of Conservative governments in the last thirty, because all these emigrants who've left for Canada and Australia have been Conservatives at heart. That's the first big difference between this country and Australia, and that colours everything. You're a Right Wing country, and we're Left Wing."

He nodded slowly, looking at her profile as she stared at the electric fire. She had very clean features, with a warm brown tint to her skin that probably came from the Solent.

"I think the historians will say that Socialism has been a good thing for England," she said thoughtfully. "All countries go through good patches and bad patches, and England has been going through a bad patch for the last forty years. It's probably not far from the end now. When we can feed our population things will suddenly improve, and the economists say that's only about five years ahead. Then, maybe, we can try free enterprise again. But in the meantime we've got to work together to get through the mess, and Socialism's probably the best for that."

"That may be so," he said. "But we Australians aren't quite in the same boat."

"You've got to try and understand," she said. "You've got to understand why England has developed differently to your country."

She turned her head to face him. He met her clear grey eyes, and he was suddenly delighted to be sitting here with her, engaged in this serious conversation. He was far happier than if they had been at the movies.

"And now you've got to try and understand what an illogical people the English are," she said. "A country so strongly Socialist as England is ought to be a republic. The Crown rules by divine right, and that's still the essence of the Crown's position in this country. That right conflicts entirely with all the principles of a democracy, especially a Socialist democracy. Any other people but the British would have done away with the Crown long ago, but the British aren't like that. They love their Kings and Queens. The British people won't have the Crown touched. They won't even have the Royal Palaces touched. When the Bevan Government tried to put the Inland Revenue into Hampton Court in 1960 it brought down the government and the Conservatives got in. It was the Queen who gave up Balmoral and Sandringham for economy, and the British people didn't like that much. The British people are completely Royalist at heart, and yet they're Socialist. It's quite illogical, but that's the way they are."

He smiled. "It's a good thing for us all that they're like that," he said. "If it wasn't for the Queen, we wouldn't have much in common with England."

She nodded. "The old King and the present Queen have been terribly wise," she said. "They've held the Commonwealth together, when everything was set for a break up. They've done a magnificent job, and in England, anyway, they've had a rotten time." She hesitated. "Kings and Queens have an easier time in Right Wing countries," she said. "That's why she gets on so well with your Mr. Hogan, and with Mr. Delamain in Canada."

He laughed, "And why things aren't so hot with Mr. Iorwerth Jones."

"I didn't say that," she retorted.

"No," he replied. "But I can see it, all the same." He paused. "English scientists, and English engineers, and the Queen," he said. "Those are the things that we like and admire in England. We don't think a fat lot of your governments."

"No . . ." She turned, and stared at the fire again. "And now this matter of the voting has come up. You've experimented in your States, and found what seems to be a better system of democracy."

He opened his eyes. "Is that making trouble over here?"

"I think it is," she said. "Yes, I think it is." She paused and then she said, "New Zealanders, and you Australians—you did this once before, when it was Votes for Women. You tried it out in one State and saw it was a success, and then adopted it for the whole country. You put us in a very difficult position over that. And now it's happening again . . ."

He asked, "Is England sorry that she got forced into giving women the vote?"

She smiled. "Of course not. The British people would be very happy with your multiple vote, once they got used to it. But it would mean great changes."

"I bet it would," he said cynically. "You wouldn't get a nit-wit like Lord Coles in charge of the Royal Air Force. You might not even have Iorwerth Jones."

"Exactly," she replied. "That's the difficulty that you Australians and Canadians have made for us, as you did over Votes for Women. You can't expect Iorwerth Jones to like you very much."

He raised his head. "Our way of doing it is right," he said. "People like that could hardly get elected to our House of Representatives. They'd never get made ministers."

She smiled at him, and he was glad of it because he was afraid that he might have offended her. "You can't expect Iorwerth Jones to look at it like that. The people have put him where he is upon the one man one vote principle. He believes in that principle, because he believes that he's the best man in the country to be Prime Minister. He probably believes this multiple vote talk to be a Tory trick to get him out of office. He probably believes that Australian and Canadian politicians are backing the Tories, to force this voting upon England by pressure from the Commonwealth." She smiled. "On top of that, your Governments must choose this time to go and give aeroplanes and crews to the Queen, to make it easy for her to go and spend more time in the Dominions."

"She's our Queen as well as yours," he said. "If she were to spend her time in each of the countries of the Commonwealth proportionate to its white population, she'd only spend about three months of each year in England. If you include the coloured peoples, you'd be lucky if you saw her for a fortnight." He paused. "As it is, she hasn't been at Tharwa for two years. Australians feel they aren't getting a square deal."

"She knows that, Nigger," Rosemary said quietly.

"She's very well aware of what Australians feel. But she's got difficulties."

"I bet she has," he said thoughtfully. "I wouldn't like her job."

"No," she said. "I sometimes think she's got the beastliest job that any Englishwoman could have."

She got up from her chair. "More coffee?"

He got up with her. "I should be going soon," he said, thinking that perhaps her job required her to be careful of her reputation, and that he must help her. "I've asked most of the questions now."

"It's early yet," she said. "Stay and have another cup of coffee. Or there's a bottle of beer, if you'd rather."

He shook his head. "I never take it."

"You don't drink at all, do you?"

He shook his head. "I couldn't afford to, when I was a boy. I wanted all my money for books and for club flying. Then when I got to be a pilot I was glad I'd never started. I think you're just that little bit better if you don't."

"Well, have another cup of coffee. It's quite early."

She went through and switched on the percolator, rinsed out the cups, and made fresh coffee. She carried the cups back into the sitting room, careful to avoid spilling.

He took his cup from her. "Thanks." And standing by the stove, he asked, "Where does the Queen stand in this matter of the multiple vote? What does she think about it all?"

The girl laughed. "I don't know, Nigger," she said. "She doesn't confide in me. And if she did, I wouldn't spill the beans to you or anybody else."

He laughed with her. "You don't have any opinions of your own?"

"Not one," she said firmly. "All the opinions that I've got are based on documents with red things stamped across the top, like CONFIDENTIAL, and MOST SECRET, and FOR HER MAJESTY'S HAND ALONE."

"All right," he said. "No more questions. I think you've told me all I want to know."

"I haven't told you anything at all," she said. "We've just been talking about England and why she's different to Australia."

He laughed. "Have it your own way."

They sat down again with their cups of coffee. "You know an awful lot about the woman's vote," he said. "Where did you get all that from—all about Australia and New Zealand?"

"One of the bits of information that one picks up and remembers," she said. "I'm a woman, so I take more interest in that than you would." They smiled. "I did History at Oxford."

"You went to Oxford, did you?"

She nodded. "I was at Somerville."

"Did you get this job from there?" he asked. He wanted to find out how old she was.

"Not quite," she said. "I did a course of shorthand typing and then got a job in the Foreign Office. I was there two years, and then I heard there was a vacancy in the Secretaries' office, and I went to see Miss Porson, and I got it."

His guess had not been very far from the mark; she would be about twenty seven. He asked, "Is your home in London?"

She shook her head. "My father and mother live outside Oxford, at a place called Boar's Hill. He's a don at New College."

"Do you sail every week end in the summer?" he asked.

"Whenever I can get away," she said. "I spend one

week end in every four on duty at the Palace. I get Monday off instead. I generally go home those week ends, and come up on Tuesday morning. I'm usually at Itchenor for the others, in the summer, or else out with Uncle Ted."

"It's dinghy sailing at Itchenor, isn't it?"

She nodded. "I've got an International fourteen footer down there, that I race with another girl, Sue Collins." She hesitated. "We were very lucky in the crash," she said. "We didn't lose quite all our money. We lost most of it, but not quite all."

"The 1970 crash?"

She nodded. "Most people I know lost everything."

"Was it as bad as that?" he asked. "I was a boy, of course —I've only heard about it vaguely."

"It was bad," she said. "Most people had a little money saved in one form or another up till then—insurance policies or something, but after that I don't think anyone had anything. I don't remember it personally—I was too young. But it was very bad."

"What caused it?" he enquired.

"I think it was the emigration," she said. "When people began emigrating it was all right at first. But then when four or five million people had left England there began to be an empty house in every street, and when that happened houses weren't worth anything, any more. Before that, people used to buy their houses—that's the way they saved money. Well, then house property went down to nothing, and that money was all lost." She paused. "Office buildings, too—they weren't worth anything, with empty offices everywhere. It ended in a general financial crash, and everyone lost all their savings."

He nodded slowly. "I don't think we've had anything like that in Australia," he said.

"I don't think you have. You've been very lucky." She

smiled at him. "The funny thing is, I don't think it hurt anyone very much. Everyone was in the same boat, and the houses were still there, and most people's jobs were still there, too. It meant that the government had to take over all the buildings in the country, of course, or they'd have fallen down for lack of maintenance. That's why practically every house and office building in the country is government owned today."

"Is that the reason?" he enquired. "I wondered about that. I thought it was just Socialism."

She shook her head. "Actually, I think it was the second Eden Government that did it."

"Are any houses being built in England now?" he asked.

She shook her head. "I don't think there's been a new house built in England for the last ten years."

"We seem to be doing nothing else," he said. "New houses going up everywhere."

"Can anybody build a house?" she asked.

"Why—yes, if you've got the money."

"How much does a new house cost?"

"An ordinary, three bedroomed, small house costs about four or five thousand pounds. That's built in weatherboard, of course."

"What do you have to do to build a house?" she asked. "How do you get the land?"

He glanced at her. "You just buy it."

"Just like that? Buy it from somebody that owns it, himself?"

"That's right."

"And then pay a builder to build the house?"

He nodded. "If you haven't got the money you go to a building society and borrow part of it. You've got to have *some* money."

"Can ordinary people save enough for that, out of what they earn?" she asked.

"I think so," he replied. "I've saved about two thousand pounds since I joined the Air Force."

She stared at him, amazed. "Two thousand pounds! But how much do you get paid?"

"As a Wing Commander, with allowances, I get about eighteen hundred a year," he said. "That's two thousand seven hundred sterling, in your money."

"But that's half as much again as Frank Cox gets!" she exclaimed.

He grinned. "I didn't know that, but I guessed it." He paused. "It's a pity, but that's the way it is. It's mostly due to the depreciation of your pound."

"You're earning more than double what a Member of Parliament gets in England," she said. "I had no idea Australian officers were paid like that."

"Our members of the House of Representatives get about four thousand, I think," he said. "You see, it's a whole time job with us, and if you want first class men to run the country you've got to pay a first class wage."

"Ours is a whole time job, too," she said a little sadly. "But we don't pay Members of Parliament like that."

He did not answer her, repressing the comment that came quickly to his mind. They sat sipping their coffee in silence for a time, and smoking. "It must be rather fun having a new house, that nobody's lived in before," she said at last. "You can have it built just as you want it, I suppose?"

"Of course. Most people build their house when they get married. They have great fun planning it, when they get engaged."

"People do that, do they? Build a new house and get married into it, and start off with everything clean and fresh?"

He nodded. "A lot of people do that. The parents usually help with the cost of it."

"Because the young man hasn't saved up enough money?"

He smiled. "Give him a chance. We marry a good bit younger than you do here."

"How old are people when they marry in Australia?"

"Oh—I don't know," he said. "I think they marry younger than they did when I was a boy. The average young man can afford the expenses of a family by the time he's twenty four, I think. I'd say that was a likely sort of age."

"And the girl about twenty?"

"I suppose so. I don't really know."

She smiled at him. "It didn't happen to you?"

"It's a bit different with me," he replied, "because of the colour." He grinned at her. "I get the money instead."

"I don't believe that's anything to do with it," she said. "You just keep that as an excuse." She paused. "I suppose that explains why your population's going up so fast, if people marry so young."

"I should think so," he replied. "Most families I know seem to have four or five children."

They sat in silence for a minute. "I don't know that I've ever seen a new house," she said at last. "I was just trying to think. I suppose you can have all the modern built-in furnishings and ventilation that you see in American magazines, if you build a house for yourself."

He glanced at her. "You *must* have seen a new house!"

"I suppose I have," she said. "I must have as a child. I can't remember one, though."

"Haven't you seen them abroad?"

"I've only been to France," she said. "It's the exchange difficulty, of course. I think I've seen new houses there."

She turned to him, smiling, "I suppose this all sounds terribly insular to you."

"Different," he said. "All my life, I seem to have been on the move. It's like that, when you're in a bomber squadron. I've never been in South America or Russia, but I've been to most of the other countries. But one airstrip's just like another, and one Air Force station like the last. I don't think I know half so much about the world as you do, sitting here in London. I mean, what makes it tick."

"I expect you do." She paused, and then she said, "I believe I'm going with the Queen to Canada."

"On this next trip—next month?" She nodded. "That'll be fun for you. You'll be going in Sugar, with Jim Dewar."

She nodded. "It's not quite certain. But Lord Marlow's getting a bit old and he's not got over his operation yet. The Queen said he'd better stay and hold the fort with the Prince of Wales, and she's taking Major Macmahon as secretary. Miss Porson has worked for Lord Marlow for forty years. She's very fit—you'd never think that she was fifty nine. Miss Turnbull comes next, and she's going with Major Macmahon, and Miss Porson's staying with Lord Marlow and Prince Charles. They want another girl to go to do the donkey work, and Miss Porson asked if I'd like to go with Miss Turnbull."

"That's fine," the pilot said. "You'll have a wonderful time."

"I'll have a lot of hard work at my typewriter in offices where I don't know where anything is," the girl said practically. "I'll be glad if it comes off, of course, because one should get *some* time off. But it's not in the bag yet. It's got to go before the Queen."

"I shouldn't think there's much for you to worry about," he said. He glanced at her, and as she was looking at the stove he let his gaze dwell for a minute. She was pretty and dignified, and thoughtful, and efficient and self-effacing; he could not imagine a better member for the Royal party. It was a pity, he thought, that this was going to be Dewar's trip.

Time to go, if he was thinking things like that. He put his cup down, and got to his feet. "I'd better be off," he said. "I've got to get down to Maidenhead, and I don't want to be late."

She got to her feet with him. "Why don't you come round to Itchenor in your boat one week end and have a go in my fourteen footer?" she suggested. "They're good fun to sail."

"Can I anchor there?" he asked.

"Moorings," she said. "We can fix you up one way or the other. You might have to lie alongside another boat."

"I'd like to do that," he replied, and he was suddenly unreasonably happy. "When are you going to be there?"

"Not this week end," she said. "I'll be on duty. I'll be going down there to the club next Friday night—Friday of next week."

"We shan't be back from Canada," he said. "We're taking Sugar over on this trial flight. Dewar has timed the take off for ten o'clock on Thursday morning."

"How long will it take you?" she asked.

"To Edmonton? About seven and a half hours, I think. There's eight hours' time difference, so we'll get there about the time that we took off, and have lunch there, and get on to Vancouver in the afternoon. We spent the next night there, and Friday night at Ottawa, and land back here sometime on Sunday morning."

"Do you know all those places?" she asked curiously.

"I've never been to Edmonton. I know Vancouver and Ottawa." He paused. "It's a pity about that week end," he

133

said. "Will you be going down to Itchenor again! I'd like to have a go on your fourteen footer."

She turned to a calendar on the mantelpiece. "I'll be down there the following week end," she said. "After that I'll probably have to lay her up, because of going to Canada."

"Can we make a date for that one?" he asked.

"Of course," she said. "Still smoking with the velocity of your flight from Canada."

"We'll have had a week to cool off," he replied. "We'll have to, because I believe the Queen's coming to inspect the Flight on the Wednesday after we get back."

She nodded. "That's right. She's looking forward to that very much. She's been talking a lot about the machines."

"Will you be coming down with her?" he asked.

She shook her head. "I shall be typing in the office. You can tell me about it at Itchenor on Saturday."

He moved towards the door. "I'll do that. Thanks a lot for all you've told me, Rosemary."

"Got all you want to know?" she asked.

He nodded. "I think so."

"That's fine," she said, "because I haven't told you anything. Good night, Nigger."

"Good night, Rosemary," he said.

Five

A WEEK later, the Queen's Flight took off from White
Waltham for Edmonton upon the training flight
arranged. They went in the Canadian Ceres with Dewar
and his Canadian crew in control, carrying Group Captain
Cox in charge, and with David and his crew of Australians
as interested passengers. They took off punctually at ten
o'clock G.M.T. and climbed to fifty thousand feet in the
first hour, leaving the rain and the clouds far below them.
They levelled off at their cruising altitude somewhere over
Northern Ireland; an hour and a half later Reykjavik in
Iceland was abeam and some two hundred miles to the
north. They crossed Greenland from the east coast in the
vicinity of Angmagsalik and went on across the Davis
Strait to Baffinland. They had a meal as they passed over the
north end of Hudson Bay, and here there was no cloud and
they looked down with interest at the passing panorama of
deserted land. Navigating by Decca and by radio bearings
they had little need for landmarks, but they identified the
east end of Lake Athabasca and started to lose height. An
hour later they came on the circuit of the aerodrome, well
known to Dewar, and put down upon the runway at a
quarter to ten, local time, a quarter of an hour earlier than
their time of take off from White Waltham.

This was the first Ceres that had visited Edmonton, and a

small crowd of pilots and R.C.A.F. officers gathered around it on the tarmac. David turned his Australians on to servicing and inspecting the machine with the Canadian crew, relieving the Canadian officers a little and enabling them to show the aircraft to their friends. No announcement had been made of the flight to the Press; they refuelled untroubled by reporters and photographers, and lunched in the R.C.A.F. mess. The Press caught up with them ten minutes before take off for Vancouver and Frank Cox made a short statement and submitted to be photographed in front of the machine with the Canadians. Then they were in the air again and climbing to forty thousand feet to clear the Rockies. An hour and a half later they put down at the R.C.A.F. aerodrome at Vancouver, and spent the night upon the station there.

Jet temperatures on the port inner engine were a little high at altitude, and they spent some time next morning adjusting the fuel pumps and doing engine runs. They took off for Ottawa after an early lunch and landed four hours later in the dark. Next day was a Saturday and they displayed the aircraft to a large number of Canadian members of the Senate and the House of Commons, now seeing the aeroplane that they had given to the Queen for the first time.

It was a disappointment to David that the Governor-General did not come to see the aircraft. Sir Thomas Forrest was a legendary figure at that time to every man who had served in the Russian war, the Field-Marshal who had come up from the bottom, who had risen from corporal to brigadier in the second war, from major to lieutenant-general in the third. At that time he had been Governor-General of Canada for about two years. David had never met him and he wanted very much to do so, but Tom Forrest was away in Winnipeg.

Mr. Delamain, the Prime Minister, entertained the officers to lunch at his residence. He was a small, vivacious French Canadian from Quebec who had worked his way up from the bottom to a commanding position in the lumber industry by the time he was forty five, and had then turned to politics. Auguste Delamain had a fat wife called Marie and eleven children, only two of whom appeared at the lunch table, and he had a fund of amusing anecdotes for the officers.

"Mr. Iorwerth Jones, he is well?" he asked. "Last time I was in England I thought he looks very poorly, and I thought perhaps he is not well. But then I hear that he has tried to nationalise your retail clothing shops and the Trades Union Congress did not approve, and so he was not allowed to do that. I think he was not very unwell, but only angry."

"The T.U.C. stood out against that one," said Group Captain Cox. "I expect they were afraid of what their wives would say."

"I asked him that," said Mr. Delamain. "I asked how English women would like to wear standard clothes all to one of six or eight designs, and he told me that it was necessary to the economic situation that they should do that. Marie was with me, and she was very rude to him, but she was very rude in French, which he does not understand, and fortunately nobody who was with us offered to translate what she had said. So we are still good friends."

Within the meaning of the act, thought David.

A little later the Prime Minister said, "Mr. McKinnon has told me that the Queen has had a heavy cold, and that she was looking tired when he saw her last week. I hope when she comes she will take a long rest. I have talked to the Governor-General, and we have discouraged all suggestions for engagements for her. She is to open the hydro-electric scheme at the Clearwater River, and the new Hospital in

Vancouver, but after that there is nothing arranged, and I hope that she will take a long rest at Gatineau. It is very beautiful up the Gatineau in the late fall, and the colours of the maples will be wonderful this year, because we have had frost." He paused. "But she is so energetic—she is always making engagements for herself. But this time she should rest."

"I wish she would rest, sir," said Cox. "She's had a very difficult time recently."

The French Canadian shot a quick glance at him. "I know that," he said. "Perhaps one day she will be able to come here and spend a long, long time with us."

The Ceres crews escaped from hospitality in the middle of the afternoon and went back to the aerodrome to prepare Sugar for the flight home. Refuelling and inspection took an hour and a half; they locked up the machine and went to the R.C.A.F. station for an early meal and bed. They were up at three in the morning and took off at four o'clock in the dark night and climbed to operating height. The sun rose an hour and a half later as they passed above the Straits of Belle Isle between Newfoundland and Labrador and started on the Atlantic crossing; flying against the sun they took five hours on the trip from Ottawa to White Waltham, and put down at the home aerodrome at two o'clock in the afternoon.

David had brought home with him from Ottawa twenty pounds of steak and a dozen bottles of claret, at that time practically unobtainable in England. He drove back to his flat at Maidenhead and put the meat in the deep freeze, and pondered for a time whether he dared call up Rosemary to suggest that she should get on the electric train to Maidenhead to come and share his meal. He resisted the temptation and cooked his *steak au vin* alone, and spent the evening thinking of all the things that he would have to tell her when he met her next at Itchenor.

The Royal inspection of the aircraft took place at White Waltham a few days later. Frank Cox had had the two machines drawn up outside the hangar and the crews paraded in front of each aircraft; it was a bright, sunny afternoon. The Royal party arrived in a big Daimler, the Queen and the Prince Consort and the Prince of Wales. Frank Cox went forward and saluted as they got out of the car, and then walked with the Queen as she inspected the parade.

At the end of the inspection she said, "Will you fall the parade out, Group Captain, and introduce the officers to me. Then let each member of the crews go to his own position in his own machine, so that I can see what they have to do."

David was introduced after Dewar, and the Queen shook his hand. She was not tall and she was definitely plump, but she was still beautiful, and clearly interested in the new machines, even excited. She asked how he was enjoying life in England, and he said, very much indeed, and she smiled, and said that she expected to see a great deal more of him. Then she passed on to the next officer and he met the Consort, a grey haired, handsome, humorous man, who asked him what he got the Air Force Cross for.

"Test flying, at Laverton, sir," said David.

"In general, or anything in particular?"

David hesitated. "I got a thing down after it got broken up a bit," he said.

The Prince of Wales beside the Consort spoke up. He was a man of about thirty five, fair haired and pleasant, in the uniform of an Air Vice-Marshal. "Was that the Boomerang?"

David said, "Yes, sir."

"I remember that, Father," said the Prince. "The

rudder came off in a dive. He landed it without a rudder."

The Consort said, "It must have been a great temptation to bale out."

"Couldn't do that, sir," said David. "It cost about a million pounds."

The Consort laughed. "They didn't give you any of it?"

"No, sir. Not even the grateful thanks of the tax-payer."

"Ah well, you got the best decoration of the lot."

He passed on to the other officers, and the Prince stayed and chatted for a moment with David. "We met somewhere in the war," he said. "I remember your face."

"At Lingayen, sir. I had No. 147 Squadron of the R.A.A.F. there."

"I remember." They chatted for a time about the war. Then the Prince said, "Is everything working out all right here, in this job?"

"Quite all right, sir."

"Getting all the stores and material you want?"

"Yes, sir. There were a few minor difficulties just at first, but Major Macmahon got those ironed out for us. Everything seems to be going very smoothly now."

The Prince said, "When the Queen goes to Canada next month with my father, Group Captain Cox is going too. You'll be left in charge here, I suppose."

David said, "Yes, sir."

"If anything should crop up that you don't feel you can handle, while the Group Captain is away," the Prince said, "you'd better give me a ring, or come and see me."

The pilot blinked a little in surprise. "Very good, sir," he said. "Thank you."

The Royal party went to the Canadian machine, and David got his own crew into Tare in their places. He stood by the fuselage door himself waiting; it was over half an hour before the Queen emerged from Sugar. He came to attention and saluted as she crossed to the Australian machine. "I'm afraid this one is exactly the same as the other, Your Majesty," he said.

She smiled. "Never mind. I want to meet your crew. It will make it so much easier to get to Tharwa, now that we have this beautiful aeroplane to go in. How long will it take us, Wing Commander?"

"About nineteen hours flying time, madam," he said. "Colombo is almost exactly half-way, and we should have to put down there to refuel. That would take about an hour."

She asked, "Could we go by night?"

"Going Eastwards the time difference makes the night short," he said. "If your time is at your own choice, it would be best to start after dinner, say at about nine o'clock at night. You could go to bed then, and have eight hours sleep before we reach Colombo at about noon, local time. You could lunch upon the ground then if you want to, and going on we should reach Canberra nine hours later, but that would be before dawn of the next day."

She said, "It sounds as if I shall be spending most of the journey in bed in my cabin."

"I should say that that's the best way to take it," he said. "The cabin is very quiet in this aircraft, and I think you would be comfortable."

"I'm sure of it," she said. She turned to the Consort. "Twenty four hours in bed with no possibility of a box reaching you, and Tharwa at the end of it. It sounds too good to be true!"

They passed into the machine laughing together, and David followed with Prince Charles. The aircraft was, in fact, a replica of the one that they had seen before, but they spent twenty minutes in it, talking to the crew. The Queen

141

spent several minutes in her cabin talking to the stewardess, a girl called Gillian Foster from Shepparton; coming out, David heard her say to the girl, "I can hardly wait to spend a night in here."

"We'll do our very best to make you comfortable, madam," the stewardess said.

The inspection over, the party left the machine, but they seemed to be in no hurry to get back to Windsor. The Queen stood with the Consort for a time upon the tarmac, chatting to the officers. To David she said once, "It makes our lovely home at Tharwa seem so close, to get into this magnificent thing and to be there in about twenty hours."

He asked her curiously, "You like Tharwa so much as that, madam? We have no autumn colours like Canada, and no high mountains."

"I know," she said. "That corner of Australia is beautiful in its own way. I am always sorry when it's time to come away from Tharwa."

At last they got into the Daimler and drove off, and even then it seemed to the officers that they were reluctant to go. Dewar turned to Cox, "Well, that went off all right," he said. "They seemed to like these aircraft."

The Group Captain nodded. "I thought at one time they were going to ask if they could have a ride in one of them. I thought they'd only be here for about ten minutes."

"They could have gone up if they'd wanted to," said David. "Tare's had her daily. We could have flown Tare." He paused. "I didn't expect them to be so enthusiastic," he said. "It must be just another aeroplane to them."

"They're only human," said Frank Cox. "Things aren't so complicated for them in Australia and Canada. Now they can get there just whenever they want to, without bothering Lord Coles of Northfield."

David drove back to his flat that evening happier in his job than he had been since he started. It had made a difference to him that the Queen had said that she liked Tharwa. He knew the Royal residence in the Federal Territory by motoring past it and looking at it from the hills upon the west side of the Murrumbidgee, two miles away. He had even studied it with field glasses, for curiosity. It was a long, white house in pastoral surroundings, set in a bowl of wooded hills and with lawns running to the Murrumbidgee river from the house. With the inferiority complex of an Australian he could see no reason why anyone should want to come to Tharwa. He had been quite deeply moved by the Queen's statement that she found it beautiful in its own way, because it was his country, and he himself would rather have lived there than anywhere else though he could not have said why.

That evening he rang up Rosemary in her flat. She said, "Hullo, Wing Commander. How did your party go off today?"

"It went off very well," he said. "I think they were pleased with everything."

"I thought they would be."

"They're bonza people," he said. "I was really impressed."

"Had you never met them before?"

"No," he said. "I'd read about them in the papers, of course. But you can't believe all that stuff."

"You can now," she said.

"That's right. Are you going down to Itchenor this week end?"

"Yes," she said. "I'm going down on Friday night and staying at the club. Will you be coming over?"

"I thought I would," he said. "I'll probably get into Wootton and lie there for Friday night, and come on to

Chichester Harbour on Saturday morning early. It's high water about midday, isn't it?"

"I think so. I'm racing in the afternoon," she said. "Would you like to crew for me?"

"I'd like to," he replied.

"I'll be looking for you in the morning, then," she said. "You should be able to pick up a mooring at this time of year."

"I'll get in somewhere." He paused. "I brought some steaks back from Ottawa, and some red wine. Will you have dinner with me on Saturday?"

"I might have known you'd do something like that if you went off to Canada. Of course, I'd love to dine with you. How did the flight go?"

"All right," he said. "We got back in one piece. I've got a lot I want to talk to you about."

"We'll talk on Saturday," she said.

He arrived in Chichester Harbour at about ten o'clock that Saturday morning, having sailed from the Isle of Wight at dawn. He dropped sailed just inside the entrance to the wide stretch of inland water and motored up the long channel to Itchenor, three miles from the entrance. He saw Rosemary put off in a dinghy from the shore as he drew near the village and scull out into the middle of the stream; he put the clutch out and she came on board and streamed her dinghy astern. "There's a yellow mooring a few hundred yards upstream," she said. "You can take that one."

She was wearing her yachting clothes, thin shirt, shorts, and blue sandshoes; she brushed his arm as they were pulling in the mooring chain together, and he found her proximity disturbing. She helped him to make up the mainsail on the boom and get the vessel into harbour trim. Then she rowed him ashore in her dinghy, and so began a very happy day.

She took him to the beach and showed him her boat; they rigged it together and waded out with it, scrambled aboard, and sailed for an hour in the Itchenor and Bosham channels while he got the hang of the boat. She let him sail it, and offered to let him sail it in the race that afternoon, but he refused, saying that he did not know it well enough and that they would do best if she had the tiller and he crewed for her. So they landed before the club, and went up to the bar for a sandwich lunch. She introduced him to a number of her friends. They raced that afternoon with eleven or twelve other boats of the same class, twice round a long course that took them practically down to the harbour entrance. They came in fourth, and went ashore for tea and gossip; then they took the sails off the boat and put them away, and rowed out to his little yacht for supper.

Again she exclaimed at the amount of meat he had aboard. "We can't possibly eat a quarter of this, Nigger," she said. "You're a floating butcher's shop."

"There's tomorrow," he replied. "You wouldn't have me starve on the way back to Hamble?"

"You won't starve," she said. "What time have you got to go?"

"I'll have to get away after breakfast," he replied. "The tide will be making eastwards by eleven o'clock." He hesitated, and then he said, "You wouldn't like to come with me?"

"I've got to be back in Dover Street without fail tomorrow night," she said. "I go to work in the morning."

"We should be ashore at Hamble by six," he said. "I've got the car there. I can run you home. I've got to be on the job on Monday morning bright and early, too."

"It would be an awfully long way out of your way to take me up to Dover Street," she said. "You could put me on the train at Guildford."

145

He grinned. "We'll argue about that. But would you like to come?"

"I'd love to, David," she said. "I'd love a day out in the Solent in this boat." She paused. "I'll have to put my fourteen footer in the shed and hose her down before I go," she said. "I shan't be sailing her again this season, because of Canada."

He nodded. "I'll come on shore and give you a hand in the morning. About half past eight?"

"Come and have breakfast at the club."

"All right. When is the Canada trip starting?"

"Wednesday morning of next week—in ten days' time," she said. "She's opening the hydro-electric thing on Thursday." The girl paused. "What's Edmonton like?"

"We didn't go in from the aerodrome," he replied. "I only saw it from the air. It looked just like any other town."

"I'm longing to see it," she said. "I've never been to America at all before. What's the Ceres like to travel in?"

"She's very comfortable," he told her. "No noise to speak of, and no vibration. The party seemed to like her all right." He poured her out a glass from the bottle of sherry he had bought for her, and a tomato cocktail for himself.

She nodded. "They liked what they saw," she said. "The Queen's been talking about nothing else."

"What did she say?"

The girl laughed. "I wasn't there, of course. I only hear that sort of thing third or fourth hand. Gossip of the servants' hall, David." She raised her glass. "Here's luck to Tare."

"I'd rather not trust to luck." He drank with her. "I'm taking Tare off on a trial next Wednesday. We've never flown her longer than an hour and a half, and we've never flown either of them in tropical conditions. The manufacturers did tropical trials on the prototype, of course. But I think we ought to see one of them function in the tropics before taking our sort of passengers about the world."

"Are you going far?" she asked.

"We shall only be away one night," he said. "I'm going down to Gambia, to Bathurst on the west coast of Africa, and spending the night there. Then next day we'll go north eastwards across Africa to Cyprus, turn there without landing, and back to White Waltham. That makes about a nine hours' flight, getting on for the maximum safe operating range."

She said curiously, "Do you feel that you're really travelling, on an enormous flight like that?"

He shook his head. "You're just flying. Usually you can't see the ground because of the cloud layer, and if you can you're ten miles up, so you don't see any detail. The sky is almost black, and the sun's much brighter. You can't see much."

"Do you get bored sometimes?"

He shook his head. "It's what I like doing. I never get bored."

Presently they went down into the little cabin and began to fry the steaks over the oil stove, with a few potatoes sliced. "One day if you get to Australia, I'll show you how a steak ought to be cooked," he said.

She smiled. "How's that?"

"Grilled, over a fire of gum tree twigs. It's very quick." He paused. "It's the best way in the world to cook a steak, and so far as I know you can only do it in Australia." He turned to her. "It's like sugaring in Canada."

"What's that?"

"You go up through the snow on skis to a little hut in the woods, and there you find an old man boiling down the sap out of the maple tree to make maple syrup." He told her all about it as they cooked their dinner: the bright snow, the bright sun, the wood fire under the evaporating pan, and the heavenly smell. "All countries have one taste or smell that others can't equal," he told her. "Grilled steaks are Australia to me. Sugaring is Canada."

Presently they took their plates and sat down at the little table to eat their meal, one on each side of the cabin. They topped up with bread and honey, and with a mug of coffee made out of a tin; then in the warmth and intimacy of the little lamplit room they sat smoking together.

"The Prince said one thing that I didn't understand," he told her presently. "When they came to see the aeroplanes. He said, if Frank Cox was away and something happened at White Waltham that I couldn't handle, I was to get in touch with him at once." He paused. "What do you think he meant?"

She smiled at him. "Just what he said, Nigger."

"What sort of thing?"

She opened her eyes wide. "He didn't tell me."

He laughed. "All right, you win. I suppose I can put two and two together for myself."

"I expect you can," she said. "You won't get far upon that flight from Gambia to Cyprus and White Waltham unless you can do that."

She stayed till about half past nine, and then made off for the shore in her dinghy. David watched her rowing off in the bright moonlight, thinking how well she managed her boat, how well her job.

He went ashore for breakfast with her and helped her with the business of putting her dinghy away for the winter. Then they sailed in *Nicolette* for Hamble, passing down the long channels of the harbour under sail this time with Rosemary on board as pilot, out through the entrance and straight out to sea over the bar, finally bearing away towards the forts at Spithead at the entrance to the Solent, with a light southerly breeze. All day they sailed together in close contact of a little yacht, doing the thing that they both loved to do, happy together.

They passed into the Hamble River at about five o'clock, and took down sail and put the sail covers on as they motored up the river to the mooring. By quarter to six they were on shore packing their luggage into the little car. They had a snack meal at the Bugle Inn upon the foreshore. While they were eating, David said, "We never saw Judy Marsh in *Red Coral*. What about going to see that before you go to Canada?"

She hesitated. "When could we go? I can't tomorrow night, or Friday. I'm going home this week end."

"I've got this trial—the Gambia affair." He thought for a moment. "I'd better get to bed early on Tuesday. Wednesday, Bathurst, and I'll probably be a bit tired on Thursday night."

"I should think you might be," she said drily. "It would have to be next week, we go off on Wednesday."

"What about Monday?"

"I should think Monday would be all right," she said thoughtfully. "Will you ring me at the Palace about lunch time? If there's an awful lot of work before we go, I might have to wash it out, David. You'd understand that, wouldn't you?"

"Of course," he said. "I'll get seats anway, and ring you lunch time on Monday."

He drove her up to London and deposited her outside her flat in Dover Street, still in her salt spotted blue jeans and rough blue jersey. She asked him in, but he refused that, thinking that she had to work next day and ought to get to bed. He drove back to Maidenhead in a dream, and thought of nothing else but Rosemary all night.

That week, with Frank Cox in command and carrying the Canadian crew as passengers, David flew Tare from London to Bathurst in five hours. They stayed, as usual, in the R.A.F. station for the night having refuelled the machine and loaded up with pineapples for private use. They took off at dawn next day and flew to Cyprus in about five and a half hours, turned over Nicosia, and landed back at their home aerodrome in England at tea time, with nothing particular the matter with the aeroplane.

He cruised alone in the Solent that week-end and found it cold and lonely.

He picked up Rosemary on Monday evening and gave her a couple of pineapples in spite of her protests that she wouldn't have time to eat them before leaving for Canada. "You can try," he said firmly. "I brought them from Bathurst specially for you, and I'm not going to have them thrown back in my face." They went and dined at the R.A.C., and this time, having no confidential business to discuss the dinner was a success. They went on to the movies to see Judy Marsh in *Red Coral* and sat very close together for two hours.

Coming out, he said, "You don't have to go home yet, do you? Let's go to the Dorchester and dance." So they went up to the Dorchester and danced together for the first time, and enjoyed it, and laughed a great deal, till the orchestra played God Save the Queen and woke them to the realisation that it was two in the morning.

He drove her back to Dover Street in his small car and parked outside the entrance to her flat; for a time they sat talking in the car, reluctant to break it up. "I have enjoyed this evening, David," she said. "It's been fun, every minute of it. It was sweet of you to take me."

"Pity it's going to be some time before we can do another," he said. "How long is she staying over in Canada?"

"About a month," she said. "I don't know the exact date when we come back, but it's before December the twentieth anyway, because her appointments start again here then. It's not so long."

"I'll probably be in Singapore or in Nairobi," he said gloomily. "Charles will want to go and shoot an elephant or something."

She laughed. "He's got to stay at home and hold the fort," she said. "He's not allowed to go away."

"Will you have dinner with me when you get back?" he asked. "The first free night, and tell me all about it?"

"I'll have dinner with you, Nigger," she said, "but I don't suppose I'll tell you about it. I never met such a nosey man as you are."

"I don't mean what the Queen did," he said. "I'm not interested in that. I mean, what you did."

"I can tell you that now," she said. "I sat in an office and took letters down for Major Macmahon, and typed them out, and put them on his desk for him to sign. Eight hours a day, when it wasn't ten."

"Doesn't he ever give you a holiday?"

"I get three weeks holiday a year," she said. "Sometimes Major Macmahon gets a bilious attack and then there usually isn't any work to do. That's an extra. They don't make me count it as a day of my three weeks."

"Perhaps he'll get a bilious attack over in Canada. Canadian food is full of grease and calories."

"I'm sure it's not."

He was very conscious of her close beside him in the little car. "What sort of scent is that you're using?"

"Bonne Nuit," she said. "It's French. It means Good Night."

"Fancy!" he said.

She stirred a little and reached for the door. "I'm not

going to sit here talking about my scent at three in the morning when I'm going away tomorrow," she said. "You can raise the matter again when I get back if you're still interested."

He got out and walked round the car, and helped her out on to the pavement. They stood together in deserted Dover Street in the pale moonlight. "I'll remember that," he said. "I'll write it down in my little book."

She said, "I expect you'll have more to tell me when I get back than I have to tell you."

"And how," he said. "More than you bargain for."

She laughed a little self-consciously, and moved towards her door, fumbling in her bag for the key. She found it and unlocked the door, and stood for a moment in the doorway.

"Look after yourself, Nigger," she said. "And thanks again for such a lovely evening."

"Thank you for everything," he said quietly. She paused, uncertain, on the threshold for a moment; then she went inside and the door closed behind her.

On the Wednesday the Queen left for Canada. The Press and the newsreel cameras were at White Waltham very early, photographing the machine and the Canadian crew. The minor members of the entourage arrived in several cars, amongst them Rosemary, who waved to David as she passed into the aircraft. Finally at ten o'clock the Royal car arrived carrying the Queen and the Consort, and followed by two other cars, one bringing the Prince and Princess of Wales and their two boys, the other bringing the Princess Royal with her husband, the Duke of Havant, and little Alexandra. There were a few minutes of Royal leavetaking and then the Queen went up the three steps into the fuselage, followed by the Consort and escorted by Frank Cox.

Dewar was waiting at the door to welcome them; in the

cockpit Johnnie Clare, the second pilot, broke out the Royal Standard at the mast at the exact moment that the Queen entered the machine, while cameras whirred and clicked outside. The door closed, and presently the machine moved forward on the taxi track towards the runway's end. The Ceres lined up on the runway, the mast and standard sank down into the fuselage, the outboard engines started, and then it was accelerating smoothly with the white plumes from the rockets leaving a long trail behind. It was airborne very quickly and the undercarriage disappeared into the wing; it put its nose up in a great climbing turn and vanished into the clouds towards the north.

David was left in charge upon the aerodrome. He escorted the Prince and the Princess back to their cars and answered a few questions from their children. Then they drove off, and he was left to cope with the reporters, some of whom had been perplexed by the direction the machine had taken. He got rid of them after an hour or so, and settled down into the uneventful routine of the Queen's Flight, waiting for a job to do.

The Trade Union Congress met at Blackpool for their annual conference next week end, and gave him something to think about. For some years past it had been usual for the more violent elements of the T.U.C. to rail against the size of the Civil List and the general expense of the Royal Family to the country, a method of blowing off steam which wounded nobody's feelings except those of the Family, who had no votes to be endangered and so didn't matter. It was undoubtedly the case that in the past the accumulation of Royal Palaces in England had represented a very minor extravagance for an impoverished country, but one by one the less essential ones had been eliminated from the List by making them self supporting in a fitting and a gracious manner as in the case of Sandringham, the permanent headquarters of the Commonwealth Coordination Council. Those which remained were fully used by various offices connected with diplomacy which could not be reduced or with the Royal Family, and the fact that they were paid for out of the Civil List was a matter of historical interest rather than evidence of Royal extravagance.

However, any stick does to beat a dog with, and for years a section of the T.U.C. had harped upon this theme. This year a fresh note was added to the melody. David Anderson, opening his newspaper one morning to read the comic strip, found that a Mr. Andrew Duncan of the National Association of Plate Benders had made a stinging speech about White Waltham aerodrome. This aerodrome, declared Mr. Duncan, comprised about twelve hundred acres of the soil of England, the property of the British people. At present it was reserved for the use of the Royal Family, who did not use it more than once or twice a year, and whose huge aeroplanes were wastefully maintained there at a vast expense; he did not say at whose expense that was. The Royal Family were keeping this land for their selfish pleasures, but if the land were freed from their tyrannical grasp and handed back to the People, it could be farmed and made to produce food to support four hundred working families. Four hundred families, said Mr. Duncan, were going hungry, eight hundred undernourished, pale-faced children were pitifully crying for the crust of bread that was not there, in order that these pampered aristocrats, these relics of an effete, outdated feudalism, might stamp upon their faces. It made his blood boil, said Mr. Duncan.

It made David's blood boil, too, when he thought of the two thousand sheep that fouled the runways and the tarmac and had to be laboriously herded to one side before the Royal aircraft could take off or land. White Waltham in the second war had been a training aerodrome; in the third war it had been expanded for operational use and it was held by the Air Ministry as a reserve field for Bomber Command. He knew that Frank Cox had had particular instructions from the Consort about the grazing; the sheep had first rights on that aerodrome, and the aeroplanes came a long way behind.

Blood, in fact, boiled freely over White Waltham, and before the day was out the aerodrome had become a serious political issue. No less than four speakers took the matter up, some vehement and some, the more effective, grieved that the Monarchy should have sunk so low. The Prime Minister and the Secretary of State for Air were both present, but said nothing to reveal the true position of the airfield to the Congress; perhaps they did not know it. Finally Lord Coles got up and assured the Congress that the matter would be looked into, and that suitable action would be taken. Mr. Iorwerth Jones said nothing.

David went out to go to White Waltham, and on the way bought all the other newspapers that he could find. *The Daily Monitor* in a first editorial said roundly that the whole thing was a Socialist plot to discredit the Royal Family, and disclosed the fact that 744 fat lambs had been sold off White Waltham aerodrome in the last calendar year, one for each of Mr. Duncan's starving children. *The Times* deplored the use of the Royal Family for political purposes, and did little else. *The Daily Watchman* said that whatever the merits or demerits of White Waltham aerodrome, it was beyond all question that the working man could no longer afford the annual expenses of Buckingham Palace or Windsor. St. James's Palace, said the leader writer, was the historic one and was quite sufficient for the Royal Residence. All other Royal palaces, castles, or houses in the country should be put to some remunerative use, or be turned over to the

Ministry of Works to house some overcrowded government department.

In the office David pored over these leading articles, with Dick Ryder, his second pilot, looking over his shoulder. "They don't like us much," he said at last.

The younger man shook his head. "Looks like they're going to winkle us out of here," he said. "Where do you think we'll go?"

"God knows. One of the R.A.F. aerodromes, probably."

"We'd have to get permission from the R.A.F. for every flight then, wouldn't we?"

David stared at him. "Theoretically, I suppose we should. They couldn't interfere with us, though."

"They hate us like hell," said Ryder. "I believe they could."

"The R.A.F. don't hate us."

"Lord Coles and the Prime Minister do. The R.A.F. would have to do as they were told, if we were on their aerodrome."

David sat in silence for a minute. "I hadn't thought about that one," he said. "Do you think that's behind it?"

"Could be. Whatever is behind it, anyway, it's not because they like having us here, or want to make our job any the easier."

David turned to the papers again. "My God," he said, "there'll be a stink at home if they touch Buckingham Palace or Windsor."

"Of course there will," the second pilot said. "But they don't think of that. They see it as an English problem that's no business of Australia. I don't believe they think of us at all when they decide these things."

David nodded. "No reason why they should. Half of them don't know where Australia is."

He spent the morning upon nominal duties, and left for

London at about noon, having Frank Cox's office in St. James's Palace to look after as well as his own. He lunched at the R.A.C. and walked down Pall Mall after lunch to the Palace, and in the two small rooms that opened on to Engine Court he set to work with the girl secretary to deal with the correspondence. At about half past three the telephone rang; the girl answered it and handed it to him. It was Miss Porson, speaking from the Palace.

She said, "Oh, Wing Commander, I'm so glad you're in London. The Prince of Wales would like to see you this afternoon."

"What time shall I come over?"

"If you would come to my office at about five minutes past four. I will take you along then."

He put down the instrument, wondering what this was all about, and went on with the correspondence. At five minutes past four he was in the Palace, clean and neat, following Miss Porson down the corridor. She took him to an ante-room and handed him over to the girl sitting in it. "I don't think he'll keep you very long."

He sat on a gilt chair in the tall room in silence for ten minutes. Tall white double doors opened into the Prince's study, from which he could hear a low murmur of voices now and then. At last the handle of these doors turned; the door opened a fraction, and then closed again. Evidently the conversation was continuing as the visitor was about to be shown out.

Finally the door opened definitely, and David heard the Prince speaking. He said, "Well, that's all I've got to say to you, Mr. Jones. If you go on with this I shall advise my mother to build an airstrip on our own land, in Windsor Great Park. And, what's more, I'll get a Canadian contractor to come here and build it."

David sat motionless, staring at the carpet beside his feet, as the Prime Minister passed by within a yard of him. The door closed again; after a minute the girl got up and went through the double doors into the room. She came out presently. "He won't be very long," she said softly. "He's just got a couple of calls to make."

The door opened presently, and the Prince of Wales appeared. He said, "Come in, Anderson. Sorry to have kept you." David went into the room, and the Prince closed the door. He was wearing a grey civilian suit, and David thought that he looked tired.

He turned to the pilot. "I've got to go to Ottawa, Wing Commander," he said. "Is that machine of yours serviceable?"

David was a little hurt. "Of course, sir. When do you want to go?"

"Can we go tonight?"

"You can go in an hour's time, sir. There's no food or drink on board, but otherwise we're ready."

"All fuelled up?"

"Yes, sir."

"Done the daily?"

"Yes, sir."

"All right." He glanced at his wrist watch. "Suppose we start off after dinner. I'll be at White Waltham about half past eight."

"Very good, sir." He hesitated, and then said, "Can you give me any idea how long the crew will be away? It's just a matter of their kit."

"They may be away some time."

"Any chance that they may need tropical kit, sir?"

The Prince thought for a moment. "I don't know. They'd better take everything."

David went out and rang up Ryder from Miss Porson's office and put everything in train; Miss Porson undertook to have the food and drink sent down from the Palace kitchens. David went back to the office in St. James's Palace and stayed there for an hour; then he drove down to Maidenhead, packed furiously for ten minutes, and was at White Waltham aerodrome by seven o'clock.

He had much to do, but he was a very happy man as he did it. All the way down from London he had driven in a dream, amazed at his incredible luck. Not only had he got a job of work to do for the first time since he joined the Queen's Flight, but it was taking him to Rosemary. He was lucky, he felt, all round. He knew that he was taking a small, insignificant part in world moving events. One day, this journey that the Prince of Wales was making in a hurry to consult with his parents would occupy a sentence in the history books; behind that sentence, unremembered and unknown, would be Nigger Anderson. It was sufficient for him; it made the job worth doing and justified the weeks and months of waiting on the aerodrome, the interruption to his career. Not only was he playing a small part in world affairs, but he was going to Rosemary. Rosemary, who had been away barely a week, Rosemary that he had not hoped to see again for over a month.

He was delighted with his luck.

At the aerodrome he met Ryder. The Ceres was already out upon the tarmac doing engine runs; he went to the machine at once with the second pilot and stood in the cockpit for a few minutes watching the engineers as they made the checks, glancing over the figures pencilled on their test sheets. They checked the fuel in each tank, the hydraulic system; they checked with the radio and radar operators that their apparatus was still serviceable. Then the two pilots left the aircraft, and went back to the office for the navigational study and the preparation of the flight plan.

Dick Ryder asked, "What does tropical kit mean? Where are we going after Ottawa?"

"I don't know," said David. "I don't think they know themselves."

"What maps ought we to take, then?"

"Better take the lot."

"We shan't want South America, surely?" The second pilot paused. "There must be a couple of hundredweight, or more, if we take everything."

David hesitated. "Take the lot," he said. "Take all we've got, and all the radio and radar stuff as well. It's no good to us here, and Dewar may want it, if we don't."

"Is Sugar at Ottawa now?"

"Should be," said David. "Unless they've sent him off upon some other job."

They set to work to make the flight plan; then David got on the telephone to Area Control and gave them details of the flight. He added a few words of his own. "This is Wing Commander Anderson, speaking for the Captain of the Queen's Flight," he said. "I don't know how you go there for publicity, but we should prefer to avoid any mention of this flight till after we have gone. We don't want a flock of reporters at the aerodrome tonight."

The control officer said, "There'll be nothing issued tonight, sir—the P.R.O. goes home at five o'clock. If anyone comes on the phone I'll stall them off until you're airborne."

"Good-oh," said David. "I'll speak again when we are on the runway, ready to take off."

The provisions came at about eight o'clock with the steward and the stewardess, who set to work to load the boxes and the thermos jars, and then to make up beds. Finally, punctually at half past eight, the car arrived with the Prince; a valet travelling with him rode beside the driver.

David went forward to meet him, and saluted as he stepped out of the car.

"Quite ready, sir," he said.

The Prince said, "What's the weather?"

"Clear and frosty for the other side, sir. We shall be out of this stuff at about twenty-five thousand feet. A probable headwind, fifty to sixty knots at cruising altitude."

The telephone girl approached, and stood on the tarmac a few yards away. "What's the E.T.A. Ottawa?" asked the Prince.

"Zero three fifteen," said the pilot. "About ten fifteen, local time. It's going to take us about six and a half hours."

The Prince nodded. "Let me know when you get in radio contact with Ottawa direct," he said. "I shall have some signals to make then." He turned to the girl. "What does she want?"

The telephone girl came up to David, and said, "*The Recorder* are on the line, sir, asking to speak to you."

"What have you told them?" asked the Prince.

"Nothing, sir. I said that Wing Commander Anderson was busy for the moment, but I'd ask him to speak."

The Prince made a grimace. "How long before we get airborne?"

"We're ready to go now, sir." David hesitated. "If you would get on board, I'll go and tell them something—stall them off."

"All right. Better not say you're taking me to Ottawa if you can avoid it."

He turned and went to the machine, and David went to the telephone. A man's voice said, "Wing Commander, I understand that you are making a flight tonight. Where is that to?"

David said, "Aw, look—I'm a serving officer, you know. You want our Public Relations Officer, don't you?"

"I was hoping that you would be able to tell me."

"I couldn't do that. I got a rocket last week for speaking out of turn. You'll have to get on to the P.R.O."

"Where is he, then?"

"Get on to Australia House, extension 643," the pilot invented. "Ask to speak to Mr. Mollison. He's there now, because I've just been speaking to him. He'll tell you the whole story." He put down the receiver.

The girl was smiling. "What'll I say when he comes on again?" she asked.

"Say that I'm in the air, and you can't answer any questions. You can pack up and go home as soon as we've gone."

He left the office, spoke for a few minutes to the foreman of the ground staff, and then went to the machine. The steward closed the doorway behind him, and he went forward towards the cockpit. The Prince stood at the door of his cabin. "Everything all right?"

"I got rid of him, sir. May we take off now?"

"Go when you like, Captain."

"Very good, sir."

David went forward and slipped into his seat, settled himself comfortably, and adjusted his belt. Then he nodded to Ryder, and the engineer started the inboard motors; they moved forward to the runway with Ryder speaking on the radio to area control.

Half an hour later they came out through the cloud into the clear moonlight at twenty-three thousand feet. Ahead of them the night was deep blue and serene. David sat motionless as the machine climbed on her course; he roused presently at a touch upon his shoulder, and it was the Prince.

"Mind if I sit here for a bit, Captain?"

"Of course, sir." Ryder slipped out of his seat. "Would you like to come here?" asked David.

"No—this 'll be all right." He slipped into the second pilot's seat; Ryder withdrew to the navigator's table and the radio operator began to get a series of bearings and positions for him.

David offered the Prince a cigarette, which was refused. It was quiet in the cockpit of the Ceres; the fine lines and the heavy structure of the windscreen to resist the pressure deadened the rush of air, and the engines were far behind. They sat in the dimmed lights of the instruments watching the blue starry night ahead of them without speaking, and the altimeter needle made circuit after circuit of the dial as they sat. The Prince sat staring ahead into the night, immersed in thought. David sat letting the machine fly herself upon the automatic pilot, relaxed, watching the hands move on the dials in front of him.

Presently he leaned back and spoke to Ryder at the navigator's table and the second pilot came and stood between the seats with the engineer by him. They levelled off the climb and stood for some minutes adjusting the engine throttles as the speed slowly rose, till finally she was steady in the cruising condition. The Prince watched this going on and asked a question or two; then Ryder and the engineer withdrew, and all was quiet in the cockpit once again.

Presently the Prince said, "Is this your first spell of duty in England, Anderson?"

"That's right, sir," he replied. "I've never been stationed in England before."

"You've spent all your life in the R.A.A.F., haven't you?"

"Yes, sir. I entered as a boy apprentice when I was fifteen years old. I got my commission from the ranks when I'd been in six years."

"And since then you've done nothing but fly aeroplanes?"

"That's right, sir."

"Lucky devil."

Presently the Prince spoke again. "If I'd had the chance, I'd have tried to do what you've done," he said quietly. "Go into the R.A.F. and try to make a go of it, and get the rings because you've earned them, not because you're heir to the Throne." He turned to David. "Some people are born lucky."

The pilot grinned. "I wasn't born lucky," he said. "I was born in a ditch, and my mother was a half caste girl. They must have told you that."

"They told us that. I still say you were born lucky. You could choose your life, and make it what you wanted it to be."

"Yes, sir."

They flew on in silence for a quarter of an hour, staring ahead into the blue, starry night. Presently the Prince slipped from the second pilot's seat, thanked David, and went back to his cabin.

Three hours after take off they were south of Cape Farewell and about an hour out from Belle Isle at the north end of Newfoundland. Radio from Ottawa began to come in loud and clear; David sent Ryder to tell the Prince and to get his signals for transmission. The stewardess brought him a tray of supper in the cockpit and he sat eating in the pilot's seat, while the Ceres flew on through the dark night to Canada. She came to take the tray as they passed over Belle Isle, and he handed over the control to Ryder and took a little stroll through the machine. Forty minutes later he began a slow let down when they were somewhere over Anticosti; they passed over Quebec in a clear sky at twenty-five thousand feet and saw the city as a mass of tiny strings of lights upon the velvety black ground. So presently they came to Ottawa and talked upon the radio to control, made one half circuit of the airfield and came in to land upon the lighted runway, six hours and forty minutes after they had left White Waltham.

They taxied Tare to the tarmac and shut off the engines; David left his seat and went aft to the Prince, who turned to thank him for the flight before he left the aircraft. David said, "I'm sorry we're a little late, sir. We lost time after passing Belle Isle; there's a cold mass moving down from the north there, that we weren't told about."

"That's all right, Captain. A very pleasant flight."

David followed him down the steps on to the aerodrome; Frank Cox and Dewar were there, and a car waiting for the Prince and his valet. When that had driven off, Frank Cox turned to David. "Good trip?"

"Quite all right. What happens to us now?"

"Wait here for orders for a day or two. I've got you accommodation with the R.C.A.F. here." They set to work to move the aircraft to the parking place and snug it down for the night under a guard of the Royal Canadian Air Force Regiment. An hour later David was going to bed, with Dewar chatting to him in the doorway as he took his shoes off.

The Australian said, "Come in and shut the door a minute." The Canadian did so. "What's this all in aid of— do you know?"

"I don't know a thing. We heard about the T.U.C. and White Waltham—that was splashed in all the papers here." He paused. "Our people hit the roof. It happened the day after we got here, and they'd had pages of photographs of the Queen and the aircraft and me and Johnny. Canada's own aeroplane of the Queen's Flight, and the Queen coming in it. You know how it is." The Australian nodded. "And then, the very next day, the row about our aerodrome in England. My God, does England stink!

165

I kept some of the papers—I'll show you. I've got them in my room."

"I'll take them for granted," David said. "I know how ours go on. One thing I will say for the Pommies; they keep their Press under control—more or less."

"What is the real position?" asked the Canadian. "Are they kicking us out?"

"I haven't an idea," said David. "I haven't heard a thing, except what's in the papers." It was quite all right to try and pump Dewar for a bit of information, but he had no intention of being indiscreet himself.

Wing Commander Dewar nodded. "You may have to watch your step with the reporters," he said. "They were on to me this morning trying to find out if I knew anything about it. Feeling's running a bit high just now."

David nodded. "I'll tell the boys." He paused. "I wish to God they'd get a better class of politician back at home," he said. "This thing need never have happened at all."

"They'll have to get some modern notions into their democracy first," the Canadian said. "They're still living in the eighteenth century."

David put his shoes outside the door for the French Canadian batman, and put his coat across the chair. "I'm going to turn in," he said. "To hell with all their politics. Where's Macmahon working? Out at Gatineau?"

The Canadian shook his head. "He's got an office in the Rideau Hall annexe, by the Rockcliffe Park," he said. "That's the Governor-General's residence. You can get him on the telephone through Rideau Hall."

"Is he living there?"

Dewar shook his head. "He's living in the Chateau Laurier Hotel—the two girls are there, too. I think he spends most of his time at Gatineau, though."

"I expect he does, with all this bloody nonsense going on."

The Canadian went away, and David went to bed, having secured the information that he wanted. He was tired with the responsibility of the flight and he slept heavily, but he set his small alarm clock for the morning and at half past seven he was speaking on the telephone to Rosemary in the hotel.

"Sorry to ring so early," he said. "I thought I'd better make it early to catch you. How are you liking Canada?"

She said, "It's grand. I didn't see much of Edmonton, but Vancouver was lovely. Dewar made up a party for us and we went over to the Island one day and drove up into the mountains and had a picnic by a lake. It was simply heavenly."

"I've never been to the Island," he said. "I've flown over it twice or three times. It looks good." He paused. "We just got in last night," he said. "I was wondering if you'd have dinner with me tonight."

She said, "I'd love to, Nigger. I don't know whether we'll be able to. It was a very busy day yesterday—I didn't get back here till after nine. And it's going to be another busy one today. Are you going to be here tonight, do you think?"

"I haven't an idea," he said. "We're just waiting for orders. I'll refuel and inspect the aircraft first thing this morning; after that we shall be standing by."

"I doubt if you'll be here," she said. "I think you may be going back to London." She paused. "I don't know anything, really," she said. "I think they're all at sixes and sevens."

"If I've got to beat it back to England our date's off," he said. "But if it's not, where shall we dine, and when?"

"Do you mind if we dine here, fairly late?" she asked. "Say about eight o'clock? It it's a day like yesterday I

167

shan't feel up to going anywhere where I should have to dress. Would you mind that?"

"Of course. Look, Rosemary—if it's a day like that give me a ring here about six o'clock and we'll scrub it. You'll want to get to bed."

"Of course not, David. It's only that I may be feeling like old Jorrocks—where I dines I sleeps. I'd love to see you and hear all your news."

"I've not got much," he said. "I'll be at the hotel about eight, then. Look after yourself."

"Goodbye," she said. "See you tonight, unless they send you back."

He rang off and went into the mess for breakfast. By half past ten the fuelling and the inspection of the machine was finished and he dismissed the crew, with warning that they should not leave the camp till further notice. Frank Cox turned up shortly before lunch in one of the Royal cars, and David reported to him. "We're in readiness again now," he said. "Any orders, sir?"

"Keep standing by," the Group Captain said. "I'm going out to Gatineau again after lunch. They're having a high level conference there now, I think. One or other of them will probably be going back tonight."

"If we're still here, in readiness, tonight, I've got a dinner date I'd like to keep at the Chateau Laurier Hotel," the pilot said. "Be all right if I'm on the telephone there?"

"I suppose so. Ryder had better stay here in the mess if you're away."

They lunched together in the mess. Frank Cox drove off again in his car, and David, left with the afternoon upon his hands, went and lay down on his bed. He had the prospect of another flight that evening back to England in front of him; although he had received no orders it was most unlikely that the Prince of Wales would stay away from

England for more than a day in the absence of the Queen. It was morally certain, David felt, that he would receive instructions very shortly to fly the Prince back that night, and in anticipation he would catch up on his sleep. He took his coat and shoes off and set his alarm for six o'clock, and lay down on the bed, and pulled a blanket over him. In ten minutes he was asleep.

He was roused at about five by Dewar coming quickly into the room. He said something, and David roused and sat up. "All right," he said. "Have you told Ryder? What time do we take off?"

"It's us," said Dewar. "I'm taking him in Sugar."

"Who?"

"Wake up, you silly bastard. I'm taking the Prince back to England in Sugar. We're pushing off at half past six."

"Well, what's happening to me?"

"I don't know. I wish to God I did. I've got Mollie's father and mother coming up here from Toronto to-morrow."

"I'll take this trip for you," said David. "We can fly tonight."

"No, that's all right, old man. I did say something to Frank, but there's more behind it than that. They've got something else lined up for you, I think. I sent a telegram to put off Mollie's people."

"You don't know what they've got lined up for me?"

"I don't."

He went out of the room, urgent and busy in the pre-parations for his flight. David got up and dressed with care; in all these swift alarums and excursions there was still a chance that he would be allowed to keep his dinner date with Rosemary, although the prospects were now getting fainter. The autumn evening was chilly and he put his greatcoat on, and went out to the tarmac where Sugar was running engines in the park.

Most of the crew of Tare were there helping to get Sugar ready for the flight; for some months the Australians had worked side by side with the Canadians in the hangar at White Waltham and though each was concerned chiefly with his own machine their loyalty to the Queen's Flight was strong. Frank Cox turned up shortly after David got out to the aerodrome, and David raised the matter of the maps with him and with Dewar.

"I've got the whole stock of maps here in Tare," he said. "I brought everything we've got for the whole world— maps, radio, and radar. How had we better split it?"

The Group Captain turned to the Canadian. "How are you fixed for going home?"

"I've got everything I want between Vancouver and White Waltham," the Canadian said. "I've got nothing else."

Frank Cox thought for a moment. "Leave the lot in Tare," he said at last. He turned to the Canadian. "If you get another job away from Canada you'll have to raise maps from the R.A.F. in London."

"Okay, sir," said Dewar. "You're not coming back with us?"

"No. I shall be staying here, or going on with Tare."

Dewar went off to his machine, and David said, "Any gen about our movements yet, sir?"

"Not yet," said the Group Captain. "They're still talking out at Gatineau. They'll probably decide something tonight."

The Australian said, "I'll stay here till Dewar gets away. After that, is it still all right for me to keep my dinner date at the Chateau Laurier? I'll be on call there."

"That's all right," the other said. "I may be in there later on myself, with Macmahon."

In the dusk Sugar was drawn with a tractor to the departure tarmac and the officers stood in a small group waiting for the passengers. At half past six exactly the Prince came with his valet; they saluted and he said a word to them, and got into the aircraft, followed by Dewar. The door closed and the engines started up and the machine moved off towards the runway; Cox and David watched the take off and watched the machine circle and head off towards the east.

At five minutes to eight David drove up to the hotel. He dismissed the taxi and went into the enquiry desk and asked for Miss Long. The clerk said, "She said, to go up to Suite 23—second floor." He went up in the elevator and found the door. Rosemary opened it to him, and he went into the sitting room with her. There was a faint colour in her cheeks, and though she was evidently tired he thought her prettier than ever.

"My word," he said, "they do you proud. *I* don't get a suite."

She laughed. "This isn't mine," she said. "It's Major Macmahon's, but he's dining at Gatineau with the Queen tonight." She hesitated. "There are so many reporters here," she said. "We'd probably have trouble with them if we dined down in the public rooms, so I asked him if we could have dinner up here. Do you mind?"

"Of course not," he replied. He took his coat off. "I shan't stay very long," he said. "I know you're tired."

She smiled. "I'm all right," she said a little wearily. "It's just being cooped up in the office gets you down a bit. I tried to go out for half an hour's walk yesterday afternoon, but there was a woman reporter just walked with me all the way. *The Daily Sun*, I think. I had to give up and

171

come back. They know there's something in the wind, but they don't know what it is."

"You've not been out at all today?" he asked.

She shook her head. "I didn't try it."

"Never mind," he said. "Let's order a drink and talk about boats."

She smiled at him and pressed the bell, and presently the sherry and tomato cocktails came, and then the dinner. They tried to keep the conversation upon boats, but the pressure of great events was against them. Once she said, "Did you hear anything about this row in England, David?"

He smiled at her. "Nothing but what's in the newspapers," he said. "We don't gossip in this servants' hall."

She laughed. "Oh, you pig. To throw that up at me!"

"Why not?" he laughed with her. "I had a very good teacher." He paused. "I haven't seen the newspapers here," he said. "Can you tell me anything about what's happened at this end, without gossiping too much?"

"I typed a communiqué this afternoon—three drafts and then the final," she said. "It's being issued to the Press by now. I can tell you what's in that."

"What?"

She said, "Her Majesty has taken the opportunity afforded by her residence in Canada to hold conversations upon Commonwealth affairs with the Governor-General, the Prime Minister, the Leader of the Opposition, and with various elder statesmen of the Federal and the Provincial Governments. These conversations will be continued as opportunity presents itself in the other countries of the Commonwealth."

"What does that mean?" he asked.

"I don't know, Nigger," she replied. "I only wish I did."

"I can tell you, or make a pretty good guess."

"What's your guess?"

"They've been debating what the hell they're going to do about England."

She sat in silence for a minute, staring at the table cloth. Then she raised her head, and said, "You're probably right, Nigger. But I'm an Englishwoman, and so is the Queen. I don't like hearing that sort of thing put into words. I don't suppose that she does, either."

"I'm sorry, Rosemary," he said. "I'm just a bloody Colonial, I suppose. Forget it."

"I can't forget it," she said unhappily. "I can't forget it, because I know it's probably true. It's just that I don't care to hear it said."

They finished dinner and got up from the table; she rang the bell and the French Canadian waiter came to clear the table. When he had gone, he said, "I'm going to beat it pretty soon, Rosemary. If I go now, will you go to bed?"

She said, "Stay till ten o'clock, David. I shouldn't go to bed before Major Macmahon comes back, because I said I'd be here to mind the telephone. He said that he'd be back here about ten."

They sat down in armchairs before the radiants of the electric stove in the ornamental fireplace. "Let's play a game of some sort, Nigger," she said wistfully. "Let's try and stop thinking about this wretched thing. Do you know any games?"

"You've not got any cards? Or chess? Or draughts?" She shook her head. He grinned and thought for a minute. "I tell you what," he said. "Suppose you got a little illness—not too bad, but just enough to make you lose your job in the Palace. And suppose you couldn't take another real job because of your bad health. And suppose then, somebody left you five thousand a year. What would you do with yourself? You tell me first, and then I'll tell you what I'd do."

She laughed. "You mean, I'd be well enough to do whatever I wanted to, but too ill to do any work?"

"That's right."

"What lovely illnesses you do think of!"

"Too right," he said. "What would you do?"

She thought for a minute. "I believe I'd have a boat like yours," she said. "A five tonner, just big enough for one to live in comfortably, or two at a pinch. I'd have a cottage with just a couple of bedrooms and a sitting room and kitchen, looking out over the sea. Somewhere near Yarmouth in the Isle of Wight, I think."

"And just live there, and sail your boat?"

"I think so."

"Wouldn't you get bored with doing nothing but that?"

"I don't know. Wouldn't I be able to do any work at all?"

"Of course not. You're very ill, you know."

She smiled. "I think one would get bored if there was no work at all. I think I'd like to do a half time job of some sort, even if it killed me."

"Very unwise," he said. "As your medical adviser I can't recommend it."

"Good thing you're not my medical adviser," she replied. "Now you tell me what you'd do. Mind—no flying. You're too ill to work."

"I think I'd get a shark boat and fit it up as a yacht," he said.

"What's a shark boat like?" she asked.

"It's a big boat, sixty or seventy feet long," he said. "It's generally got one big diesel in it—I'd like to have two smaller ones. It's got a high bow and a low stern, with a steep sheer, rather like some of your English fishing boats, with a little wheelhouse at the stern. They're splendid sea-boats; you could go round the world in a shark boat."

She laughed. "Do you want to go round the world, David? You must have been round it about twenty times already."

He laughed with her. "Ah, but that's flying. You never see anything when you're flying." He thought for a moment. "I don't know that I want to go round the world in my shark boat," he said. "I'd like to cruise in it about Australia. Tasmania's full of lovely creeks and harbours. And then up north, it would be tremendous fun to cruise about the Celebes, and the Sunda Islands, and the Moluccas, all the way to Borneo. That's a huge cruising ground that no one ever visits." He paused. "Years ago," he said, "during the war, I was flying a new Hatfield up to Luzon in the Philippines. I put down at Darwin for fuel, and after that we'd got enough fuel to fly low, so I went at about a thousand feet all the way, just for fun. I've never seen anything so lovely. After Timor it was just hundreds and hundreds of islands, the Celebes and the Moluccas and the Philippines, all coral islands, so it seemed, and nobody much living on them. I always promised myself that one day I'd go there in a boat."

"I'm not sure that you aren't cheating," she said. "There's not much difference between going in a boat and going in an aeroplane. If you're too ill to fly, are you well enough to go in a shark boat?"

"Of course," he said. "It's only work that makes me go all queer."

"You wouldn't have a place on shore at all?"

"I don't think so. You could live on a shark boat."

"And you wouldn't want to do any work?"

He grinned. "Getting a small yacht from A to B through a lot of uncharted coral reefs is work enough for me."

"I wouldn't be happy without some kind of a job to do,"

she said thoughtfully. "However interesting the rest of it might be."

He glanced at her. "You'd better come and cook for me on the shark boat."

"You wouldn't want an invalid cook, liable to die on you at any moment," she laughed.

"I don't know," he said. "We'd be a couple of old crocks together, with ten thousand a year."

"You might have a lot of fun on ten thousand a year," she said reflectively.

"We could have a lot of fun together on a darn sight less than that," he replied.

She coloured a little, and said nothing. She sat staring at the elements of the fire, and he sat silent, noticing the curl of her hair behind her ear, the soft lines of her neck, wondering if he had said too much. She stirred at last, and looked at her wrist watch. "Quarter past ten," she said prosaically. "I'm going to have a cup of tea before going to bed. Will you have one, David?"

He got to his feet. "Don't you think I'd better go home?" he said. "You ought to get to bed, and so ought I. I may have to work tomorrow, and you certainly will."

The door of the sitting room opened, and they turned towards it. Macmahon walked in with the Group Captain.

Frank Cox turned to the pilot. "The Queen's changed her plans," he said. "She wants to go from here to Canberra, in Tare."

Six

THE pilot stood in thought for a moment by the fire-place. Then he said, "Which way round?"

"You know the form better than I do, Nigger," the Group Captain said. "Which way would you rather?"

Macmahon asked, "What's the point at issue?"

David turned to him. "I should think it's practically the same distance going east or west from here to Canberra. No—wait a minute—seventy-five west and a hundred and fifty-two east——" he stood for a moment in thought. "No, it's much shorter across the Pacific. It just depends if there's enough fuel held on Christmas Island."

He glanced at the Group Captain. "You don't want to land outside the Commonwealth? There's fuel for us at Honolulu."

"Christmas Island would be better. Can you make Christmas from here in one hop?"

"I'm not sure," said the pilot. "I'll have to get down to it on the maps. If we can't we could refuel at Vancouver. We can do Christmas to Canberra all right, provided that they've got the fuel there."

"Four thousand gallons, and a hundred and fifty gallons of oil?" The pilot nodded. "I'll get a signal off at once."

"If there's no fuel there," the pilot said, "we'd better go the other way about. In that case, we'd better go back to White Waltham, and then on with one stop at Colombo."

"Not England," said Macmahon.

David looked up quickly. "Oh. Well, Malta. There's all the fuel that we'd need at Malta."

The Secretary said, "I think the Pacific route would be the better. Is there an alternative if there should be no fuel at Christmas Island?"

The pilot bit his lip. "Fiji, from Vancouver," he said. "That's the only one that keeps inside the Commonwealth. I'm not sure if that's too far for us or not. You'll have to let me go and work it out." He turned to the Group Captain. "What time does she want to start?"

"As soon as possible, I think."

"West about," said David. "If it's Christmas, I think we'll try and get there in daylight. Take off about nine-thirty, after breakfast?"

"I think that would be all right. Have you been to Christmas?"

David nodded. "I've been there three times. It's just a staging post, you know, on an island that's a coconut plantation. I don't know that it's been used much since the war. The R.A.A.F. still have a detachment there." He paused for a moment in thought. "Food," he said. "We'd better stock up here for the whole trip to Canberra. We shan't get much at Christmas, and we'll only be there to refuel for an hour. How many people will be coming?"

"The whole party," said Macmahon. "Eight passengers and the Group Captain."

From the background Rosemary said quietly, "Am I going, Major?"

"Of course. Couldn't do without you."

The pilot said, "I'd better go and do my sums." He turned to Cox. "Would you ring Ryder for me, sir, and tell him that I'm on my way out? Then if you could check up on the fuel held at Christmas, I can ring you about midnight and we'll make the definite decisions. Will you be here?"

"Yes, I'll be here."

David turned to Rosemary. "Thanks for the dinner, Miss Long. See you in the morning." He put his coat on, and went out.

A reporter intercepted him while he was waiting for a taxi, and got a rude rebuff. He drove out to the aerodrome and worked for half an hour with Ryder at the navigator's table in the Ceres, for the maps had been left in the aircraft. They walked back to the mess across the frosty tarmac under a bright moon, and talked again by telephone to Frank Cox in the hotel suite. Christmas Island, it appeared, had fuel; they confirmed the take off time as nine thirty and rang off, Cox to ring the Consort at Gatineau and David to start negotiations with Area Control for clearance to fly over the United States. Their course crossed the Pacific Coast in the vicinity of Los Angeles.

He slept then for a few hours, but he was out on the aerodrome at seven with the crew as the machine was prepared for flight, checking the navigation and the flight plan with Ryder. At half past eight he sent the crew to breakfast, and at nine-fifteen the machine was drawn by the tractor to the tarmac.

News of the Queen's departure had got around, and a crowd of several thousand people had assembled on the aerodrome to see her go. A detachment of the Mounted Police were there to keep the tarmac clear, and to control the press photographers and the television crew.

It was a bright, sunny morning with a sharp nip in the air. The first car to arrive was that of the Governor-General, known to soldiers and airmen throughout the Commonwealth as Tom Forrest. He got out and greeted Frank Cox genially, and walked to the machine, a powerful, fresh-faced, friendly man. He was introduced to David and shook hands with him, and made a quick inspection of the aircraft before the Queen came. Then they went out and joined Mr. Delamain and several members of the Cabinet upon the tarmac.

The Royal car arrived, and the cameras whirred and flash bulbs flared as the Queen stepped out, followed by the Consort. David had only seen the Queen once before when she had inspected the new aircraft at White Waltham; in comparison with her appearance on that happy afternoon she now seemed tired and worn. There was a short period of shaking hands and leave taking upon the tarmac, and then she hurried into the machine with only a brief smile towards the crowd.

The rest of the party were already on board. Frank Cox and David followed the Queen and Consort through the door, which closed behind them. David waited till the gangway was clear and the Queen in her cabin; then he went forward and settled into his seat with Ryder by his side. The roof trap above their heads was open, and the Royal Standard flapped above them lazily in the light airs.

Frank Cox came up the alleyway behind them, and David looked back at him over his shoulder. The Group Captain said, "Ready to go now. Take off in your own time, Captain." David nodded, and turned to his job.

An hour later they were cruising at their operating height in brilliant sunshine, above a white, flocculent cloud floor far below. He left the control to Ryder and walked aft down the length of the machine. He stopped and talked to Macmahon for a little and to the middle aged Miss Turnbull, and finally he came to Rosemary.

"Getting on all right?" he asked.

"Fine," she said. "Where are we now?"

"I should think we're somewhere over the bottom end of

Lake Michigan," he said. "We go a little bit north of Chicago."

"You can't see anything, can you?"

He shook his head. "You might see something of the Rockies in a couple of hours' time," he said. "The gen is two tenths cloud at Denver. But it won't look very interesting."

"Where is Christmas Island, Nigger?"

"Twenty degrees south of Hawaii," he said. "We get there in about ten hours from Ottawa, at half past seven by your watch, more or less. But there's nine hours time difference and we're going with the sun, so it will still be the middle of the morning when we get there."

"Oh dear. How long do we stay at Christmas Island?"

"Only just an hour or so—the time it takes us to refuel. Then we go on again another seven and a half hours to Canberra. We might be there about four in the morning by your watch."

She smiled at him. "It's going to be a terribly long day."

"I know," he said. "We'll have lunch in about a couple of hours' time. I should try and sleep a bit, if I were you."

He made sure that she knew how to adjust the reclining chair. "I'll come along after lunch," he said, "if everything's all quiet, and you can come up forward and sit there a bit. It makes a change, and I can show you where we're going on the chart."

"I suppose you get a marvellous view from the cockpit?" she said.

"Too right," he replied. "Miles and miles and miles and miles of nothing at all."

She smiled. "Can't you see the ground?"

"Not at midday," he said. "Not very much. At sunset or at sunrise you see plenty. But at this height the sun's so bright and the sky so dark—we don't bother much about the ground."

"How high are we?" she asked.

"About forty-eight thousand," he told her. "We go up slowly as the flight goes on and the machine gets lighter."

He went on aft and spoke for a time to the steward and the stewardess about the meals. Then he asked, "What's Her Majesty doing?"

"She's lying down, sir. I made up her bed."

"She's all right, is she? Not sick, or anything?"

The girl shook her head. "I think she's just very tired, sir. She said she hadn't been sleeping well."

The doctor was the eighth member of the Royal party, a Harley Street physician, Dr. Mitchison. David stopped by his chair on his way back to the cockpit and had a word with him, and was reassured. He went on forward; passing the Consort's cabin the door was open, and the Consort standing in it. He said, "May I come up to the flight deck, Captain?"

"Sure, sir," said David. For a quarter of an hour he discussed the navigation with the naval officer, and then for a time they played with the periscopic sextant and took a line of position. The machine hung suspended in the sky, apparently motionless; it needed careful scrutiny of the cloud floor below to detect any forward movement at all. Slowly they crept across Iowa and Nebraska.

The Consort stayed with David for an hour, sitting in the pilot's seat, learning the function of the many instruments and flight controls. "I'd like to bring the Queen up here when she gets up," he said. "She's a bit tired now."

"Of course, sir."

The Consort went back to his cabin presently, and David sat at the control while Ryder rested on one of the berths at the rear of the flight deck. The stewardess brought him a tray of lunch and he ate it in the pilot's seat as they passed over Arizona with the grey and red mountains showing far below. Frank Cox came forward and relieved him at the control, and David went down aft to Rosemary. "We're just going to cross the coast," he said. "Would you like to come up to the office now? There won't be anything to look at for a long time after this."

She said, "I'd love to."

He took her forward to the cockpit and sat her in the second pilot's seat. Frank Cox retired aft with the expressed intention of going to sleep, and David sat for an hour or so with Rosemary at the control. He showed her everything, but it was academic instruction in a way, because the aircraft pursued a steady and undeviating course in the control of the automatic pilot. "I'd let you fly it for a bit," he said, "but the Queen's asleep, according to the stewardess. We'd better not wake her up by rocking the ship."

The girl said, "Don't do that. She's been looking terribly tired the last two days. I don't believe she's been sleeping."

"She's asleep now, so Gillian says."

"I know. Don't do anything to wake her."

"What's the trouble?"

"Charles, I think."

"What's he been up to?" She was silent, and then with a sudden intuition he asked, "Doesn't he want the job?"

"Some thing like that—I don't know," she said. "It's something very serious, whatever it is. We'd better not talk about it, David."

He grinned at her. "What a bloody nuisance children are! I don't know why anybody ever has any."

The girl sat in silence for a minute or two. Then she said, "It's so awful, David, because she's such a nice person, herself. If she was arrogant or proud, it 'ld be easier in a way, because then one wouldn't feel so terribly sorry for her. But for such a simple, decent little woman to have these huge responsibilities and difficulties, and all the family troubles mixed up and a part of it . . . it's too bad."

"She was brought up to the job," he said uncertainly. "It's not so bad for her as it would be for you or me."

"I don't believe that makes a bit of difference, really," she said. "You can't train people out of being hurt by things."

Presently Ryder appeared, to take over the control, and Rosemary went aft to her seat. David lay down on the berth and slept for an hour; when he woke up it was four o'clock and time for afternoon tea. He drank a cup of tea and washed his face, and then went to the navigator's table and set to work to check up the position. He got a stern bearing from San Diego and a cross bearing from Hawaii and drew a little circle round the intersection on the map, and then took a sun sight with the sextant and worked a line of position. He stood looking at the chart for a few minutes, and worked out an E.T.A. Everything was in order, and he turned to the radio operator. "You should get Christmas pretty soon."

"I've got them now, sir, but not strong enough to take a bearing. I'll get a bearing in a quarter of an hour, I think."

"Let's know what it is when you've got it."

At six-fifteen by Ottawa time the flight deck woke to life. David and Ryder settled into their seats, the flight engineer came to his desk of controls immediately behind them, power was reduced and the machine re-trimmed, and they started to let down towards Christmas Island six hundred miles ahead. The sky was cloudless here, and the sun almost overhead, for it was midday in October practically on the Equator. Below them was the hazy

184

cobalt of the sea, merging to grey mist at the horizon all around.

There was a stir on the flight deck, and David looked round, and the Queen was at his elbow, with the Consort behind her. He half rose in his seat, but she said, "Don't move, either of you. I can see quite well, standing here." David sank back into his seat obediently; when climbing or letting down, the Ceres was rather less stable than in cruising trim, and he preferred to stay at the controls with Ryder by his side.

She said, "What a wonderful view you have, Captain. It's quite the best place in an aeroplane."

He said, "There's not very much to look at now, madam."

"I know," she said. "There never is when you fly. What sort of a place is Christmas Island, Captain? Have you been there before?"

He said, "It's just a coral island, rather a big one. I've been here several times. It's got coconut plantations round the lagoon. It's quite big for one of these coral islands, about fifteen miles long and ten miles wide. The airstrip's on the north coast."

She asked, "Do many people live there?"

"Not many," he replied. "When I was here last there were only about fifty natives on the coconut plantations, and an Australian manager. There's a District Officer, but he lives at Fanning Island about a hundred and eighty miles away; he comes over now and then. There are generally two officers and about fifteen men of the R.A.A.F. on the airstrip."

"I'm longing to see it."

She asked a few questions about the instruments, but they did not mean a great deal to her, and presently she thanked the pilots and turned to go back to her cabin. As she turned, David said, "Would you like to fly a circuit round the island before we land, madam? I could send and tell you when it comes in sight, if you'd like to come up and see it from here. Or I can fly so that you can see it from the cabin window."

She said, "That's very kind of you, Captain. I should like to come back here."

Three quarters of an hour later, at four thousand feet, he asked Frank Cox to tell the Queen that Christmas Island was in sight. She came back to the flight deck and stood between the pilots, staring at the island brilliant in the sun, the emerald and azure tints in the lagoon, the white coral sand. David banked the Ceres round in a wide turn and passed over the airstrip at about a thousand feet. The Queen said, "What a lovely little place! Who lives in the white house by the lagoon, the one with the tennis court?"

"That's the District Officer's residence," David said. "I don't know if he's here now—I don't think he is. I think if he was here we should see his launch in the lagoon, but I don't see anything like it."

She stood staring at the island, and while she stood looking David went on turning, so that he made two full circuits before she withdrew her gaze. "It would be wonderful to spend a few days here," she said quietly. "To have a little time." She turned to David. "Thank you, Captain. You can go in and land."

She went back to the cabin, and David flew to the east end of the island with Ryder talking to the control on the radio. He turned over the sea throttling back and trimming for the approach speed of about two hundred knots and came in for a straight approach on the airstrip. Ryder gave half flap and then full flaps, and David motored the Ceres in just above the coconuts and put down on the runway, ten hours out from Ottawa. There was a thatched building with a utility outside it; he turned and taxied over to that while

Ryder poked the Royal Standard up through the hatch. Eleven airmen and one officer stood stiffly to attention in front of the building, as a guard of honour.

The engines stopped; the door was opened and a couple of Fijian natives rolled a gangway forward directed by the officer and the steward at the doorway, and the Queen stepped out to receive the salute and to inspect the guard. The rest of the party followed down the gangway, stretching and savouring the earth again, and David turned to the refuelling with his crew. He saw the Queen and the Consort talking to Macmahon and Frank Cox and the local officer. Then they all got into the utility, with the Queen and the Consort in the cab with the local officer, and Frank Cox and Macmahon in the truck-like body behind.

Fuelling was troublesome on Christmas Island. The kerosene was all in forty gallon drums, and nearly a hundred of these had to be pumped into the machine with a small portable motor pump. It was clear that the operation would take several hours, and David was about to send a message to Frank Cox to tell him there would be a long delay when the Group Captain returned and came to David, working in an overall with his crew.

He said, "We're going to stay here a day or two, Nigger."

"Thank God for that," said the pilot. "I was just going to tell you that we can't take off much before dark, with this pipsqueak pump and all these bloody drums."

"Well, you can take your time. We shan't be going on today. The Queen and the Consort and Macmahon are moving into the District Officer's house. I've fixed up accommodation for the four women in an empty hutment in the camp. You and I, and Ryder, and Dr. Mitchison, go to the mess. The rest go to the camp with the R.A.A.F. bods."

The pilot stood in silence for a moment, conning over his

187   G

various duties that required adjustment. The aircraft would be all right, the accommodation seemed to be fixed. "We'll have to make a lot of signals," he said. "We'll have to make them quick. We're due in Canberra eight hours from now. There'll be a scream if the Queen's missing, oh my word."

"I know. I'll look after those."

"What about rations?" asked the pilot. "There's sixteen —no, seventeen of us. That must double the white population. Is there enough food?"

"The officer here, Flight Lieutenant Vary—he says that's all right. They've got a lot of tinned stuff in reserve."

David nodded; that was likely at a remote staging post like Christmas Island where crews might be stranded many weeks with a defective aircraft, or where strategic movements might bring many aircrews suddenly. "All right," he said. "We'd better send all the food we've got in the machine up to the District Officer's house. It'll be better stuff than R.A.A.F. rations."

He glanced at the Group Captain. "What's it all about? Why are we stopping here?"

"I don't know." Frank Cox hesitated, and then he said, "She's got an awful lot on her plate just at present. I think she wants a rest and time to think about things, where she hasn't got to meet people and put on an act all the time. As soon as she saw this place she wanted to stop here."

Within a quarter of an hour each member of the party was aware of the change of plan. Most of them welcomed the idea of a couple of days idleness, bathing and sunbathing on a Pacific island; the most delighted people of all were the R.A.A.F. detachment, who were normally stationed upon Christmas Island for nine months at a time and had seen their last aeroplane five months before when a bomber on a training flight had spent a night upon the airstrip. They were bored with sunbathing, bored with football, bored with playing housey-housey; they crowded round the Ceres to examine it and touch it and smell it. They could not do enough to entertain the visitors in their pleasure at new faces and new voices.

David knew Flight-Lieutenant Vary slightly, a fresh faced youth spinning out his time upon the island, only anxious to get back to flying duties. He got his crew fixed up in their accommodation; it was arranged that the four women should take their meals with the officers in the little mess, to the evident pleasure of the officer and the disappointment of the airmen. They met together for the first time for lunch about two hours after landing; the visitors were inclined to be sleepy, and with one accord retired to their beds after the meal, to sleep and drowse away the heat of the day.

The pilot came to life about an hour before sunset and got up, put on a clean tropical suit, and went into the tiny mess room. He found Flight Lieutenant Vary in consultation with the Philippino cook boy, trying to concoct a dinner worthy of the Royal entourage. It was a task that might have daunted a better caterer than Vary, but he was tackling it with enthusiasm. "I thought we'd start off with crayfish mayonnaise," he said. "We've got some tins of crayfish, and some tinned tomatoes, and we've got some real lettuces. We've killed a couple of chickens and we'll have those for the main course, with tinned peas and sweet potatoes. And after that, Aguinaldo knows a wizard sweet made of young coconut, icecream, and creme de menthe."

"Don't bother to push out the boat for us," the Wing Commander said. "We'll eat what you eat normally."

The boy looked disappointed. "It's not much trouble," he said. "I'd like to try and do things properly, for once. It isn't often that one sees a girl like Gillian Foster in a mess like this. Do you know, she comes from Shepparton—her people have a station there, and I'm from Swan Hill, only a hundred and twenty miles from where she lives. Bit of a coincidence, isn't it?"

It was obviously such a pleasure to him to try and put on a good dinner that David said no more to damp the project, but praised his work. "They've got a lot of Chinese lanterns in the store that they bring out for Christmas Day," Vary said. "I wasn't here last Christmas, but I've seen them. Do you think that's a good idea?"

Rosemary came into the mess with Gillian Foster and they discussed the Chinese lanterns and decided to have one to shroud the naked bulb that dangled above the table on its length of flex. The stewardess went off to the District Officer's house to see about her duties over there, and as the sun sank to the horizon David and Rosemary walked along the shore at the head of the beach. They laughed a little together about Mr. Vary. "He's taking this dinner very seriously," the girl said. "We must show that we enjoy it. He's going to such a lot of trouble."

"He's having a marvellous time," the pilot said. "I know what it is. I spent six months once on Keeling Cocos Islands, but this one's worse. I'd never want to have a job like that again."

They strolled slowly through the grove of casuarina trees that fringed the sand of the lagoon. The lagoon was roughly square in shape. Two coral reefs ran out from the mainland to the north and to the south, covered in sand and coconut trees, and these formed the entrance to the lagoon facing to the west; in the entrance gap was a small coral island. "That's Cook Island," said the pilot. "Captain Cook discovered this place on Christmas Eve—that's why it's called Christmas Island." He paused. "You see the two points of land on each side of the entrance? The north one—

that one—that's called London. The other one, the south one, that's called Paris."

"Who called them that, Nigger?"

"I don't know. They're always called London and Paris. Someone who was stationed here, I suppose."

"He must have been very lonely," she said.

"Yes. I dare say he was. It's bad enough now there's an airstrip here. It must have been lonely here before."

They strolled on, and now they were in sight of the District Officer's house. Strolling towards them were another couple, arm in arm, a tall, slight, grey haired man and a short, plumpish woman in late middle age, both dressed in tropical white. The pilot said, "Look. Had we better go back?"

Rosemary said, "No. Just walk past naturally, Nigger."

The Queen stopped as they came up and said, "Good evening, Captain. Good evening, Miss Long. Isn't this a beautiful place?"

"I think it's simply lovely," said the girl. The pilot smiled. "I've been telling Rosemary about London and Paris, madam," he said.

"London and Paris?"

He explained the names and the Queen laughed. "How absurd!" She asked about the accommodation. "I do hope everybody's going to be comfortable," she said. "I've been feeling rather bad about it—the accommodation. It's all right for us, of course. We've got the dearest little house."

Rosemary said, "I think everybody's very happy, madam. Everyone I've spoken to seems to be enjoying it so far."

David said, "The R.A.A.F. are perfectly delighted."

"I am so glad. I wish we could see more of these small places. I don't think any of my family have ever been here, even when it was British."

Rosemary asked, "When did it become Australian? I'm

afraid I thought up till yesterday that it *was* British."

"1961," the Queen said. "Nine years after I came to the throne. We transferred all the Line Islands to Australia in 1961. It makes a much more sensible arrangement." She paused, and then she said, "Do either of you two play tennis?"

Rosemary hesitated, and then said, "I'm an awful rabbit."

"I play a bit," the pilot said. "For fun."

"I expect you're much better than we are," the Queen replied. "We discovered four tennis racquets in the house. Two of them have got broken strings, and they're all a bit soft; I suppose that's the climate. Would you two like to come and try a set or two with us tomorrow evening?"

"We'd love to," said Rosemary.

"Oh, that will be nice. Say about half past four. That will give us about an hour and a half before sunset. I always think that one should try and take some exercise each day when one is in the tropics. But it's so seldom possible to do it."

They parted, and strolled on in different directions. For a time David and Rosemary walked together in silence. "She's such a *human* little woman," the girl said at last. "It's bad luck, having a job like hers."

In the dusk they turned and walked back to the mess. Dinner was arranged for seven o'clock in order that Gillian Foster could get over to the District Officer's house to help to serve the meal there at eight o'clock. It was a very merry dinner in the mess, with Australian sherry, Australian claret, and Australian port. Under the Chinese lantern the thick plates and the service cutlery looked almost delicate, and the crayfish mayonnaise made by the Philippino boy was delicious, if rather heavily spiced to hide the slight metallic taste. Rosemary said crayfish disagreed with her, and didn't have any. They drank the health of the Queen with more sincerity, perhaps, than usual in a mess, and then Frank Cox proposed the health of the Mess President for the good dinner. There was nothing much to do after they had finished eating except to sit out on the verandah and talk, looking out over the lagoon in the bright moonlight. Everyone was tired with the long day and the flight from Ottawa; one by one they made excuse and slipped away. By half past nine David was in bed.

In the middle of the night the pilot had a horrible dream.

He dreamed that he was dying. It seemed to him that he was lying on a bed in a dark room, and he was very cold and sweating at the same time. He had an appalling, tearing pain in his abdomen and his legs seemed to be paralysed, and everything about him stank. His body stank of stale sweat, the bed stank of dirty linen, and there was a vile, unnatural flavour in his mouth and nose. He knew in some way that this disgusting fragrance could relieve his pain and he struggled feebly to move his hands to renew it, but no motion came to his muscles. He knew that whiskey hot and burning in his throat would ease the pain and quench the filthy stink that he was lying in, and he struggled to ask for whiskey, but no sound would come, for he was practically dead.

There was a man sitting by the bed side and holding his hand, and this man was out of his mind. His hand was as hot as David's was cold, and both were sweating freely so that it was as if they were holding hands beneath the water. This man was ill and wandering in his mind; he was a priest, too, and a good cobber who got beds for fellows with bad ears, but he was away out of his mind now and wandering in a crazy world of harps and angels' wings.

There was a woman there, a sister from a hospital who could do nothing to relieve his pain because a crocodile had eaten her medicine case, and so she had gone to sleep; she sat there at the table with her head upon her arms, and he was left alone with the mad priest in the darkness. The place that he was in was a tumbledown house or shack upon an island in the middle of great floods and all the animals in the world had come through the darkness and the floods, running and creeping and hopping and crawling to this small place in the wilderness. They had come because death is a great mystery, and animals are curious about the mystery as well as men, so they had come to see him die. There they were, grouped in a circle round the house in the intermittent moonlight, and they were getting closer every minute because there was nobody but a mad priest awake in the house, and they were not afraid of him. Presently, when he died, they would come into the room to watch him die; he would know the moment when they came into the room, and they were getting closer every minute. The tearing, tearing pain.

Animals were right. Cobbers they could be sometimes; they never did you any harm unless you went for them. Two hundred and thirty horses at Wonamboola station he had had; dumb brutes but they never called you Pisspot, only if they got frightened they might go wild on you and hurt you without meaning. He wasn't afraid of animals; let them come into the room and watch him die if they wanted. Sooner the better. His body was contorted once again with the intolerable pain.

In the darkness there was a glow of light, like a bloke that might be holding half an inch of candle in a saucer, where the edge of the saucer hid the candle and the flame and you could only see the glow. And in this glow there was a face, yellow and wrinkled, the face of an old Chinaman floating in the air before his eyes. The face floated before his eyes in the darkness, and the lips moved, and they said, "You want a pipe, Stevie?"

The words somehow meant relief. He tried to speak but no sound came; he looked imploringly into the eyes, and the face said, "Or-right, I get you pipe." There was a period then, while some familiar movements were going on quite close to him, that promised a relief from pain, and then the vile fragrance that he welcomed was upon him once again, and in his mouth, and in the back of his nose. Now he could relax, free from the pain. Now he could turn to the dream, England, and Ratmalana, and Fairbairn aerodrome at Canberra, all across the world, backwards and forwards, all across the world and carrying the Queen. Christmas Island in the middle of the Pacific, and being in love.

Christmas Island. The pain hit him like a blow, and he opened his eyes, groaning and muttering with the pain. He was in a strange room that he did not recognise, but it was different from the hut in the middle of the floods, and there was moonlight in the room, and a glow of electric light under the door. Through the thin partition he heard a voice say, "Somebody else is having trouble in here. Who's sleeping in this one?"

He heard Rosemary say, "That's Wing Commander Anderson."

The door opened and the light was switched on, and he sat up in bed, his stomach cramped and tense with pain. Dr. Mitchison in his pyjamas stood in the door, with Rosemary in her dressing gown behind him. The doctor said, "Are you feeling all right?"

"By God I'm not," the pilot said. "I'm feeling awful."

"Stay there a minute, and I'll get you something." The doctor vanished up the corridor, and Rosemary stood in the doorway looking at him, and she was laughing; even in his pain he thought how charming in her dressing gown she looked. "What's happening?" he asked.

She said, "It's the crayfish, I think, Nigger. Everybody's been in trouble except me—I didn't have any. It must have been a bad tin."

He licked his lips to try to clear the foul taste from his mouth. "I had an awful dream," he muttered.

"What about?"

"I don't know. I was dying in a hut with a mad priest, and a crocodile had eaten all the medicines." The doctor came back carrying a tumbler half full of water with a white powder in it, that he was stirring with the handle of a toothbrush. "Drink this," he said. "If it makes you sick, come along at once and I'll give you some more."

The pilot took it from him. "What is it?"

"Diazentothene. It'll put you right if you can keep it down."

He drank, and handed the glass back to the doctor, who went out quickly to another patient. David said to Rosemary, "Do you say everyone's like this?"

"Everyone who ate the crayfish. It's ptomaine poisoning or something. Mr. Vary and Miss Turnbull are the worst, Nigger. They're really bad."

Nausea seized him, and he got quickly out of bed. "I'm another one," he said. "I'm sorry, but I've got to run."

Nobody in the officers' quarters got much more sleep that night, except Rosemary, who went back to bed after an hour or two when everything was under control. It was a white and shaken party that crept out on to the verandah one by one next morning as the bedrooms grew too hot to occupy with comfort; they sat in deck chairs in the shade in the breeze in the lightest of clothing, gradually recovering. Rosemary went up and reported their troubles to Major Macmahon at the District Officer's house, who came down to see them. There was nothing to be done except to let nature and modern drugs take their course. Most of the party lunched on diazentothene and brandy, though the stronger ones pecked at a milk pudding. Rosemary finished up the cold chicken.

David felt better after lunch. He dressed in a clean tropical uniform and went out in the utility to the airstrip to inspect the aeroplane and see that everything was in order there. He came back to the mess at about four o'clock and found Rosemary sitting on the verandah alone. "I went up to the District Officer's house and saw Philip," she said. "I asked if we could be excused from tennis, and he said we'd have the mixed doubles tomorrow. I was wondering how you'd feel about a bathe."

"I'm feeling all right now," he said. "I'd like a bathe." So they changed in their rooms and walked down to the beach, and lay together in the lukewarm water on the silvery white sand. There were reported to be sharks in the lagoon from time to time, and so they did not venture far from the shore.

A quarter of a mile up the beach to the north of them were three or four men of the R.A.A.F. detachment bathing in the shallows. A quarter of a mile to the south of them in front of the District Officer's house a small shade had been created at the head of the beach by slinging a tent fly between the casuarina trees, and in this patch of shade a middled aged woman and her husband were sitting in bathing dress in deck chairs. They had evidently been bathing, because their towels hung draped upon the ropes supporting the tent fly, but now they were just sitting together, looking out over the lagoon.

David rolled over in the water, and looked at them, and said, "I wonder what they're talking about."

"England," said Rosemary. "I wonder if this is a good place to make decisions about England?"

"What's wrong with it?"

She turned to him in the water. "It's too lovely, I mean, just look at it." She glanced around at the blue, sparkling sea, the white beaches, the olive green groves of the coconut palms. "It's like something out of a theatrical set. England is grey industrial cities—Leeds and Bradford, Newcastle and Birmingham. That's the England that really counts, and it's got nothing in common whatsoever with a place like this. Do you think that one could make a sound decision on what's best for Manchester, on Christmas Island?"

He glanced at her, and his glance strayed for a moment to her white skin, and the soft curves of her figure. He recalled himself to the subject under discussion. "She hasn't got to decide what's best for Manchester," he said. "She's got to decide what's best for the Commonwealth. Quite a lot of the Commonwealth consists of places like this—England's only just a little of it." He paused. "And anyway, she can't sit and think quietly anywhere else, without being badgered all day."

"I know," she said. She turned to him. "I went up there this morning to see Major Macmahon, and I asked if there was anything that I could do—washing or ironing her clothes or anything like that while Gillian Foster and the maid are ill. He said he didn't think she wanted anything, or to be bothered at all. She was sitting out there on the beach with Philip all this morning, and she's been there all this afternoon."

"We'll know some day what it's all about," he said. "Forget about it now." He glanced again at her fair skin, now flushed a little. "You're burning," he said. "You'll be badly burned if we stay out in this sun. Let's get into the shade."

She looked down at her arms and legs. "I suppose I ought to. I'm not used to this." And then she looked at him, "You're much browner."

"Too right," he said equably.

"I didn't mean that, David," she said. "You're sun burnt too, aren't you?"

He glanced down at his body. "I don't think so," he said. "I think this is about as pale as I ever get. It's nearly a year since I left Australia. I go a lot darker than this in the summer, if I do a lot of bathing or sunbathing."

"You're looking disgustingly well now, anyway," she laughed. "You're looking just like an Englishman who's come back from a summer holiday in the south of France."

"Permanent sunburn," he replied. "I can recommend it. Won't come off." He glanced at her. "You're like something off the lid of a chocolate box."

She laughed. "Anyway, nobody would think, to look at you, that you'd been writhing in agony twelve hours ago."

"My word," he said. "I was crook. The things I dreamed about!"

They sat down on the sand in the shade of the trees. "You said something about your dream last night," she said. "Something about dying in a hut with a mad priest."

"My word," he said again, "it was a bad one, that."

"Do you dream much in the ordinary way?"

He shook his head.

"Tell me about the mad priest."

He sat silent for a time, looking out over the lagoon. At last he said, "It sounds a stupid thing to say, but I was very frightened. I don't know that frightened is the word. It was a sort of horror of the state that I was in."

She looked at him curiously, impressed by the seriousness of his manner. "Was it as bad as that, David?" He nodded. "Tell me about it."

He told her.

In the end she said, "Dreams always come from memories, don't they? Things that have happened to you, and that you've practically forgotten. And then they crop up in a dream, all higgledy-piggledy."

He said, "I know that's supposed to be the explanation. But none of these things ever happened to me."

"You can't remember anything that could be the origin of your dream? Not any part of it?"

He shook his head. "Nothing at all."

She smiled. "Then I should forget the dream as well."

"I'm going to," he said. "I'm going to forget it as quickly as I darned well can. And I can tell you this—it'll be a long time before I eat another crayfish, even if I've seen it caught."

From behind the point called London at the entrance to the lagoon a big motor launch appeared, a diesel engined vessel ninety or a hundred feet in length. She came in at a smart pace between the land and Cook Island and headed into the lagoon, and revealed herself as a seaworthy, businesslike vessel painted white and in need of a new coat of paint; she flew the Australian blue ensign at the stern. Rosemary said, "Oh, look what's coming!"

He smiled. "I'll give you three guesses who that is."

She said, "The District Officer from Fanning Island?"

He nodded. "Probably. He'll never have had a thing like this happen in his diocese before, and he never will again."

"He must have got a shock when he heard that the Queen and the Consort were living in his house on Christmas Island, and he was a hundred and eighty miles away and not there to receive them and do the honours."

"He probably thinks it's some sort of a deep plot to do him out of a knighthood."

The vessel slowed as she came into the lagoon and brown sailors appeared on the foredeck and began to unlash the anchors and take stoppers off the chains. Then Rosemary said, "Oh, David—look!"

She caught his arm, and he thrilled at her touch. He

glanced down at her hand, and then up again to see what had excited her. Three white men in spotless tropical suits had appeared on deck, and two white women dressed as for an afternoon function, with wide Ascot hats and gloves in hand, ready to come on shore to be presented to the Queen.

"Oh . . ." she said. "He's brought his wife and all sorts of people with him." There was a world of disappointment in her voice. "Oh David! Even in a place like this she can't live simply—not even for a day!"

He said uncertainly, "They won't bother her much, will they? They'll have to stay on the yacht."

"They're lowering a boat," she said dully. "They're all coming on shore. She can't receive them sitting in a deck chair in her bathing dress." They glanced up the beach, but the deck chairs were empty, the occupants had already gone into the house. She said furiously, "Oh, people are such *fools!* They won't give her a chance!"

They sat silent in the shade of the casuarina trees and watched the boat row ashore to the small jetty in front of the District Officer's house, loaded with the men and the women in their best frocks. Major Macmahon walked down from the house to meet the party on the jetty and stood in talk with them, and Rosemary woke suddenly to a realisation of her duties. "My God," she said suddenly, "I ought to be there helping to keep these blasted women off her." She grabbed her towel and ran back to the R.A.A.F. mess. David sat on upon the beach for a few minutes, watching the party as they left the jetty and walked up to the District Officer's house; then he, too, walked slowly to the camp. He passed Rosemary in a clean white frock hurrying to her job.

That evening before dinner, as David sat on the verandah sipping his tomato juice while the others drank gin, Frank Cox came to the mess and called him aside. "We're going on tomorrow, Nigger," he said. "Take off at about nine o'clock."

"For Canberra?"

"That's right. Is everything fit to fly tomorrow?"

"Oh yes." He paused. "She's going straight to Tharwa, I suppose?"

"That's right. It's going to be a bit difficult here, now that these people have turned up. There isn't really the accommodation on the island for us all."

"Can't they sleep on their bloody yacht?"

"Well—they can, but I understand it's a bit primitive. Anyway, the Queen wants to go on. She can shut herself up at Tharwa and see nobody at all. There's not the organisation or the layout here to secure her privacy."

The pilot nodded. "What's Rosemary doing?"

"She's been shepherding the women around. She's gone off to the yacht with them now with Macmahon. They're having dinner on board."

"Any idea when they're coming on shore?"

"The boat was ordered for nine o'clock."

David nodded. "I'll walk down and meet her. It's a bit dark for her to walk back through the trees alone."

He strolled down after dinner to the jetty and sat on a bollard in the darkness. The rising moon made a glow in the sky behind Paris. The lights of the yacht were bright in the middle of the lagoon, and over the still water he could hear the sound of voices and laughter. In the District Officer's house behind him there were now no lights except one in the kitchen at the back of the house. He could not see the deck chairs in the darkness, but he guessed that they were occupied.

Presently, as he waited, there were steps upon the jetty behind him, and he got to his feet. The moon was not yet up, but in its coming light he saw the Consort and the

202

Queen. She said, "Is that Commander Anderson?"

"Yes, Your Majesty. I was waiting for Miss Long to see her home."

"How nice of you. I was so sorry to hear about the crayfish. Are you all right now, do you think?"

He laughed. "Oh, yes. Dr. Mitchison fixed us up. Fixed himself up, too."

She said, "I was so sorry when I heard about it, because I know you sent us up the tins out of the aeroplane. But for that we might have had the crayfish, too."

He said a little awkwardly, "Oh, that's all right."

They stood looking out over the lagoon as the moon rose in sight. "It's a very lovely place," the Queen said. "I'm so glad to have had this time here. Some day I should like to come back here again."

"It's the best place to refuel between Canada and Australia," the pilot said.

The Queen turned to the Consort. "Perhaps we might have a little house of our own, if we come here often. A very little house, with just two bedrooms, where we couldn't entertain."

He said, "I should think that would be possible, my dear."

On the yacht there was a sound of voices upon deck, and a light at the companion ladder showing the boat manned below it. They saw Macmahon and Rosemary get down into the boat, and watched it as it pushed off, with a rhythmic beat of oars.

"They're coming now," the Queen said. She turned to David. "I am sorry that it wasn't possible for us to have that game of tennis," she said. "I was looking forward to it. We must have it one evening at Tharwa. Would you bring Miss Long one evening, and have supper with us afterwards?"

"I'd like that very much," he said. "I'm sure she would, too, madam."

"She's been such a help to me today," the Queen said. "I'll let you know which evening when we get to Tharwa. Good night, Commander."

"Good night, madam."

They walked off into the shadows of the casuarina trees, and he stood waiting for the boat. Presently he was walking slowly back along the beach with Rosemary. "How did your party go off?"

"Oh, all right," she replied. "They're quite nice people, but of course they just can't understand that she's got to have a rest sometimes, and muck about like other people, and do what she wants. She was terribly good with them, of course—she always is. And they were so excited at meeting her . . ." She paused. "One couldn't be bad tempered," she said quietly. "It's just the way things are."

He looked down at her as they strolled together in the moonlight. "I don't believe that you could be bad tempered any time at all," he said.

"You're wrong there," she replied. "I had a vile temper when I was a child, and I've got it still."

They strolled along the beach a little way in silence. "The Queen wants us to go and play tennis with her one evening when she gets to Tharwa," he said presently.

"The Queen does? When did you see her?"

"Just now, while I was waiting for you to come ashore. She walked out with Philip to the jetty."

"She wants both of us to go?"

"That's right. Tennis and supper."

The girl said in wonder, "But she hardly knows my name. It's all right here, of course. But Tharwa—well, it's different. It's more like the Palace."

"She said that you'd been such a help to her today," the pilot said. "You've got to allow her to be grateful."

"I know. It's just that it takes a bit of getting used to.

204

I mean, I'd never have thought of such a thing in London."

He smiled. "Nor would I. I don't know what Aunt Phoebe at Chillagoe would say if she knew that I was having supper with the Queen. Maybe they'd promote her to serve in the bar."

She stopped, and laid her hand upon his arm. "I don't like to hear you talk like that, David," she said. "Aunt Phoebe's your mother's sister, so she's almost certainly a nice old thing, half caste or not. But anyway, she's just a measure of what you've achieved. You started further back than most people, and you've worked up to the point when your own country puts you forward as the best man that they've got to serve the Queen. If she wants you to have supper with her, it's because she wants to know you better, for the sake of your achievements. Don't be cynical about it."

He turned and faced her, and took both her hands in his. "Look," he said huskily, "I think it's time we had a talk about things."

She raised her eyes to his. "What sort of things, David?"

"I want to clear the air about this colour business," he replied. "I want to know if you could ever bring yourself to think of marrying me."

Seven

SHE stood in the slanting light of the low moon, looking up at him. "If I wanted to marry you, I'd marry you for what you are and what you've done, David," she said. "I wouldn't mind about the colour. But I'm not marrying anybody yet."

He smiled down at her. "How long is Yet?" he asked.

She looked down at her hands that he was holding. "It's a long, long time," she said. There was a pause, and then she raised her head and faced him. "I don't want to make things difficult for you, David," she said. "I know you're fond of me. A girl knows that, and it's made me very proud that you should like me. But now I've got to tell you I'm not marrying, not for a long time, anyway. Perhaps it would be better if we didn't go about so much together."

"I think it would be worse," he said.

"I'm not so sure," she replied. "You *must* try and understand that I'm not marrying anybody, David—anybody at all. If I was, I'd probably jump at the chance of marrying a man like you. But there's no question of it. So far as I'm concerned, marrying is out."

He stood looking down at her, holding her hands, puzzled by her attitude. At last he asked her, "Can you tell me honestly and truthfully that it's not the colour? If that's really in the back of your mind, I'd like you to tell me now.

Because that would be definite and final, and I wouldn't worry you again."

She shook her head. "It's not the colour."

He felt he had to press the point, to search her mind before they went on any further. "Suppose some day you were to marry me, and we had a kid," he said. "You might have a dark baby."

She nodded. "I've thought of that. I don't think that would worry me, David. Honestly, I don't think the colour comes into it." She paused. "You see, if I were to marry you—ever—it would be because I was proud of you, and because I was in love with you. I'd be marrying one of the coming men in the Royal Australian Air Force. I don't believe I'd care about the colour any more than you do. I'd probably be more troubled about leaving England to go and live with you in Australia than I would be about the black baby."

"Brown," he corrected. "I'm not as black as all that."

She said seriously, "But you can get a throw-back."

"Well . . ." She looked up at him, and became aware to her amazement that he was laughing at her. "That depends on you."

"On me?"

"You want to read up your genetics, if you're thinking of marrying a quadroon," he said.

"I'm not. But if I was, what ought I to read?"

"A gentleman called Edward M. East. You can only get a really dark child if both parties have a touch of the tar-brush." He grinned down at her. "I didn't think you had."

"I haven't—not that I know of, anyway."

"Too bad. If you married me and we had a kid, it couldn't possibly be darker than me. It 'ld probably be a good bit lighter."

"But you're not dark at all!" she exclaimed.

"Perhaps you've got a touch of the tarbrush you don't know about," he suggested helpfully. "You could get a black baby that way, but you won't get it any other." He paused. "Not unless you adopt one."

"I don't know that this is very desirable conversation," she remarked. "But tell me David—if a throwback doesn't happen, why does everyone believe it does?"

"It's been a useful superstition to a lot of half caste women living in coloured countries," he said. "It explains a lot of things that might want a bit of explaining any other way."

She burst out laughing. "Oh David! Do you mean to say that's all there is to it?"

"That's right." And then, more seriously, he said, "It's true, Rosemary. If we had a lot of kids, most of them would be light in colour probably, but one or two of them might be as dark as me."

She laughed up at him. "You're going too fast, Nigger. It was only one just now. But I'm telling you there aren't going to be any at all."

He drew her a little closer to him. "Why not?"

She stood quietly in his arms, watching the yellow path of moonlight on the calm water of the lagoon. "If I married anyone I'd want to make a job of it, and make a home, and have kids like a normal girl," she said. "I'd have to give up my job at the Palace to do that—one couldn't possibly do both. And this isn't a good time to chuck that up."

"You'll have to chuck it up some day, if you're ever going to marry," he said. "Of course, you'd have to give a good long notice, so that they could get someone else of the right sort."

She shook her head. "I wouldn't do it."

They stood in silence for a minute. Then she turned back to him, and put her hand upon his shoulder. "I want you to understand about things, Nigger," she said quietly. "I know you've been getting fond of me, and perhaps I'm a bit fond of you. If we gave up thinking about anybody but ourselves—if we turned thoroughly selfish and behaved like people on the movies—we might get to feeling we were passionately in love, and then we'd have to marry or do the other thing. I'm not going to relax like that. I'm not going to leave Major Macmahon's office at a time like this, or any time until this thing is over. As far as I can see, it may go on for years."

"They could get someone to replace you," he said. "I could be replaced in my job. No one's indispensable."

"I know," she said. "That wouldn't stop me hating myself if I left them now." She raised her head. "I don't know if you realise quite all that's going on, Nigger," she said. "The Queen's in the middle of a first class constitutional crisis. The job of ruling England has become so unattractive that her children won't take it on—not one of them. That's the long and the short of it."

"Is that really true?" he asked.

She nodded. "If she was to die tonight, there'd be abdications—one after another, and the Monarchy in England would come to an end. You just can't treat people the way she's been treated. If you could see some of the things I've seen in the State papers in the office—the way these stinking little politicians write to her, as if she was nobody at all . . ." She paused, and then she said, "She must love England very, very much, or she'd have chucked her hand in before this. It's not as if she was a coward."

"I didn't know it was as bad as that," he said.

"Of course you didn't. I wouldn't have talked about it now, Nigger, but for us—personally. I want you to understand why I'm not even thinking of marrying anybody till all this is over. I know they could replace me. I'm only a cog in the machine, but I've been there three years and I'm run in now, and working smoothly. If I left, it would be one more worry for them. And there's another thing—I've got to know so much. If I left, they'd be anxious that I might start gossiping, perhaps, or they'd be worried that the new girl might not be discreet." She turned, and looked out over the still lagoon. "I couldn't have that happen. If I miss the chance of marrying you I may be sorry for it all my life, and that's just something that 'll have to be borne. But I'm not leaving the party at a time like this."

He stroked the soft, shingled hair at the back of her head. "How long do you think it's likely to go on for?"

There was a pause, and then she said thoughtfully, "She's got something that she's working at. Some constitutional change. I don't know what it is, or how long it will take her to get the Monarchy into a state when Charles will agree to take it on after her time. I don't know what's in the wind, or how long it will take her to achieve it." There was a little silence, and then she said, "She had several long talks in Ottawa with Mr. Delamain and with the Leader of the Opposition—Mr. Macdonald, and with the Governor-General. Now I suppose she's going to Canberra to do the same things there. She's got something in her mind that she's discussing with the senior politicians all around the Commonwealth. Some constitutional change to make the Monarch's life more bearable in England. I don't know what it is, David. If I did know, I don't think I could tell it, even to you."

"No," he said thoughtfully. "The less said about these things the better."

She smiled up at him. "I had to talk to you about it," she said. "I know you thought I wouldn't marry you because of the black baby."

"Brown," he corrected her. "Not browner than me."

"That's hardly brown at all," she said. "There's nothing in that one. You do believe that now, don't you?"

"Of course."

"If I've been talking about things I ought not to have repeated, please try and forget them, David. I had to tell you, to explain why I'm not marrying now, or for some quite indefinite time. Otherwise, I know you'd have thought it was something to do with you."

"I shan't talk," he said. He looked down at her, smiling. "Do you know this is the first time I've ever asked a girl to marry me?"

"Is it, David?"

He nodded. "I've never met anyone before that I thought wouldn't mind about the colour. I've never been certain, like I've been with you." He touched the hair at the back of her head again. "You needn't be afraid I'll run away," he said. "This thing can't drag on for longer than a year or so. I'll be here when you feel you're free enough to marry."

"I may never feel that, David."

"Too bad," he said quietly. "But that's one of the chances people like us take, when we start working for a Queen."

Presently she stirred in his arms. "We've got to get to bed," she said. "You've a long way to fly tomorrow."

He released her a little, and they stood looking at the moonlit scene. "Just look at it!" he said. "We've got everything laid on—a coral island, a moon, a calm lagoon—everything you'd want for a stage love scene. We're a couple of silly mutts, if you ask me."

She laughed with him, and freed herself from his arms. "I don't want a stage love scene," she said. "When I get it, if I ever do, I want it to be real."

Presently they walked back slowly to the camp through the deep shadows of the casuarina trees, hand in hand.

David was up early next morning, preparing for the flight to Canberra. They ran the engines of the Ceres at about seven o'clock, shut down after the test, and topped up the machine with fuel; then they went to breakfast. At half past eight the passengers began to assemble on the airstrip, a long business because there was only the one motor vehicle upon the island. At nine o'clock the Queen and the Consort drove up with Macmahon; they said goodbye to the District Officer and Flight Lieutenant Vary, and the little crowd of onlookers, and got into the aircraft. The door shut, the engines started up, David swung the Ceres towards the far end of the airstrip and presently took off. Ten minutes later Christmas Island had faded into the grey haze on the horizon behind them.

The flight to Canberra was uneventful. David saw nothing of the Queen or the Consort during the flight; Rosemary came forward to the cockpit for a few minutes, but there was nothing to be seen but wastes of cobalt and grey sea, and she spent most of the flight dozing in her chair. They passed a little to the north of Fiji about lunch time and spoke to the control by radio telephone, and went on across an empty sky. At half past three by Christmas Island time, in the vicinity of Lord Howe Island, David began a slow let down as they approached the coast of Australia in the vicinity of Newcastle. He was warned by radio to expect a fighter guard of honour, and shortly before they reached the coast he made contact with the fighter leader on the radio telephone; the twelve machines appeared and took station on each side of the Ceres, six to port and six to starboard, so that they flew on across Australia in a V formation with the Ceres leading at the apex of the V. He dismissed the escort as he came in to Canberra in its bowl of hills, and they peeled away up into the clear blue sky and formed a circle over Fairbairn airport six thousand feet above him as he came on to the circuit for the landing. From the cockpit as he moved around the circuit he could see a great crowd of people in the enclosures, waiting to greet the Queen. He lined up on the runway, brought the Ceres in on a long, slow descent, and touched the wheels down gently on the tarmac, seven and a half hours out from Christmas Island. Ryder stuck the Royal Standard up through the hatch, and they taxied in to the ceremonial welcome.

David and Ryder stayed in their seats in the cockpit while Frank Cox ushered the Queen and Consort from the aircraft to face the battery of still, movie, and television cameras, to meet the Governor-General, the Prime Minister, the Cabinet, and the Leader of the Opposition, and to inspect the guard of honour. Finally they drove away in state in an open car to the Royal Residence at Tharwa, hiding their fatigue and bowing and smiling to the crowds that lined the road. The rest of the party left the aircraft then and drove away in cars, but there was no rest for the crew of Tare. They had to face what the Canadians had faced at Ottawa, because this was Australia's own aircraft that Australia had presented to the Queen, flown by Australians and bringing the Queen to Australia for the first time. The Australian Press were out to make the most of it, and David had first to face the cameras and the microphones to make a little speech, praising the aircraft and explaining that the delay at Christmas Island, in Australian territory, had not been due to any mishap or defect, but because the Queen had wanted to visit one of the Line Islands as a part of her policy of getting to know the smallest portions of her Commonwealth.

The welcome went on for hours. Every member of the crew in turn had to go before the cameras and the microphones, and mostly they were eager to do it, knowing that their wives or girls or parents would be proud to see them on the screen in their home town. All the members of the crew had friends among the R.A.A.F. squadrons stationed on the aerodrome and many of them had relations in the crowd, so that people were in and out of the machine all afternoon inspecting her in every detail. The cabins of the Queen and the Consort were kept locked, on David's order; he felt that there were limits to the display that could be allowed.

Finally at about five o'clock they put an end to it and cleared the people out. The Ceres was taxied to the far end of the aerodrome and put into the hangar of the Queen's Flight under guard, to be refuelled and inspected in the morning. David and Ryder drove in an R.A.A.F. car to the Canberra Hotel, where rooms had been reserved for them.

The Royal party were divided between Tharwa and the Canberra Hotel, while the aircrew were accommodated at the aerodrome. Macmahon and Dr. Mitchison were at Tharwa; Frank Cox and David and Miss Turnbull and Rosemary were at the hotel, a pleasant, rambling collection of single storey buildings radiating from garden court-yards bright with flowers. David had a shower and changed his clothes, somewhat tired, more by the welcome to Australia than by the flight from Christmas Island. Presently he went out to look for the rest of the party; sitting in a long chair in the verandah round the garden court from which his corridor radiated, he found Rosemary.

"Hullo," he said. "Are you here, too?"

She nodded. "I'm in the next corridor. I saw you come in, so I waited for you here. It's a very lovely place, this, Nigger."

He was delighted that she should have waited for him, and sat down beside her. "You like it?"

She said, "It's so beautiful. Nobody ever told me that Australia was beautiful, like this."

He smiled. "I don't know that we're very good at.

214

propaganda. I love it, of course. I wouldn't want to live anywhere else. But then, I was born here, and it's my country."

"Is all Australia like this?" she asked. "All the habitable part?"

"I think Canberra is better than most of it," he said. "It's fairly high up, for one thing, and it's got a good rainfall. All the eastern coastal strip grows flowers like this, of course—or it could do, if people planted them." He paused. "The middle's very dry, but bits of West Australia are lovely."

"Big bits?"

"About as big as England."

She laughed. "It's so difficult to realise what distance means in a country like this."

He nodded. "I hope the Queen will go and spend a few days in West Australia this time. She hasn't been there for three or four years." He turned to her. "Have you seen Tharwa yet?"

She nodded. "I drove out there with Major Macmahon this afternoon, to fix up the office. There's a car calling for us each morning at nine o'clock to take us out there."

"How did you like Tharwa?"

"I only saw a little corner of the house," she said. "I just got a glimpse of the gardens and the lawns. It's a really lovely place, David. Do you know who designed it?"

"They had a prize competition, about 1959 or 1960," he said. "A chap called Somerset who lived at Wangaratta won it—quite an unknown architect in a small country town. He got the right idea, didn't he?"

"I should say he did. It's lovely—simple and dignified. And it fits the landscape so well. Did he do a lot of buildings in Australia?"

"He was just a house designer up till then," the pilot said.

"He only did one thing after Tharwa—the Town Hall for Port Albert. That's the port they ship the brown coal from, in Victoria. Port Albert Town Hall's rather like Tharwa. He died before it was finished."

She asked, "What happens up in the mountains behind Tharwa?"

"Nothing very much," he said. "A few sheep stations in the valleys. Some timber cutting in the forests. Trout in the rivers, and ski-ing in the winter."

"How far does that sort of country go?"

"Behind Tharwa? Oh, three hundred miles or so. Then you'd come to Melbourne."

"And not many people in all that country?"

"Not many." He changed the subject. "Have you got any idea how long we're going to be here?"

She shook her head. "She's got the Governor-General coming to lunch at Tharwa tomorrow. Apart from that, there don't seem to be any engagements yet. I think she's just resting, trying to make up her mind about something."

"You'd say we'd probably be off within a week?"

"I should think so, David, but I really don't know. I don't suppose she even knows herself. I shouldn't think she'd want to be away from England very long."

"Africa, do you think?"

"I don't know. Could we do that direct?"

"We can make Cape Town from Perth," he said. "It's just about the limit of our range. Durban would be easier."

"I think she may want to go home direct from here," the girl said.

"Too bad," he replied. "I had hoped that we'd get enough time here for you to travel round a bit. Sydney's a good city and so is Melbourne. And I'd like to show you just a bit of Queensland."

She turned to him. "David, have you got any relations here?"

He grinned at her. "You mean, Aunt Phoebe?"

"Besides Aunt Phoebe."

He shook his head. "We're all Queenslanders. I don't think any of my people live so far south as this. My father and my mother are both dead, you know."

"I didn't know," she said. "I'm sorry."

"I've got a brother who makes shoes in a Brisbane factory," he told her, "and my sister Annie's married to a chap who keeps a garage in Rockhampton. I've got an uncle who keeps a silk shop in Townsville—my father's brother. That's about all there are of us—there are plenty more, of course, but those are the important ones."

"I suppose they'd be thrilled to come down here to see the machine and meet you."

"I know," he said. "That's why I was asking just now how long we'd be here. Uncle Donald would come down, I know."

"We may hear something tomorrow," she replied. "I've got a kind of feeling that she won't stay very long, and she'll want to get back straight from here to London."

They dined with the others, and went early to bed.

There followed three days of waiting for the crew of Tare. They refuelled and inspected the machine, and did a little maintenance work, and then there was nothing to be done but to sit waiting for orders and gossiping in the R.A.A.F. mess. Rosemary was out at Tharwa all day, and in the evenings she told David a little of what was going on. On the first day the Queen had seen nobody but the Governor-General for lunch; but the second and third days had been busier. Mr. Hogan the Prime Minister and Mr. Cochrane the Leader of the Opposition had lunched together with the Queen, in itself a curious circumstance, and had stayed for several hours, till nearly five o'clock. The Vice-Chancellor of the University had dined at Tharwa, and other visitors had been Sir Hubert Spence, a Judge of the High Court, Murray Gordon the research professor of Political Economy at the University, the Professor of History, and several other gentlemen of the same calibre.

At lunch time on the third day Frank Cox appeared in the R.A.A.F. mess. "Got a job for you tomorrow," he said to David.

The pilot nodded. "London?"

"Not yet. Melbourne."

The pilot raised his eyebrows. "Not very far. What time do we take off?"

"Ten o'clock. They want to come back in the evening, taking off probably about six o'clock." He paused. "Which aerodrome will you use?"

"Berwick," said the pilot. "Essendon and Moorabbin are for regular airlines only. Get the cars to Berwick—oh, about ten forty-five."

Half an hour later Rosemary rang up from Tharwa. "David," she said, a little breathlessly. "You know that game of tennis we were going to have? Well, it's tonight."

"My word," he said. "All among the Ambassadors and Prime Ministers?"

"I don't think so. She came into the office just before lunch and wanted to know if you and I would go up and play tennis with them, and have supper afterwards. I said we would."

"I'd have thought she'd have forgotten that," he said in wonder. "She'd have every right to."

"She's not that sort," the girl said. "I didn't think she'd forget. She wants to start playing about five o'clock. Shall I fix a car for you at the hotel at quarter past four?"

"Thanks, Rosemary. I'll have to see about borrowing some clothes and a racquet."

Tennis that evening was not of a very high order. The Queen at the age of fifty-five liked playing on a grass court for an obvious reason, and she played as a plump woman of that age might be expected to play. Rosemary was not a great deal better, sailing dinghies being her pastime, so that the ladies were fairly evenly matched. The Consort, lean and athletic still, played a remarkably good game and kept David on the jump, so that Royalty defeated the common clay six three, six four.

Two sets were enough, and in the fading light they strolled through the rose gardens to the wide lawn before the house, and down towards the river. As they went the Queen said, "Is everything all right for us to go to Melbourne tomorrow, Commander?"

"Quite all right, madam," he said. "We shan't be able to get up to operating height, so we shan't go very fast. It will take us about fifty minutes, I should think."

"It seems such a waste to take such a beautiful aeroplane for such a little journey," she remarked. "But it wouldn't be fair to ask Sir Robert to come all this way."

"Sir Robert?" he enquired.

"Sir Robert Menzies," she said. "He's such an old man; I don't know how many years he was Prime Minister before he retired. He was Prime Minister when I came to the throne, and before that. I always try and see him when I am in Australia. But he's eighty-eight this year. He keeps remarkably well, but it's really not fair to ask him to travel, at his age. So I'm having lunch at his house in Toorak with him tomorrow, and Mr. Calwell is lunching with us there as well. He lives in Melbourne, too."

"I didn't know Calwell was alive still," the pilot said in wonder.

219   H

"Oh dear, yes. He's only eighty-six. So funny. In the House those two were political enemies all their lives. Now they can't fight each other in the House any longer, so they meet and have a game of chess each week, and quarrel over that." She paused, and stood staring over to the evening lights upon the wooded slopes of Mount Tennant. "These old men have seen so much, and learned so much," she said quietly. "I always learn something by talking to old statesmen. They get objective when they've been retired a year or two, and then they're really useful."

She turned to Rosemary. "This is your first visit to Australia, isn't it?"

"Yes," she replied. "I've hardly been out of England before."

They turned, and walked back up the lawn towards the long, white house in the evening light. "Do you like it here?" the Queen asked.

"I've only seen Canberra and Tharwa," the girl said. "What I've seen is simply lovely, of course."

"You should see more than that," the Queen said. "Why don't you come with us to Melbourne tomorrow? I expect Commander Anderson would give you lunch in Melbourne, if you ask him very nicely. We shan't be starting back before the evening."

The girl said, "It's terrible kind of you to suggest that, madam. I think I ought to see Major Macmahon, and find out how much work there is to do."

"We'll speak to him this evening," the Queen said. "I can't believe that there's a great deal of work when we're away."

David said smiling, "It's a bit unethical for me to leave the aeroplane on a strange aerodrome to take Miss Long to lunch in Melbourne."

"Oh nonsense, Commander. You've got Mr. Ryder to

leave in charge. If you say any more I shall begin to think that you don't want to take her."

The pilot grinned. "I wouldn't like you to think that, madam."

"I should hope not."

Rosemary coloured a little; to break the conversation she stopped, and turned, and looked around. It was very quiet and peaceful in the summer evening light, with the gum trees fringing the river, and the blue, forest covered hills around. "It's a beautiful place," she said quietly. "I don't think I've ever seen anything quite like this in England."

The Queen said, "No, my dear. There's nothing quite like this in England. I love England, and English scenery, very very dearly, but I love coming here to Tharwa, too." They walked a little way towards the house in silence. "I think I like Australia because it's new," she said after a time. "It's like opening your diary at a clean page. I always feel when I come here that I can start again, and try and do a little better in this clean, new place."

They went into the house, and the Queen took Rosemary away towards the bedroom side. David had brought uniform with him in a suitcase, but the Consort said, "We're not changing tonight. There's quite a heavy day tomorrow, so we thought a little exercise and bed early tonight would be about the mark." So presently they all assembled in the Consort's study for cocktails and sherry; a liveried manservant was despatched for a tomato juice for David.

The Consort asked, "Do you never drink these things, Commander?"

"No, sir."

"How very wise." The Consort sipped his sherry. "Is that policy or disinclination?"

"Disinclination," said the pilot. He hesitated. "I've always been afraid of drink," he said. "I think it might get

221

hold of one. I've never started. I think I'm different to other people in that way."

"It's quite true," said Rosemary. "He doesn't drink at all. I believe he's the only man I know who doesn't."

"I'm very glad to hear it," said the Queen. "I shall feel safer than ever when we're flying, now."

David smiled. "I think that must be the reason why they picked me for this job, madam. I can't think of any other."

"Nonsense," said the Queen. "I know why they picked you."

Macmahon joined them before dinner, and gave his agreement to Rosemary's day off. They dined at a small table in the bow window of the big dining room and talked principally of Australian gardens and flowers, and of the Queensland drought. They had coffee in the Queen's drawing room, and then David and Rosemary took their leave, and were driven back to the hotel at Canberra.

They took off from Fairbairn aerodrome next morning punctually at ten o'clock, and flew across the mountains at ten thousand feet with an escort of four fighters of the R.A.A.F. to Berwick, twenty miles to the south east of Melbourne; over the aerodrome the fighters peeled away up into the sky and David put the Ceres down and taxied in. There were few people on the aerodrome because this visit was incognito and no mention of it had appeared in the Press, and the aerodrome was one used only for charter work and private flying. Four cars were waiting on the tarmac; David parked the Ceres near these cars, stopped engines, handed over the machine to Ryder, and followed Frank Cox and Rosemary out down the steps. To his relief there were no pressmen there, and no photographers.

The Queen was talking to two very old men standing by one of the cars, one of them rather stout. David, standing with Frank Cox and Rosemary, could hear what she was saying. "You shouldn't have come out," she said. "I was coming to you."

He recognised the Menzies features in the stout one, who replied, "I hope I'll never be so old as not to be able to drive out to meet you, madam." The other said, "Too right."

The Queen said, "Well, I'm not going to have you standing about in this wind, either of you. Do you want to see the aeroplane? It's a lovely thing, the most comfortable aeroplane I've ever travelled in, and so fast, too. We came from Ottawa to Canberra in less than eighteen flying hours."

"My word, that's going," said old Mr. Calwell.

The Queen turned, and saw David. "Come here, Wing Commander." To the two old men she said, "This is one of your own countrymen, the captain of the aircraft. Wing Commander Anderson, Sir Robert Menzies and Mr. Calwell."

David asked, "Would you like to see over the machine?"

The old men glanced at each other. "One aeroplane's just like another to me," said Mr. Calwell. "I've seen enough of them to last my lifetime."

Sir Robert said, "I can imagine it." He paused, and let his eye run over the great silvery thing. "Such a pity Dick Casey died," he said quietly. "He would have been so interested to be here, and to have seen the Queen come to Australia in an Australian aeroplane of the Queen's Flight, with an Australian crew . . ." He turned to the Queen. "This was his private aerodrome in the early days, you know, madam—he owned a lot of land round here. He had an aeroplane of his own, and he went on flying himself as a pilot till he was over seventy—his wife was a pilot, too. I often used to come here in the Forties, but I never went up with him. He had a wooden hangar just over there beside the show ground, where the Shell depot is."

The Queen cut short this flow of reminiscence by shepherding the old man back into the shelter of his car. She got in after him herself, and the Consort and Mr. Calwell got into another car, and both drove off out on the Melbourne road.

There was a third car waiting on the tarmac. David said to Rosemary, "This one is ours." The chauffeur opened the door for her, and David got in beside her, and they followed the other cars up to the Princess Highway and the road to Melbourne.

Rosemary said, "I feel an awful fraud. Do you think this car is ours for the whole day?"

"I should think so," he replied. "It's got to bring us back to Berwick by about five o'clock, or the Queen won't be able to go home. What would you like to do?"

She thought for a minute. "I'd like to drive through Melbourne and see what kind of a place it is." She turned to him. "I'm so very ignorant," she said. "It's on the sea, isn't it?"

"That's right," he said. "Not the open sea. It's on a great big circular bay, Port Phillip Bay, at the north end. It's about forty miles from the sea proper."

"Do people sail there, like we do at home?"

"My word," he said. "We've got all the small racing classes that you've got at home. I've got a Dragon laid up here, in the Brighton Club."

She looked up at him in wonder. "You told me once you used to sail a Dragon. Is she here?"

He nodded. "This is my home town. I mean, I'm a Queenslander by birth, but most of my Service life has been in and around Melbourne. I was stationed at Laverton before I came to England."

She said, "Could we go and see your Dragon, David? I'd love to see an Australian sailing club."

224

"Of course," he said. "I'd like to go and have a look at her myself. It's a year since I saw her. We'll drive through the city and have lunch somewhere, and then go down to Brighton."

"Is that far?"

He shook his head. "It's only a few miles out of town. It's a suburb—quite a good one."

She looked about her with interest as they drove in through the outer suburbs. "Such a lot of new houses," she said. She turned to him. "David, could we stop and look at one?"

He said, "Of course." He leaned forward and spoke to the driver. "That's one that's practically finished—there. Stop at that one."

They got out of the car, and she looked around at the littered garden plot. "I suppose all this builder's mess is inevitable," she said. "It must take an awfully long time to get the garden right, though."

She stood looking around. "And anybody who has the money can just buy a bit of land, like this, and build a house on it, like this?"

"That's right," he said.

"And then it's your own property, and you can do what you like with it—sell it, or alter it, or live in it, or let it for as much as you can get? Without asking the Ministry?"

"I think that's right. I've never heard that you have to ask anybody."

"It would be fun," she said, "to have a house that was really your own, like you own a boat."

The door was open, and the painters and the electricians were in putting the finishing touches. The girl said, "Can you spend as much as you like on it? I mean, if you wanted one really lovely room, with a stainless steel floor and mirrors all round and a sunk alabaster fishpond in the floor with a glow of light shining up through it—could you have it?"

He laughed. "I don't think there's anything to stop you, if you'd got enough money and you wanted to spend it that way."

"I just wanted to know," she replied thoughtfully. "I don't want a stainless steel floor with a fishpond in it, or mirrors all round. But it's nice to know that you could have it if it was what you really wanted more than anything."

They wandered from room to room. The detail fittings intrigued her, the design of the taps and the latches and the kitchen sink. "Of course," she said, "we just don't get new things like this in England, because there aren't any new houses. The taps and the sink in our house must be sixty or seventy years old. Things like that never wear out."

She turned to him. "David, how much would a house like this cost? I mean, a brand new house, like this one."

"Three bedrooms," he said. "There's nothing particular about it. I should think it 'ld cost about four or five thousand pounds."

She looked up at him, smiling. "If you ever married anyone, could you afford a house like this?"

He grinned down at her. "Yes," he said. "We could afford a house like this."

She turned away. "I didn't say that," she remarked. "I said, you."

They got back into the car and drove on into Melbourne. "There's nothing much about this city," he said. "It's not particularly big, only about two million people. But to my mind it's got everything you want, clubs and theatres and picture galleries and concerts. And—I don't know, but it's a gracious place, with plenty of parks and wide streets. I've seen a good bit of the world, but I think I like Melbourne just about as well as any place I know."

226

By the end of the day she was inclined to agree with him. They lunched at a small Greek restaurant where he was known to the proprietor, who made a fuss of them because his name had been much in the papers in connection with the Queen's unexpected visit to Australia. From there they drove to the Treasury Gardens, where he showed her Captain Cook's cottage, saved by a generous benefactor from demolition in Whitby and reverently transported stone by stone twelve thousand miles to be re-erected in the Antipodes that he explored. They drove then to the Royal Brighton Yacht Club, and here the smell of salt water and seaweed, and varnish, and clean timber brought nostalgic memories of Itchenor to Rosemary. "Oh David—there's an International fourteen footer—and there's another!"

"That's right," he said. "They've got a class of them here."

"I never knew that," she said in wonder. "I mean, I always thought of them as English boats."

He laughed at her. "That's why they're called International."

They ducked under the bows of vessels laid up in the boat shed and came to his Dragon standing on shores at the back, covered in dust. "This is *Ariadne*," he said. "That's her mast and boom." He pointed to the spars on racks beside the vessel on the wall.

"She's just like an English Dragon," said the girl. She stepped back and looked critically at the hull. "They *have* got beautiful lines."

"She's a bonza thing to sail," the pilot said. "She must be forty years old, I think, but she's perfectly sound still." He caressed the topsides with his hand, and smiled at the girl. "It's nice to see her again, and know she's waiting for me when I get back to Australia."

She stood studying the boat for a moment. Then she

said, "You're longing to get back here, aren't you?"

"It's my own country," he replied. "I wouldn't have missed this job in the Queen's Flight for the world. I'm glad I didn't turn it down when it was offered to me—I very nearly did. I think I'm beginning to understand a bit more about England, too. But I'll be glad to get back here again one day, and get this thing out, and sail her." He patted the boat. "Would you like to get up into the cockpit? It may be a bit dirty."

"I'd like to see what she's like on deck, David." So he got a ladder and they climbed up into the cockpit, and she brushed the dust off the varnished coaming and sat looking up and down the deck. "She must be very fast," she said. "I'd love to have a sail in her one day."

"I hope you will," he replied.

She disregarded that. "What did you mean just now by saying that you were beginning to understand about England?" she enquired. "Are you getting to like it a bit better?"

He thought for a moment. "I'd never want to live there," he replied. "I think there are better places to live, and this is one of them. No—what I mean is this. There's so much in England to admire and like. Their technical achievements, their courage in the bad conditions they've had forced on them, the Queen herself. There's a good deal to dislike, their political system, their subservience to civil servants. I'm not sure that we've got the right to pat ourselves on the back, here in Australia, because we've not got those bad things. Maybe it's just the luck of the game, and if we couldn't feed our people out of what we grow ourselves we'd get to be the same as England."

She smiled reflectively. "There, but for the Grace of God, goes Australia," she said.

"What? Well—yes. I feel that if we'd had as bad a spin

228

as England we might be in the same boat. We're basically the same people, and we'd probably react in the same way."

She smiled. "You don't think that Australians are a superior race of people?"

"I used to think that," he said candidly. "I used to think we'd got a know-how of government that England had lost, and that's what made this country happier and more prosperous. But now I'm not so sure. Compared with England, we're still backward in the sciences and the techniques. I'm not sure that things aren't just easier here because it's still an empty country, because it's still expanding, because almost anyone with any guts can start up a new business and see it prosper. More saucepans wanted every year, more food, more power, because more people. I'm not sure that it's really any virtue in ourselves, although we like to kid ourselves it is."

She repeated his words. "Just the luck of the game."

"That's right. How do you like it here?"

"I've only seen the very top layer of it, David," she protested. "I've been here for about four days, and all I've seen is the Canberra Hotel, and the Royal Residence, and the restaurant we lunched in, and this boat shed." She laughed. "I'm not going to even think if I like it or not. I'll say this— that I never knew it was so lovely, or that so many flowers grow here, or so many flowering trees. But it would be silly if I said I liked Australia when I've only seen the bits of it I've seen."

"That's true," he admitted. "You want to live on a station for a year with nobody to talk to but the cattle and the sheep, and have a drought and a couple of bush fires."

She laughed. "If I did that I'd probably be glad to get back to my flat in Dover Street."

She got up, and he held the ladder for her while she went down. They walked around and found the foreman and talked a little about *Ariadne*, and then they went into the club house and had tea in a window looking out over the bay. Then it was time to get into the car for the drive back to Berwick.

A considerable crowd had collected at the aerodrome by that time, with a number of pressmen, for the news of the Queen's visit had got out. Rosemary passed through the crowd unchallenged and got into the machine, but David had to submit to the photographers and to an interview. He cut it short and went into the machine to see about his business, and presently the Queen and Consort drove up and posed for a moment for the cameras, and then got in. Frank Cox came forward and spoke to the pilots, and David swung the Ceres towards the runway and presently took off. At ten minutes to seven, in the evening light, he put her down at Canberra.

Next day Frank Cox came to him at lunch time in the mess at Fairbairn aerodrome. "It's back to London next," he said. "Tomorrow or the next day. They want a proposal for the best time to take off."

The pilot nodded. "They'll want to get back in the evening, I suppose?" he said. "Land at White Waltham about seven o'clock?"

"I should think so. That would give them a night's rest before they start on anything."

"Ten hours time difference," said David. "Refuel at Ratmalana. Two equal legs of about ten hours, allowing for average headwind going westwards. Do they want to stop in Ceylon?"

The Group Captain shook his head. "They want to go straight through, and get back to London as soon as possible."

"Well, say an hour at Ratmalana. That makes twenty-one hours on the way, less ten, leaves eleven. I'd like an hour

230

for contingencies, perhaps. Take off from here at seven in the morning would get them to White Waltham at seven in the evening."

"Daylight all the way?"

"That's right." The pilot paused. "You can usually do a daylight flight going westwards, with our cruising speed."

"I'll tell them. They'd better have a cup of morning tea at Tharwa, and then breakfast on board."

"That's right," David said. "Breakfast at eight o'clock, when we level off for cruising. It's a bit awkward for them on the climb, because of the tables." He thought for a moment. "Twenty hours," he said. "Breakfast and four other meals. What'll we make it? Four lunches?"

"I should think so. See if you can make them a bit different."

David nodded. "Two hot and two cold. I'll see the stewards, and get that worked out. When can you let me know the time of take off definitely?"

"No snags with the machine?"

"No. We'd be ready to go now. It's just the food."

"I'll ring you about four o'clock this afternoon."

He rang later, and confirmed the flight for England for the next day. David briefed his crew; in the evening light they had the Ceres drawn out of the hangar and did an engine run, and finally topped up with fuel for the flight to Colombo. It was seven o'clock when he got back to the hotel; he found Rosemary waiting for him in the lounge as he passed through.

He stopped by her. "I won't be a minute," he said. "I've just got to wash."

"It's all right," she said. "I saw the head waiter, and they're keeping dinner for us. Australians dine early, don't they?"

He came back to her in five minutes, and they went in to

the meal. The dining room was emptying; he glanced around, but there was no one seated near them. "Back to London," he said. "Has it been announced yet?"

She shook her head. "It's to be released for the nine o'clock news. It's going to cause a lot of disappointment here, they say."

He nodded. "It's bound to. She's not been here for two years, and it's much longer than that since she was over in West Australia. Now, when she does come, she has to go back to England after less than a week. People are bound to be disappointed."

"Australians aren't the only ones to be disappointed," the girl replied.

"Who else?"

"She is," the girl said. "She's not going back to England for a holiday."

"I suppose not."

They ate in silence for a few minutes. Then Rosemary said, "Tharwa isn't going into mothballs."

"What's that?"

"The cars are staying in the garage and the staff are being kept on in the house. It was all on a care and maintenance basis before we arrived. They had an awful job getting it ready for her this time—everybody worked all through the night. If we hadn't stopped at Christmas Island nothing would have been finished. It's not so easy on the domestic side when she can suddenly make up her mind in Ottawa that she's coming to Tharwa after two years, and she can arrive less than a day later."

"I never thought of that," he said. "The house isn't being put on care and maintenance this time?"

She shook her head.

"Does that mean that she's coming back here pretty soon?"

"It could mean that," she said. "It may be Charles or Anne. But anyway, the house is being kept open."

He smiled. "Perhaps Uncle Donald 'll see the Ceres after all."

"Perhaps I shall see Uncle Donald," she remarked.

He glanced at her. "If she comes back here after doing what she's got to do in London, would you come with her?"

"I might. It's all worked quite smoothly this time. Macmahon seems to be able to handle all her work, and if he came he'd probably want me. I can't see Lord Marlow travelling about much, at his age. Besides, I don't think he'd go down so well here as Macmahon. He's too much the old aristocrat."

David nodded. "He wouldn't go down here. Macmahon's all right."

They finished the meal, and went out into the cloister around the garden courtyard, and sat down in long chairs with their coffee. "I'm going to bed as soon as I've drunk this," the pilot said. "I've got a call in for five o'clock. There's a car coming for me at five-twenty."

The flower beds were scented in the warm darkness. "We shan't be able to sit out like this tomorrow night," the girl said. "It will be nearly midwinter—only three weeks before Christmas."

"I bet we strike a packet of misery going in to White Waltham," David remarked. "We'll have a freezing fog and zero visibility. If it's like that, I'll probably divert and take them in to London Airport, where there's proper ground control for radar landings."

In spite of the early hour, there was quite a crowd at Fairbairn aerodrome next morning to see the Queen depart. When the Royal car drew up before the aeroplane the Queen and the Consort got out and talked for a time with the

Governor-General and the Prime Minister while the cameras whirred and flash bulbs exploded around. Then they got into the Ceres and the door closed behind them; Frank Cox came forward and spoke to David, and the pilot started the inboard motors and swung the machine towards the runway. Five minutes later they were in the air with a fighter escort at each wing tip, climbing to operating altitude over New South Wales.

The weather was bright and cloudless over central Australia. Over the scarred earth of Broken Hill they levelled off for cruising; the Queen sent a radio message of thanks to the fighter escort, who peeled away and went down to land, and the Royal party went to breakfast. Oodnadatta on the railway line that runs south from Alice was passed at about nine o'clock, and then there was nothing before them but the golden and pink wastes of the Australian desert. They flew on steadily, monotonously, and came to the Indian Ocean at about eleven o'clock near a place called Marble Bar, and the sea lay in front of them. David handed over the control to Ryder, lunched, and went to lie down for a time. They passed over the other Christmas Island and flew roughly parallel to the coasts of Java and Sumatra and about a hundred and fifty miles south of them, droning along in a cloudless sky all the afternoon. At four o'clock by Canberra time they began to lose height for the landing at Colombo and had afternoon tea, and an hour later David put the Ceres down upon the runway of Ratmalana aerodrome, ten hours out from Canberra. It was then a little after noon, by local time.

At the Queen's request no announcement of her passing visit had been made to the Press and there was no crowd at the aerodrome, and only one photographer exercising his scoop, but there was a little party grouped around the Governor-General and the Prime Minister waiting to welcome her upon the tarmac. The Queen and Consort got out and stood talking with them in the shade of the airport buildings while the Ceres was refuelled and inspected; in fifty-five minutes David reported to Frank Cox that they were ready to go. Ten minutes later they were in the air again, and climbing up to operational height over Cape Comorin on a course for the Persian Gulf and Cyprus. A direct course would have taken them over Kurdistan and the Black Sea, still territories that were somewhat hostile and disturbed, and better avoided by the Queen of England in her flight.

It was about eight o'clock in the morning by Greenwich time when they took off from Colombo. They moved on across the Arabian Sea, weary now; most of the passengers were dozing in their seats, and the Queen and the Consort had retired into their cabins. On the flight deck Frank Cox and David and Ryder were taking three-hour watches at the controls though there was little to be done; the machine flew steadily upon course in the control of the automatic pilot. At half past eleven they came to the Gulf of Oman at the entrance to the Persian Gulf and passed over the town of Muscat; at one o'clock they flew over Kuweit. An hour and forty minutes later Cyprus was beneath them and they altered course for London. At four o'clock they were in the dusk a little to the south of Belgrade and an hour later, in the vicinity of Munich, David started to let down upon the long descent at the flight end. And here they ran into trouble.

They had advised the London Area Control for air traffic of their estimated time of arrival, and had asked for weather 'actuals'. The radio operator passed a slip of paper to David in a few minutes, and he bent over it upon the chart table, with Frank Cox by his side.

They studied it together in silence. "Typical December

evening," the Group Captain said. There was low cloud over the whole of southern England with fog patches; at London Airport the cloud base was at eight hundred feet and visibility upon the ground six hundred yards. There were icing conditions at two thousand feet.

David nodded. "I think we'll ask to be diverted to London. I don't like White Waltham much for instrument landings in this sort of stuff. London's better for us on a night like this."

The Group Captain nodded. "I agree."

David made his signal, and waited for the answering approval and information of the other traffic in the air. No answer came for ten minutes, during which they were approaching England at six hundred miles an hour and losing height at the rate of a thousand feet a minute. The pilot frowned a little, and repeated his request for a diversion to London Airport, stating his altitude and his position, and his estimated time of arrival.

The answer came at last. 'Maintain altitude thirty thousand feet diversion approved to Driffield, Yorks, cloud base at Driffield three thousand feet visibility five miles.'

The two officers stared at this in consternation. "For Christ's sake," said Frank Cox. ''We can't take them to Yorkshire!"

The pilot bit his lip. "That's what it says."

"Is airline traffic going in and out of London?"

David turned to the radio operator. "Airline traffic seems normal at London, Cap," the man said. "I can hear them talking on the V.H.F. They're landing normally."

"Make this signal," said Frank Cox. '' 'Request per-. mission to land at London Airport with Royal passengers.' Sign it, Captain of the Queen's Flight."

David said, "Shall we level off at thirty thousand, sir? We're getting near that now."

236

Frank Cox hesitated. In the air and approaching a congested traffic area at night it was imperative that the instructions of the ground control should be obeyed implicitly; no one knew that better. He nodded, unwilling. "Level off at thirty thousand, but hold your course," he said.

David went and spoke to Ryder at the control, and came back to the chart table. The answering signal came back in a couple of minutes.

It read, 'Permission not, repeat not, granted to land at London Airport because of unknown experience of Australian crew. Proceed to Driffield and state estimated time of arrival.'

David flushed angrily. "I think you'll have to handle this one from now on, sir," he said.

"It's a put up job," said the Group Captain quietly. "Somebody's out to make trouble for them." He thought for a minute. "Make this signal: 'Australian crew full trained instrument landings by B.O.A.C. to B.O.A.C. standards. Request permission to land at London Airport.' "

The officers waited in silence by the chart table till the answer came. It read, 'Names of crew do not appear on current certification lists. Permission not, repeat not, granted for landing London account of deteriorating weather conditions. Proceed to Driffield and state estimated time of arrival.'

Frank Cox said, "Alter course for Driffield, Nigger, and give them your E.T.A."

The pilot went in silence to the chart table, and ran out the new course, and made the signal, and gave the course to Ryder at the control; then he relieved him and slipped into the first pilot's seat himself. He was no longer angry, because he knew that no complaint could lie against him, or

237

against his crew. He knew that the B.O.A.C. training staff at Hurn, at an investigation, would vouch for their competence. This was something bigger than that. This was some petty mind at work, some small, powerful official saying to the Queen, "Well, if you insist on flying with these Colonials you must expect to suffer some slight inconvenience, you know. Why can't you leave the Commonwealth alone, and stay in England?" David wondered if Lord Coles was the small, petty mind.

Behind him, Frank Cox took the signal log from him and went aft with it. David turned in his seat to look after him, and through the open door that led into the cabin he saw him knock at the Consort's door. He tightened his lips at the thought of this welcome home that England was giving to the Queen, and turned to his job with a heavy heart. Here was no fighter guard of honour for the Queen, here was no Prime Minister waiting on the tarmac to greet her. Here was something very, very different.

He broke through the cloud ten miles short of Driffield at about two thousand five hundred feet, and the aerodrome lay before him, the runways and the taxiways lit up. Driffield was an R.A.F. station, and David wondered why it had been chosen for the diversion of their flight, unless it was that it was nearly forty miles from the main railway line at York, and so presented the maximum fatigue and inconvenience to the Queen at the end of her long journey. He brought the Ceres round upon the circuit, lined her up three miles outside the boundaries of the aerodrome, and put her down upon the runway, twenty-one and a half hours out from Canberra.

He parked the aircraft on the tarmac where a little group of officers were waiting by a couple of cars, and stopped the engines. He slipped out of his seat, put on his cap and straightened his tunic, and went aft into the saloon. The

Queen, coming out of her cabin, turned to speak to him. "Thank you so much, Commander Anderson," she said. "It's been a very easy flight."

He said, "I'm very sorry about this diversion, madam. It's going to put you to a lot of trouble, I'm afraid. We'll try and make sure that it doesn't happen again."

"Don't worry," she said quietly. "I know it's nothing to do with you. Thank you for a very safe and pleasant journey." She turned, and left the machine.

He stopped by Rosemary's seat and helped her with her hand luggage, and followed her down the steps on to the tarmac. A bitter wind from the North Sea whipped round them in the darkness. He said, "You're going on to London with the Queen, I suppose?"

"I think so, Nigger," she said. "I believe we're driving into York to catch a train at ten-twenty. What will you be doing?"

"I shall stay here with the aircraft," he said. "We'll fly her down to White Waltham tomorrow. If we're allowed to fly at all in England," he added bitterly.

"I wish I was coming with you," she said wearily. "It'll be three in the morning by the time we reach King's Cross."

He left her then, to arrange with the R.A.F. to hangar the machine; he stayed with the party till the tractor had drawn the Ceres under cover and the doors were shut. Then he walked over to the R.A.F. mess. He found that the Queen and the Consort were dining with the R.A.F. Commandant in his house; the rest of the party were already at dinner in the mess. Transport to York had been arranged for eight forty-five.

He had a few words with Frank Cox before he left for London with the party. "I'll ring you tomorrow morning, here," the Group Captain said. "About eleven o'clock, I should think. As soon as I've got clearance for you to fly down to White Waltham."

David asked directly, "Is White Waltham still open to us, sir?"

"I haven't heard it's not. Have you heard anything?"

"No. I just wondered."

"I think that's going to be all right. . . . I don't think you need worry about this, Nigger. It's just another pin-prick. It's nothing to do with you or with your crew. They could have found out all about you from B.O.A.C. if they didn't know already." He paused. "No, it's something quite different, that's to do with the Queen. I'd forget about it, if I were you."

"It'll be a long time before I do that," the pilot said grimly. "She's my Queen as well as yours, you know. I'm not a bloody Pommie."

The Group Captain looked up at him, startled. "That's a point of view I hadn't thought about."

"It's about time somebody started thinking about it," David said. "My Queen's dead tired now, and some Pommie bastard's forcing her to travel for six hours longer, by car and train, in the middle of the night, for no reason at all. I don't like it. My High Commissioner won't like it, either. And Canberra won't like it, when they hear what's happened."

There was a short silence. Then the Group Captain looked up, smiling. "Difficult, isn't it?" he remarked.

"Too right, it's difficult," the Australian said. And then he added, "All Pommies aren't bloody. I used that as a kind of figure of speech."

"Most Aussies are bastards, though," said the Group Captain. "Prickly bloody types to deal with."

They laughed together over a cup of coffee.

Next day David flew Tare down to White Waltham.

He found Dewar there with Sugar, rather envious of the Australians in their flight around the world, and anxious to hear all about it. David spoke to Frank Cox upon the telephone and received his permission to lay up Tare for a comprehensive inspection by the manufacturers that would take three days, and set this in motion with the firm. On the following day he flew the machine to Hatfield in the morning and handed it over to de Havilland's, and returned to White Waltham by road.

That afternoon he got a telephone call from the High Commissioner's office, making an appointment for him to see Mr. Harry Ferguson next afternoon. He had been summoned to similar appointments with the High Commissioner several times during his service in the Queen's Flight, to report on his work and upon any organisational difficulties that might have arisen, and he had shown him over Tare at White Waltham. It was natural that the High Commissioner should want an account of the flight to and from Australia. David rang up Rosemary to ask her to dine with him that evening, and made an appointment to pick her up at her flat at seven o'clock.

Mr. Ferguson, fat and genial in a grey suit, made David welcome and sat him down in the chair on the other side of the desk. As David had supposed, he wanted to know all about the flight, and he was particularly interested in Christmas Island. "What's it like there?" he enquired. "I've never seen it. I don't suppose many other people have, either."

"It's a pretty little place," the pilot said. "Just one of these coral atolls. The strip's all right, but refuelling arrangements are a bit antiquated. If we're going to go there often, we should have proper fuel storage tanks, and a modern pump and hoses. They'll probably be needed for strategic reasons, anyway."

241

"Will you write me a report on that, Commander?"

David made a note in his diary.

"I've never been to any of those coral islands," said Mr. Ferguson. "I'd like to go, one day. Where did the Queen stay?"

"In the District Officer's house." David told him all about it, and then he went on, and told him how much the Queen seemed to have enjoyed the day's rest on Christmas Island. "If she's likely to be travelling from Canada to Australia much," he said, "she'll be going there pretty frequently, because it's the natural refuelling point for us. I know she'd very much appreciate a little house there of her own."

Harry Ferguson raised his eyebrows. "She would?"

David told him of the conversation that he had overheard between the Queen and the Consort. "It's a long way from Ottawa to Canberra," he said. "Even in a Ceres, it's eighteen flying hours, and that's a long trip for a woman of her age without a break. Nine or ten hours at a stretch is quite enough. If she had a little house there—just a little one, with two bedrooms only—she'd probably use it, and stay there a day to break the flight. Will she be going that way often?"

"She may. Under the new arrangements, she may well be doing that trip every three or four months."

David did not like to ask what new arrangements those might be. "I should think the Federal Government might cough up a little weatherboard house," he said.

"I think they might," the High Commissioner said. "Who would provide the service?"

"She'd have the steward and the stewardess out of the aeroplane," the pilot said. "She won't need any more than that. She's got her own maid travelling with her, too."

They discussed it for a little. "Will you put all this in

242

your report?" the High Commissioner said. "It's little things like this we want to know." David made his note. "Now, what's all this I've heard about the trouble you had landing in this country? This business about going up to Yorkshire?"

David told him.

In the end, Harry Ferguson said, "I see. London Airport is a civil airport, and they demand first class instrument landing certificates for pilots landing there in bad weather conditions. And those certificates are only issued to civil pilots. They got you on that."

"That's right," the pilot said. "Service pilots don't use London Airport in the normal way, and they don't have civil licences. That was the excuse for sending us to Driffield, which is an R.A.F. aerodrome—because we're an R.A.A.F. crew."

"Wasn't there an R.A.F. aerodrome closer than Yorkshire?"

"There must have been," the pilot said. "Dozens of them."

"Did they know that you were trained by B.O.A.C. to the standard of their crews?"

"They must have known," the pilot repeated. "We told them in the signals. I've got the copies here." He passed them across the desk to the High Commissioner, who read them carefully. "Anyway," he said, "B.O.A.C. didn't train us down at Hurn. We trained them."

Mr. Ferguson laid the papers down. "I see. Somebody was just being awkward."

"I think so," said the pilot. "Frank Cox thought that somebody was out to make things difficult and tiring for the Queen. Teach her not to go flying with Colonials again."

"I see."

243

There was a pause, and then the High Commissioner said, "How do you feel about the British now, now that you've had more experience of them?"

The pilot grinned. "I think their policemen are just wonderful," he said. And then he added, more seriously, "I've got nothing to complain about, sir. This is the first unpleasantness we've had. I don't think this was aimed against us, as a crew."

Mr. Ferguson inclined his head. "No," he said thoughtfully. "I think that it was probably upon a higher level than that."

They discussed a little routine business, and David left Australia House and walked down the length of the Strand on the way to his club. There was a raw nip in the air, and a light, foggy drizzle that struck chill after the warm benison of Canberra. The people in the streets looked pale and stunted in comparison with the glowing health of his own countrymen, and yet there was an air of purpose and determination about them that was always novel to him. Again he was torn between dislike and admiration for them; no negligible people, these. These were the people who produced the Ceres, and a thousand other marvels that his country could not match.

He walked to his club in Pall Mall and sat looking at the weekly reviews to bring himself up to date with the temper of England since he had gone away. Something had evidently happened in the House of Commons that had brought the subject of multiple voting to the forefront of the news, but he could not gather from the weekly papers what that was. He sat with a cup of tea, turning over the reviews. There was much talk in the Conservative papers about electoral reform, and there were bitter articles in the Labour papers about an audacious attempt on the part of the Tories to kill democracy and to regain an obsolete form of government by privilege. It was all rather unhappy reading, a record of disunity on fundamental principles that he could not recall in his own country; he put the papers aside with a sigh, nostalgic for the country on the far side of the world that he had left so recently.

He called for Rosemary in her flat at seven o'clock. She took him to a very small, very discreet little restaurant in Shepherd's Market, where the tables were widely separated to enable the patrons to talk confidentially, where the proprietor exhibited sheer genius in circumventing the rationing restrictions, and where the bill was in line with the benefits of the establishment. He handed her coat to the waiter, and they sat down with a glass of sherry and a tomato juice. He asked her, "What was the journey down to London like?"

"There was a fog," she said. "We didn't get into King's Cross till after half past three."

"You had a sleeper, I suppose?"

She shook her head. "They couldn't lay it on at such short notice. They put on an extra first class coach for us. She was looking awfully tired when we got to London."

He bit his lip. "I'm very sore about all this," he said. "It was so totally unnecessary."

"It wasn't your fault," she said. "A report came through the office this morning from the Air Ministry. It wasn't anything to do with you."

"I know. That doesn't stop me being sore. Do you know who the nigger in the woodpile was?"

She hesitated. "Forget about it," she said at last. "It's not a thing that concerns either of us."

"All right." They sat in silence for a time. Presently he asked, "Did anyone come to meet her at King's Cross?"

"Charles and Anne came," she said. "It was very sweet of them to turn out at that time in the morning."

245

His lip curled a little. "No Prime Minister? No one from the Cabinet?"

"No."

He said no more, and presently the hors d'œuvres were served. When the waiter had gone away, he said, "I've been reading the weeklies to find out what's been happening while we've been away. There seems to be a lot going on about this multiple voting."

She nodded. "I think there is."

"The Government seem very bitter."

"Yes," she said, "they are. People are usually bitter when they see something threatened that they believe in with all their hearts and souls. And this Government believes in the old principle of one man, one vote. They believe in that very sincerely."

"And is that threatened now?" he asked.

"I think it is, Nigger," she said seriously. "Somehow, I don't believe it can go on much longer here."

"What's going to stop it?"

"I don't know. Perhaps the quality of the people."

He could have made a bitter and a scornful remark at that, but he didn't do it because Rosemary was English, and he loved her. And as they ate in silence he thought about her words, and about the purpose and determination of these people. Perhaps she was right; perhaps the English really had a quality that would ultimately lead them out of difficulties. He did not care to ask her what she meant just then, so he turned the conversation and began to tell her about the proposal to put up a little house on Christmas Island for the Queen to use if she went there again. "I was going to put forward that as a suggestion in my report, and Harry Ferguson said he'd endorse it." He looked at her diffidently. "Do you think that's all right?"

"Oh Nigger, she'll love it!" the girl exclaimed. "It'll

246

come out of the blue, as a suggestion from the Australian Government, will it?"

"I should think so," he replied. "You don't think it would be speaking out of turn if I put it in the report?"

"Of course it's not." She turned to him. "She's in such difficulties here," she said. "A little thing like that would make a world of difference to her. Just the thought that somebody, somewhere, is trying to make things easier for her, even if it's on the other side of the world and in the middle of the Pacific."

"Do you think I might tell that to Harry Ferguson—verbally? There's something about giving twice if you give quickly."

She smiled. "It's in all the Latin textbooks." She thought for a moment. "I don't see why you shouldn't tell him if you're seeing him again, but he's probably got a good idea of it already."

"He speaks to Canberra almost every day," the pilot said. "He could probably fix up a little thing like that up on the telephone."

They finished their meal and sat smoking over their coffee. "My father came up yesterday," she said presently. "He spent the night in the flat with me, on a camp bed in the sitting room. He doesn't very often come to London, but I can't get down to Oxford this week end—I'm on duty. He wanted to hear all about our trip."

"Has he gone back now?" David asked.

She nodded. "He went back this morning."

"I'd like to meet him some time."

"I want you to," she said. "I wanted him to stay tonight and come and dine with us here, but he had to get back—he's got tutorials or something." She paused. "He talked for a long time last night before we went to bed. He'd got some very interesting things to say."

"What about?"

"Just everything," she replied vaguely. "About this miserable crisis. About England. He thinks the people of this country are getting better and better."

The pilot wrinkled his brows in perplexity. "Better?"

She nodded. "He said that all the duds were going, and they'd been going for a long time now." She stirred her coffee thoughtfully. "Of course, Daddy's sixty-three and he can remember quite a long time back. He fought in the second war, in the Royal Armoured Corps. He was talking a lot last night about the things he saw when he was a young man. About the sort of people who got out of France and Holland when they were invaded, and the sort who stayed behind."

"Oh?"

She nodded. "He said that when a country was invaded by the enemy, the first to go were the very intelligent and patriotic and adventurous people, who left because they were resolved to go on fighting with the Allies, fighting from a better ground. But after that, he said, the refugees consisted of the timid people, and the selfish people, and the people who put moneymaking first; people who would never fight for their own country or for anything else. Daddy hasn't got a lot of use for refugees. He said that after those had gone, France was a better place. The people who stayed on under the Germans were good, steady people mostly, people who weren't going to be kicked out of their country by any invader, people with guts and common-sense." She paused. "He said that that's what's been happening in England for the last twenty years. All the timid people and the selfish people have been getting out."

The pilot glanced at her, interested. "That's quite a new one to me. Did he mean that the average of the British people was sort of worse twenty years ago than it is now?"

"That's what he said," she replied. "He said he notices it in the young men coming up to college. They're better types now than they were thirty years ago, when he went back to Oxford after the second war. They've got more character. They think for themselves more—they don't take anything for granted, like they used to. That's what he said."

"I wonder if that's true?" the pilot remarked.

"I think it's probably right," the girl said slowly. "Daddy's no fool, and he rubs shoulders with a lot of first class people up at Oxford. And it fits in, too. Adversity makes people better sometimes, makes them cleverer and tougher. It might happen with a country, just the same."

"Do you think that's got anything to do with all this fuss about the multiple vote?" he asked.

"I think it has," she said. "I think Iorwerth Jones is running into difficulties he didn't quite expect."

Eight

FOR the next few days David saw little of Rosemary. He went with his crew to Hatfield and fetched Tare back to White Waltham, and with Frank Cox began the business of obtaining British civil instrument landing certificates to enable them to use London Airport in emergency. They went together to the Air Ministry and were received by a bland civil servant of medium grade, who suggested that the requirements of the regulations would be met if the Australians and the Canadians abandoned their Service ranks during their employment in the Queen's Flight and requalified as civilian pilots for all grades of licence, a proceeding which would have taken all their time for about six weeks. Dewar and David said that this seemed rather unnecessary, and the official said that he was sorry, but that he was bound by the rules of his department. David and Dewar went away and put the matter in the hands of their High Commissioners.

A few days later, quite abruptly, they were summoned to the Ministry again. This time they were received by a much higher official, the Second Secretary. He greeted them very genially, and said that he was glad that the matter of their licences had been adjusted. Upon his desk he had a set of civil licences already made out for all the members of the

Australian and Canadian crews; first class master pilot's licences for Wing Commander Dewar and Wing Commander Anderson, and a sheaf of civil pilot's, radio operator's, and engineer's licences for all the other crew members. The officers gathered up this mass of paper, somewhat dazed, and retired with it to the Royal Aero club.

"Bit of a change of tone," said David. "What's done that?"

"God knows," said Dewar. "I asked Frank, but he went all cagey. I think they've got the wind up over something." There was a pause, and then the Canadian said, "Did he tell you I'm for Ottawa again?"

"No. When are you going?"

"Tomorrow night. I'm taking Charles over—with all his family."

David stared at him. "How long is he going for?"

"You can search me. I'm taking off at eight o'clock tomorrow night, with the Prince and Princess, three children, valet, maid, secretary and three quarters of a ton of luggage. After that I'm waiting there for orders."

"Nothing about that in the papers, is there?"

"Not yet. Keep it under your hat."

"Of course."

That was on December the 10th. David turned up next evening with Ryder to see Sugar leave and to assist if necessary. There was no hitch; the Prince of Wales arrived with his family and suite in three cars and got out on the dark, windy tarmac by the aeroplane, and got into it quickly. The door was shut, the inboard engines started, and Sugar moved towards the runway. Frank Cox and David stood watching the tail light as it dwindled in the sky upon the way to Canada, and then turned to the warmth and brightness of the office.

In the office Frank Cox turned to him, and said, "Your turn next, Nigger."

David asked, "Is anything laid on?"

"More or less. The Havants are going to Kenya, to Nyeri."

"When?"

"Friday or Saturday. No date has been fixed yet. Probably Saturday, I should think."

David nodded. "We'll be ready. Are we staying out there, or coming straight back here?"

"Coming straight back," the Group Captain said. "There may be another job quite soon after that."

The pilot laughed. "One's enough to worry about at a time. This Nyeri trip. There's a strip at a place called Nanyuki that they use, isn't there?"

"That's right." They turned to the files, and Cox pulled out the chart and details for Nanyuki. "Have you been there?"

David shook his head. "No." He studied the runway details, the altitude, and the surrounding terrain. "We'll be all right to put down there in daylight," he said. "We'll be flying light by the time we get there—seven or eight hours. I wouldn't try it for the first time in bad weather, or at night. Nairobi's the alternative, I suppose."

They spent a quarter of an hour studying the route. "Well, that's all right," the pilot said at last. "Take off at seven in the morning. If that's too early for them, then it's a night landing at Nairobi. In that case they'd better stay the night there, and go on next day by car."

Frank Cox jotted down the figures on the back of an envelope. "They could leave here late at night, and make a night flight," he said. "Take off at eleven and arrive at nine in the morning. That might be better for them—let the children sleep all night."

"All the family going?"

The Group Captain nodded.

The pilot eyed him, smiling a little. "First the Prince and all his family, and then Princess Anne and all hers. Looks like a general evacuation."

"It may do," said Frank Cox. "But that's nothing to do with us."

"No. Well, that's the dope, sir. We can do it day or night, whichever they prefer. I'd like a day's notice, because of the food."

"I'll let you know in good time," said the Group Captain.

"The boys were asking about Christmas leave," said David. "They've most of them got relations in this country."

Cox shook his head. "There'll be no Christmas leave for your crew, Nigger," he said. "At least, I don't think so. I think you may be off upon another job." He paused. "I'm sorry."

"It's not important," said the pilot. "They'd rather be working than just sitting around. Where's that one to?"

"I don't know yet. I don't think they've made up their minds."

It was announced next morning in the Press that the Prince and Princess of Wales had left with their family to spend the Christmas holidays at the Royal Residence at Gatineau, where little George and Alice would have their first ski-ing lesson. *The Times*, in an editorial, commented upon the happy effect on Commonwealth relations of these domestic movements of the Royal Family from country to country. No mention, however, was made of the forthcoming visit of the Princess Royal and the Duke of Havant to Kenya.

That day, Thursday, David rang up Rosemary at the

Palace and suggested they should dine together. "I'll be going away soon," he said. "What about tonight?"

She said, "It's just a question of getting off, Nigger . . . Things have been busy recently. I didn't get back to the flat till after ten o'clock last night."

"My word," he said. "You must be very tired."

"I'm all right." There was a pause. "I don't like to say we'd dine at Mario's—the place in Shepherd's Market—in case I can't get there."

"What 'ld you do by yourself?" he asked.

"Oh—I'd just cook up something in the flat and go to bed."

"I can cook," he said. "I do want to see you, because of what's going on. Would you think it out of order if I came up with some tins of things and waited for you in the flat, and cooked you something there? I won't stay very long."

"Oh David!" she said. "That's a good idea. I wouldn't have to worry about being late then. Can you really cook?"

"Too right I can," he said. "How will I get into the flat?"

She told him about the caretaker in the basement who had a key. "I'll ring her up and tell her it's all right to let you in," she said. "I'll try and be back by seven, but I don't know if I'll make it. Don't go reading all my love letters."

"Of course I shall," he said. "It's not often a bloke gets a chance like this."

He drove up to London in the late afternoon with a small suitcase full of tins that he had brought back from Australia in the Ceres, paid a supplementary visit to Fortnum and Mason's, and went to the flat. The caretaker let him in and he put down the suitcase on the table, and looked around with pleasure, carefully studying her pictures and her books. A quarter of an hour later he woke up and took his jacket off, and began to investigate the resources of the little

254

kitchenette. He unpacked his case and planned the meal, and then he found the cutlery and cloth and laid the table. He deviated from the path of rectitude then to peep rather shyly into her bedroom, but he did not go beyond the door and closed it again, feeling guilty.

When she came hurrying back to the flat she found the table laid and the fire lit, and a glass of sherry ready poured out for her with a plate of caviar on biscuits beside it. She was cold and weary as she came in from the street, and there were these good things, and a delicious smell from the kitchenette, and Nigger Anderson, big and dark and cheerful and comforting. "Oh Nigger," she said, "how simply wonderful! What's that you've got cooking?"

"Casserole of pheasant," he said. "Are you very tired?"

"Not now," she said. "I never smelt anything so good."

"It's the wine," he said. "Australian wine. I always put a good dollop of wine into a casserole. It covers up a lot of the deficiencies."

"And caviar!" She went into the bedroom and threw off her coat; in a few minutes she came back to him, her eyes shining. "You can't think what it means to come back to a warm room, and a meal all ready made!"

He handed her her sherry and took his own tomato juice. Together they nibbled the caviar biscuits. "Very busy today?" he asked. He studied her as she sat opposite him; there were fine lines of fatigue around her eyes and her mouth.

"A bit," she said. "Let's not talk about it just yet, Nigger. Not till I'm warmed up."

He nodded. "It's different to the Canberra Hotel," he said. "It was just comfortably warm then, to my way of thinking."

She nodded. "It was lovely there. It's so difficult to realise that it was only ten days ago, and that it's all there

255

still, the same flowers even, on the same stalks in the garden." She stared at the glowing radiants of the fire. "I love England," she said thoughtfully. "But I'm beginning to realise that there are other places one could get to love as well."

"England in spring is just a fairyland," he said. "I'll give you that. But anyone can have it at this time of year, so far as I'm concerned."

She laughed, and sipped her sherry. "Where did you get the sherry from, Nigger?" she asked. "It's not mine, is it?"

He shook his head. "It's a South Australian wine—quite a cheap one. Do you like it?"

"I think it's very good. I suppose you brought a lot of stuff back in the aeroplane, hidden away somewhere?"

He laughed. "I should think we had half a ton of food on board, between the lot of us. Food and drink. I told each member of the crew that he could bring a hundred pounds—weight, that is."

"Oh Nigger!"

Presently she said, "You're going away again tomorrow, aren't you?"

"Tomorrow or Saturday," he said. "I've not heard yet."

"I think it's tomorrow," she replied. "Major Macmahon was talking to Lord Marlow about it just before I came away. Princess Anne wants to go tomorrow, late at night."

"Have they told Frank Cox?"

"I think they were ringing him about the time I left."

He nodded. Ryder would take the message if it came that evening, and warn the crew. And while the thought was in his mind, the telephone rang. The girl got up and answered it, and handed the microphone to him, smiling. "It's Flight Lieutenant Ryder," she said.

He spoke to his co-pilot for a few minutes, and set the necessary arrangements in train. He put down the instrument, and she was standing by his side; she had finished her sherry. "Let's eat, Nigger," she said. "I can't stand being tantalised by your casserole any longer. I'm just drooling at the mouth." So they dished up the casserole and the creamed potatoes and the peas, and he opened half a bottle of claret for her, and they sat down to dinner.

He had tinned peaches and tinned cream for her as a sweet, both from the other side of the world. Over the peaches she said, "I suppose you'll stock up again tomorrow or the next day, in Kenya, David?"

He laughed. "I suppose so. I think I'll go on to Nairobi when I've put them down at Nanyuki, and let the boys have a night's rest. We've got to refuel somewhere before starting home—there's no fuel at Nanyuki. Make a daylight flight home on the Sunday, and get in well before dark this time." He smiled. "I don't want to end up in Driffield."

"That won't happen again, Nigger," she said. "Not that one, anyway."

"They gave us all our licences in a great hurry last Monday," he remarked. "Did something blow up in your place?"

"I don't know," she replied. "I know Philip sent for Lord Coles on Saturday and he had him in the study for nearly half an hour. I don't know what they said, of course. I only know Lord Coles had a smile on his face when he went in, and he hadn't got it on when he came out."

"Too bad," said the pilot. He paused, and then he said, "Charles is in Canada with all his family by now, and with three quarters of a ton of luggage. I'm taking Princess Anne to Nyeri with Havant and all *their* family, and I suppose there'll be three quarters of a ton of luggage going with them, too."

The girl nodded.

"There'll only be the Queen and the Consort left in England, in the direct line of the Monarchy," he said.

Rosemary dropped her eyes, and studied the dish in front of her. "That's happened often enough before."

"Maybe. But Frank Cox wants me back here quick from Kenya, because there may be another job for me to do."

The girl glanced at him, troubled. "You think too much, Nigger," she said. "You go putting two and two together when there's no occasion to. You don't have to know what's coming, and it's better not to, sometimes."

He smiled at her. "I'm not prying into the secrets of the Royal Family," he said. "I'll do what I'm told to do when the time comes, and I'll ask no questions. I'm thinking about you and me. Will you be coming too, this time?"

"I think so," she said slowly. "Whatever comes out of this, I think Major Macmahon will be with her, and I'll be with him."

"Fine," he said. "That's all I want to know."

She sat in silence for a time. "David," she said at last, "I want you to be very, very careful in the next few days. People may try to get things out of you, but they mustn't. People may try getting at your crew in some way—I don't know. They might try and put the aeroplane out of action, even. Funny things are going on that I can't possibly talk about, even to you. But if you want to do a good job for the Queen, be very, very careful in the next few days, till after Christmas."

He met her eyes. "Thank you," he said quietly. "I'll remember that."

They got up from the table presently, and stacked the dishes for her caretaker to wash up in the morning. Then she poured out cups of coffee for them from the percolator, and they went back into the sitting room, and sat down before the fire again. "You're very tired," he said quietly. "You must go to bed and get a long night's sleep. I'm going home when I've drunk this."

"I'm not tired," she said. "It's just that it's a bit of a strain on all of us, with all this going on."

He smiled gently. "You've had three years of it," he remarked. "I think that's enough for anyone, but possibly I'm biased."

The girl said simply, "She's had thirty years of it, David."

"It's not always been like this, though, has it?" he remarked. "I mean, this is a specially bad time—this trouble with her ministers?"

She nodded. "I think it is. But the work's always been too heavy for one woman, David. Even in the easy times, the mass of State papers that she's got to read and sign, the mass of things she must attend to personally, the stupid social functions that she must attend. It's been too much for anyone, for the last hundred years. Ever since the Monarch became serious and responsible, he's been grossly overworked. It's nothing new, this thing." She paused. "Prince Albert died of overwork, Albert the Good. Victoria could only tackle it alone by withdrawing from society completely. Edward the Seventh and George the Fifth— they neither of them made old bones; they worked at their desks all day until they went to bed to die. George the Sixth worked himself to death, like Albert the Good. Elizabeth and Philip have had thirty years of it, longer than any of the others except Queen Victoria. They've stuck it out—they've been able to carry the job because they've worked together as a team, and they've done marvellously. But they can't carry it much longer. They're getting old now, David, old before their time."

There was a silence. "Well, what's the answer?" he

asked at last. "When she dies, will the Monarchy break up? Is she the last King or Queen of England?"

"Not if she can help it," the girl said. "You see, if that happened it would mean the end of the Commonwealth."

She got to her feet. "Don't let's talk any more tonight, David," she said. "I can't keep secrets from you, and I've got to keep them a bit longer. You do understand, don't you?"

He rose, and stood beside her. "Sure," he said. "It's time you went to bed. Will you sleep all right, with all this on your mind? I'll go out and get you something, if you'll take it."

She smiled. "I'll sleep all right. I've got some stuff to take if I can't, but I hardly ever use it. You've got to get a good night's rest yourself. You'll be up all tomorrow night, won't you, flying to Kenya?"

He nodded. "I'll be right. I've got a straight job with no worries, nothing to lose sleep over." He smiled down at her. "You're my only worry at the moment."

She reached out impulsively and took his hand. "Dear Nigger . . ." She smiled up at him. "It was very sweet of you to come this evening, and it was a lovely dinner."

He took her other hand and drew her to him; she relaxed into his arms and put her face up, and he kissed her. She stood for a few minutes nestling in his arms while he kissed her face and stroked her hair; then she withdrew a little. "We mustn't start doing this," she said quietly. "Not yet."

He smiled down at her. "It's a bit late to say that," he replied softly. "We've started."

"I know," she said. "But we mustn't go on."

His arm was still around her shoulders. "We can take it easy till things straighten out a bit," he replied. "But you won't forget this, and I won't either. We go on from here till we get married, and it can't be too soon for me."

260

"Dear Nigger . . ." she said again. And then she looked up into his face. "We won't wait any longer than we've got to. It may not be so long as I thought once."

"How long?"

"She may be in calm water in a few months' time," the girl said. "I could leave her then." And then she withdrew herself from his arms, and only held one of his hands. "You're making me talk again," she said. "I mustn't talk, David. Please."

He smiled at her. "I'm going to go away," he said, "and you must go to bed. Wish I was coming with you."

She laughed. "David! If you talk like that I'll think I'm not safe with you in the flat."

"No more you are," he said. "You're taking a great risk." He turned and picked up his uniform coat and cap. "It's girls like you," he said, "that make boys go wrong."

"We'll go wrong one day," she said, "when she's in calm water. I'll promise you that."

"That's a bet," he said. He bent and kissed her lightly on the cheek. "Good night, Rosemary."

She said softly, "Good night, David dear. Look after yourself on the way to Kenya."

He drove back to Maidenhead in his small sports car in a rosy dream, but not so far lost to the world that he was unmindful of her warning to be careful. He slept soundly in his bed, but by ten o'clock next morning he was back in London, in an office in Shell House, and closeted in privacy with the Chief Aviation Representative, a Mr. Corbett. To him he disclosed the fact in strictest confidence that he was leaving on a long flight that evening. "I want a couple of empty tank waggons down this afternoon, and an oil truck," he said. "I want every drop of fuel and oil pumped out of my Ceres and inspected by someone on your staff with some kind of a sample analysis. I don't want to find when I

switch on another tank that there's water or sugar or some
other damn stuff mixed up with the fuel, or the oil. Then
when you give it a clean bill, we'll pump it back again into
the aircraft." He paused. "And I don't want it talked
about."

Mr. Corbett raised his eyebrows. "I'll come down
myself."

The business took about three hours that afternoon; by
five o'clock the aircraft was refuelled and given a clean bill.
David had the whole crew at the hangar while this was going
on except the stewards; when the tank waggons had gone he
sent half of the crew away to get their luggage and stayed in
the machine with the other half; he was taking no chances.
At ten o'clock they pulled the Ceres from the hangar with
the tractor and ran each engine for a few minutes; while they
were doing this a closed van loaded with luggage arrived.
At a quarter to eleven the Princess Royal with the Duke and
their three children drove up, followed by another car with
nurse, maid, and valet. Frank Cox and David met them on
the tarmac and showed them into the machine; then Frank
Cox got out, the door closed, and David went forward to
his job.

It was a blustery, moist night on the ground, and they
entered cloud at about a thousand feet. They broke out of
the last layer at about sixteen thousand, and climbed up on
their course in the bright moonlight. Princess Anne came
forward to the cockpit with her husband for a few minutes
and talked to the pilots, but there was nothing to be seen but
the blue night and the bright moon and the cloud floor far
below, and presently they went aft to lie down.

They left the cloud behind as they passed southwards,
and at midnight they came to the Mediterranean and got a
glimpse of the lights of Genoa between the parting clouds.
At one-fifteen they crossed the end of Sicily somewhere

near Catania, and at two-fifteen they crossed the coast of Africa at Benghazi. At four-thirty their radio bearings showed Khartoum abeam and some three hundred miles to the west of them, and here they met the dawn, for they were flying to the south east. An hour later David started on the long let down, and at six-fifteen he picked up the black line of the airstrip on the north side of Mt. Kenya. He approached it cautiously in wide descending circuits, for he had never been there before, and at six-thirty-five by Greenwich time he touched his wheels down on the tarmac and taxied to the cars parked by the runway. On the ground it was nine o'clock in the morning, and the African sun was already hot.

He stood for a few minutes on the tarmac talking with the Princess Royal and her husband, and with the sleepy children only just awake. Then they got into their cars and were driven off towards Sagana and the Royal Residence, and the Australians were left to make their way on to Nairobi for refuelling, and thence to England. They accepted an invitation to breakfast from the local Police Commissioner who had it organised for them, and they showed a few local farmers and planters over the machine, including two negroes who spoke perfect English. Soon after eleven they took off for Nairobi, and put down there half an hour later.

They refuelled the machine and went to the hotel in which accommodation had been booked for them. By seven o'clock next morning, local time, they were in the air on their way back to England. They put down at White Waltham shortly after noon by Greenwich time, and David had the Ceres refuelled and inspected that same afternoon, Sunday December the 17th, and made ready for another flight. That evening he rang up Group Captain Cox, and reported readiness again.

263

To his surprise, he found Sugar in the hangar, back from Canada. During a pause in the work he asked Wing Commander Dewar what had brought him back.

"Brought the Governor-General," the Canadian said laconically.

"Tom Forrest?"

"Field-Marshal Sir Thomas Forrest to you," said the Canadian.

"What's he come back for?"

"He didn't tell me."

"Anyone come with him?"

"Nosey. No, he came alone. How did your trip go?"

"Just like that," said the Australian. "We got there, put some juice into the thing, and turned round and came back."

"Exciting, isn't it?" said the Canadian.

"Like hell. Give me Luna Park."

Later on, he talked privately to Dewar in the office. "I got the wire there may be trouble in this bloody country," he said. "There's just a possibility of sabotage on one or other of our aircraft. Seems like the Monarch's getting a bit too independent in her movements, with our aircraft here, to suit some of the Pommies." He told Dewar about his precautions with the fuel. "I'm worried about people getting in at night," he said. "There's only the one watchman."

The Canadian said, "Think some of us ought to be here nights?"

"I think we should. Run some kind of a guard."

"I'll row in while I'm here, with my boys," said Wing Commander Dewar. "I'm going back to Ottawa tomorrow, though. Seems like I've got to stand by there for quite a while. I'll keep half of my crew on guard tonight, though."

David thought for a moment. "Better not if you're flying

tomorrow. I'll keep half mine here, to watch the two machines. I'll fix up something better in the morning. Are you taking anybody over with you?"

The Canadian shook his head. "Going over empty, far as I know at present."

David stayed in the hangar that night with three of his crew, running a four hour watch with two awake on guard and two asleep in the flight deck of Tare. By eleven o'clock next morning he was in Australia House, waiting to see Vice-Admiral Sir Charles O'Keefe of the Royal Australian Navy. Charlie O'Keefe knew all about Nigger Anderson, and had flown with him once in the third war. He greeted him cordially, and offered him a cigarette.

The pilot said, "I'm in a bit of a spot, sir, and I can't say much about it, I'm afraid. What I want is a guard for my machine, in the hangar at White Waltham, and I don't want to ask the R.A.F. for it. The aircraft is Australian property. I was wondering if you could spare a party from one of the Australian ships over here."

"I see," said the Admiral. "How long do you want them for?"

"Till after Christmas," said the pilot. "Say about three weeks, to make it safe."

"*Gona*'s in Portsmouth dockyard till the middle of January. When do you want them?"

"This afternoon if I can have them, sir. I'm afraid I've got no accommodation, though."

"They can sling hammocks in your hangar?"

"Oh yes, they can do that."

"Can do. Two officers and fifty ratings be enough?"

"That's ample, sir."

"They'll be there this evening, Wing Commander. You don't have to say any more."

Three trucks full of sailors, rations, and hammocks turned

up at the hangar that afternoon, and took a load off David's mind. In the evening he drove over to the little Grace and Favour house that Frank Cox lived in on the edge of Windsor Great Park, and presented the *fait accompli* to his chief. "I hope you don't mind all these Australian sailors in the hangar, sir," he said. "You see, Tare's the property of the Australian Government, and I wasn't quite happy about things."

"I see," said the Group Captain quietly. "That's the line you're taking, is it? That they're just there to look after the property of the Australian Government?"

"That's right, sir. I hope you don't think I've been acting out of turn."

"Of course you have," the Group Captain said. "It's absolutely watertight." He paused, and then he said, "How did you get the idea that a guard might be a good thing?"

"I'm a very nosey person, sir," the pilot replied. "I'm not an English gentleman."

Frank Cox laughed. "An Aussie bastard is the right term, I believe."

"That's right," said the pilot equably. "I'm an Aussie bastard, so I've got a nose for what the other bastards may be up to."

He drank a tomato juice cocktail with his chief before starting back to Maidenhead. "Got anything to tell me about this other job?"

"Not yet."

"I suppose Tom Forrest will be going back to Ottawa some time. Will we be taking him?"

"You're fishing," said the Group Captain. "I don't know myself yet, Nigger, and if I did I wouldn't tell you or anybody else before it's necessary."

The pilot laughed. "Sorry. I wasn't fishing really. I'd like to take Tom Forrest somewhere."

With most Service men of that generation, he had a veneration for the Field-Marshal. Like Nigger Anderson himself, Tom Forrest had come up from the bottom. Tom Forrest was the son of a man who ran the boilers of a little laundry in Roundhay, a suburb to the north of Leeds. He was a Territorial week end soldier before the second war and rose to the rank of corporal in the first days of the war; by the end of it he was an acting brigadier. In 1946 he succeeded in staying in the Army with a permanent commission as a captain, and he entered the third war as a major. He came out of it as a lieutenant-general, and it is perhaps an indication of the quality of the man that all through his career, from laundry to general, he had been known to everybody as Tom Forrest. Such political opinions as he held were mildly socialist as would be expected from his origin, but he was the confidant of princes, and in particular he was a great friend of the Prince of Wales. In another sphere, he was liked and respected by most of the members of the Cabinet, and he was generally with Iorwerth Jones to watch the Cup Final at Wembley. He was now sixty-one years old and he had been Governor-General of Canada for about two years, a competent and a popular representative of the Queen in the Dominion.

That day was December the 18th, a week before Christmas. David drove back from Windsor in his little sports car, and deviated from his road home to Maidenhead to look in at the hangar at White Waltham aerodrome. A hundred yards from the hangar a naval sentry stopped him, a dark figure in a long blue coat with a white webbing belt, and David saw the rifle with fixed bayonet pointed at his chest. He was held there while a runner went to fetch the officer, to his intense pleasure. The sub-lieutenant came and released him, with apologies, and got told to do that every time.

Presently David found himself back in his little flat. He

cooked himself a scratch meal; in normal times he would have gone and had a meal at one of the hotels, but now he preferred to stay at home rather than risk contact with a possible reporter in a public place. When he had eaten and washed his few dishes, he settled down to read the papers for an hour before bed.

That day was a Monday, and he had taken Princess Anne to Kenya with her family on Friday night, too late for editorial comment in Saturday's Press. Monday's papers, which he was now reading, reflected a growing uneasiness about the movements of the Royal Family. It was right, said *The Times* that the family should make frequent visits to the Dominions and no doubt the clear air of Sagana would be good for little Alexandra's cough, but it would be regretted that circumstances prevented the reunion of the Monarch with her family for the festivities of Christmas; it would be the first time within living memory when the Royal Family had not been together in England at this season. Moreover, said *The Times*, there were certain dangers apart from the breach of precedent in too wide a dispersal of the Royal Family within the Commonwealth; it did not require a very vivid imagination to visualise a chain of events which could leave England with no Monarch and no heir in the country, and without even a Council of State.

The Recorder was more outspoken. It carried a banner headline right across the page, PRINCESS ROYAL TO KENYA. It followed with a factual account of the departure of the Princess with her family for the Royal Lodge at Sagana, and reminded its readers that the Prince and Princess of Wales had left for the Royal Residence at Gatineau a few days previously. The editorial was headed succinctly, HAPPY CHRISTMAS? It pointed out that the Prince of Wales and the Princess Royal preferred to spend Christmas in the Dominions rather than in England. No doubt, said *The Recorder*, many readers would agree with them, for after thirty-seven years of Socialist mis-rule England was no longer the happy place it once had been. Yet, said the leader, the hearts of all right thinking people would go out to the Queen, separated from her family at the time of the greatest festival of the Christian year. It would be a sad thing for England, said *The Recorder*, if it should come to pass that in future years the Royal Family should find themselves assembled at this joyous season in one of the Dominions, if the Christmas broadcast of the Queen should be delivered at the Royal Residence at Tharwa near Canberra, and recorded, and relayed to England at a suitable time distorted with howlings and half incomprehensible with static.

David laid down the paper thoughtfully, wondering if *The Recorder* had hit the bull's eye. It was very possible they had. He and his crew of Australians, and the aircraft, were at readiness to fly at any time, a fact that might well be known to the staff of *The Recorder*. It was difficult to keep a thing like that entirely secret from an experienced and skilled reporter. It would easily be possible for the Queen to get to Tharwa before Christmas, and Australia and New Zealand were now the only major countries owing her allegiance that had no member of the Royal Family in them. He sat for a long time, troubled and thoughtful, and then picked up *The Sun*.

The Sun at that time carried no leading articles, but merged its reporting with opinion. It printed a three column heading, WHAT'S THE MATTER WITH ENGLAND? It said that plain, honest working men could see no sense in gallivanting off to places like Canada and Kenya for Christmas. Let the Royal Family go to these places if they must, said *The Sun*, but the British working man would spend his Christmas in the way that suited

English people best, in the good fellowship of the village inn or in the happy relaxation of the cinema.

David dropped his eyes to the bottom of the page, to the strip cartoon of Jane, still in the throes of an adventure that had deprived her of most of her clothes.

That week was an uneasy week in England. Every visit to Buckingham Palace seemed to make the headlines, and the visitors were many, from the Archbishop of Canterbury to Tom Forrest, from Iorwerth Jones to Group Captain Cox. In general the leader writers kept silence, so that an impression was created in the country that something was about to happen, though nobody quite knew what it was likely to be. Gradually the rumour spread around that something serious was likely to be announced by the Queen in her Christmas broadcast speech. Nobody knew where this rumour had come from, but it was widely repeated, and added to the tension of the week.

On the Wednesday David began to be troubled by reporters, when a representative of *The Sun* called at his flat and asked if he had any statement to make about future journeys. He said he hadn't and referred his visitor to the Queen's Private Secretary, but when he went out to get his car from the garage to drive to White Waltham a photographer was waiting and took a number of pictures of him as he walked down the pavement and got into the car.

He rang up Rosemary that day, and dined with her at Mario's in Shepherd's Market in the evening. He found her looking white and exhausted, and decided at first sight of her to cut the dinner short and take her back to the flat directly they had dined. Because of her evident fatigue and strain he did not broach the subject of their job, but talked to her about boats and cruising grounds around the coast of England most of the time.

She said once, "I went home last night, just for a few hours."

He was surprised, for it was the middle of the week. "To Oxford?"

She nodded. "I shan't be able to get down there next week end, or for some time after that."

He nodded, thought for a minute, and then said, "Will we be together?"

She smiled at him. "I think so."

He smiled back at her. "Well, that's all right. Things might be a lot worse."

She found his hand and pressed it. "I know." And then she said, "You've not had any orders yet, Nigger?"

He shook his head. "So far as I've been told, we're here for the next six months."

She nodded, and then she said, "I hear you've got a lot of Australian sailors in the hangar guarding the machine."

He grinned at her cheerfully. "Somebody told me to be careful," he remarked. "I can't remember who it was."

She smiled. "We're a couple of busybodies, I suppose. But I'm glad you did it."

"Does the Consort know about it?"

She shook her head. "I don't think they know. Frank Cox told Macmahon, but I don't think he let it go any further. I think he was quite pleased you'd done it. It's one anxiety removed, at any rate."

They talked about other things, and presently she said, "Where will you be on Friday, Nigger?"

"At White Waltham," he replied. "I don't know that I'll be anywhere else."

She said, "My father's coming up on Friday. I *would* like you to meet him, and there may not be another chance."

"I want to meet him. What's he coming up for?"

"He's got a meeting with Tom Forrest on Friday. I think he's lunching with him at the Athenaeum."

"Does your father know Tom Forrest?"

"Daddy's met him once or twice. But he wants to meet Daddy now. Daddy's Professor of Political Economy, you know. He rang up Daddy, and so Daddy's coming up on Friday."

"I see." Wheels within wheels; was Rosemary's father mixed up in the English crisis? No business of his, however. "It's going to be difficult for me to get up here on Friday," he said, biting his lip. "I told Ryder he could have Friday evening off to go and see some friends in Hampstead. We can't both be up in London at the same time. When's your father going back?"

"He's got to get back to Oxford on Friday night."

The pilot sat in brooding thought for a minute. "I can't make it," he said at last. "I'm sorry, Rosemary. I'll have to be at home on Friday night, sitting at the telephone. I can't risk not being there if any orders come, with Ryder out that night."

"Of course not, Nigger." She paused, and then she said, "If I came down with Daddy by train to Maidenhead, could we have dinner in your flat?"

"Of course," he said. "Could you get off for that?"

"I think so," she replied. "I do want you to meet him before we go."

He did not care to pick her up upon her indiscretion. "I could get one of the boys to drive him on to Oxford in my car after dinner," he said, "and bring the car back. He could drive you to the station, too, to get a train back here. But it's an awful bind for you, at such a time as this."

"I'd like to do it," she replied. "It 'ld make a bit of a change."

He took her back to her flat after dinner, and helped her

out of the small car on to the pavement in Dover Street. She asked if he would like to come up for a little, but she was obviously tired, and he refused. He kissed her in the darkness of the doorway and said good night, and she opened the door with her latch-key.

"Good night, Nigger darling."

"Good night, Rosemary. Sleep tight."

The uneasy days went by, and at ten minutes to seven on Friday night David stood in the cold, windy darkness upon the platform of Maidenhead station, waiting for the electric train from Paddington. It came in with a glow of lights and a sighing of pneumatic brakes, and he stood by the ticket collector watching for Rosemary with her father. She was not there, but an elderly man in an old raincoat and a battered felt hat stopped by him. "It's Wing Commander Anderson?"

He glanced sharply at the man, and saw her features in his face. "That's right," he said. "Are you Professor Long?"

"That's right. Rosemary said I was to tell you that she's got to go back to the Palace tonight. So I thought I'd better come and meet you, anyway. We may not have another chance for some time. I knew you by the colour of the uniform, of course."

David said something or other in reply, and guided Rosemary's father to the car. As they drove the short distance to his flat he said, "I'm sorry she's got to work tonight. She's working much too hard."

"Ah well," her father said, "it's not much longer now." The pilot did not answer that.

In the flat he gave Professor Long a glass of sherry, and with his own tomato cocktail in his hand he turned to face him. "In a way, I'm glad you've come alone this evening," he said. "We'll probably be able to talk more freely. Did Rosemary tell you that we want to get married?"

The older man smiled. "She did say something about it."

The pilot said directly, "Did she tell you that I'm not pure white? That I'm a quadroon?"

"She did."

"What do you think about that, sir?"

The professor shrugged his shoulders. "I've got a lot of more important things to think about than that. To start with, have you ever been married before?"

"No. I never came within a mile of it. It's not so easy when you've got a touch of colour."

The other smiled. "You've started on the awkward subjects, so we may as well clear the decks of all of them." He asked two further questions, and the pilot grinned, and answered them. "Well, that just leaves the colour. I think that's Rosemary's affair and nobody else's."

"You wouldn't mind about it very much, yourself? I'd rather know now if you take a strong view about boongs."

"Boongs?"

"Coloured people. It's a word we use up in North Queensland, where I come from."

"I see. I think the view I take is this: that if you're regarded as suitable to serve the Queen as intimately as you do, you're suitable to be my son-in-law, if Rosemary wants to marry you. That covers it, so far as I'm concerned."

David had got Jim Hansen, the Australian steward from Tare, to come in and serve the dinner; he sat down with Rosemary's father to a dinner of clear soup, English chicken, Australian ham, and a fruit salad of mangoes and pawpaw and fresh apricots from Kenya served with Australian cream and sugar. Sitting over coffee at the conclusion of the meal, when the steward had left the room, the older man said, "You've had no orders yet?"

The pilot shook his head.

"I think I'd better tell you what I told Rosemary this afternoon," her father said. "These are difficult times, and she's mixed up in great affairs. I told her that if she finds herself in some far country where she feels she has to stay for months, or even for years, and if she wants to marry while she's out there, she mustn't let thoughts of her mother and myself stand in her way. Naturally, we should like to see her married. But if that's not possible, she mustn't hold up anything on our account. Rosemary's got her own life to lead, and if she wants to marry while she's out there, she'll have our blessing."

David said, "It's very good of you to take that line about it, sir."

He asked David one or two questions about his education and his early life and they talked about North Queensland. "Rosemary told us most of this," the older man said once. "I shall be sorry for our own sakes if she makes her life in Australia, because my wife and I are English. We shall never leave Oxford. But in another way, I think she may be doing the right thing. She's had a hand in great affairs as a young woman. If she goes to Australia with you, she's going to the coming centre of the Commonwealth, where all the great affairs will happen in the future, and before she's old."

David glanced at him curiously. "You think that, do you, sir? You think Australia will be the centre of the Commonwealth in years to come?"

"I do. What's the population of Australia now?"

"About twenty-seven million, I think. It's changing pretty rapidly. It was twenty-three million at the last census, but that's some time ago."

The don nodded. "That's about right. And what do you think it will be, ultimately?"

275

"It's hard to say," David replied. "It's all a matter of the water, I think. When I was a boy people were still saying that twenty-five million was the limit. But in my lifetime the Snowy irrigation scheme has been completed, and the Burdekin, and half a dozen others, and now they've got this nuclear distillation of sea water in the North, around Rum Jungle, and that's getting cheaper and cheaper. People are saying now that the limit may be fifty millions, but others say a hundred and fifty millions."

The professor said, "Whether it's fifty millions or a hundred and fifty doesn't matter much. England can feed thirty millions, and when the population of this country gets down to that figure things will suddenly improve, and England will be a happy and prosperous country again. But your country will always have the advantage of population, and the great advantage of strategic safety. And on top of that, you've got a system of democracy that works."

"You mean, the multiple vote?"

The older man nodded. "How many votes have you got?"

"Me?" asked the pilot. "I'm a three vote man."

"Basic and education?" David nodded. "What's the third?"

"Living abroad," the pilot said. "I got that for the war."

There was a short pause. "If everybody of your type in England had three votes instead of one," the don said heavily, "there'd be no question of a Governor-General."

David sat silent. So that was what was in the wind. There was to be a Governor-General in England as in all the other Dominions, a buffer between the elected politicians and the Queen, selected by the Queen for his ability to get on with the politicians of the day while serving her. Somebody who could take the day to day hack work of Royalty off her, who could open the Town Halls and lay the foundation stones and hold the Levees and the Courts and the Garden Parties, and leave the Monarch free for the real work of governing the Commonwealth. And as he sat there pondering this information, the pieces of the puzzle fell together in his mind. Tom Forrest was the man chosen to be the first Governor-General of England, Tom Forrest who had worked his way up from the bottom, Tom Forrest who was honoured and respected as the soldier who had led the British people to victory in the last war, who had been Governor-General in Canada for the last two years, who was a friend of the Prince of Wales. And at that thought, another piece of the puzzle fell into its place; with Tom Forrest or somebody like him between the Monarch and Iorwerth Jones, perhaps the succession would be less distasteful to Prince Charles. Perhaps that was what Rosemary's father meant. Perhaps a Governor-General in England was a condition that the heirs to the Throne had made, as an alternative to abdication. Perhaps the row over White Waltham aerodrome had been the last straw laid upon Prince Charles by the Prime Minister; perhaps it had even been intended to be so. Perhaps David had flown Prince Charles to Canada to speak both for his sister and himself, to tell their mother that they would not have the job.

All this passed through his mind in a few seconds while Rosemary's father sat in thought before the fire, heedless of his indiscretion, or perhaps thinking that the pilot must already have heard about the changes that were to be made. "One man one vote has never really worked," he said quietly. "It came in at a time of liberal social awakening in the middle of the nineteenth century. The governing elements in this country leaned over backwards to redress

277

the wrongs that previous generations of their class had wrought upon the common man, and they made all men equal in deciding the affairs of the country, relying on the veto power of the House of Lords to put a curb on irresponsible elected politicians. The thing looked promising for a time, while the educated and travelled members of the House of Lords still held the veto. But they never reformed the House of Lords, so in the end that restraint had to go, and then the system ceased to work at all."

He turned to David. "I doubt if history can show, in any country, at any time, a more greedy form of government than democracy as practised in Great Britain in the last fifty years," he said. "The common man has held the voting power, and the common man has voted consistently to increase his own standard of living, regardless of the long term interests of his children, regardless of the wider interests of his country." He paused. "When I was a young man we lost the Persian oilfields and the Abadan refinery," he said. "In the last year of operation of that company the shareholders took four million pounds out of the profits, the Persian Government were given sixteen millions, and the British Government took fifty-four millions in taxation. The Persian Government revolted, and we lost the entire industry, refinery, oil rights, and all, because we were too greedy. Since then it has been the same melancholy story, over and over again. No despot, no autocratic monarch in his pride and greed has injured England so much as the common man. Every penny that could be wrung out of the nation has been devoted to raising the standard of living of the least competent elements in the country, who have held the voting power. No money has been left for generous actions by Great Britain, or for overseas investment, or for the re-equipment of our industry at home, and the politicians who have come to power through this system of voting

278

have been irresponsible and ill-informed, on both sides of the House."

He paused. "You people in the Antipodes have been wiser. Perhaps it was easier for you, by reason of your economic situation. But until this country follows your example once again, as they followed it in instituting the secret ballot and in giving votes to women, I cannot see a very satisfactory future here."

He knocked his pipe out. "I should be getting back to Oxford," he said. "I wanted to talk to you about these things a little, because it is because of them that I am reconciled to Rosemary going to Australia, and marrying there if she should decide she wants to do so. I think your country it on the right road to greatness. I don't think this one is."

He got to his feet, and David got up with him. "Is this what you've been telling Tom Forrest, sir?" the pilot asked.

The don smiled. "More or less," he said. "More or less. When one holds certain prejudices very strongly one is apt to shoot them off at everyone one meets. Especially as one gets older."

David lifted the telephone and rang Flight Sergeant Syme, who was to drive the professor back to Oxford in David's car. And while they were waiting for the car they talked of minor matters. "I should have got in touch with you earlier," the pilot said. "I should have met Rosemary's mother. But things have been a little difficult in the last week or two, and now it looks as if I shall be off again quite soon."

The older man said, "Never mind. In your appointment you will probably be back in England in a month or so, before Rosemary, and you can come and see us then."

The car came, and David went down to the street and saw the professor off to Oxford. He went back to his empty flat and stood before the dying fire for a long time, conning over what he had learned and speculating upon what it meant to him. If the Queen were to announce the appointment of Tom Forrest as Governor-General in England, it meant that she would leave England herself almost immediately; she would hardly remain in the country after the appointment. In the year that he had been in England he had learned sufficient of the temper of the country to realise that the shock would be immense. That, then, was why Rosemary had told him to be very, very careful—and another piece of the puzzle fell into its place. Rosemary, of course, knew everything that was going on. She must have known of this for weeks and weeks, perhaps even when they were in Ottawa. No wonder she was looking white and strained.

The shock to the British people would be immense. Under that shock, a few small sections of the people might well lose their heads, behave wildly and do foolish things. There would be sections of the British people who would turn against the Commonwealth, the Commonwealth that had seduced their Queen away. Strong hatreds would arise, and ugly things might happen. The distinctive Australian Air Force uniform might prove a liability; an Australian aeroplane might be exposed to sabotage. He knew that in a week or so England would settle down and would regain her traditional balance, but anything might happen in the first few days. These overworked and undernourished people were in no condition to think clearly and objectively under a great shock.

He thanked God for the warning Rosemary had given him, for the wisdom of the Australian naval officer that had given him the sailors as a guard for the machine against a danger that he had not understood himself and that he could not have explained. His duty was to keep the aircraft safe and efficient, with its crew, ready to take the Queen wherever she wished to go. But as he stood there by the dying fire, his sympathies were with the British; did ever a people have the wind so strongly in their face? For forty years they had battled for existence in a world adverse to the economy by which their nation had been built up. They had battled on tenaciously, closing their ranks and pulling together in the Socialism suited to their hard and bitter struggle. They had made mistakes—what nation does not?—but they had performed prodigies of skill and production which had served only to reduce the pace of their decline and make it manageable. Now as a reward, their Queen was withdrawing from them a little, that the dynasty might continue and the Commonwealth be held together. Poor, badly used British people! Poor, harassed, anxious Queen!

He shook himself, and went to bed, troubled and depressed. It was his duty to protect himself, his crew, and his machine against anything that the British might do in the first angry shock. But now, whatever they might do, he felt he would be sorry for them.

Next day was Saturday, the day before Christmas Eve. Normally he would have given the crew Saturday and Sunday off, but he had arranged to have them at the hangar that week end. He was at the hangar as usual at half past eight; at ten o'clock he got a telephone call from Frank Cox asking him to come to London, to St. James's Palace.

He went into the office in Engine Court an hour later. Frank Cox was waiting for him, and he closed the door carefully behind the Australian. "They're leaving for Canberra on the evening of Christmas Day, Nigger," he said. "Is that going to be all right with you?"

The pilot nodded; everything that he had heard in the last few days had led him to expect this. "We'll be right," he said. "What time do they want to go?"

"What time is best for them?"

"Any time would suit us," David replied. "Do they want to stop in Colombo?"

"Not this time," said the Group Captain. "They owe Ceylon a visit, and they're planning to go there for a fortnight or three weeks in February. But she's altogether too tired now for that. She wants to go straight through to Tharwa and rest there for a time."

The Australian nodded. "Allowing an hour for refuelling at Ratmalana, if we took off at nine o'clock, after they've had dinner, we'd get to Canberra about four in the morning. I told her that once before, and it's probably the most restful way for her to tackle it. But we can take it any way she likes."

Frank Cox said, "She's doing her broadcast at three in the afternoon, as usual. She's going to speak for about twenty minutes. Philip wants to get her away fairly soon after that. Not immediately, but fairly soon. How would take off at six o'clock suit you?"

"Suit me all right," the pilot said. "We'd refuel at Ratmalana about breakfast time and get to Canberra about one in the morning. It would be dark then, of course. We couldn't have the fighter escort that they like to give her."

"She doesn't want it, Nigger. Not this time. She doesn't want any ceremonial at all. She's a very tired woman."

David nodded. "It might be rather a good thing for us to put down at one in the morning," he remarked. "Not many people will turn out at Fairbairn in the middle of the night."

"No. I'm seeing Philip this afternoon, and I'll suggest take off at six o'clock on Christmas evening. Now, how little notice do you have to give your crew?"

"How little?"

"Yes, for security. It's very important that nothing of this should leak out before."

The pilot stood in thought for a minute. "I'd like to have Shell check our fuel again before the flight," he said. "Pump it all out and pump it in again, like they did before. If they start on that on Christmas morning they'll be finished by dinner. I could warn the crew then, and send them back to get their gear. That's enough notice for them." He paused. "There's the food, of course."

"I'll see to the food." The Group Captain stood in thought for a minute. "Too bad if anything happened to the crew," he said. "Could you send them all round together in a truck, with two or three of your Australian ratings with them? Let them go to each man's lodgings in turn?"

David nodded. "I'll think up something on those lines. Leave it with me, sir. I'll have the machine and the crew in readiness for take off at six o'clock. We don't have to tell them before dinner time." He paused. "Luggage at about five-thirty?"

Frank Cox nodded. "I'll be having the whole party assemble at the Palace with their luggage. Send it all down together."

"How many in the party?"

"Identical with the last Canberra trip. Eight persons and myself."

"Miss Long coming this time?" He could not resist that.

"Oh yes—she's coming."

They talked for a little longer about the practical details of the flight, and then David took his leave. As he was going out of the door, Frank Cox said, "Oh by the way—have you seen *The Sun*?"

"No."

The Group Captain turned to his desk, and opened the paper in the middle. There was a very large picture of

283

David, looking rather annoyed, striding down a Maidenhead pavement to fetch his car. Underneath was the caption, "WHERE WOULD HE BE GOING TO? Wing Commander Anderson R.A.A.F. of the Queen's Flight."

David looked at it in silence for a minute. "Not much secrecy about our movements now," he said.

"I know," said Frank Cox wearily. "But we've got to go through the motions."

In Engine Court David hesitated, irresolute, wondering whether to ring up Rosemary and try to make a date with her for dinner. In the end he decided to leave her alone; with only two days to go she would be working at top pitch and an interlude with him would only upset her at a time when she could not afford to be upset. He took a taxi from the bottom of St. James's to Shell House and found an official in the Aviation department keeping watch over the holiday, and through him he arranged for the work down at White Waltham upon Christmas morning.

He drove down to the aerodrome and warned the crew for a day-long inspection of the aircraft on Sunday. That day they worked from morning till evening, Christmas Eve, and found nothing wrong. They left the Ceres all night guarded by the sailors, and on Christmas morning they returned for the work of emptying the fuel, analysing it, and refuelling.

At midday the Shell employees drove away in their empty tank waggons to a belated Christmas Day, and David assembled his crew in the fuselage of the aircraft, with the door shut. "We're going home this evening, boys," he said. "Take off at six o'clock, with the Queen on board, via Ratmalana." He told them of the arrangements he had made for them to collect their gear. "I want the truck back here by a quarter to three, and after that nobody's to leave the hangar."

Flight Sergeant Syme said, "Can we listen to the Queen speaking, Cap?"

He nodded. "There's a radio in the office. We'll listen to it all together there."

That afternoon they assembled in the bare, utilitarian little office in the hangar, seven young men and one girl, in the dark blue uniforms of the Royal Australian Air Force. Outside the office, the silver bulk of the Ceres loomed immensely, fuelled and ready for flight. The young men stood or sat upon the edge of tables, grave and serious, aware that they were to hear something very important, not knowing what it was.

The radio boomed out the striking of Big Ben, the announcement was made, and the familiar voice began to speak to them, stumbling a little now and then from sheer fatigue.

By the time she had finished, Gillian Foster was in tears.

Nine

AT five o'clock they pulled the Ceres out of the hangar with the tractor, swung her round, and ran the engines. They shut down after a short trial, satisfied that everything was in order, and David sat on in the pilot's seat for a time, his mind running over the machine searching for anything that might have been neglected, any inspection that had been left undone. Below upon the tarmac the Australian sailors had been thrown round the machine in a cordon, to prevent anybody from approaching it in the darkness.

An airline bus from B.O.A.C. came to the hangar presently, a device adopted by Frank Cox to avoid notice. He was travelling in it himself with all the passengers except the Queen and the Consort, and with all the luggage. David went down to meet them, and watched Ryder as he superintended the loading of the suitcases into the aircraft. He said a word or two to Dr. Mitchison and to Macmahon, and suggested that they get into the aircraft out of the cold wind. Then he turned to Rosemary.

"You'd better get in, too," he said. "You're looking very tired."

She said, "I'd like to stay out here for a few minutes. It's fresh here. I've been cooped up in the office for so long." She paused, and then she said, "You heard the broadcast?"

"We heard it all together in the hangar here," he said. "It was very moving."

"Was it a surprise to you?" she asked.

He shook his head. "I knew more or less what was coming. I don't think any of the boys did, though."

"How did they take it?"

"You mean, about Tom Forrest? They thought it was a grand idea. But they're Australians, you see, and we're used to having a Governor-General. I don't think it matters how they took it. It's how the British are going to take it that's the important thing."

"I know." She stood for a minute bareheaded, letting the clean, cold air blow through her hair, refreshing her. "I believe the people of England are adult enough now to realise that it's necessary," she said. "They certainly weren't when she came to the throne, thirty years ago. Daddy says they've changed a great deal in her reign, since he was a young man."

"It was a marvellous speech," he said. "Who wrote it for her?"

She sighed. "Everybody," she replied wearily. "Lord Marlow wrote one and the Consort wrote another. And then Tom Forrest had a talk to Daddy, and he sent in one that was practically pure Daddy—every word of it. Major Macmahon had a go at putting them all together for her, and then old Sir Robert Menzies wrote her about three thousand words from Melbourne, some of it quite good. We've been working at it for a fortnight, Nigger. I must have typed it fifteen or twenty times. I've woken up in the middle of the night, over and over again, and found myself repeating bits of it."

He pressed her hand in the darkness, and she smiled up at him. "It's over now," he said. "It's a marvel that such a fine speech could be made up out of so many bits and pieces."

287

"It wasn't," she replied. "She scrapped the whole lot on Sunday morning, and sat down, and wrote it in her own words, in her own handwriting. After that, she wouldn't let anybody change a thing. I typed it out from what she wrote on eleven quarto sheets of notepaper, and there wasn't an alteration or an erasure in the whole of it."

They stood there in the darkness, hand in hand. "You were right about Tharwa," he said presently. "Right about it being kept open, I mean. She'll only have been away about three weeks."

"I know. It's better for her to be out of England now, and see what boils up under Tom Forrest. Some of the Labour back-benchers will be furious."

"With her?"

She looked up quickly. "Oh—no. With the Government. With Iorwerth Jones." She paused. "A good bit of it leaked out yesterday, and there was a lot going on behind the scenes. But it was too late then."

"I see . . ." He knew too little of the British political scene to venture any comment. All he said was, "Tom Forrest 'll have quite a bit to do."

She nodded. "*He* won't care. He's speaking on the radio on Wednesday night."

"Do you know what he's going to say?"

She shook her head. "If he says all that he put into her draft speech, he'll start something. And he's quite capable of doing it. He's a fan of Daddy's."

A chilly December wind blew in a sharp gust round about them, and she drew a little closer to him. "You ought to get inside," he said gently. "You're very tired, and you'll catch a cold if you stay out in this. When you get out of the machine it will be warm and sunny, with all the flowers out. Remember the courtyard of the Canberra Hotel?"

She nodded. "I hate leaving England," she said in a low

tone, and he bent to catch her words. "But this is an end to all the backward glances and irresolutions. This is the end of something that began in 1867, when a lot of generous idealists gave one vote to every man."

He led her to the aircraft and up the steps into the cabin, and Gillian Foster took charge of her and took her to her seat. David went down again on to the tarmac and glanced at his watch; ten minutes to go before the Royal car was due. He walked underneath the engines, vaguely uneasy, and stood looking up at each of them in turn. It was quite unusual for him to have the needle before a flight; he had flown so often and so far that he was long past that. Everything had been inspected and everything was right, but he was troubled by an anticipation of danger. The tyres, perhaps. He walked over to the great wheels and passed his hand over the treads, from the ground in front to the ground behind, standing upon tiptoe to reach the topmost point. The tyres were perfect, as with his intellect he had known they were. And still he had the sense of danger strong upon him.

He walked over to the gangway where Frank Cox was waiting for the Queen, and stood with him. Exactly at six o'clock the lights of the big Daimler appeared upon the road outside. It stopped at the sentry post where the naval officers were waiting for it, and then came on, and drew up by the aircraft. The two officers stood at the salute as the Queen and the Consort stepped out.

The Queen said good evening to them, and walked to the gangway; Frank Cox escorted her up into the aircraft. The Consort stopped for a moment and spoke to David. "Where did all these naval officers and ratings come from?" he enquired.

"They're from H.M.A.S. *Gona*, sir. She's in Portsmouth now."

"Did you produce them?"

"I asked Vice-Admiral O'Keefe for them. They've been here a fortnight."

"They're all Australians, are they?"

"Yes, sir."

"I see. Perhaps that was wise. Thank you, Wing Commander."

He went up the steps into the machine, and David followed him. Jim Hansen, the steward, closed the door behind them, and David went forward to the cockpit to join Ryder. Frank Cox came forward in a minute. "Take off in your own time, Captain." David nodded, and started the inboard engines.

Ten minutes later they were on the climb, heading rather to the east of south upon a course for Cyprus. They flew through layer after layer of cloud in the darkness, till finally they broke out into moonlight and clear skies at about twenty-two thousand feet over northern France. The pilot sat motionless at the controls as the machine climbed higher, still troubled and uneasy in his mind, with the sense of danger strong upon him still. He was one quarter Aboriginal, not wholly of a European stock, and in some directions his perceptions and his sensibilities were stronger than in ordinary men, which possibly accounted for his excellence in flying and for his safety record. That evening he sat at the controls with the unease growing stronger in him every minute, and when at last they reached their operating height and levelled off to cruise, somewhere in the vicinity of Lake Constance, he handed over the control to Ryder, and went aft.

In the flight deck everything was normal. He stopped by the flight engineer's table and peered at the instruments himself, and read the flight log carefully. There was nothing there. He sat down by the radio operator and looked through his log, and peered at the green traces on the cathode tubes, and checked a position on the Decca apparatus. There was nothing there. He passed into the cabin and walked slowly down the length of it, looking for a cracked window perhaps that would release the pressure, or for some danger of fire, but everything was in order. The steward and the stewardess were serving dinner; the Queen was in her cabin with the door closed. He stopped Gillian Foster and nodded to the door. "Everything all right in there?"

The girl said, "Quite all right, sir."

"Had her dinner?"

"Yes, sir."

"Eat it?"

"Oh yes, she ate it nearly all. She had a glass of claret, too."

He passed on down the gangway between the seats. Rosemary looked up at him and smiled, but he hardly saw her. There was something, somewhere, something very wrong. His eyes searched everywhere, the ventilators for some issue of smoke, the door latches, the carpets on the floor. He stopped and sniffed keenly for a trace of kerosene, but only smelt good cooking.

Jim Hansen was in the galley. He said, "Everything all right here?"

"We could do with a bigger stove, Cap," said the man. "It's not so easy serving a hot dinner with just the one hot plate and the oven. Think we could get a bigger stove put in?"

He said something absent minded, and went on. Both toilets were vacant, and he looked into each of them, but there was nothing there. He went aft again into the luggage compartment and stood looking at the piled suitcases in the bins, strapped down with webbing straps. Everything

K*

seemed in order, but there was something very, very wrong.

The luggage was one thing he had not checked, and nobody had checked of his own crew. He would not rest, he knew, until he had satisfied himself that that was all in order. He pulled a notebook and a pencil from his inner breast pocket, and went forward to the cockpit again, to Ryder at the controls. "How many ports have you got on board, Harry?"

"Two suitcases and a haversack. What's this about?"

"Just making a check up. Are they labelled with your name?"

"The suitcases are. The haversack is in the top bunk there."

He passed on down the aircraft from bow to stern, listing the names of everyone on board with their luggage. He did not disturb the Queen or the Consort, but he got the list of their luggage from the maid and the valet. When he came to Frank Cox, the Group Captain asked, "What's this for, Nigger?"

"I want to count it all up," the pilot said. "I'm not comfortable about this flight. I've got the heebie-geebies."

Frank Cox glanced quickly up at him, and got out of his seat. There only remained the steward and the stewardess to question, and the pilot turned again to the luggage compartment. "Give me a hand," he said to the steward. "I want to check the cases off against this list."

The Group Captain followed them into the luggage compartment and the three of them began to unlash and to sort out the luggage.

A quarter of an hour later they came on a discrepancy. There were four cases labelled E. C. Mitchison, as against three on the list.

"Doctor's made a mistake," said Jim Hansen cheerfully. "He's got four instead of three."

The pilot said, "Slip up and ask him to come down here and identify them."

When the doctor came, David asked, "Are those your four cases?"

"That's not mine," said Mitchison. "Not the green one. The other three are mine."

"It's got your name on it." They showed him the label.

"I'm sure it's not mine," he said. "I only brought the three. I've never seen that before."

David picked it up, laid it on the floor of the gangway, and stooped to undo it. He found it locked. He thought for a moment, and then went forward into the cabin. Over the entrance door there hung a steel bar with flattened ends; the sort of thing used to open packing cases. It was painted red, and it was there for the purpose of opening the door from the inside if it should be jammed tight in its frame by the distortion of the fuselage in a crash.

He pulled this out of its clips, and went back to the suitcase. With two vigorous heaves he broke the hasp, and lifted back the lid. Inside he saw a bundle of sacking. He felt a hard object wrapped up in it. Gently he unwrapped this object, moving it as little as possible, and took it very carefully in his hands, while the others crowded near to see.

It was a metal box, apparently of heavy gauge brass with soldered joints. It was about twelve inches long, eight or nine wide, and about five inches deep. It weighed twelve or fifteen pounds.

Very carefully he lifted it above his head, and looked beneath it. There was no apparent opening, no lid. It seemed to have been soldered solidly together, and not designed to be opened at all.

Very carefully he put it down upon the sacking in the open suitcase.

Frank Cox said quietly, "We'll have to get rid of that, Nigger."

The pilot stood silent for an instant. "We'll have to go down," he replied. "We can't jettison out of the pressure shell. We'll have to go down to seven or eight thousand feet. The Queen." He could not risk giving the Queen the diver's bends by opening the pressure hull at any greater altitude than that.

"How long will it take you to get down?"

"Seventeen or eighteen minutes." The pilot turned, and went forward swiftly to the flight deck, and spoke quickly to the startled engineer and to Ryder at the controls. The inboard engines died, but the outer engines were kept going at reduced revs to maintain the cabin pressure. The air-brakes on the top surface of the wing crept out, the nose went down a little, and the Ceres steadied at a rate of descent of three thousand feet a minute.

David went quickly to the navigator's table and looked at the map, and while he did so the radio operator gave him a new fix by Decca. They were about a hundred miles south west of Belgrade, and over the Jugoslav mountain ranges with peaks up to ten thousand feet. He laid off a quick course towards the Adriatic and the Ionian Sea, passing over Brindisi in Italy. He said to Ryder, "Steer two hundred true," and watched to see the aircraft steady on that course. He turned, and Frank Cox was beside him.

David put a finger on the chart between the toe of Italy and Greece. "We'll drop it somewhere here, if the bloody thing doesn't go off first."

The Group Captain said, "It's not making any noise, so it's not a time clock. I can't see any breathing holes in it, so it's probably not a barometric fuse. I think it's probably an

294

acid fuse, acid eating through a strip of metal of some sort. If that's so, it'll be pretty far gone, and we'll want to be careful how we move it. Think we'd better land at Brindisi or Bari?"

The pilot hesitated. "I've moved it once, and it's not gone off," he said. "I'm quite game to put it out of the machine myself."

"Where would you put it out?"

"Put down the undercarriage and take off the inspection cover for the forward oleo leg," he said. "It'll fall clear of the machine from there, behind the front wheel." He paused. "We can land at Brindisi," he said. "I've been there before. There's a long runway roughly east and west. I think it's lit."

Frank Cox bit his lip. "There's the publicity . . ."

"I know. We'll have to make our minds up pretty quick." It would be in the newspapers all around the world, that the Queen of England had had to land in Italy to remove a bomb from her aircraft. "I'm quite prepared to drop it out myself," he said again.

"I can't decide this," said the Group Captain. "I'll have to ask the Consort. I think we ought to land."

He hurried aft, and David turned quickly to his list of aerodromes along the route. Brindisi was lit upon request for night landings, and was habitually used by the Italian Air Force. He called the second engineer, who was already out of his bunk, and went down with him to the forward luggage hold, now empty, to the inspection plate above the undercarriage leg. "Loosen up these studs," he said. "Be ready to open up this pretty quick when I tell you, after I've put the undercarriage down. I may want to drop something out."

He went back to the flight deck; they were now down to about twenty thousand feet in clear air; ahead of them a little starry cluster of lights showed upon the land, which must be Brindisi. He turned to meet Frank Cox. "She won't have it," the Group Captain said. "She won't land. We've got to put it out of the machine over the sea."

David nodded. "I've got Cummings ready to take off the plate, down in the forward hold," he said. "If you'll go down there, I'll go aft and fetch it along." He grinned. "Keep our fingers crossed."

He turned to Ryder. "Steer south now, one eight zero true. You'll come out over sea again in a couple of minutes. Go on down like this, and level out at seven thousand feet. Then decompress. Then reduce speed to two hundred knots and flaps half down. Then lower the undercarriage. Carry on like that until I tell you."

The second pilot repeated the instructions, and David went quickly aft through the saloon to the luggage bay. Jim Hansen was still there standing guard over the suitcase. He was very white, and David grinned at him. "We'll get rid of this thing pretty soon, now," he said.

"I've been saying me prayers, sir," the lad remarked.

"Well, keep on saying them for about five minutes longer." The pilot stopped, and took the metal case in both his hands, wondering if this was the end of it for all of them. He raised it to the level of his waist, and turned, and walked forward into the saloon, and up between the lines of seats. As he passed Rosemary, he heard her say softly, "Good luck, Nigger."

He came to the cabins, and the Queen was standing at her door with the Consort at her side; she was in a white, flowered dressing gown. She said, "Is that it, Commander?"

He paused for a moment. "That's it, madam. We'll be rid of it in a few minutes now."

She said quietly, "I am so very sorry for you all. This

wouldn't have happened if I hadn't been on board."

He left her, and went forward walking very carefully; although if it went off in any part of the machine it would mean certain death for all of them, it seemed to him to be important to remove it from the Queen as far as possible. The forward hold was reached by a hatch in the flight deck under the engineer's seat covered by a hinged duralumin flap, now open. Below were two ladder rungs on the side of the aircraft and then the floor of the hold, with not more than four foot six of headroom. The radio officer came forward and offered to hold the thing for him as he went down. David made him sit upon the floor and put it in his hands, and went down through the hole, and standing on the floor below reached up and took it from him. The boy went back to his desk, streaming with sweat.

Crouched down by the inspection plate were the Group Captain and the engineer, Cummings. David moved very cautiously towards them in the dim light, stooping almost double, terrified of stumbling or hitting his head against some unseen beam and dropping the box. He knelt down beside them with it still unshaken in his hands, and said, "Well, here we are. What's the betting the bloody thing goes off before we get it out?"

"Five to one on," said Cummings.

The Group Captain said, "What's our altitude now?"

"I don't know," said David. "We must be pretty well down. I didn't stop to ask."

They waited, tense and motionless as the minutes crept by. It would be bad luck, thought David, if the thing went off now . . . His wrists ached with holding it. When suddenly the attitude of the machine began to alter and a change in the whisper of the air told that she was slowing down, it came almost as a surprise. He glanced at Cox, and met his eyes.

"Levelling out," said the Group Captain.

The pilot nodded. He knelt by the inspection plate noting the phases of the manoeuvre, the hydraulic whistle as the airbrakes went in, and then the groaning of the flap motor as the flaps went down. Finally came the action they were waiting for, the clank and hiss immediately beneath their feet as the undercarriage fell, and the shock as it was locked in place. In the semi-darkness David said to Cummings, "Get that plate off now."

The engineer worked methodically, removing the studs one by one and putting them with the washers into the breast pocket of his overall. He hummed a little tune about love as he worked. Finally the last stud was removed, and he freed the plate.

A great rush of air came upwards through the hole, as solid as a wall. It beat about them in the narrow space, insensate; David was forced backwards, still holding the metal case desperately horizontal. In the roar of the entering air he signed to Cummings to put the cover back. The engineer laid the plate beside the hole and slid it forward with the weight of his body on it and, half sitting and half lying on the plate with Frank Cox helping him, he got half a dozen of the studs back into place. The bay seemed strangely quiet after that blast of air.

The Group Captain said, "We'll never get it out through that, Nigger. It wouldn't fall."

The pilot knelt in thought. "I wonder where the hell that air was going to?" he said. And then it came to him that after decompressing perhaps Ryder had opened the cockpit window at his side, because air coming into the machine must be going out somewhere. He mentioned this to Cox, and then he said, "If I shut this hatch above us, and see everything battened down, and stall her—could you get it out then, sir?" In stalling, the machine would be poised momentarily at barely a hundred knots, before she fell into a dive and the speed rose again.

"Are you happy about stalling her at night, at only seven thousand, Nigger?"

David nodded. "I've stalled her on instruments several times. She comes out in about three thousand feet."

The Group Captain bit his lip.

The pilot said, "Would you like to ask her if she'd rather change her mind and land?"

"She wouldn't do it. She'd say, go ahead and stall it. She won't land anywhere outside the Commonwealth."

"There's Malta," David said. "We could make Malta in about fifty minutes, at low altitude."

The Group Captain was silent, and David was sorry for him in the decision that he had to make. At last he said, "We'll try stalling it, Nigger. Do it yourself, and send Ryder aft first to tell them to hold on to something. If I can't get it out safely I shan't try. In that case, we'll go on to Malta."

The pilot said, "Okay, sir. I shan't be able to give you much of a signal. I shall pull up pretty sharply, about thirty degrees nose up. I think you'll be able to get it out then, at the top. But if you have to hang on to it, get yourself wedged tight. She'll go sixty or seventy degrees nose down before she starts coming up. She'll probably spin a bit."

He went up into the cockpit, and put down the hatch under the engineer's seat to check the rush of air in when they took the plate off again, battening down Frank Cox with the engineer in the forward hold. He went to Ryder at the controls, and glanced at the window, but it was shut. He discussed the position briefly with the younger man. "The air was going backwards through the ventilation system," the younger man said. "It was going in here, instead of coming out." He pointed to the punkah louvre in front of him.

David spoke to the engineer, who shut off the ventilation trunk at the main. Then he sent Ryder aft through the machine to tell the passengers to fasten their safety belts, and to explain personally to the Consort and the Queen what he was going to do. He sat at the controls settling comfortably into his seat and fastening his own belt, and turned out the flight deck lights, and adjusted the dim instrument lights. Then he put on a little power and climbed to about nine thousand feet.

Ryder came back and slipped into the seat beside him.

"Everything all right aft? All ready for it?"

"Quite all right, sir."

"Okay. Don't touch your controls unless I tell you."

The pilots sat together in the dim light, peering forward into the darkness. They were flying between two layers of cloud; there was a very faint light from the setting moon away on their right hand, but there was no horizon and no means of judging the attitude of the machine except by the instruments. David set the gyro to zero, checked the flap setting, throttled the outer engines, put the nose up a little, and slowed the machine to about a hundred and eighty knots. He held her so for a whole minute, to give Frank Cox and Cummings notice that the stall was imminent, and to give them time to take the plate off.

As he sat there in semi-darkness concentrating on the small illuminated horizon bar before him and the aero figure on the gyro, he suffered an experience that he had had before in difficult test flying, and that he welcomed. He saw the instruments with only a small portion of his mind. Only a small portion of his being was seated in the cockpit beside Ryder, holding the controls. The rest of him seemed to be seated in mid-air forty or fifty feet above and behind the rear fin and rudder of the machine. From there he could see the whole aeroplane spread out before him, from wing tip to wing tip. He could see the four engines, the elevons, the flaps, the long line of the fuselage tapering to the nose, the fin and rudder itself. All this was clearly visible to him in every detail; it was blueish grey in colour, slightly luminous. Beyond the aeroplane he could see the horizon clearly defined in two shades of grey, a light grey above that was the sky and a darker grey below that was the ground. With the small portion of his mind he knew that the horizon bar had tilted very slightly; from his heavenly seat he saw the left wing drop a little. He moved his hand a little and saw the elevons move a fraction under his control, and he levelled the wing up upon the grey horizon.

Then with the small portion of his mind he saw the second hand of the clock upon the panel creep to the end of the minute he was giving Frank Cox to prepare. In his heavenly seat he moved his hand and throttled both the inner engines, and he saw the glow from the exhaust tubes on the wing deepen in tone, and die. He pulled back gently with both hands and saw the luminous blue nose of the machine rise to the horizon, and then he pulled back firmly and lifted it right up into the air. It was all so easy when you could see the whole aeroplane spread out in front of you, in this way.

For a second the Ceres hung poised nose up at a steep angle, virtually standing on her tail. It was incredible to see a blue aeroplane stand up like a fish rising to a fly. Then the nose dropped violently and a wing dropped; with the small portion of his mind the pilot saw the horizon bar rise and tilt quickly, and the gyro move around. From his heavenly seat David saw the wing drop and the spin commence, and he was amazed at the rapidity and violence of the rotation. Seated behind the aeroplane, however, and with everything in view, it was easy to correct. His hand and foot moved gently and he saw the tail pipe of the port outboard engine glow and rise in colour till a long streak of blue flame came from it, and he saw the rudder move a few degrees to bring the wing up. She was nearly vertically nose down now, but let her go. Poor old thing, she needed her speed. The spin was nearly checked, a trifle more from the port inner engine . . . so. He pulled the throttles back and the glow from the tail pipes died, and now she was diving straight for the dark ground, and the turn had stopped. From his seat up in the air behind her he could see the flaps half out, and he noticed that they were bending slightly with the pressure of the air at the increasing speed; he put his hand to the flap control, and saw them sink back into the wing. He could sense the relief in the machine and feel a gladness in the structure, and now he eased back very gently on the wheel again, watching the line of the blue wings as they rose up towards the grey horizon, and correcting now and then gently to keep them level. The dark ground slipped backwards underneath them a long way below, and now she was nearly horizontal again. He pressed forward slowly on the throttle levers of the inner engines as the blue wings met the light grey of the sky, and moved his hand upon the trimming wheel to keep them so.

Gradually his being came back to the cockpit, the vision faded, and he was trimming the machine to fly steadily at five thousand feet. He turned to Ryder by his side. "Keep her at about two hundred and thirty," he said. "I'm going to see what's happened down below."

He slipped out of his seat, and went to the hatch and opened it. Group Captain Cox stood up in the hole, and heaved himself out on to the floor.

"Get rid of it, sir?"

The other nodded. "It fell away quite clear," he said

standing up. "If anything the air was blowing out this time, instead of coming in. I got it out before you actually stalled her, before she got to the top." He grinned. "I got the wind up that you'd catch it up in your dive."

"You didn't see what happened when it hit the ground?"

Frank Cox looked at him, astonished. "We were in thick cloud!"

"Yes," said the pilot. "Yes, of course we were."

Frank Cox dusted his uniform a little, and straightened his tie. "I'll go back and tell them it's all over and done with. Cummings is putting back the studs."

"Get up to operating height again, and set a new course for Ratmalana?" said the pilot. "We use a lot of fuel down here."

Frank Cox nodded. "Get on up. I'll come and check the fuel reserve with you when I've had a drink."

"I think we'll be all right," the pilot said.

"Have you had any dinner?"

"Not yet. You might ask Gillian to bring me a tray here."

He went back to his seat, but handed over to Ryder, and sat resting, tired with the strain of the last hour. He sat watching the second pilot and the engineer get the aircraft into climbing trim and take her up, and presently they broke out above the clouds again to the glory of the setting moon upon their right hand side. Then Gillian brought him a tray of dinner with a cup of hot coffee, and he ate it, and felt better.

They came to operating height somewhere over Rhodes at ten minutes past nine, and put the machine into the cruising trim. David checked the fuel with Frank Cox, with Bahrein in mind for possible refuelling, but they came to the conclusion that they would still have adequate reserves to reach Colombo in spite of the two climbs, favoured as they were with general tail winds when flying east. Frank Cox volunteered for a watch at the controls, and Ryder went to lie down, and David strolled aft down the saloon for another cup of coffee.

The doors of the Queen's cabin and the Consort's cabin were both shut. He found Rosemary awake, and paused by her. "Fun and games," he said. "We do see life in this job."

She cleared the seat beside her. "Sit down a bit, Nigger," she said. "Or have you got to go back?"

He motioned to the stewardess to bring him the coffee there, and sat down by Rosemary. "What was it like back here, when she stalled?" he asked. "Did anyone fall over, or get hurt?"

She shook her head. "Ryder and Jim Hansen came along and saw that we were all strapped in, and collected all the loose cases," she said. "I think Fethers was sick." Miss Fethers was the Queen's maid.

"I'm sorry," he said. "I'll have a word with her as I go back. It was the only way we could get rid of the damn thing. I think I'll suggest we have a hatch made right aft somewhere, by the tail, in case we ever have another one." He sipped the coffee. "You were all right?"

She nodded. "Did she swing round when she went down? Something funny happened, didn't it?"

"She got in a bit of a spin," he replied. "They do that very easily, these things. They're quite all right when you understand them."

He sat with her a little, and pressed her hand discreetly between the seats. "Try and get some sleep now," he said. "It'll be dawn in a few hours. You've had enough excitements for one day." She smiled at him, and he got up and went back to the flight deck, pausing to talk a little to Miss Fethers.

304

In the blackness of the night they passed over Nicosia and Beirut and Basra, and went on down the Persian Gulf past Bandar Abbas. As they cleared the Gulf of Oman the sky lightened ahead of them, and forty minutes later the sun rose over the Arabian Sea. Soon after that, David put the Ceres on the long let down that would bring them to Colombo at a moderate height, and had another cup of coffee and a few biscuits.

He was sitting eating these in the pilot's seat when Frank Cox came to him. "The Queen's coming in here," he said. "She's been talking to the passengers and the stewards in the saloon. She wants to talk to the rest of you here, on the flight deck. I'll take over. Get that chap out of bed and get them all lined up. She's coming in here in five minutes time."

David got out of the pilot's seat and Frank Cox got in; they exchanged a few words about the course and rate of descent. There were a few minutes of hurried putting on tunics and straightening ties, and then the door opened, and the Consort and the Queen were there. The flight deck of the Ceres was not very spacious, and with eight people standing in it it was definitely crowded. The Queen stood close against David, for all the room he tried to give her, and her head came hardly to the level of his shoulder.

She said in the clear voice he knew so well, "First of all, I want to thank you all for what you did a few hours ago. When the Federal Government first suggested that they should give this aeroplane for the use of my Flight and that they should man it with an Australian crew, I knew that I should fly very safely. Now I have seen it proved. I do not think I can say very much more than that, except that I thank you with all my heart."

She paused. "And now I have a command for you, and it is this. You are not to talk about this bomb that was put into the aeroplane. You are not to say a word about it to your wives, or to your sweethearts, or to anybody at all. You are not to talk about it even between yourselves. It is to be forgotten. This is a royal command from myself to you, and if anybody should break it I shall be very severe. The world outside this aeroplane is not to know that this has happened."

She smiled at them. "But since we are friends, and since you boys have saved my life, I will tell you why this is. There have been two attempts upon my life since I came to the throne thirty years ago, and this is the third. It is one of the occupational hazards of the throne of England, or of any other throne, that poor, distraught, unbalanced people think that their troubles will be rectified if they can kill their Monarch." She paused. "In the previous two instances of my own experience I could feel nothing but pity for the people who tried to kill me, when their cases were investigated and disclosed. It has always been the same, because political murder has never been a fashion in our Commonwealth."

She looked around the faces of the young men. "I am convinced that this attempt upon my life, and yours, will prove to be the work of some unhappy person who deserves our sympathy. Unfortunately, it has come at a troubled time in England, when feelings are running high. It would not assist England to regain her balance if it should become known that my life has been attempted. Rather, the schisms which may heal in a few days might well become deeper, to the damage of England, to the damage of the Commonwealth. And so, it is my royal command to you that this thing is to be kept secret, absolutely. And this secrecy is to endure until I die." She smiled faintly. "After that, you can talk all you want to."

She looked at David. "Do you understand that, Captain?"

306

"Yes, madam," he said. "I shan't talk."

She looked at Ryder. "And you, Mr. Ryder?" And so she went to every member of the crew with the direct question, and David was surprised to see that she knew all their names.

In the end she smiled at them, and said, "That is all, except, thank you again." She looked up at David, "Captain, will you please come to my cabin."

He followed her out of the flight deck and to her tiny cabin, and the Consort entered it with her, and David followed, and the Consort closed the door. And then she said, "Of all the people in the aeroplane I feel that you deserve our special thanks, Captain, for the care and the intuition that led you to discover our danger and for the skill with which you handled it. I have been thinking over what is the best way for me to recognise your services. Normally, I should have liked to bestow on you the Air Force Cross, for acts of gallantry and devotion to duty not in face of the enemy." She smiled. "But I see you already have it, and a bar to the Air Force Cross would be so unusual, I think, that it might lead to enquiry."

"Too right, madam," he said. "There aren't very many of those."

"So, Wing Commander," she said, "we have decided to commemorate your services by giving you a greater voice in the affairs of your country than is held by other men, since it appears to us that in wisdom and good sense you merit that distinction. We have confidence that the qualities that you have shown will be of value in matters of State far removed from aeroplanes or flying. So, we have instructed our Secretary to draw up a Royal Charter for our signature, granting to you the Seventh Vote in elections for the Federal Government of Australia, and in elections for the government of any State of Australia in which you happen to reside. We do this with gratitude to you, and from the bottom of our heart."

She held out her hand, back upwards, and he divined what was intended, and bowed low, and kissed it rather clumsily.

They landed at Ratmalana in Ceylon at about nine o'clock by local time. The Governor-General and a small crowd of politicians and a guard of honour were on the aerodrome to greet the Queen. She stepped from the machine looking as fresh as a daisy, smiling and composed, the tired, anxious woman that the pilot knew all put away. He was amazed that she could do it, at the strain that Royalty imposed, but he had other things to think of. While the Queen was conversing with the Cingalese politicians and while refuelling was going on, David had every article of luggage taken out of the machine, with every food container and every kit of tools. When all these things were lying on the tarmac in the shade of the wing, he went through the aircraft on a tour of inspection with Frank Cox and Dick Ryder. Together they opened every box and cupboard and compartment in the aeroplane; by the end of half an hour they were satisfied. Then, as each piece of luggage was brought into the machine they opened it and searched it with the assistance of the owner before clearing it for the luggage bay. When finally they were ready to take off again, they did so with the knowledge that the aeroplane was free of any further surprises.

They took off at half past ten by local time, having spent longer than usual upon the ground over this business. For five hours they moved in brilliant, burning sunshine under a deep blue sky, with nothing to be seen but an appearance of the sea immediately below. The passengers were all exhausted with the strains prior to the commencement of the flight and with the reaction from the emotions of the first stage. The Queen and the Consort kept to their cabins, probably resting in bed; the others lay dozing in their reclining chairs, impatient for the journey to end. Even in the flight deck reaction was evident; David himself was sleepy, and as soon as operating height was reached he took an hour's sleep upon one of the bunks.

They crossed the coast of West Australia at half past three by Colombo time, but it was already evening in Australia and soon after they began upon the desert crossing the sun set behind them and to starboard. They went on in the light of the rising moon, and now David took a couple of Benzedrine tablets, and offered them around the crew. A meal served to pass the time, and three hours after sunset they began the long let down that would end up on the circuit of Fairbairn aerodrome, at Canberra. At midnight, local time, they saw the lights of the city ahead of them as they approached at seven thousand feet, mindful of the hills around, and made a close circuit of the lighted airport, dropping off height at two thousand feet a minute. Then they were on the final circuit at a thousand feet with flaps half down and speed reduced to a bare two hundred knots, and at fourteen minutes after midnight David brought his Ceres in on a long, straight approach and put her down upon the runway.

A few cars were waiting for them on the tarmac, but only a few because nothing had been published about the Queen's arrival. The Governor-General was there to meet her, and Mr. Hogan the Prime Minister, but it was all very informal, and after a few words with them the Queen and the Consort drove off in a car for Tharwa. The rest of the party for the Royal Residence followed with the luggage in a small bus, while David and Ryder taxied to the hangar of the Queen's Flight and saw the aircraft drawn in under cover.

Rooms had been reserved in the Canberra Hotel for the

same members of the Royal party, and David drove there when he had seen his crew accommodated, at about half past one in the morning. It had been a hot day in Canberra with the thermometer up somewhere in the nineties, and the night was warm and balmy, and scented with the fragrance of the gum trees and the wattles. He walked up the steps into the lounge of the hotel carrying his suitcase, and there in the desert of small tables and empty chairs Rosemary was waiting for him. A great Christmas tree stood in the lounge beside her, decorated with imitation frost and snow.

She said, "We've got the same rooms as before, Nigger. I got them to produce a couple of bottles of lemonade out of the ice chest. I thought you'd like a drink of something."

He said, "You shouldn't have stayed up."

"I shouldn't sleep if I went to bed just yet. I thought it would be nice to sit out in the garden for a bit, till we get sleepy."

He nodded. "Let me go and put this case down, and wash my face. I'll join you in five minutes."

When he came to her again, he found her sitting in a deck chair in the garden quad, with a tinkle of water by her where somebody had left a sprinkler on all night. He sat down by her side, and took the glass she handed him. "Well, here we are again," he said.

The girl said quietly, "It hardly seems possible, that we've been so far, and lived through so much. It's only three weeks since we were here, David. And everything is just the same. And everything has changed so much in England in that time . . ."

"It's a quiet place, this," he replied. "A place free from great excitements and emotions, free from the strain of not having enough money, a place where one can sit and think." He turned to her. "It's a wonderful experience to go to England and get mixed up in great affairs. But when you've had the great affairs, this is a better place to be."

"I believe that's what she thinks," the girl said slowly. "I'm not sure that isn't why she likes it here."

She turned to him. "What day is this, David?"

He thought for a minute. "Christmas Day was Monday," he said. "This is Wednesday morning."

"Then it's this evening that Tom Forrest is broadcasting in England," she said. "Can we listen to that?"

"Oh yes—it'll be put out on the short waves and re-broadcast here—a thing like that. The A.B.C. will have it on their programmes. What time is he speaking?"

"At nine o'clock—after the nine o'clock news."

"That will be seven o'clock tomorrow morning here," he said.

"Will it? Can we listen to it here?"

"I'll find out about it," he assured her. "I'll see if I can borrow a portable. It's going to be very important, is it?"

She nodded. "He seems to have got Daddy on the brain. I don't know what he isn't going to say, now that he's left alone and in the saddle."

"Probably a good thing."

"I think it may be," she said slowly. "I think it may be time that somebody spoke plainly to the people."

They sat in the quiet darkness for a time, not speaking, listening to the tinkling of the water. Presently she said, "We must go to bed, David. You must be terribly tired." She got to her feet. "Come on, or you'll be asleep here."

He got to his feet with her. "I'm right," he said. "I shan't want rocking, though."

She looked at her watch. "What's the time? I've still got London time."

He smiled. "I wouldn't know. Some time in the middle of the night." He yawned. "Perhaps you're right about bed."

"Sleep in tomorrow," she said. "I'm going to. She said she didn't want any of us up at Tharwa till the day after—Thursday."

He said reflectively, "She'll have heard Tom Forrest by that time. Does she know what he's going to say?"

"I doubt if she does. She doesn't usually know what a Governor-General's going to broadcast, not in any detail."

He took her arm. "Go on to bed," he said gently. "There's no sense in brooding over what's happening twelve thousand miles away."

"No sense," she repeated. "No, no sense at all."

She turned to him. "David, were you very frightened when you found that thing in the machine?"

"I think I was," he said. "I thought that we were all going to be killed."

She nodded. "Would you have minded very much?"

"I would," he said. "Very much indeed."

She leaned a little towards him. "I don't think I would. I'm not sure that she'd have minded, either. It's such a sad time, this. Everything changing and coming to pieces in England. I sometimes feel I don't want to see any more of it."

"I'd have minded," he said. "If she'd been killed in my aeroplane, with me, it would have been my fault. I was the captain, and she was my responsibility. I wouldn't want to die like that." She nodded. "And there's another thing."

"What's that, David?"

He smiled down at her. "If I'd been killed I couldn't have married you and bullied you into giving me a family. And I'm still hoping to do that one day."

"What a thing to say!" She slipped into his arms and put her face up, and he kissed her. "I don't think it 'll be long now," she said at last. "I think she'll probably be here for something like six months. If that's right, I could chuck the job in and not hurt her."

312

He kissed her again. "It can't be too soon for me."

Presently they walked arm in arm to her bedroom door, and kissed again in the passage. "Good night, David," she said. "I won't ask you in. Not while I'm on her staff."

He grinned. "No," he said. "You watch your step when you hand in your notice, though."

She laughed. "Good night, Nigger, dear."

"Good night, Rosemary. Sleep well."

He did not see her before he went out to the aerodrome next morning at about ten o'clock, to put in hand the routine inspection and refuelling of his machine. In the R.A.A.F. mess he got hold of a copy of the *Canberra Times*, black with headlines about the Queen's Christmas broadcast, about her arrival in Australia, about the appointment of Tom Forrest and about the political repercussions in England. In the mess he found the officers talking of nothing else, but conversation ended suddenly as he came into the ante-room, and everybody studiously avoided asking him any questions. It was a heavy, embarrassing atmosphere, and he was glad to leave after lunch. He went back to the hangar for an hour and did the necessary paper work in connection with the flight, and then he left for the hotel in one of the two cars allocated to the Queen's Flight.

Rosemary was out, and he did not find her again till he was sitting in the lounge before dinner, relaxed in a loose tropical suit beside the great Christmas tree decorated with tinsel and cotton wool snow. She came to him there, cool and fresh. "I went down with Gillian to bathe," she said. "We had a lovely swim. Have you been back long?"

"I came back about four o'clock," he said. "I got a portable radio. He's coming on the air about quarter past seven tomorrow morning, by our time. Where would you like to listen?"

"Not in a public place," she replied. "I think we may be going to get a bit of a shock."

He raised his eyebrows. "That so?"

"I don't know. He's a very strong character, and Daddy's been stuffing him up with all his ideas. Let's listen in one or other of our rooms, Nigger. I'll be up before then."

He nodded. "All right. I'll bring it along to your room soon after seven. What do you want to do tonight?"

"Let's do something to take our minds off it," she said wistfully. "Let's try and think of other things tonight."

"Like to go to the pictures?"

"Wouldn't it be awfully hot?"

"No," he said. "There's an open air cinema—you'll probably want a coat. It can get chilly in the evening here, even after a day like this. We're two thousand feet up, you know."

"I've never been to an open air cinema," she said. "Do you know what's on?"

"Vivienne Walsh and Douglas Mason in *Heart's Desire*," he told her. "I don't think it's one of the best."

"Vivienne Walsh is good," she replied. "Let's try it, Nigger. We can always walk out if it's too awful."

"I don't think people do that here," he replied. "I think that's a Pommie habit. We'll probably get a reputation for snootiness. Douglas Mason's from Adelaide, you know. Local boy makes good."

She laughed. "Let's go, anyway."

So they went to the movies after dinner and sat holding hands in the cool darkness under the stars while the Californian idyll unfolded before them. They sat it out in unsophisticated pleasure, insulated by it for the moment from the great events developing upon the other side of the world in the bleak wind and sleet of London in December. It stayed with them while they walked back arm in arm to the hotel through the scented night, while he kissed her good night before her bedroom door.

He went to her room next morning just after seven o'clock, fully dressed and carrying the radio, which he had already tried out in his own bedroom. She was dressed and waiting for him, but her room was still in intimate disarray, the bed unmade, her pyjamas thrown down upon the sheets, the faint scent of her powder in the air. He forced his mind from these distractions, and put down the radio and turned it on. "He's coming on in a few minutes," he told her. "They announced it at half past six, and again at seven."

Operatic music filled the room; he adjusted the volume and they settled down to wait. Presently the announcer spoke, and then, after a pause the room was filled with the harsh, virile tones of the Field Marshal who had risen from the laundry.

They sat listening in silence. Reception was fairly good, and only a few sudden surges in the volume indicated that the speaker was on the far side of the world.

Once Rosemary said impetuously, 'But he can't *do* that," and David grinned, and said, "He's done it." Then they were silent again.

Twenty minutes later the harsh voice ceased, and David turned the radio off. "Well, that's it," he said. "He's given them electoral reform, or else."

"He's got no right to say a thing like that," she expostulated. "England *is* the Commonwealth. He's got no right even to suggest that the other countries could do without her."

"He didn't exactly say that," the pilot replied thoughtfully.

"It's what he meant," she said indignantly. "He as good as said that if they didn't do something about electoral reform they'd never see the Queen again! He needn't have said that about the secret ballot and the women's vote, either."

David grinned. "He certainly hits pretty hard." He sat in silence for a minute. "Did you notice that he said that 'I have summoned *my* Parliament to meet on Monday'. *His* Parliament. I suppose it is, now."

"I think it's simply outrageous," she said angrily. "It's the Queen's Parliament, not his."

"He's her representative."

She paused for a moment. "I suppose legally he may be right, but it's not the thing to say. He's not the King, and he's no right to speak like one." And then she said, "Parliament is in recess till January the 24th. He can't go summoning them back like that, at three days' notice."

"He's done it," David said again. "I suppose he knows his stuff upon the legal side."

She said thoughtfully, "The Monarch can summon Parliament at any time, of course, and tell them to debate anything. But he's not the Monarch—or is he?"

He laughed. "He's certainly behaving like one."

"But he's running directly against all Government policy. This Government won't support that kind of an Address from the Throne, or Governor General's speech, rather."

"He'll probably get himself another Government, then." He paused. "I never did much history," he said. "But I reckon that it's no new thing for the King to be up against the House of Commons."

"It's not," she replied. "But we outgrew that sort of trouble centuries ago."

"That's what *you* think."

There was a pause, and then he said, "He's a shrewd and a clever man. And he's a good one, too, and he's got nothing to lose. He didn't ask to be made Governor-

General of England, and if he gets the sack I don't suppose he'll burst into salt tears. He's free to do exactly what he thinks is the right thing, and if he gets bumped off or gets the sack for doing it, that's too bad. But he's got nothing to lose."

"No," she said. "He's got nothing to lose." She paused, and then she said, "I wonder if that's what's been wrong with the Monarchy in England? Too much to lose?"

"In what way?" he asked.

She said slowly, "It's only the Monarchy that holds the Commonwealth together. If there was no Monarch the countries of the Commonwealth would fall apart, and each go its own way. The Queen knows that well enough, and she'll never have that happen. She'd never force a quarrel with the House of Commons to the point when she and all her family would abdicate, because that 'ld mean the destruction of the Commonwealth. I wonder if that's prevented her from ruling England as a Queen should rule?"

"You mean, Iorwerth Jones could twist her tail as much as he damn well liked?"

She flushed a little. "I think that's what I mean."

"Well," he said, "he won't twist Tom Forrest's tail. If he wants a head on collision with the Governor-General he can have it any time, and it looks to me as if he's got it now."

She said, "I wonder . . ." and then stopped.

He glanced at her in enquiry. "What do you wonder?"

She smiled, a little whimsically. "It 'ld be a funny thing if England got a King again this way. A King that could really rule by staking his job against these whippersnapper politicians, and keep them in their place. A real Monarch for a change, the first since Queen Victoria."

They sat in silence for a time. "I wonder what's going to

happen on Monday?" he said at last. "When Parliament meets? He's giving them the Governor-General's speech in person—didn't he say that? Where does he do that?"

"In the House of Lords," she replied. "That's what the Queen used to do. I suppose he'll give them another dose of the same medicine then. Electoral reform, or they can kiss the Queen good-bye. I wonder how he dares to say a thing like that! I wonder if she knew about it when she left, that he was going to carry on like this?"

A phrase came back into the pilot's mind. " 'That while Her Majesty would wish to visit every one of her Dominions from time to time, she would devote the greater part of her attention to those Dominions most advanced in their political development.' "

"That was it," the girl said. "How dare he say a thing like that!"

He grinned. "He's got guts, and he's injuring nobody if he gets sacked. You can say a lot of things and get away with it if you're a free man." They sat in silence for a few minutes. "Stirring times," he said at last. "I don't suppose anything like this has happened for a long, long time in England."

"No," she replied. "We're living in history, Nigger. What's happening now will be in all the history books in twenty years time, for better or worse. And we're in the middle of it, you and I. We shan't be in the books, because we're not very important people. But we're in it just the same, in it up to the neck and all the time."

He took her hand. "Too right," he said. "Wouldn't it rile you?"

"What, David?"

He smiled down at her. "To have all this nonsense going on just as we decided to fall in love."

"It's more important than us, David."

"Not to me, it isn't," he replied.

They went to breakfast together, and afterwards he saw her off to Tharwa in the car. He did not see her again till dinner time, when they met in the lounge. She was evidently tired, but not exhausted. Over the meal she told him what she had been doing. "I've got a new office, with three typists from the pool," she said. "In the South Block, up on Capital Hill."

"Not at Tharwa any more?" he asked.

She shook her head. "It's the correspondence. There were over eighteen hundred letters in the post this morning, most of them from cranks. We can't cope with that in the Residence. Turnbull and I have been doing nothing else all day but glance them through, and sort them out into the ones that need a special answer and the ones that don't. She took about a hundred and fifty of the most important ones out to Tharwa to Macmahon this evening. Tomorrow I'll start answering the others with the girls from the pool."

He stared at her. "What a job! I suppose you use a standard letter for each one?"

She shook her head. "She won't have that. They've all got to be individual, but we try and get it into one sentence, or two at the most." She paused. "They all start, 'I am commanded by Her Majesty the Queen,' of course. One's bound to say the same thing over and over again, but we try and vary it as much as possible. There just aren't enough words, though, to make each one different."

"How long will it go on for?" he enquired.

She shrugged her shoulders. "Macmahon thinks we'll probably be back to normal in a month. They'll probably go on at the rate of a thousand a day for the next week, and then they'll start tailing off." She smiled. "But we've only got ten thousand sheets of the Royal notepaper, so we'll get a break in a few days. We sent off the printing order today, but it may take a fortnight. It's the holiday season here, of course."

He asked in wonder, "How many did you get done today?"

"Oh, hardly any," she said. "We're only just getting organised. A good girl can do about a hundred and fifty a day. I'll probably ask for a couple more girls if we get a heavy mail tomorrow. It'll ease up before long."

He saw little of her for the rest of the week. The Consort turned up at the aerodrome unexpectedly with Frank Cox on Friday, apparently for no other purpose than to look at the aeroplane and to give David a general invitation to use the swimming pool at Tharwa any time he cared to do so. This was a good offer, because at the New Year Canberra was hot with the thermometer over ninety in the shade each day, and the city had grown more quickly than the swimming pools. Tharwa was twenty miles out, it was true, but when you got there the pool was a pool to dream about, shady and spacious and deserted, at the bottom of the rose garden.

The pilot said, "It's very good of you, sir. Can I take Miss Long?"

"Of course."

They walked around the aeroplane for a few minutes, watching the polishers at work upon the wing. David asked, "Any idea when the next job's likely to be, sir? If there's likely to be a fortnight or so, I'll give some leave."

Frank Cox said, "Stay in readiness for a bit longer, Nigger."

"Very good."

The Consort asked, "Could you make Kenya direct from here, Captain? It may be necessary for you to go and fetch Anne from Sagana, and bring her here."

"I can't make that direct from here," the pilot said.

320

"We'd have to refuel somewhere on the way. Keeling Cocos islands would be best for that, I think. From here to Nanyuki would be about fourteen flying hours."

"Not more than that?"

"No, sir. It's not very far." He paused. "I was looking at that route the other day, as a matter of fact."

"There's no difficulty about it?"

"None at all," the pilot said. "We're ready for that any time you say."

"I'll let you know."

Rosemary had an afternoon off on Saturday because the pool typists did not work at the week end. She did a little in her office, and David picked her up at the South Block at about twelve o'clock and drove her out to Tharwa. They lunched with Macmahon in the Secretary's apartments, and changed there, and went out in bathing costumes and dressing gowns down through the rose garden in the hot sun to the pool.

They spent the afternoon there, alone and undisturbed. Sitting in deck chairs by the water's edge they talked a little about great affairs. "I haven't seen her since we arrived," the girl told him. "But Macmahon and Turnie say she's looking very much happier. She talks to Lord Marlow in London on the telephone every evening, and she's had one talk with Tom Forrest. She got a great bundle of the London papers by air yesterday, and there was another today. There's an awful lot going on apparently, about electoral reform."

David asked, "Multiple voting, like we have?"

"I think that's the idea. I haven't seen the papers myself. Macmahon says it's a pity that Tom Forrest said what he did about the secret ballot and the woman's vote. He thinks that may have got people's backs up in England."

"Why would it?"

She looked up at him, smiling. "You can't expect England to tag along after Australia *all* the time, Nigger."

He laughed. "Not *all* the time," he said. "Just once more. After all, we've tagged along after England in a thousand different things, and very glad we've been to do it."

"Yes," she said, "that's true enough. But English people may not see it quite that way. To them, culture and political development is a one way street."

In the evening he drove her back to Canberra. Macmahon had told them that the Queen was going to the new cathedral, St. Mark's, on Sunday morning, her first public appearance since her arrival in Australia. David and Rosemary went to swell the entourage, and sat in a pew immediately behind the Queen and the Consort, with Miss Turnbull and Macmahon and Dr. Mitchison. Rather to David's surprise the entire crew of Tare turned up, led by Ryder, and by a quick adjustment of the seating by the sidesmen they were seated in the next pew again behind the Queen, so that in all three pews the worshippers gave thanks for a deliverance they could not talk about.

She would not go driving with him after lunch. He wanted to take her to Letchworth where a new estate of houses of a good class was going up in the Yarrow Road just outside the Federal Territory, hoping to tempt her with one of them, but she wouldn't play. "I've got to work this afternoon, Nigger," she said. "It'll be quiet in the office, and I can get ahead with some of the mail. One really hasn't time to give each letter proper attention when you've got five girls to keep going. Jennifer Menzies is coming in to help me."

"Who's Jennifer Menzies?"

"She's some connection of the old man—great niece or something. She's one of the pool typists."

"Is she good?"

The girl nodded. "She's absolutely first class—a head and shoulders above the rest. It was her idea, this going in this afternoon to get down to it quietly."

"Australian?"

"Yes. She's a Sydney girl. She was in England for three years, at Girton." She hesitated. "It just crossed my mind that if I turned the job in, in a few months time, she might be the right person to take it on."

He grinned. "I'm glad to see you're thinking on the right lines." He thought for a minute, and then said, "Would she be the first Australian ever to work on the Queen's personal staff?"

"There's you," she said.

"Apart from me. I mean, on her private affairs."

"I think she would," the girl said. "I can't remember having heard of anyone except English people. I don't think that should be an obstacle, though."

He grinned at her again. "It sounds to me a very dangerous experiment."

"You're a pig to laugh at me," she said. "As a matter of fact, I believe the Queen would like her."

He saw little more of Rosemary till dinner time on Monday evening, when they met as usual in the lounge. "I'm going out to Tharwa this evening," she told him. "There's a car coming for me at eight o'clock."

He was concerned for her. "There's such a thing as limiting the hours of work," he remarked. "You won't do anybody any good if you crack up."

She smiled, "I shan't crack up," she said. "But this is the big night."

"Tom Forrest's giving his Governor-General's Speech?"

She nodded. "Nine o'clock by our time. She's speaking to Lord Marlow after it's over, and she wants us to take down the conversation so that she can look it over quietly. Then the debate in the Commons begins at one in the morning by our time, and she'll be speaking to him every hour or so from then on. She wants all those conversations taken down."

He could not interfere in such affairs. "You're not going to get much sleep," he said gently. "Is there anything at all that I can do to help?"

She pressed his hand. "Dear Nigger. No, you can't do anything, no more than I could help you when you stalled the Ceres. We've each got our job that we can do for her, and mine will be over before long. Nobody thinks the debate 'll run into a second day. It's one thing or the other now."

"He'll never unseat the Government," he said. "They've got a majority of over two hundred in the House of Commons."

"I know," she said. "But he's gone over the head of the Government by broadcasting to his people. I don't know what's going to happen, but everybody thinks it's going to happen quickly."

He gave her dinner and took her to the car and saw her off for Tharwa. He gossiped with Frank Cox for a time, and together they explored the possibility of listening to Tom Forrest making his Speech in the House of Lords. But either no broadcast was taking place or the Australian stations were not relaying it, and presently David went to bed. He had a copy of the Reader's Digest, and he read this for a time in bed, and presently he slept.

He got up at six o'clock. He had arranged with Rosemary that she would slip a note under his door when she went to bed if there was any important news, but there was no note there. If the House of Commons met at one o'clock in the morning by Australian time, they would have been debating for five hours. He decided that they would probably go much longer than that, and went and had a shower, and shaved, and dressed.

While he was putting on his jacket a note was pushed under the door. He opened it, and there was Rosemary. "It's over, Nigger," she said. "The Government was defeated on an amendment to the Address in Reply."

She was pale and tired, with dark rings under her eyes, but she was jubilant. "What does that mean?" he asked.

"Iorwerth Jones' Government has resigned," she said, "or it's resigning now. It's all over bar the shouting."

He was amazed. "But how did that happen, with the majority they had?"

She laid her hand against the jamb of the door to steady herself in her fatigue. "Nearly half the Labour members voted for the Opposition amendment," she said. "Two hundred and nine of them voted against their own party, and fifty-eight abstained. There was a majority of over two hundred and fifty for the amendment—that's for electoral reform."

"Why did they do that?" he asked·

"It's the Queen," she said. "It's been a terrible shock to the people, the Queen going and the Governor General being appointed. We've not heard the whole story yet, by any means. But the bulk of the Labour back benchers knew the feeling in their constituencies, and there doesn't seem to be any doubt about it now. The country wants electoral reform."

"What happens next?" he asked.

"There'll be another Labour Government," she said. "It's only on this one issue that the country differs from Iorwerth Jones. Tom Forrest's going to send for Mr. Grayson and get him to form a Labour government pledged to introduce a multiple voting system."

He made a gesture of distaste. "Another Labour government?"

She nodded. "It's the only thing for England, Nigger. When things are really tough you've got to pull together, and share what you've got. It's got to be another Labour government. But from now on, things will get better and better. England's on the right road now, at last."

He nodded. "Maybe." And then he said, "You'll have to get to bed and get some sleep."

She nodded. "I'm going to pull down the blinds, and sleep all day."

He took her to her room. "Have you had any breakfast?" he asked.

She said, "I had some snacks in the middle of the night."

He paused at her door. "Can I get you something now—a tray?"

She smiled at him. "Dear Nigger. I could drink about a pint of milk and eat a few biscuits. I don't want any more than that."

He nodded. "You get to bed, and I'll get it. How long will you be?"

"Five minutes," she said. "I shan't be longer than that."

He went to the kitchen, and met the staff just coming on duty. He persuaded them to give him a jug of cold milk and a plate of biscuits, and carried them through the hotel back to her room. She was in bed and sitting up in a hot weather nightdress which rather disturbed him, but she was evidently very tired and he repressed the sally that came into his mind. "I got your breakfast," he said. He put it down upon the bedside table.

She said, "Thank you so much. I'm going to sleep the clock round, I believe." She took a sip of milk. "David, have they said anything to you about going anywhere?"

He nodded.   We're staying in readiness to go to Kenya to fetch Princess Anne here."

"Oh—they've told you. She's going to have a talk with Anne this morning. Charles is on his way here now, with Wing Commander Dewar."

That was news to the pilot. "Is he?"

She nodded. "She spoke to him about an hour ago, just before I left. She's getting them all together for a sort of family conference."

"He'll be here tomorrow, then. Coming by way of Christmas Island?"

"I don't know—I suppose they would be, wouldn't they?" She paused. "You may get your orders today, Nigger, and be off before I come to life again. If that's so, I shan't see you till Thursday, probably."

"Wednesday," he said. "It's not more than a two day trip, provided that they're ready to start when I arrive."

She drank a little of the milk. "Sit down and talk to me for a minute, Nigger, till I go to sleep," she said. He sat down on the bed, and took one of her hands, and so they sat in silence for a time.

"You're very tired," he said quietly. "Will you stay in bed tomorrow, too, if I'm away?"

She smiled. "It's the reaction. But I'm nothing like so tired as she is, Nigger. I don't believe that she's slept properly for the last month."

"I know," he replied. "But two wrongs don't make a right. If she's as tired as that she'll need a rest, and she won't need you in the office."

"She needs a rest all right," the girl said. "But this is the climax of it, and from now onwards both the Queen and England will be in calm water."

He stroked her hand, "Would you be able to leave, and marry me?"

M

She nodded. "I think so. I think when we've all recovered from this thing a bit I could have a talk with Macmahon, and then perhaps start training up the Menzies girl."

"Will she be staying here some time?" he asked.

She nodded. "She won't go back to England until England's settled down, and probably not till they've had a general election under the new franchise. She's got to go to Ceylon for a fortnight pretty soon, and I know she wants to go to Borneo. But this will be her home and her main base until the autumn, or your spring. It's not a bad time for a change of staff, if there's to be one."

He smiled slowly. "I think that's a good idea," he said.

She smiled with him. "I think that, too." She drank the last of the milk and put the glass down, and sat holding his hand. Presently her eyelids dropped, and she jerked herself awake.

He bent and kissed her. "Go to sleep now," he said softly. "If I have to go to Kenya or across the world before you wake again, you know that I'll be thinking of you all the way, and counting the hours till I can get back here again."

She clung to him for a minute. "Dear Nigger. Don't be away too long."

He kissed her again, and put her down sleepily upon the pillow, and she turned on her side and sighed with the relief of relaxation from strain. He got up from her side and went to the window and pulled down the venetian blind to darken the room, adjusting it carefully to let the air blow through. In the half light he paused by the bed on his way to the door, but she was already breathing evenly and deeply, already practically asleep. He moved to the door and opened it gently, and went out, and closed it carefully and silently behind him.

He was tired with the strain himself, and now he knew for certain that a new flight was close at hand, when he would have to stay awake for many hours. He went back to his bedroom and pulled his own blind down, and lay down on the unmade bed again for an hour's sleep before the ardours of the day.

He knew as he drifted into sleep that he was one with Rosemary. Together they would make one splendid person; apart both had been incomplete. He would wake presently and go away and leave her, and while he was away he would be thinking of her all the time, as she would be of him. He would go thousands of miles away from her in a few hours so that a quarter of the world would lie between them, but he would come back again and find that other half of his new self, and they would be complete.

He slept very deeply. In his sleep he seemed to be drifting further and further away from her, and growing weaker and weaker. The time of separation grew immensely; it was no longer two days as he had thought it would be, or three days at the most. She was receding from him in time as he slept; he struggled to wake, but he was now too weak. She would be there for him to find again, and love, but many years away. As he grew weaker she receded further; when first he slept he knew that she was only a few yards away, and if he needed her she would come. But now he needed her, needed her infinitely badly, and she could not come to him, and with the agony and disappointment he heard himself sobbing, and he felt the tears as they streamed down his face.

He needed Rosemary, and she could not come for thirty years or more. Only the animals had come, standing outside in the rain among the floods to watch him die. Only the animals and a dazed, delirious old Bush Brother who sat holding his hand while he sweated with malaria, touching

329

him with a hand that shook from time to time with fever chills.

He did not need the parson or the animals; he needed only Rosemary, and she was now too far away in time for her to be able to help him. There was a steady drumming sound, incessant, like a low kettledrum, drumming him out of life. He knew that he was finished and that Rosemary was very far away; he would find her again some day, but she could not come to help him now. His lips moved once again, and muttered, "Rosemary."

"She'll come," I said wearily. It seemed I had been saying that all night.

Sister Finlay moved beside me, and she took his hand from mine, and held the pulse while she looked at her wrist watch in the grey light of the dawn. I sat there in the chair beside the bed trying to focus my eyes upon the scene, utterly exhausted.

"He's practically gone now," she said softly.

She stood holding his wrist, motionless. I got up stiffly and she made a movement to assist me, but I put her aside, and she turned back to Stevie. I stood there in the doorway looking out into the clearing, and it was still raining. The wild dogs and the wild pigs, and the cattle, and the wallabies stood in a circle round the house in the grey, rainy dawn, their heads all turned to us in adoration, watching the majesty of his passing.

Ten

SERGEANT DONOVAN arrived about midday, with Hugh McIntyre, the manager of Dorset Downs, and one of his black stockmen. They came in a boat from the station homestead, a flat bottomed skiff that they had poled through the channels and the floods. Donovan had left Landsborough at dawn on horseback and had tried to ride to us, but the horse would not cross the deeper channels, probably because of the crocodiles, so he had gone round by the station track to Dorset Downs to get help, and the boat.

It was only a small boat, and it was leaking rather badly; moreover, the rain still poured down and added to the water in the bottom. Liang Shih flatly refused to leave his home, and I think perhaps this was a relief to Sergeant Donovan, because when the five of us got into the boat we only had three inches freeboard, so that we had to sit very still and bale a good deal with an old cigarette tin. Hugh McIntyre promised to send the black boy back next day with a few gallons of kerosene for Liang, and I believe he sent some flour and sugar too.

Before leaving, we buried Stevie on the far side of the clearing, where the animals had been. The Sergeant wanted to leave that till the next day because they were all rather foolishly concerned about my health. But I knew that once I got to Dorset Downs they would put me to bed, and nobody would read a burial service over the man. So I insisted that we should bury him before we left, and in fact, it didn't take very long because the grave began to fill with water when it was little more than two feet deep. We had to let it go at that and bury him so, and I repeated the essential parts of the service while the sister held me by the elbow and the men stood by bareheaded in the rain. We put a little cross of branches up to mark the spot and blazed a couple of the trees in case the cross got washed away, and then they made me get into the boat and we started back towards the homestead.

Last month, at the May races in Landsborough, the first race meeting of the year after the wet, I took up a collection for a headstone for the grave. I took it up each evening in the bars of the hotels at about seven o'clock, because men drinking in a bar are free with their money at that time of night and everyone remembered Stevie. I had to drink more beer than I enjoyed, but I went on till I had collected sixty pounds by the third night, because headstones are rather expensive in a place like Landsborough on account of the high cost of transport. I sent the order off to Cairns immediately, and I hope that it will be here in a month or two, and we can take it out to Dorset Downs and set it up.

I had this matter of a proper headstone very much in mind from the first, and even in the boat on the way back to Dorset Downs, feverish as I was, I was troubling myself about the inscription. The surname was Anderson, of course, but I had difficulty in sorting out in my confused mind whether it was Stephen or David, or Stephen David, or David Stephen. In the long journey down the channels and the floods I tried to ask Hugh McIntyre and Sergeant Donovan about this, but I was really rather ill by that time, I suppose, and I couldn't make them understand what it was that I wanted to know. I think they thought that I was wandering, because they kept saying things like, "You'll be

332

right," and "Not so long, now," and presently I gave up the attempt.

Dorset Downs homestead stands on a little hill, and we had to disembark from the boat about a mile from the house. I should have had difficulty in walking so far, but the men were most kind; they sent the black boy running to fetch down a quiet old horse for me, and when this came they put me up on it and so I came to the house on the hill. Hugh McIntyre is a bachelor and there is normally no woman there except the gins, but they put me to bed, with Sister Finlay in the next room to me, and there I stayed for the next four days till I was quite recovered.

They have a radio transmitter worked from batteries at Dorset Downs, so they were able to talk to Landsborough after the morning and the evening schedule from Cloncurry. Sergeant Donovan left on horseback for the town the morning after we arrived, but there was nothing urgent in the hospital to require the Sister, and so she stayed with me at the station for the whole four days. By that time I was very anxious to get back to Landsborough. I had missed one Sunday through my infirmity, which worried me a good deal, and I had left my parish magazine half written and so missed the weekly aeroplane that takes it into Cairns each month to be printed. I was most anxious to get back to my work, and when we had some sunshine on the morning of the fifth day I insisted that I must return.

We went on horseback, of course, Sister Finlay and myself, with John Collins and Harpo, both stockmen from the station, to ride with us and bring the horses back. The water was not more than a foot deep on any part of the track so that we had quite an easy ride, but it took us about three hours, and though we walked the horses the whole way I was rather tired when we got to Landsborough. Sister Finlay refused point blank to let me go back to my vicarage and insisted that I should go into hospital for a few days, and as at any rate I had got back to town I let her have her way.

Sergeant Donovan came up to the hospital the day after we arrived. I was still in bed because the sister had taken away my clothes, a gesture that was kindly meant but really quite unnecessary. I was anxious to get something organised about the headstone, because a grave out in the bush is very apt to become obliterated and forgotten, whereas I have noticed that if it has a headstone stockmen sometimes stop there as they pass by in the course of their work, and dismount and leave a flower or two upon the grave, or even say a prayer if they are quite sure that nobody is looking, which is very good for the stockman. So I talked to Sergeant Donovan about the headstone and the inscription.

"I am most anxious that he should not be forgotten," I told him. "There was a great deal of good in Stevie."

"Aye," said the Sergeant non-committally. "He was all right."

"I had a great respect for him," I said. The Sergeant was looking at me a little curiously. "There's a verse from the Wisdom of Solomon that I should like to see upon the stone."

"What's that, Mr. Hargreaves?"

I said, " 'Having been a little chastised they shall be greatly rewarded, for God proved them and found them worthy of Himself'."

There was a pause. "Aye," he said at last, "that might do."

I was a little disappointed that he did not display more enthusiasm, but mounted policemen in North Queensland are not noted for their lyrical outbursts. "There's one thing that I'm not clear about," I said, "and that's his name. The surname was Anderson, of course, but was he Stephen or David?"

The Sergeant stared at me. "You've got that all mixed

up, Mr. Hargreaves," he said slowly. "He wasn't Anderson. We haven't got an Anderson in Landsborough. His name was Stevie Figgins."

"But he told me that his name was Anderson!" I exclaimed. "Nigger Anderson. They called him Nigger, because he was a quadroon."

He shook his head. "Stevie Figgins," he repeated. "I can show you on his pension papers, in his own handwriting. Did he tell you that his name was Anderson?"

I nodded. "Most definitely."

"A bloke like that, he'd say anything when he'd a skinful, Mr. Hargreaves. When did he tell you that?"

"In Liang Shih's hut, before he died," I said.

He smiled. "He wouldn't be himself then," he said gently. "Maybe you weren't quite yourself then either, Mr. Hargreaves, with the fever and that. I can tell you, Stevie Figgins was the only name he had, and he wasn't a quadroon, either."

I was silent for a long time, re-arranging my ideas. At last I said, "Do you know anything about his wife?"

"I know a little bit," he said. "They used to fight like cat and dog twenty-five years ago, when he was manager of Wonamboola Station. It was probably that that started him upon the booze and lost him the job. She left him then, and later she got run over by a truck in Sydney, and died. That might have been in 1930 or soon after."

"They didn't live in Canberra?" I asked.

He laughed. "Canberra? Never come within a mile of it. They weren't that sort of people, Mr. Hargreaves."

"Did they have any children?"

"Not that I ever heard of. They might have done, but if there were any they never showed up here. Far as I know, there weren't any relations. It doesn't matter, because he'd nothing to leave."

He went away presently, and I was left to try to reconcile what he had told me with my memories. I found it better to cling to the sheet anchor of reality. Sergeant Donovan was a competent and level headed young man, and I was forced to accept that what he had said about Stevie was almost certainly correct. It tallied, moreover, with my own experience of Stevie up to the night when he had died on Dorset Downs. And as regards that night, I had to admit that for most of it I was running a very high fever, myself.

I took the matter a stage further with Sister Finlay when she brought me a cup of tea that evening. "Sister," I said, "I want to ask you something. Did you hear any of that long story Stevie told me before he died?"

She stared at me. "What story? I didn't hear any story."

"After we put the light out, to save the torch," I said. "I asked him about his relations, and he began telling me about . . . all sorts of things."

She shook her head. "He didn't say anything. I'm sure of that, Mr. Hargreaves."

"Nothing at all?"

"I don't think so. You were sitting there holding his hand, but neither of you said a thing."

"Are you quite sure of that?"

"I'm quite certain," she said, smiling. "I was much more worried about you than I was about Stevie, because he was going to die in any case. You went to sleep, Mr. Hargreaves, and I didn't wake you because I thought it was such a very good thing for you. You slept the whole night through."

It was fantastic, because I had seen *her* asleep. "You're sure you didn't go to sleep yourself?"

She was affronted. "Mr. Hargreaves! I've never slept upon a night case yet, and I hope I never shall!"

"I'm sorry," I said. "I can't make it out, because I

336

thought he told me a long story, all about himself."

"You were very ill," she said. "I should forget about it, if I were you. I may have dozed a little once or twice, but I was up and walking about every half hour, having a good look at you and at those wretched animals. Liang and I gave Stevie a couple more of those pipes at about two in the morning, right under your nose, but you never woke."

That seemed conclusive, anyway. "The animals were there?"

"Oh, yes, they were there. Liang said he's seen them do that before when they're all stranded together on an island, in the wet."

"Do what?"

"Stand looking at the house. It didn't seem to worry him, but if I'd had a gun I'd have soon driven them away. I don't like wild animals as much as that."

I was silent.

Presently she said, "Whatever you think he told you, I should forget about it, Mr. Hargreaves. People often think funny things when they're running a high temperature, and it doesn't mean anything at all. It's part of the clinical condition, part of the disease, that you get mild delusions. When the body's sick it can't help affecting the mind sometimes, just a little, and when the body gets well the mind gets well again too, and much more quickly."

"I see that, Sister," I said. "It was a very odd experience, and I hope I don't have another one like it."

"I'm sure you won't," she said. "You're getting on splendidly. We'll have you up next week."

In spite of my protests, she kept me in bed for five or six days longer, partly, I think, because she knew that I would want to go back to my vicarage as soon as I was well. When finally I got back there I found that a transformation had been made. There was glass in all the windows of the one

337

room that I occupy, and a coat of colour wash had been put upon the walls, and there was a proper bedstead out of one hotel and a cane easy chair out of the other, and a brand new kerosene stove that gives out a tremendous heat and keeps me very warm and cosy in the wet. The people had done all this for me completely of their own initiative, and I must say that I was very much affected.

I settled down then for a very comfortable and lazy couple of months. It is usually April before one can get motor vehicles about again in the Gulf Country, and although when I was a younger man I used to go on travelling on horseback all through the wet I now feel that I am getting a bit old for that. I settled down instead to write a series of articles for my parish magazine, so that I could issue it each month throughout the dry without wasting too much time in writing during the season when the roads are fit for travelling.

We do not very often see strange faces at Landsborough in the wet, of course. But one day about the end of February or the beginning of March a strange aeroplane flew in and landed at the aerodrome, quite unexpectedly. It turned out to be a Dakota of the Department of Civil Aviation on loan for a period to the Department of Works and Housing. The passengers and crew came into the Post Office Hotel to spend the night, and I met them there when I went down to have my tea.

They turned out to be a party of surveyors and architects from the head office of their Department at Canberra; they had spent a couple of days at Brisbane on the way up, and had flown direct from there to Landsborough. Everybody was naturally curious to know what they had come for, and they were forthright people who made no bones about their business. They had come up to reinstate the aerodrome at Invergarry.

I sat at table with the man who seemed to be the head of the party, a grey haired man of fifty-five or so, a Mr. Hutchinson. "There's no secret about it," he said. "It's all been in the papers, though perhaps you haven't heard about it here. It's in connection with the expansion of the R.A.A.F.—we've got to open up some of the old war-time aerodromes again and make them suitable for squadrons to occupy upon a permanent basis. It's a big programme—means permanent buildings and hangars. It'll take about five years to complete, perhaps longer. Take Invergarry, as an example; that's the one that we're going to see tomorrow. I understand there's nothing there at all."

I shook my head. "I passed by it about three years ago."

"You did? There's nothing there, is there?"

"Nothing but the runways," I replied. "They were all right then. But there aren't any buildings."

"None at all?"

"Nothing."

He turned to one of the others. "It's as you said, Harry. The Americans took everything away." He turned back to me. "You'll think it's funny that we shouldn't know," he said, "but these were American airstrips in the war against Japan, and we never had very much to do with them. And they're not in places that one goes to every day."

We talked a little about the job they had to do. Working from the basis of the existing runways, which they had to survey and to map, they had to start in and design a complete new station for the R.A.A.F. out in the middle of the wilderness, capable of accommodating one squadron as a start and for expansion at some later date to take a Wing. "It won't all happen overnight," said Mr. Hutchinson. "It will be five years at least before a squadron gets there with its aeroplanes, working as we do under peace time conditions. It might be longer than that."

I asked quietly, "Will they have helicopters there?"

"Helicopters? Oh, I don't know about that. Medium bombers is the intention, I believe. Most stations seem to have a helicopter or two about the place these days, though."

"They're useful for communications work," one of the others said.

I sat with them at table for some time after the meal, because the only other place to go was into the bar, and none of the surveyors seemed to be fanatical beer drinkers. And sitting so, and thinking over what they had told me, I thought it best to have the whole of it, and I asked Mr. Hutchinson. "Do you people know Canberra well?"

"We all live there," he said. "We moved up from Melbourne last year. But I've been there off and on about eleven years."

"Do you know a place called Letchworth?"

"Too right I do," he said. "It's just outside the Federal Territory, in New South Wales."

"Do you know the Yarrow Road in Letchworth?"

He wrinkled his brows. "Can't say I do. There's only one or two roads there at all. Simon might know—he worked in Canberra before he joined us. Simie, know the Yarrow Road, in Letchworth?"

A red haired young man spoke up. "What about it?"

"There *is* a Yarrow Road in Letchworth, is there? Mr. Hargreaves was asking."

"There's going to be," the young man said. "It's not built yet. It's not even pegged out, far as I know. It's one of the roads running up the hill away from the railway line, all going to be called after places in England. You'll find it marked on the twenty-five inch plan, dotted."

I asked. "There aren't any houses on it yet?"

He shook his head. "It's all virgin bush. It's not even

scheduled for construction yet, Mr. Hargreaves. How did you get to hear about it?"

I said vaguely, "A chap I know was talking about a house he wanted to build some day, on Yarrow Road."

Mr. Simon smiled. "He'll have a long time to wait."

"Have you got any idea when it's likely to be made?"

He shook his head. "You tell me first how fast Canberra's going to grow. It'll have to be a city of three or four hundred thousand people before Yarrow Road gets built, I'd say."

Mr. Hutchinson said, "Ah, no. Long before that."

There was a short, desultory dispute. "What's the population now?" I asked.

"Twenty-five thousand." He paused. "It might be built in twenty years from now, the way things are going on. Mind you," he said, "it'll open up some fine positions for houses when it *is* built. There'll be a good class suburb up there on the Yarrow Road one day. But not just yet."

I went back to my vicarage that night troubled and perplexed.

I had no time to brood over these matters, however, because even in the wet I find my life at Landsborough surprisingly busy. Not only were there the usual occupations such as the morning service for the children, and the visiting, but soon after I came out of hospital they elected me on to the Shire Council, a considerable honour and one which gave me a good deal of say in municipal affairs. I took advantage of the position to press for the institution of a School of Arts, which might be called a public library in other places, and at the same time I was trying to get organised a branch of the Country Women's Association. All this meant a good deal of work in canvassing opinion amongst uninformed people, and a good deal of scratching round for funds, and a good deal of correspondence with outside bodies in Brisbane and other cities. I found myself kept very fully occupied on all this work and I was glad that it should be so, because I would not like the people to get the impression that their vicar just sits down with his hands folded in the wet when it is impossible for him to get about the parish.

Everything comes to an end at last, and about the middle of March we got a succession of fine, cloudless days with a bright, hot sun. We got a storm or two after that at the tail end of the monsoon, but by the end of the month cars were beginning to move about in the immediate vicinity of Landsborough and the water was off most of the roads. By the middle of April trucks were running through to Cloncurry again, and I was able to get about my parish.

I had a great deal to do, of course. The small radios and the aeroplanes had kept me fairly well aware of what was going on, and there were a number of children born during the wet to be baptised, and a few graves to be blessed. I went first to the east, to the Newmarket River district of my parish. Travelling conditions were not very good, and I had to miss one Sunday at Landsborough, because it was about a hundred and thirty miles to come back and there was so much to be done down there I thought I ought to stay and clean up all the spiritual requirements of the people in that part of the country. I was away upon that journey for eleven days, and although the country down there was still very wet I kept remarkably well, being quite restored to health after my long rest.

I got back to Landsborough on the Saturday, and I had to stay in the district for a week, because there was no transport going to the Blazing River till the following Monday. I filled in the time by visiting the stations around, spending a night at Dorset Downs where Hugh McIntyre very kindly lent me a horse and a black boy as a guide to take me out to Liang Shih's house.

We started at dawn, and it took us about three hours to get there through the bush. When we came to the house on the rising bit of land between the waterholes, we found that Liang was already busy in his garden. The receding floods had left a layer of fine mud over everything, and Liang had already hoed and planted an acre or so, and was busy on another plot as large again. It was pleasant to see the little lettuces all coming up, and the neat garden, all bright and fresh in the warm sun.

I got down off my horse and the boy took him, and Liang left his work and came to greet me. I chatted with him for a little, and told him that I had come to see what needed doing to the grave, since I was in the neighbourhood. We walked over to it together. The cross had gone, knocked over by some animal perhaps and washed away, but the covering of soil still hid the body, or perhaps Liang had attended to that, because there was fresh soil on the top. He had driven stakes in around the grave and against these stakes he had erected a wall of old corrugated iron sheets, discarded from some roof because of the many rust holes in them, so that the grave now lay within a small rusty iron enclosure. He had not replaced the cross, but at each corner of the enclosure he had planted what I took to be a gladiola.

I was touched by the care that he had taken over the remains of his old friend, and I said something to that effect, but I could make no mental contact with the Chinaman. I asked if he would mind if we put up a headstone on the grave, and he shrugged his shoulders, as if to indicate that we could do what we liked. I asked if he intended to get somebody else to come and live with him, and he said no, but gave no reason. He did not seem to be prepared to discuss his life or his personal affairs at all, though I think he was pleased to see me. I asked if I could send him anything out from the town, and he said that he would be coming into town in a few days and he could shop himself. He had found Sister Finlay's medicine case as the floods went down, and he gave me this to take to her, much ruined by lying in the water for three months.

So I left him and rode back to Landsborough with the black stockman, getting there soon after midday. I turned the horse over to the boy to take back home with him, and after dinner I walked up to the hospital and gave Sister Finlay her case. She made me stay and have a cup of tea with them, and while we were drinking it I told her about the grave.

"I'm glad it's being looked after," she said. And then she said, "He was an awful nuisance to us, but one misses him. He wasn't such a bad old man."

"I think there was a lot of good in him," I said. "I found him rather an attractive character in many ways."

"If only he hadn't *smelt* so bad," said Templeton.

I started off next week upon my second journey of the year, southwards and westwards of Landsborough, travelling for the first day in the mail truck which was running again. We didn't get along very fast, because traffic was beginning to move about the roads again after the wet, and hardly an hour went by but we would meet another vehicle. When that happened we stopped, of course, and had a gossip for a quarter of an hour because there was so much news to be exchanged, and he would have a drink with us out of our bottle of rum and we would have a drink with him out of his, and so we would drive on after a time. I left the truck that evening to stay with Mr. and Mrs. Cooper at Sweet River, and held a Communion service and a christening of an Abo child next morning; in the afternoon Fred Cooper drove me on to Marriboula, where old Mrs. Foster had died of pleurisy about a month before.

344

I went on like that for a day or two, and it must have been on May the 9th or 10th that I was at Blazing Downs for the night, staying with Mr. and Mrs. Taggart. A stock route passes across one end of Blazing Downs about twenty miles from the homestead, and amongst the other gossip of the district they told me that there was a mob of about twelve hundred beasts passing across their property on their way to railhead at Cloncurry from some station up in the north east. I asked who the drover was, thinking I might know him.

"Jock Anderson," Joe Taggart said. "Ever meet him?"

I shook my head. "I can't say that I know the name." The only Anderson I knew belonged to something quite unreal, that I had resolutely put out of my mind.

"I don't know him well," said Joe. "He's a Scot from home, from some place in the Highlands. Works mostly in the Territory, but he comes down here once in a while."

"Has he got much of an outfit?" I asked.

"He got Phil Fleming with him," Joe said. "Old Harry Fleming's boy, at Camooweal. Got three or four boongs along, too."

There was nothing particularly interesting in that, and we went on to talk of other things. I spent the night with the Taggarts, and Joe offered to drive me on next day to Wentworth, a matter of thirty miles or so, which was most kind. I arranged to hold a Communion next morning after breakfast because it was a week day and work had to get started, and then there were a couple of Aboriginal children to be baptised before we could get on the road.

We were sitting gossiping over the remains of breakfast when we heard the sound of a horse down by the stockyard. I could not have distinguished it from one of the station horses, but Joe said at once, "Wonder who that is?" We had not very long to wait, because a tall, fair haired man,

345

bearded, in a dirty blue shirt and strides walked awkwardly on to the verandah, and hesitated when he saw us sitting at the table.

Joe got up to greet him. "Come on in, Jock," he said. "Just in time for breakfast." He shouted through to the pantry, "Sunshine, go over to Cookie and ask him to give you another breakfast for Mr. Anderson."

He turned to me. "This is Jock Anderson, Brother. Jock, this is Brother Hargreaves, from Landsborough."

The tall man shook hands awkwardly. "They told me you would be coming," he said, and it was very evident that he was Scotch. "I was wondering now, would ye have time to ride over to the camp with me, Brother, to baptise a child?"

From behind me I heard Mrs. Taggart give an audible sniff.

I smiled. "Always got time to baptise a child, Jock," I said. "Whose child is it? Yours?"

"Aye," he said steadily, "it's mine. The wife's down there in the camp with it."

I was surprised at that, because the Taggarts had not told me about any woman in his droving outfit. Mrs. Taggart got to her feet and called for Sunshine, her Abo maid, and began picking up the dirty dishes with a bit of a clatter, so that I got an inkling of the trouble. The girl came with a plate piled high with sausages and plains turkey and potatoes, and I sat talking to Jock Anderson while he demolished this.

"I was going on to Wentworth today, Jock," I said. "You're somewhere down that way, aren't you?"

"I am eighteen miles to the north of Wentworth homestead," he told me. "Forbye, I took the liberty to bring a second horse up with me, Brother, in case you would have time to come." He hesitated. "If you would ride over with me I will bring you back here before dark. If you would care to stay the night, I would take you on to Wentworth in the morning. But we have only a rough camp."

"That's all right," I said. "I've got a swag with me." I turned to Joe Taggart. "I should think that's the best thing I can do, Joe. Save you taking me all that way in the utility."

We discussed it for a little, and it really seemed the best thing to be done. I wondered a little why he had not brought the mother and child over with him to save me the journey, though I thought I knew the reason. However, we settled that I should go back with him to the camp, although I could see that Joe was troubled about the conditions I would meet.

I turned to Jock Anderson presently. "I'm just going to celebrate Holy Communion, Jock," I said. "Would you care to join us?"

He said awkwardly, "It is many years since I took the Lord's Supper."

"Time you did, then," I replied. "We'd be very glad to have you."

Before the service, Joe Taggart took me aside. "I'm sorry about that chap, Brother," he said. "He's living with a yeller girl. I'd have told you last night, only the wife's funny about that sort of thing. I should have told you that he'd got a gin down in the camp. I never thought of this."

"That's all right," I said. "I suppose that's why he didn't bring the baby here?"

He nodded. "The missus wouldn't like it, and it wouldn't do, with all these other boongs. It's best the way he's done it, but I'm sorry that it's giving you such a lot of trouble."

"It's no trouble at all," I said. "It's what I'm here for."

"I'm afraid you'll have a rough night," he complained.

I laughed. "It's not the first time I've stayed in a drover's camp, Joe, and it won't be the last."

347

We started off about the middle of the morning, after my Celebration and the christening. Jock Anderson had two horses but only one saddle, because it is a little awkward to lead a saddled horse for any distance. He insisted on me taking the saddled horse and we slung my bedroll across the saddle in the front and tied it down with thongs; although he was riding bareback he carried my little case of sacramental vessels. So we rode away from Blazing Downs.

He did not talk much on the way. I asked him where he had come from, and he told me that he had spent the wet at Robinson River two hundred miles or so to the north-west, being under contract to take a mob of store cattle from Wollogorang to railhead directly after the wet. He had been about three weeks on the road, and he expected to get his mob to the Curry in about another twelve days if the going was normal; after that he had to hurry back to Robinson River to fetch another mob from there. He had four men in his outfit besides himself, and about thirty horses. He seemed a steady and responsible sort of a man, apparently in demand by station managers; probably he was making good money, though he was very seldom in a town to spend it.

We rode into his camp a couple of hours before sunset. He was camped by a waterhole with cattle and horses everywhere, of course. Normally he would have been travelling, but he had rested that day in order to get hold of me. His camp consisted of a tent for himself and his wife, and a humpy shelter made of gum tree boughs for his white ringer, Phil Fleming; his three Abos had swags and slept under the stars.

There was a rough cookhouse arranged against a bank, with a fireplace made of a few stones and a couple of iron bars, and here the girl was tending the fire. She was a half caste, a coffee coloured girl, very quiet and rather good looking. Perhaps in my honour she was wearing a bright red dress, and her long black hair was done up in a sort of coil around her head. I think this was unusual, because when they struck camp next morning she was dressed in a man's clothes, in ringer's strides and a check suit. She served as the camp cook, and cooked for all of them.

She had the baby in an old American Army jungle hammock, which seemed to me a good sort of a cot for an infant on the trail; it had a waterproof roof to keep the sun off him and mosquito netting to keep off the flies, which were bad in that camp. They opened up this thing to show him to me, a well developed boy several months old, not very dark in colour. I said, "My, he's a fine chap. When was he born?"

"January the 9th," said Jock. "At Robinson River, at about five in the morning."

January the 9th, I thought, was the third day after Epiphany, and five o'clock in the morning was the time when I had stood up, dazed and weary, to find the animals still standing round the house. It was a coincidence, of course, that this man's name was Anderson; I had decided that I must put such thoughts out of my mind, and there was no going back upon that resolution. I stared down at the baby. "He looks very well," I said. "What are you going to call him?"

The girl looked up at her husband with one of her rare smiles, and he laughed self-consciously. "The wife had an idea when he was born she'd like to call him Stephen. But I thought that I would choose to name him David, after my father. We're agreed upon that now."

It was imperative that I should hide any perturbation that I might feel and carry on with the business in hand as if there was nothing unusual about it. I turned to the girl. "You are quite happy about that name?" I asked.

She nodded. "David is his name."

"David's a good Christian name," I said mechanically,

349

and while I gained time to collect my thoughts I glanced at the girl's hand. There was a wedding ring. I asked, "You two are married?"

"Aye," he replied. "Brother Fisher married us last September, over on the Roper River." Not before time, I thought, and yet I thought the better of Jock Anderson for marrying the half caste girl who was to bear his child.

There was no more to be said about it and my duty was quite plain; it was to baptise this child into Christ's holy Church. There seemed to be nothing to be gained by delaying, and so I told Jock Anderson that we would have the service right away before we ate, and he told the mother. Thinking back, I cannot remember that she took much part in our discussion; she was a very quiet girl, who spoke remarkably little, and that in a low tone. He gave her name to me for the register, Mary Anderson.

There was a little difficulty about the godfathers and godmothers, because Jock had made no provision at all for those. Phil Fleming was there, a black haired, lean, gangling lad of twenty who had little idea of what a godfather should do. It was impossible to suggest one of the black boys, of course, and Phil declared himself willing, so I had a talk with him privately and tried to make him understand what he was taking on. There was no godmother at all, but Mary was understood to say that her sister Phoebe would be godmother and that she had done it before, and so I allowed the mother to stand proxy for Phoebe, who apparently was working in a job at Chillagoe.

They had a clean bucket, and I washed it and filled it with rather muddy water and set it on a tucker box draped with my little altar cloth, to serve as a font. I arranged this in front of a couple of gum trees near the water's edge on clean ground a little way away from the camp, we drove away the cattle, and then I got them all together and showed them where to stand and what to do, and I began my service.

I have administered the Baptism of Infants many hundreds, perhaps thousands of times since I was ordained, and one would have thought that at my age I would have understood what the words of the service meant. Moreover, I have schooled myself to think about the words that I am saying as a trick to prevent the service from becoming mechanical, and this concentration had never before led me into any surprises in the Baptism of Infants. But when I came to the passage which commences, 'Give Thy Holy Spirit to this infant, that he may be born again, and be made an heir of everlasting salvation,' I had to stop, because suddenly I wondered what on earth I was talking about. It seemed to me that I had never said those words before, and I had to look at my prayer book to assure myself that there was, in fact, no error before I could collect my thoughts and go on with the service.

There were cattle all around us in the evening light, standing knee deep in the water, moving around with squelching noises, or lying chewing the cud. The smell of them was strong all over the camp. I coaxed the godfather through his responses and went on, and presently I took the child from his mother's arms and held him in my own, and I baptised him David.

That was virtually the end of it, but that I had the same trouble with the words of the Thanksgiving, parts of which seemed to hold meanings that I had never seen in them before. And finally it was all over, and the child was back in his jungle hammock, and the mother was busy at the cooking place with supper, and I was folding up my altar cloth.

The supper was the usual thing—a roast of salted beef with potatoes, home-made bread, butter, and quantities of strong sweet tea from a billy, served on tin plates and in tin

351

mugs, and eaten sitting on the ground. The light was failing as we ate and the mother lit the hurricane lamp; in the last of the daylight I chose a spot under a tree to sleep, and unrolled my swag and made my bed ready.

I knew that they would go to bed early, for they would be up long before dawn cooking the breakfast and striking camp, in order to get the cattle mustered with the first of the light and get them on the road. But while the mother tidied up the supper things and nursed her baby at the door of the tent, I sat with Jock Anderson upon a log, smoking a last pipe with him before turning in

"He's a fine child, Jock," I said. "You must be proud of him."

"Aye," he replied. And then he said, "He'll have a hard time with the colour."

"I wouldn't worry too much about that," I said. "It's not so important as some other things. He's got a good mother."

"Aye," he said, "she's a good girl." He paused, and sucked his pipe. "I don't know what the folks at home would say. They'd never understand, Brother. A man lives year after year and never sees a white girl that's unmarried, and gets terrible lonely in the bush. And she's a good wife."

"I'm sure of that," I said. "A white girl could never stand this kind of life. You ought to think about some settled job, Jock, for the child's sake, now. Especially if you're going to have any other children. Your wife's doing wonderfully well—I can see that—but every girl should have a settled home when children come."

"Aye," he said slowly, "that's a fact. She tells me that she's in the family way again already." He paused. "Jimmie Beeman, manager at Tavistock Forest, he said he'd offer me the job of head stockman, last year. He'll be at Croydon races, and I'll see him. Maybe I'll break up this outfit, and go there."

"He knows about Mary, does he?"

"Aye. He doesn't mind about the colour."

I said, "I should do that, Jock. You oughtn't to ask your wife to go on droving with you with another baby on the way. It's not fair to a woman, that. If Jimmie Beeman wants you at Tavistock, I should go there. He's got a house, hasn't he?"

He nodded. "I'll think on it, Brother. He's got a two roomed house out past his stockyard."

"He'd probably build on another room if he knew that you'd stay a year or two," I said. "I'll have a talk with him next time I'm round that way, if it 'ld help." I paused, and we sat smoking, looking out across the waterhole in the still moonlight. "You know that girl he married?" I said presently. "Nan Fowler, daughter of old Jim Fowler on the railway at Julia Creek?" He nodded. "She was a school mistress at Charters Towers," I reminded him. "They'll be having their family along with yours, and she might start a bit of a school. You want to think about these things, now you're a father."

"Aye," he said slowly, "that's a fact. I dunno that schooling 'll be much use to him, though, with the colour." He paused. "He's a fine bairn," he said presently. "As fine a bairn as I ever saw. He'll be a big fellow when he grows up. He'll make a good stockman, or a drover maybe."

"You can't tell," I said quietly. "You ought to give him a good schooling. You never know what people will turn into. He might rise to be anything before he dies."

We knocked our pipes out and turned in soon after that. I lay in my swag for a long time before sleep came watching the brilliant Queensland stars through the fine tracery of the gum leaves. I knew then that a corner of the veil had been lifted a little for me by Stevie Figgins under the hand of God, and I am still puzzled to know why this thing was done.

Because it means that I have been honoured in a way beyond my station in life; I am an obscure and unimportant man, a man like a million others doing the job each day that comes to hand, and not doing it very well. Who am I that God should pick me to reveal His wonders to?

And who was Stevie, to whom the full revelation had been made? But here I feel I am on firmer ground, because it is the way of God to deal with poor and humble men. If the Scriptures teach us anything, it is that God speaks seldom to the wise men or to the great statesmen. For His messages he speaks to poor and humble men, to outcasts, to the people we despise.

So there it is, and I can add no more to this account. I have written down what happened, and it has eased my mind to do so, and I shall now lock these exercise books away, put the whole thing out of my mind, and go on with my job here in this scattered parish. All that this strange experience has taught me has gone to confirm what I think I already knew, secretly, perhaps, and deep down in my heart. If what I think I have been told is true it means that we make our own Heaven and our own Hell in our own daily lives, and the Kingdom of Heaven is here within us, now, for those who have gone before.

AUTHOR'S NOTE

As a background to this story, I have tried to picture the relations of the countries in the British Commonwealth as they may be thirty years from now. No man can see into the future, but unless somebody makes a guess from time to time and publishes it to stimulate discussion it seems to me that we are drifting in the dark, not knowing where we want to go or how to get there.

The Monarch is the one strong link that holds the countries of the Commonwealth together; without that link they would soon fall apart. If any forecast of Commonwealth relations in thirty years time is to be made, it is vacant and sterile unless also it contains a forecast of the position of the Monarch, and gives warning of the strains and tensions that in thirty years may come upon that very human link.

Since personal strains and tensions must inevitably affect the future of the Commonwealth, it seems to me that fiction is the most suitable medium in which to make this forecast. Fiction deals with people and their difficulties and, more than that, nobody takes a novelist too seriously. The puppets born of his imagination walk their little stage for our amusement, and if we find that their creator is impertinent his errors of taste do not sway the world.

NEVIL SHUTE

THE HISTORY OF VINTAGE

The famous American publisher Alfred A. Knopf (1892–1984) founded Vintage Books in the United States in 1954 as a paperback home for the authors published by his company. Vintage was launched in the United Kingdom in 1990 and works independently from the American imprint although both are part of the international publishing group, Random House.

Vintage in the United Kingdom was initially created to publish paperback editions of books acquired by the prestigious hardback imprints in the Random House Group such as Jonathan Cape, Chatto & Windus, Hutchinson and later William Heinemann, Secker & Warburg and The Harvill Press. There are many Booker and Nobel Prize-winning authors on the Vintage list and the imprint publishes a huge variety of fiction and non-fiction. Over the years Vintage has expanded and the list now includes great authors of the past – who are published under the Vintage Classics imprint – as well as many of the most influential authors of the present.

For a full list of the books Vintage publishes, please visit our website
www.vintage-books.co.uk

For book details and other information about the classic authors we publish, please visit the Vintage Classics website
www.vintage-classics.info

Classics website
www.vintage-classics.info